Storm Shells

G.J. Walker-Smith

Storm Shells

Print Edition

© 2013 G.J. Walker-Smith

Cover by Scarlett Rugers, http://www.scarlettrugers.com
Formatting by Polgarus Studio, http://www.polgarusstudio.com

Other Books by G.J Walker-Smith
Saving Wishes (Book One, The Wishes Series)
Second Hearts (Book Two, The Wishes Series)

Contact the author:
https://www.facebook.com/gjwalkersmith
gjwalkersmith@gmail.com
gjwalkersmith.com

For my Dad, the best storyteller I know.

CONTENTS

Prologue
Alex

Charli's mother is a ballerina. That meant that Charli was supposed to possess natural talent when it came to dancing.

She didn't.

My kid became the first child in the history of Mrs O'Reilly's dance class to be expelled – at the ripe old age of five.

Joyce O'Reilly broke the news to me when I arrived to pick Charli up. "Come through to my office for a chat, Alex," she said, leading me across the hall by the elbow.

Rumour has it that Mrs O'Reilly used to be some kind of showgirl back in the day. If that was true, teaching raucous little girls twice a week in the town hall was a bit of fall from grace.

We ended up in the back room, which wasn't really an office at all. It was a storeroom packed full of chairs and Christmas decorations.

"Has something happened?" I asked, a little afraid.

Joyce looked at me with sheer pity and closed the door. That was not a good sign. "Little girls are like flowers," she announced, extending her arms. "With a little encouragement, they usually bloom."

"But?"

"Your sister is not a bloomer," she said, dropping the theatrics. "Trying to help Charli blossom as a dancer is like trying to grow a flower in the desert. It isn't going to happen. She doesn't follow instruction and she's disruptive in class."

I widened my eyes, pretending it was the first time I'd heard someone make that statement.

"There was an altercation with another student this afternoon," she added. "I'm afraid that was the end of the line. I'd prefer it if she didn't return to class next week."

"What do you mean by altercation?"

Joyce's mouth formed a grim line. "I'll let Charli explain."

"I'll have a word with her," I promised, making a grab for the door handle.

"Alex, there's a karate class here on Wednesday afternoons. Perhaps she'd be better suited to the martial arts," she suggested.

"I'll look into it," I muttered, escaping the room.

Crossing the big empty hall was like being on parade. Little girls and their mothers scowled at me like I was the enemy. I couldn't wait to hear Charli's explanation. Obviously she'd done a real number on someone.

I didn't have to wait long to find out who it was. Jasmine Tate was sitting on a chair holding an icepack to her eye, wailing like the world was ending. Charli came out of nowhere and launched herself into my arms. I carried my little terrorist to the door without saying a single word.

It wasn't exactly a clean getaway. Meredith Tate cornered me at the car. "You need to instil some manners into that little brute before it's too late, Alex," she hissed.

Charli's grip on my neck got tighter and she buried her head in my shoulder.

"Mind your business, Meredith," I grumbled, opening the car door.

She edged closer to me, furiously wagging her finger. "It is my business! That little delinquent just gave my daughter a black eye."

I lowered Charli into the car, ordered her to put on her seat belt and slammed the door closed.

"I will handle it," I told her, doing my best to ignore the brutal glare she was throwing my way.

"Make sure you do."

It was a pointless argument that could've continued all day. I let Meredith claim the win by having the last word, and got the hell out of there.

* * *

We didn't go straight home. We went to the beach because that's the place we were both at our calmest. I didn't let Charli get out of the car straight away. I gave her the disappointed stare-down through the rear vision mirror while I interrogated her.

"It wasn't my fault," she insisted. "Jasmine stomped on my music box."

"So you stomped on her head?"

She shook her little head so hard that her pigtails flicked her face. "No. We danced with wands today. I hit her with mine."

"Mrs O'Reilly doesn't think you should dance any more," I said dully.

"Good. I hate it."

I was relieved. I hated it too. Joyce O'Reilly's dance group was practically a cult. The only ones more imperious than the tiny dancers were their mothers.

"Show me your box," I ordered, getting a little off-subject.

Charli unbuckled her seat belt, rummaged through her school bag and presented me with her beaten-up box.

It was destroyed. She'd been carting it everywhere since she was three years old. To her, it wasn't just a music box. It was a wish box. Every wish she'd ever collected was stored in it.

"Jasmine didn't break it," I told her.

"Did too," she insisted. "She jumped on it."

I tried to straighten the broken lid enough to close it while I worked on my lie. "No, it burst at the seams, Charli. It's just full."

"Too many wishes?" she asked, leaning through the gap in the seats to get a better look at it.

I nodded, hoping she was buying the story. "You've got too much in here." I held up a little plastic horse. "What's this?"

"It's a white pony."

"You can wish on horses?" I asked sceptically.

"Only white ones – if their tails are black."

"I see." I continued sifting through the box. "What else is in here?"

"Storm shells. Lots of them," she replied proudly.

I smiled. "What would a little girl like you know about storm shells, Charli?"

She clambered between the seats to sit in the front, reached into the broken box and pulled out a seashell.

"You can only collect them after storms," she expertly explained, "or they don't work."

"What do they do?"

She held two fingers up. "They give you two wishes. You already know that, Alex. You told me."

"You're right. I forgot. Sorry."

"Can you fix my box?" she asked hopefully.

"I don't think I can. It's just too full."

She leaned across to peer into the box in my lap. "It's not that full."

"Sure it is. It's not the shells that busted it open. What about all the wishes you can't see?"

I glanced across to see her imagination working overtime. Her little face was etched with concentration.

"Like stars and birthdays?"

"Exactly. It's chock full, look." I handed her the box.

"What can I do?" As always, she sounded desperate for answers, and as always, I had to think quickly to come up with one.

"We'll bury it in the garden," I suggested. "When you want to spend your wishes, we can dig it up again."

* * *

The plan of spending the rest of the afternoon at the beach was abandoned. We went back to the house and spent the last hour of daylight digging a hole in the garden. I wrapped the broken box in a plastic bag and placed it in the hole.

"I'll miss you, box," Charli said tearily.

I felt bad for her. If Jasmine Tate had been in the vicinity I might have thrown her into the hole too. I put my arm around her. "You can dig it up when you're ready. It's always going to be there," I promised.

"Okay," she sniffed.

"But meanwhile, Charli, no more fighting with Jasmine. It's not nice."

"Okay. I'll be nice to her."

I wasn't buying it for a second, but I let it go. It wasn't her first run-in with Jasmine Tate, and I doubted it would be the last.

December 10
Adam

There's a certain type of pain that you can get used to, especially when you feel like you deserve it. And I most definitely deserved it.

In order to live through it, I had to get out of the apartment. I made the decision to move back in with Ryan just two days after Charlotte left.

Packing wasn't something I thought I could handle so I did what every twenty-three-year old man would do in a crisis. I called my mother.

I was lying half dead on the couch when she arrived.

"Adam, get up," she barked, storming in as if she owned the joint.

Mom isn't one for wallowing. She's British. She has the stiff-upper-lip thing going on. She's not especially sympathetic either, especially when she's pissed. The only thing I'd ever done that infuriated her more than marrying Charli was let her go.

I was no longer the good son.

She stomped to the windows and pulled up the blinds. It made little difference. The weather was as gloomy as I felt. "You are a foolish man," she scolded. "You've made your bed. Now sort yourself out and figure out how to lie in it."

"By myself is how I'm going to be lying in it, Mom."

I sounded pathetic. I probably looked pathetic too, but I gained no sympathy from the queen.

"Stupid boy," she growled, stamping out of the room.

* * *

My mother stayed with me for hours that morning, trying to put my life back in order. From the couch, I could see her down in the bedroom, packing Charli's belongings into boxes. It was brutal.

She eventually reappeared in the room waving something at me. "Adam, what are these?"

I lifted my head, glancing at the rings in her hand. "Her wedding rings."

My mother pushed my feet off the couch and sat down beside me. "You mean to tell me that girl had these beautiful rings and wouldn't wear them?"

"They didn't fit her, Mom," I muttered. "Nothing about this life fit her. Send them to Alex too."

Finally she took pity on me. "I can't bear to see you like this," she said gently. "Why don't you just call her?"

"No."

"Fine." She jumped to her feet. "I shall call her myself. Maybe I can talk some sense into her."

As far as I was concerned, Charli had already come to her senses. That's why she left my lying, scheming ass.

"You can't call her," I mumbled.

"Watch me," she said, holding her phone to her ear.

I did watch her – and the look of horror that swept her face a few seconds later. It was a perfectly understandable reaction. Charlotte's phone was charging in the kitchen, right where she'd left it. Now it was bouncing around the counter playing the ringtone she'd assigned to the queen – the theme tune from Psycho.

Mom ended the call. "Some days I could wring that girl's neck."

"But you miss her, right?" I asked, almost smiling.

"I do," she admitted. "Terribly."

* * *

I was hoping Ryan wouldn't be there when I moved back in. But not only was he there, he had company.

7

My brother has a thing for blondes – the dirty kind – the kind who see no shame in parading around someone's apartment wearing only a towel.

Thankfully Ryan was fully dressed, lounging on the sofa. His plaything was in the kitchen.

"You're moving back in?" he asked, sounding less than thrilled.

"Yup." I kicked the front door shut with my foot and lowered the box I was carrying to the floor. "Rule change."

I didn't need to elaborate. Ryan knew exactly what I meant. When we'd lived together before, we had a very strict policy about random half-naked blondes roaming the apartment, especially the dirty kind.

"Have you met Isobel?"

The blonde, who was fussing around in the kitchen, looked up at the sound of her name. She waved across at me. "Hi'ya," she greeted in a strong cockney accent.

"Hello." I looked at Ryan, smirking. "Broadening your horizons, I see. Shopping internationally now?"

"English girls are spectacular, Adam. It's the Australians you have to be wary of."

I shoved his feet off the coffee table and sat next to him. Both of us idly stared at dirty Isobel.

"Australian girls don't make you food," I muttered. "You make *them* food."

Ryan lazily cocked his head. "Isobel's a stewardess. It's in her nature to serve."

"You really are a dick, you know that?"

"So are you. That's why you're moving back in here all sad and alone."

He made a valid point. I settled further into the sofa and sighed. Was I going to enjoy rooming with my slut brother again? No. But this was my new mediocre life. Until I could figure out a way back into La La Land, this was it for me.

December 10
Charli

Mitchell Tate always seemed to get me at my worst, but as usual he didn't complain. Pathetically, he was probably used to it.

He'd borrowed Melito's jeep to make the long journey to the city to pick me up. I was glad we had a long ride ahead of us. It gave us time to catch up.

Kaimte was still blissfully laid back, and so was Mitchell. The only aspect of his simple life that had altered was the absence of a few of our friends. Zoe and Rose had returned to England six months earlier, keen to get back to the real world. If Mitchell was heartbroken, he didn't let on. "They still email me," he said, shrugging.

"Do you ever write back?"

A huge grin swept his face. "I will, one day."

Bernie and Will were also gone. They'd moved further north, skipping out late one night to avoid paying rent arrears to Leroy. Melito and Vincent were still there though, and made a big deal of my arrival by inviting us to a barbecue on the beach later that night.

Mitchell agreed instantly, rattling off a list of names of people he wanted me to meet. Like any transient town, there was a constant influx of new friends to replace those who'd moved on.

"So you're still happy here?" I asked, pacing his tiny shack.

He set my suitcase on the wooden floor. "It's the happiest place on earth. Give it a day or two and you'll remember why."

* * *

Within ten minutes of arriving at the shack, we were in the surf. Every particle of stress within me dissolved the second the water washed over me. Mitchell and I spent the next hour lolling near the water's edge, tumbling in the low breaking waves and talking.

He was surprisingly curious about my New York life and all things Adam. "I thought you loved him." He said it as if he was reminding me of something I wish I hadn't said.

"I do," I explained. "Completely and utterly. He just needs to learn how to love me."

Mitchell frowned, shaking his head. I couldn't blame him for being confused. "How long are you going to wait for that to happen?"

"I haven't thought that far ahead."

"Don't give him too long, Charli. Live your life. It's not your fault he can't get his act together."

I loved Mitchell Tate. Not in the desperate-complete-absolute Adam Décarie kind of way, but I loved him. I wondered how things would have worked out if I'd loved him à la Décarie.

The girl who landed him would never endure living in a big city. She'd permanently live on a beach somewhere, never knowing the trappings of wealth or the pressures that come with it. On the downside, she wouldn't own a single pair of shoes or a hairbrush for the rest of her existence.

"Heads up," he called, warning me of the next wave. We both dug our hands into the sand, anchoring ourselves as it washed over us. I came out of it spluttering, making Mitchell laugh. "That was number nine, Charli."

Alex first told me about the ninth wave theory when I was a kid. Of course he'd claimed it as his own, but plenty of diehard surfers and sailors are believers. The ninth wave is supposedly larger than those preceding it, making it the rogue of the set. Once it passes through, a new set begins.

I coughed again. "I'm a little off my game, I guess."

"I'm not sure what your game is any more," he teased. "You're just a skinny girl who's forgotten how to count water."

"Do you reckon you can fix me?" I sounded surprisingly serious considering the idiocy of his statement.

He smiled. "You'll be okay. Just go back to the beginning. Think of Adam as your ninth wave. The worst is over. Now the count starts again."

"You think I should go home, don't you?"

He nodded. "Alex will be glad to have you back."

For the first time in a long time, I was open to the idea. Spending time with the one person who never let me down definitely had its appeal.

December 10
Adam

Dirty Isobel eventually checked out, leaving Ryan and me alone for the first time in as long as I could remember. And it was weird. Especially when he started talking.

"So. Have you heard from Fairy Pants?"

"No."

"Do you expect to?"

"No."

"Well, I'm here if you want to talk about it," he offered. "I'd be happy to shed some light on why she dumped your ass."

It had been a long time since my brother and I had come to blows. I glanced at him from the corner of my eye, wondering how I'd fare if I punched him. I decided against it. It might make living together awkward.

"Thanks, but I don't need your input on this one."

Ryan leaned forward and dropped the TV remote on the coffee table. "Were you really expecting things to turn out differently?" he asked. "If you were looking for a compliant little Stepford wife, you married the wrong girl."

"Shut up, Ryan."

He grinned, sardonically enough to make me reconsider smacking him. "So what's the plan for winning her back? It better involve buckets of glitter and butterfly dust or you're screwed."

I'd heard enough. I was almost out of the room when he spoke again.

"I was kidding, Adam. Charli doesn't want glitter. She has enough floating around her brain already. Don't go the gimmick route. It's not her style."

Infuriated, I turned back. "How the hell would you know what Charli wants? Why would I take the advice of someone who wakes up next to women he's known less than twelve hours?"

"We're not talking about other women." He shrugged. "We're talking about your wife. She's not that complicated. Charlotte made it very clear what she wanted. Everyone heard her say it but you."

He was wrong. I'd heard it a million times. All she'd ever wanted out of the deal was me. It was the one thing I'd never been able to wholly give her. That's why I was on my own.

* * *

I wasn't looking forward to the Christmas break. School was a great distraction for me. I headed to the library after my last class, determined to load myself up with enough study to tide me over until classes resumed in the New Year.

I found a quiet corner, settled in and began poring over the notes I'd taken in class. Even I knew it was excessive but I literally had nothing else going on.

Just as I was getting into it, a girl dumped her book bag down, sending my papers flying across the desk.

"Hey," she greeted, either missing or ignoring the destruction she'd caused. "It's Adam, right?"

I gathered my papers. "Yes, and you are?"

"Trieste Kincaid." She sat. "I know, I know, you're probably thinking I was named after the city in Italy, but I wasn't." I wasn't thinking anything other than who was this girl and what the hell did she want? "My dad has a thing for the bathyscaphe called Trieste," she continued. "You know, the one that explored the Challenger Deep back in the sixties?"

Overloaded, I'd lost the ability to think. "What's a bathyscaphe?"

She giggled, a sharp sound that made everyone in the library look up. "Come on, Adam, keep up. It's a submersible deep-sea research vessel."

I stared at her, trying to clear my head of the nonsense. The fidgety girl with the runaway mouth didn't seem fazed in the slightest. "Trieste, do I know you?"

"Not yet," she replied. "But you will soon. You're my new mentor. My third, actually. The other two quit."

Signing up for the peer-mentoring program had been Parker's brainwave. At the time I'd been less than enthusiastic. Now, sitting beside the hyped-up Trieste, I was even less enthusiastic.

"Look," I began, trying to come up with a way of letting her down gently. "I'm really busy and –"

"You're my last hope. If you dump me, they're kicking me out of the mentoring program."

She looked so pitiful that I thought she might cry. I had no idea how I'd handle her if she did – especially if she cried as loudly as she laughed.

"What are you working on at the moment?" I asked, taking a softer line.

She recovered instantly, unclipped her bag, took out a heap of papers and dumped them in front of me. "Constitutional Law."

"So, do you need help?"

She giggled again and I dropped my head, shushing her before we both got kicked out. "No. I have excellent grades."

"So what do you need from me then?"

"I'm not sure yet, but I'll let you know. It'll just be great to know a friendly face."

I wasn't friendly. I thought I'd made it obvious that babysitting a first year student was not high on my agenda.

"Where are you from, Trieste?"

She couldn't have been local. The fashion police would've hunted her down by now. I'd never seen anyone pull off the toggle beanie look, least of all one with ears. Her thick black-framed glasses were a cute look, though.

"Army brat." She pointed at herself. "A bit of here, a bit of there."

I learned a lot about Trieste in the next minute and a half. She was twenty-one, but seemed much younger. She was on a full scholarship, and looking for a part-time job. She learned nothing about me and I planned to keep it that way. I figured I could help her out with a bit of study over the next few weeks and palm her off onto the next unsuspecting mentor.

After the quick Q and A session, I started packing my gear. I was confident of making a clean getaway until Parker approached the table. I would've dealt with a thousand Triestes over him. I hadn't seen him since the Christmas party from hell.

"Hey," he said.

I didn't reply. I just stared at him.

The mistress of idle chatter beamed at him and held out her hand. "Hello. How are you? I'm Trieste."

He rudely left her hanging.

"What do you want?" I snapped.

"I was just wondering how you were doing," he said quietly. "We haven't seen much of you lately."

"There's a reason for that."

He nodded, looking slightly penitent. "How's Charli? Have you heard from her?"

If that was his idea of small talk, he was a bigger douche than I'd given him credit for.

"Who's Charli?" asked Trieste, oblivious.

I glanced at her, then at Parker. "Don't you have somewhere else to be?"

I must've sounded as furious as I felt. He walked away. He was a dick, but he wasn't stupid.

Parker was barely out of earshot before the interrogation from Trieste began. "Who's Charli?" she repeated.

"Do you have to know everything?"

She tilted her head. "I like to know everything. My brain's a big sponge. I need information to live."

"Charli is my wife," I muttered.

Her eyes widened and she pushed her glasses up the bridge of her nose. "You have a wife? Wow. You're kinda young for a wife." She pointed at my hand. "I saw the ring but I thought it was one of those purity rings. You know, the ones that signify sexual abstinence?"

I almost laughed for the first time in days.

"Where is she?"

"Who?"

She rolled her eyes. "Your wife, Charli."

I wished I knew. "She's travelling. She likes to travel."

"She left you, didn't she?" she asked sympathetically. "Why did she leave you?"

Answering her made absolutely no sense, but I did it anyway. "She saw through me."

"Oh, that sucks," she replied, making me smile.

"You have no idea."

December 18
Charli

I hung out with Mitchell for a week before leaving Kaimte, feeling no less wrecked than when I'd arrived. Mitchell drove me to the airport and stayed with me until my flight was called. He hugged me, wished me luck and told me he loved me.

"One of these days I'll visit you in when I'm in a better place," I whispered.

"Your happiness doesn't depend on him, Charli. Remember that."

Very occasionally, Mitchell Tate could be an extraordinarily profound man. I wished I was better at taking his advice.

The jolt to my tired body as the plane touched down in Hobart bordered on brutal. I recovered quickly, grabbed my bag and stood in the aisle, desperate to get off the plane. I loved to travel, but I'd never been especially good at it. It seemed to take me days to get over long-haul flights. Alex vehemently believed that salt water cured everything. I had a better theory. Chocolate cured everything, and luckily for me I was back in the land of the Caramello Koala. When I spotted the vending machine on my way to the car rental desk, the koalas were practically screaming my name. I pumped a handful of coins into the machine and pocketed an obscene amount of chocolate for the journey home.

Finally free of the airport, I ambled across the car park with my head tilted toward the sky. The mild summer morning had a bite to it that only came with Tasmanian weather. It was like nowhere else on earth. I smiled to myself, realising I was travelled enough to make such a claim.

I was officially on home soil, just over an hour's drive from Pipers Cove and more importantly, Alex.

* * *

I drove south in the unimpressive little white hatchback I'd hired, inhaling the cool air through the open window while I munched on my fourth koala.

As far as I could tell, the only thing that had changed in this tiny pocket of the world was me. Two years earlier I'd been desperate to leave, but as I got within the last few kilometres of the Cove, I was getting jittery, excited – and nauseas.

I looked at the growing pile of wrappers on the passenger seat and regretted my binge. Now I *really* wanted to get home and my eagerness to get there was reflected by my driving. I didn't even look down to check my speed until I noticed the blue and red lights flashing behind me.

"Oh, crap," I muttered, coming to a stop on the gravel verge. I used the time that it took for the policeman to approach my car to practise my please-don't-give-me-a-ticket speech. I hadn't had to use it in a long time.

The constable didn't look much older than me. He seemed awkward, like he was still getting used to his starchy new blue uniform.

"Good morning," he said politely. "Where are you headed?"

"Hi. The Cove." I pointed ahead through the windscreen as if he needed direction.

"And where are you coming from?"

It occurred to me that a smart mouth might not work in my favour but I couldn't help myself. "Africa, actually."

"I see." His lips formed a tight smile. "And did you speed the whole way?"

I didn't answer him. I had other things on my mind – like what the rental company would charge me if I vomited in their car. I threw open the car door and he took a quick step back to avoid being hit by the door. He took another leap back as I lurched out of the car and threw up all over the ground. "I'm so sorry," I mumbled, humiliated and convinced he thought I was drunk.

"Can I get you something, Ma'am? Some water, maybe?"

I tilted my head to look at him. "No thank you. I'm okay."

"Good. In that case, can I see your licence please?"

I straightened up and grabbed my bag off the passenger seat, sending koala wrappers flying in all directions. "For a second there, I thought you were going to take pity on me and not write the ticket."

"Being ill doesn't excuse the fact that you were doing a hundred and seventeen in a hundred zone." He clicked his pen authoritatively.

"Have you had a good look at this car?" I asked. "There's no way I could have been going that fast."

His smile broadened but he continued writing. "You don't remember me, do you, Charli?"

He kept writing while I stared at him. "Should I?"

Finally he stopped scrawling, tore the ticket off the pad and handed it to me. "Flynn Davis."

My eyes widened. "Floss and Norm's grandson?"

He handed me back my licence. "The one and only."

I hadn't seen him in years. I remembered the times he'd visited his grandparents over the holidays. Flynn was a couple of years older than me, which is as good as decades when you're children. I'd never known him well. All I really remembered was his penchant for heavy metal music and Floss threatening to cut his long hair with garden shears.

"I didn't recognise you without your Metallica shirt and duffle coat."

He blushed. "Well, we all go through an awkward phase."

"Don't worry about it," I replied. "I think I'm still in my awkward phase. So are you living in Pipers Cove now?"

"Yeah, I'm renting a house on the beach. It keeps me out of trouble."

"I thought being a policeman would keep you out of trouble."

"What about you, Charli?" he asked, ignoring my smart-arse comment. "Are you just visiting?"

"For a while," I said vaguely.

Flynn stepped back and I wondered if I looked like I was about to vomit again. "Well, I'll let you get on your way. Drive safe, okay?"

I turned the key and the little hatchback purred to life. "Of course I will," I replied, pointlessly revving the powerless engine. "Look at the car I'm in."

* * *

I had no idea where to find Alex. I decided to try the house first because it was on the way into town. My promise to the rental company of driving only on sealed roads went out the window as I bounced the little car up the gravel driveway. I almost hoped Alex wasn't there. Seeing my out-of-practice driving skills would probably lead him to confiscate my keys. As I got nearer, I saw a shiny new red ute parked at the house. It had to be his. He would've traded up at least twice in the time I'd been away.

As I got out of the car, Alex stepped out on to the veranda and a weird, silent standoff ensued as we stood staring at each other.

My father looked exactly as he had the last time I'd seen him. His sandy hair was still unkempt and boyish. He wore faded jeans and a once-white T-shirt that had been destroyed by his tinkering in the shed.

I didn't know whether to go to him or not. Alex just looked baffled, leaving me convinced that he'd forgotten who I was.

"Hi, Dad," I said in a tiny voice.

He snapped out of whatever confusion was plaguing him and bolted down the steps without touching any of them, slowing his roll as took the last few steps toward me. "You're really home!" He took my face in his hands.

I nodded and his hands moved with me, until he let go to pull me into a bone-crushing hug. I endured it as best I could before wriggling free and drawing a long, steadying breath.

"Are you tired?"

"Deathly," I replied, mustering my best smile. "It was a long way home."

"Come inside," he ordered, draping his arm around my shoulder as we walked. "I'll make you lunch and then you can sleep."

* * *

The house looked different. The ugly but comfy brown leather lounge suite was gone. In its place was the pristine white suite from Gabrielle's cottage. Some of her artwork hung on the walls, and the once unimpressive bookshelf was now stuffed full of books. Those were the most obvious changes, but a hundred others were subtler.

The last thing I wanted to do was appear miffed. Alex had every right to move Gabrielle in. No one deserved happiness more than him and the Parisienne.

"Is Gabrielle here?" I asked.

"She has an appointment in Hobart this morning. I'm glad we have a few hours alone, though. It'll give us time to catch up. We have a lot to talk about."

"I have a lot to tell you," I replied, following him to the kitchen.

For two people who had a lot of talking to do, not much was said over the next few minutes. I felt calm just being in the same space as him. Alex set about making sandwiches while I sat at the table.

"How long are you home for, Charli?" Alex set a huge plate of food in front of me. He pulled out a chair and joined me at the table, demanding an answer by staring at me.

"For a while, if that's okay."

"You can stay forever. This will always be your home."

"Thank you," I muttered, lifting the top of my sandwich to check the contents. He'd made me tuna. My stomach lurched and I pushed the plate to the centre of the table and pinched my nose.

"Do you have something against tuna?"

"Today I do. I've been scoffing chocolate the whole way from Hobart."

He dropped his sandwich on his plate. "Are you going to puke?"

"I wasn't even thinking about it until you mentioned it."

"Can I get you something?"

I shook my head. "I'm okay. Just tired. I really need to sleep."

He nodded but I could see the tension in his jaw. We'd hardly spoken in months. I'd arrived home unannounced and he had no clue why. He didn't want to me sleep. He wanted answers.

Thankfully, he didn't push the issue. I followed him down the hallway to my bedroom. I was hoping it had remained untouched, but there were shades of Gabrielle all over the place. A large easel stood near the window, accommodating a cool abstract painting that she hadn't finished. Pots of paints and brushes littered the dressing table. I could overlook her arty junk, but I couldn't ignore the pungent smell of turpentine that hit me the instant I walked in. I pushed the curtain aside, slid the window open and waved my hand as if I could somehow pull the breeze into the room.

"Sorry, Charli," Alex muttered, scooping pots of paint off the dressing table. "Gabi likes to paint in here, something about the light being good."

I turned and smiled at him. He deserved to think I wasn't upset by the hostile takeover of my room. "I don't mind. I just want to sleep."

He gave me a smile that I knew wasn't real and backed out of the room, pulling the door closed behind him.

As exhausted as I was, sleep was impossible. As soon as I laid my head on the pillow, the ear-splitting sound of cracking wood invaded the silence. I ignored it for as long as I could before admitting defeat and getting up. I ventured outside to confront the axe-wielding maniac working the woodheap.

"I thought you said you were tired," said Alex, pausing only momentarily to ask the question before swinging the axe over his head and belting it into a log.

I winced as it made contact. "How can I sleep with this racket going on?"

"I chop wood, Charli. It takes my mind off my errant daughter." He set another log on the chopping block. "If I didn't chop wood, I'd go insane."

"I'm home. You can stop worrying now."

"You'd think so, wouldn't you?" he asked. "But you're here, and I'm still driven to smash wood."

I stepped off the veranda. "What do you want me to say, Alex? I don't know what you want to hear."

He slumped forward, leaning on the butt of the axe and wiping sweat off his face with his T-shirt. "How about the truth, for once? I've barely heard a word from you in months. When we do speak, you tell me everything is fine. Then you rock up here out of the blue, looking pretty damned dreadful if I'm honest, and still insist everything is fine. Clearly you're lying. I don't know what to do about that."

I had no clue where to begin so I put the ball back in his court. "Ask me anything. I won't lie."

"Fine," he grunted, dropping the axe. "Let's start with the crux of the problem. Where's Adam? I know you've left him. FedEx delivered a heap of boxes addressed to you a few days ago. I was curious so I opened one. It was full of your stuff."

That revelation was like a dagger through my heart. My New York life had been packed up and mailed back to my father less than a week after I'd left. I'm sure Colin the delivery guy was paid well to remove all traces of Charlotte Décarie.

"I have no regrets, Alex," I said, sounding remarkably sincere.

"You married him, Charli. That should be a big regret. What went wrong?"

Sucking in a long breath, I explained as best I could. Telling my father that Adam never intended leaving New York was a horrible admission to make. It felt like I was scoring points for the opposing team.

"So are you done now?"

"Probably not."

"Oh, come on," he growled, leaning down to pick up the axe. "Giving him another chance is like reloading the gun for him because he missed you the first time."

"You're never going to understand," I said roughly. "You never understood."

"Make me understand. And make it quick, I'm nearly out of wood."

I glanced at the less than impressive woodpile. In all my years, I'd never seen it that depleted. He'd picked a crappy time to let it run low.

"I can't explain it, Alex. I just love him."

"Are you furious right now?" he asked. "Do you see how horribly he treated you?"

"Yes." I practically whimpered the word.

"Don't be that girl, Charli. I raised you better than that."

"I'm not that girl, Alex," I huffed. "And I'm not a seventeen- year-old kid any more."

He swung the axe again belting the log so hard that even he seemed to flinch. "You're still my kid, Charli."

* * *

Defeated, I headed back to my room, lay on the bed and instantly fell into the deepest sleep I'd had in weeks. It was after four when I woke. The Parisienne was home. I could hear her musical voice coming from the lounge.

I got up quietly and peeked into the room. Gabrielle perched forward on the couch. Alex was crouched in front of her, resting his forehead on hers, mumbling something probably designed to calm her. She was crying.

I wondered why. Had my homecoming rained on her parade that much?

I cleared my throat. By the time I reached the couch, Gabrielle had pulled herself together. "Charli," she crowed, jumping up and pushing Alex aside.

"Hello, Gabrielle."

She threw her arms around me. "You look wonderful," she said, pushing me away and holding me at arm's length while she examined me. Clearly she was lying. Everyone else thought I looked pale and skinny.

"Thank you," I replied. "So do you."

Despite her red face and puffy eyes, she did look beautiful. I wanted to ask why she'd been crying but couldn't bring myself to do it. I didn't think it had anything to do with me. I hadn't been in town long enough to reduce her to tears.

"We have been waiting for you." She sat on the white couch and pulled me down beside her. "I want to hear all your news."

"What do you mean, you've been waiting for me?"

She looked embarrassed. "Please don't think I've been prying. Boxes of your belongings have been arriving all week, so I called Adam. I was worried."

My concern was reserved entirely for him. "Did he sound alright?"

Her perfect face lit up. "Fine," she assured me, patting my hand. "He is terribly sad, but he's coping."

It peeved me that she'd made it sound so final. I glanced at Alex, noticing his rigid expression. I focused back on Gabrielle. "I'm glad," I said, mainly for Alex's benefit. "I want him to be okay."

* * *

The Parisienne's bright mood lasted for the rest of the day. Whatever had upset her had passed. I kept her company in the kitchen while she conjured up a grand homecoming dinner.

Coq au vin was a meal that should have knocked me on my chocolate-overdosed butt, but I managed to eat everything on my plate. It was the first real meal I'd had in days and I instantly felt better for it. I went to bed early, feeling well, content and glad to be home, but I woke at five in the morning raring to go. I stayed in bed as long as I could stand before heading to the kitchen. I was on my second bowl of cereal when Alex trudged in.

"Charli." He yawned my name. "Are you alright?"

"I'm great!" My tone was much too chirpy for that time of morning.

Alex joined me at the table. I slid the box of cereal, a bowl and the carton of milk across to him.

"You look much better today."

"I feel better."

His lazy half smile looked more like a smirk. "I'm pleased to hear it. Do you have plans for the day?"

"I thought I might come to the café with you."

He frowned down at his bowl as he unloaded the box of cereal into it.

"Are you sure you want to? This place hasn't changed much in the time you've been away." I knew what he was hinting at. They were sparkly, overly made-up and once upon a time the two scariest girls I'd ever known, Jasmine and Lily Tate.

I was actually hoping the Beautifuls hadn't changed, because I most certainly had. I'd dealt with much bigger and badder than them since leaving town. "I'm up for it, Alex."

"Go and get dressed then. I'll give you ten minutes."

I only needed five.

* * *

The drive to the café was reminiscent of old times, especially when Alex ordered me to put my seatbelt on. I tried to adjust the settings on the stereo and had my hand slapped. I pressed the button on my door and opened my window. Using the control on his side, Alex wound it up and locked it. "Don't touch anything," he ordered, making me giggle.

We pulled into the car park, and Alex's rushed pace seemed to wane. He made no attempt to get out of the car.

"Are we just going to sit?"

"For a minute. There's something I want to tell you before we go in."

"Is it about Gabrielle?" I asked, wondering if he was about to explain her teary mood from the day before.

He pulled a face like he was chewing on broken glass. "No. Why would you think that?"

"She was crying when she came home yesterday," I told him. "I wondered if it was something to do with me."

He was shaking his head before I'd finished speaking. "No, nothing to do with you. She was having a bad day, that's all."

Gabrielle was the queen when it came to enduring bad days. She taught high school students, for crying out loud. Alex's weak explanation wasn't convincing, but quizzing him was pointless. "So what is it, then? What do you have to tell me?"

He started bouncing the bunch of keys in his hand. "I want you to put things in perspective and keep an open mind."

I couldn't think of anything he needed to tell me that was so dreadful that I needed a pep talk prior to hearing it. "Just spit it out, Alex."

He glanced at me only briefly. "Nicole's back in town."

The mere mention of her name infuriated me. I shifted, making the leather seat squeak.

"When did she resurface?" I didn't mean to sound so indignant. I wanted to give the impression that I was unaffected by anything to do with Nicole Lawson. As far as I was concerned, my ex-best friend was a thief and traitor who deserved to be left rotting in my past.

"She's only been back a few weeks. She feels terrible about what happened."

I glared at my father, fighting the urge to slap the side of his head.

"How would you know how terrible she feels?" I asked sourly. "Nicole doesn't have a contrite bone in her body."

"She's been working hard to make amends, Charli."

"Working here?" My voice sounded higher than usual as disgust set in.

He nodded but wouldn't look at me. "She's always been a hard worker and she needs the money. Everyone deserves a second chance."

She shouldn't have needed a penny. Nicole skipped town with her loser boyfriend and thirteen thousand of Adam's hard-earned dollars. If Alex had been privy to that information he might have reconsidered his stance on second chances. But he knew nothing about her thieving ways. All he knew was that she'd blown me off and done a runner with Ethan Williams.

"I believe in second chances, Alex," I said sincerely. "I just don't believe everyone deserves them."

Alex looked at me. "Keep an open mind, Charli. Hear her out. That's all I ask."

"I'm not interested in making peace with Nicole Lawson."

* * *

Unlike the house, the café hadn't changed at all. I was glad Gabrielle hadn't made her mark. The beach café with the chequerboard flooring, dark wood countertop and pale blue walls was still entirely Alex's domain.

I perched on the wicker stool at the counter while Alex set about opening up for the day. It was then that I noticed the brand spanking new coffee machine. I rushed around the counter to admire it. Out of habit, I switched it on. "Let me make you a coffee."

My enthusiasm stunned him. Alex sat on the stool I'd just vacated and watched silently as I brewed him a near perfect latte, complete with rosetta design in the froth. It smelled divine, and I took the unusual step of making myself a cup too – perhaps to prove that the fancy pattern wasn't a fluke.

"Since when have you been such an accomplished barista?" he teased, turning his cup to examine it from all angles.

"Since I married a New Yorker," I said, butchering the American accent.

He grimaced. "I'm confused by the way you talk about him, Charli." He picked up a spoon and scooped it through his cup, toying with the froth. "You're not supposed to like him so much after being duped."

"That's a nasty way of putting it, Alex."

"How else would you describe it? Would you have married him if you'd known he wasn't ever going to leave New York?"

I could feel the conversation heading to a place I didn't want to visit. Whether he realised it or not, he'd landed on the very heart of the betrayal. We were literally standing at the altar when Adam had reiterated his promise of travelling with me when he'd finished law school. I was in love, excited and completely convinced. Adam, on the other hand, was lying through his teeth.

I didn't answer him and the silence spoke volumes.

"That's what I thought," he said, way too smugly.

I shrugged. "It'll be okay in the end."

Alex didn't smile until I did. "In a million life times, I'll never figure you out."

I couldn't expect him to. I had trouble understanding myself most of the time. "I know what I'm doing, Alex," I lied.

"Charli, you've never had a clue what you're doing. That's what makes you dangerous. I've been keeping a jar of bail money on top of the fridge since you were twelve years old for that very reason," he grumbled, heading toward the back room to collect the newspaper deliveries.

I moved one of the wicker stools to the business side of the counter. I would have been perfectly content to sit there all morning, but the jingling bell at the top of the door snapped me back to reality. Nicole Lawson strolled in, stopping dead in her tracks when she saw me. I watched the colour drain from her face as her eyes darted in every direction but mine. I didn't share her nervousness. I had no urge to run and hide, probably because I wasn't a lying, backstabbing thief.

I stared her down, studying her closely. Nicole was much thinner than I'd ever known her to be – Kinsey Ballantyne thin. She was wearing cargo shorts and a black camisole top, the exact same outfit I was wearing. There was a time when I would've found the coincidence funny. Now it irked me. Her long brown hair was pulled into a high ponytail. I was glad I'd worn mine down.

"Charli," she said timidly, taking a few measured steps toward the counter. "I had no idea you were coming home."

"I was going to email you and let you know but then I remembered how much I hate you." Her already shaky expression crumpled and for some reason, I almost felt bad. *Almost.*

"For what it's worth, I'm sorry."

"It's not worth anything at all, Nicole."

She walked over to the counter and I considered screaming at her to get the hell away from me.

"I'd really like the opportunity to explain."

"Look, you might have been able to talk Alex around but it won't work with me." I leaned across the counter, trying my hand at being scary by lowering my tone. "I know *everything*, Nic. Alex wouldn't have given you your job back if he knew *everything*."

She nodded, resigned. "I know that. I'll tell him the whole story if you want me to."

My skills at bullying obviously needed some work. She didn't seem at all concerned by Alex finding out the true extent of her treacherousness.

I straightened up. "I really don't care one way or the other. Tell him, or don't tell him. Just stay away from me."

She sat opposite me, ignoring my demand. "Please, just hear me out."

"We're not friends any more, Nicole," I said harshly, "which means I don't care what you have to say. There's nothing to explain."

Her eyes drifted downward, focusing on the wooden countertop as she traced the grain with her fingertip. It was then that I noticed her loser boyfriend's name tattooed in ugly black script on the inside of her wrist.

"That's a nice touch," I taunted, pointing to her tattoo. "You let your boyfriend brand you. How sweet."

She pointed at my wedding ring. "So did you, apparently."

Although secretly pleased she hadn't become completely devoid of all personality, I didn't want to deal with Nicole for another second. Convincing Alex to take time out of his day to drive me back to the house was simple. I pulled the jetlag card, and didn't feel the tiniest bit guilty doing it.

* * *

Thanks to Gabrielle's decision to spend the day Christmas shopping in the city, I had the house to myself. I should've used the time to unpack or prepare dinner, but I didn't. I snooped around the house like a crook, counting changes that the lady of the manor had made in my absence.

Everything was entirely too neat. Even the linen cupboard had undergone a makeover. Everything in it was impeccably folded and colour coordinated. I moved to the kitchen, setting my sights on the overhead cupboards. One by one, I opened them, studying the contents. Most of our tableware had come courtesy of Floss Davis and her generous desire to cook for us a few times every week for fifteen years. We very rarely returned her dishes, meaning we had more Pyrex than we could ever use. Not any more. The cupboards now boasted a bewildering array of stylish cookware. I scowled, cursing the Parisienne as I slammed the doors shut. I was being most unreasonable. It wasn't my house any more. I hadn't lived here for a long time, and I wasn't entirely sure I could live here again.

I opened one last cupboard and groaned at the sight of three perfect rows of matching drinking glasses sitting upside down on the shelves. I counted eighteen. Alex barely knew eighteen people, let alone eighteen people who'd all be in our house wanting a drink at the same time. I took my time righting every single glass. "There," I muttered, standing back to admire my handiwork. "Much better."

Being unpleasant is tiring. After my mini crime spree, I lay down on the too-white couch and crashed. The day slipped away until the sound of Gabrielle walking in roused me. I sat bolt upright, giving her a fright.

She squealed, somehow managing to sound demure. "I didn't realise you were here, Charli. I thought you left with your father this morning."

"I did but he brought me home," I replied sleepily.

"Is the jetlag getting the better of you?"

I nodded. "I was going to make a start on dinner but –"

"It's fine. I'll take care of it," she replied cutting me short.

At that moment I realised I hadn't come home. I was a visitor in *her* home.

"Gabi, where's my stuff?" She looked at me, forcing me to elaborate. "You said my stuff arrived from New York."

"Oh. Yes, of course." Her porcelain cheeks flushed a pretty shade. "I asked Alex to take them to the cottage. I hope you don't mind. It's just that there isn't much room here."

I shrugged. "Would it be okay if I go and sort some of it out?"

"Of course." Gabrielle opened the drawer of the hallstand, picked up a bunch of keys and held them out to me. I thanked her, made a vague promise not to be too late back and slipped out the door.

If the desire not to be in the house persisted, there was a fair chance I was never going to return the little rental car. I wondered how Adam would feel about the continual charge on his credit card.

I pulled onto the driveway of the white brick cottage. It looked remarkably cheerful and bright, considering it had been vacant for a year and a half. The red tin roof had been recently repainted and the fussy gardens were well maintained. I wandered along the cobbled path, admiring the gorgeous hedge of lavender leading up to the house. I loved the cottage. No wonder Gabrielle couldn't bear to part with it. What I couldn't understand is why she'd moved in with Alex. The Parisienne had Décarie powers. Why hadn't she convinced him to move in there?

The inside looked exactly as it had when I'd last been there – except homier, thanks to Alex's ugly brown lounge suite that now took pride of place in the centre of the lounge room. I found my stack of FedEx boxes in the bedroom that Adam had once stayed in. Each box was addressed to Charlotte Décarie. I sat on the floor, reached for the closest box and tore the strip of tape off the top.

I instantly knew that none of it had been packed by Colin the delivery guy. Between each item of meticulously folded clothing was a layer of pink tissue paper. It wasn't Adam's style either. For a split second I considered calling him to ask who'd boxed up my life, but I thought better of it. I probably didn't want to know.

I couldn't deny it. I owned some gorgeous clothes. I held up one of my favourites, a white shift dress. As much as I adored it, I knew it wasn't worth taking out of the box. I was hardly going to get much wear out of it here. I managed to find a handful of casual dresses that were much more Pipers Cove and far less awesome. Perhaps I was a little more Charlotte Décarie than I cared to admit. I bundled up the clothes and shoes I wanted to take and headed home.

Thankfully, Alex was there when I arrived. Spending time alone with Gabrielle was borderline awkward.

"Hey," he beamed. "Did you unpack your boxes?"

I looked at the bundle in my arms. "Some. I'll get to the rest of them another time."

"How did the garden look?" he asked, sitting on the couch next to Gabrielle. "I should really go and mow the lawn on the weekend."

I dumped my clothes down on the other couch and sat down.

"Why didn't you move into the cottage?" I asked, perplexed. "It's such a pretty house."

The Parisienne's eyes lit up. "My sentiments exactly."

Alex groaned and sunk into the cushion, taking her with him. "Let's not go there again."

"It came down to the shed, Charli," purred Gabrielle, wriggling free of his hold on her. "He has a grander shed to play in here."

"There's nothing wrong with the shed at the cottage," I muttered, a little too defensively. "A run-down old boat was brought back to life in that shed."

"*Très vrai*," she agreed, smugly.

"English," Alex prompted.

"Very true. She said very true." I didn't doubt my translation for a second because I knew I was right. What I didn't know was what part of my brain it had come from.

"Impressive, Charli." Alex raised an eyebrow.

Gabrielle followed up with a huge burst of French. I shook my head at her, befuddled. "I have no idea what you just said." My bilingual moment was well and truly over. Both of them dissolved into laughter. I disappeared into the kitchen to escape.

One change in the house that I did welcome was the well-stocked fridge. I stood staring into it for a long time, marvelling at the fact that there were three different juices to choose from. Settling for run-of-the-mill orange, I grabbed the carton and opened the cupboard to get a glass.

Each of the eighteen perfectly matching glasses was upside down again.

"Let the games begin," I whispered, stretching up to right them.

* * *

I managed to lie low for two whole days. Going to the café held no interest for me. Nicole was a full time employee. Alex's pleas to make nice were starting to annoy me so much that I'd come close to telling him the whole truth about her more than once. Staying away was beneficial for all of us.

With limited options, I had only one outing planned for the day. Valerie Daintree, the postmistress from hell, had left a message on the house phone letting me know that she was holding some mail at the post office for me. No amount of begging and pleading could convince my father to collect it on my behalf. "Charli, I wouldn't face Val if the mail was addressed to me," he mocked. I considered leaving it there but curiosity eventually won out.

I stopped along the way to fill up the rental car with petrol. I was mindlessly watching the numbers tick over as I pumped fuel when the once gorgeous black Audi A6 pulled up at the bowser next to mine. It wasn't gorgeous any more. It was hardly even an Audi any more. Judging by the multiple scratches and dented bumper, the poor car had had a hard life in the two years since Adam had sold it.

"Charli? Is that you?" asked Lily Tate, stumbling as she got out of the car. In fairness, high-heeled espadrilles would make walking a difficult task for anyone.

"It's me, Lily," I listlessly confirmed.

She squealed, rushing at me. "Oh my God!" She drew me into a tight hug, squeezing me half to death. "Are you home for Christmas?"

Home for Christmas, I repeated in my head. Why didn't I think of that? I'd picked the perfect time to leave my husband and skulk home to my father. I didn't even need to come up with an elaborate lie. I was home for the holidays.

I grinned at her. "Yes. Yes I am."

"Cool. Where's Adam?"

"In New York."

"When's he getting here?"

"Lily, did you do something different with your hair?" Sometimes it was a blessing that Lily Tate had the concentration span of a gnat. It made changing the subject a breeze.

"I did," she crooned, fluffing her fingers through her mid length shag. "Is it that obvious?"

I narrowed my eyes, pretending to ponder her question. Lily Tate's once brassy blonde hair was now dark chocolate brown. A blind man would have considered the change obvious. "It's pretty, Lil."

The pump clicked in my hand. The car was good to go. I began walking into the shop to pay. Even without turning around, I knew she was tottering along behind me.

"Charli," Lily called, just as I got to the door.

I drew in a long breath and turned to face her. "Yeah?"

"Did you know Nicole is back too?" A scandalous grin crossed her almost-pretty, overly made-up face. I frowned, but it had nothing to do with her question. It occurred to me that I had an opportunity to milk Lily for information.

I'd assured Nicole that I wasn't interested in hearing anything to do with her life on the run. That was a lie. I was desperate to know one thing. "Lily, what happened to Ethan? Did he come home too?"

I wanted to hear that he'd left Nicole high, dry and penniless in some dodgy foreign country. Hearing that he was holed up in prison somewhere would also have appeased me.

Lily's grin morphed into an unattractive duck-face pout. "Nicole came home alone. All we know is that the day after she got here, she went to the police station and took out a restraining order on him. Even if he does come back, he can't go anywhere near her."

"Yeah, right," I scoffed, dismissing her claim as shameless gossip. Even if it was true, there's no way Nicole would have told the Beautifuls.

"It's the truth!" she shrieked. "Jasmine's fiancée told us and –"

"Wait," I stuttered, putting my hand up. "Jasmine's engaged?"

Forget Ethan Williams. I wanted to know which poor sucker had agreed to take on Jasmine Tate for a lifetime.

Lily nodded so ardently that her huge silver hoop earrings got caught in her hair. "Yes, she is. Remember Norm and Floss's grandson?"

I cast my mind back to the meek constable who'd busted me for speeding a few days earlier. "Flynn Davis?"

She burst into a fit of hysterical giggles. I had no choice but to wait for her to compose herself to hear the answer. "Not Flynn, silly. The older one, Wade."

I couldn't recall ever meeting Wade. I barely remembered Flynn. I was curious to know more, but grilling the junior Beautiful for more information would have been an ordeal. I offered my congratulations and made a quick excuse to leave.

"I'll tell Jasmine you're back," called Lily as I walked away. "We can all catch up. It'll be just like old times."

I cringed. I hadn't missed the old times one little bit.

* * *

Postmistress Val was remarkably pleasant to me. She welcomed me home, told me how grown up I looked, and chastised me for wearing too many layers of clothing on such a lovely day.

"I'm acclimatising," I told her, forcing a smile in case she thought I was giving her attitude. Thankfully she smiled back. In fact, her expression didn't sour once until she asked me to pass on her regards to my father.

I waited until I was back in the car before opening my mail. The first parcel, a big manila envelope, was full of paperwork pertaining to Billet-doux. Little yellow 'sign here' stickers dotted every page. A handwritten note in Ryan's angry scrawl was pinned to the front page.

Tinker Bell,

For the most part, your defection has improved our business relationship considerably. Unfortunately, as co-owner, I still require your signature on certain documentation. Sign these papers and return them to me at your earliest convenience. That means today. Pretty please.

Ryan

I hadn't put any thought into how leaving New York would leave Ryan in the lurch. I suddenly felt bad, grabbed a pen from my bag and spent the next ten minutes signing paperwork in the name of Charlotte Décarie. Ryan had covered all bases by including a self-addressed envelope. I repackaged the papers, ventured back into the post office and returned them to the arrogant control-freak sender.

I didn't open the second parcel until that night when I was alone in my room. I tore the strip off the top and out tumbled my curly fry rings. I searched the empty package for a note but there was nothing – and it unfairly chipped at my heart. The finality of the gesture was heartbreaking.

Ignoring the hurt, I slipped the rings onto my finger and held my hand up to the dull light from my bedside lamp. They were far more ostentatious than I remembered, but still incredibly beautiful. And for some weird reason, they no longer slipped off my fingers when I wore them.

I fell asleep still wearing the rings that I'd only managed to grow into once I abandoned the union they represented.

December 21
Adam

My plan of avoiding Trieste until classes resumed in the New Year fell apart quickly. She'd been given my phone number.

"I thought we could meet today," she suggested, during an obscenely early morning call that woke me up.

"Trieste, do you have any idea what the time is?" I asked, making a mental note to block her number.

"Ah, twenty-two minutes past seven."

"On a Saturday," I added, as if it made a difference.

"I didn't think you'd have plans, considering you're recently separated and all. There's no point moping around by yourself." The nerve of the girl was astonishing. "I have an essay due that I could do with a bit of help with. I have to submit it tomorrow."

I let out a long disgruntled groan. It should've been enough to make her to hang up and forget ever calling me again. But she didn't. I found myself agreeing to meet her that afternoon.

* * *

Trieste had the gall to keep me waiting. I was just about to give up on her when she came running down the sidewalk with an armload of books.

"You're late." I tapped my watch. "I can't wait around for you all day."

"I know, I'm sorry. I had a job interview that ran over time."

I took the stack of books from her and stood nodding as she rattled off the reasons why she didn't get the job at the café she'd applied at, followed by the reasons why she didn't want it in the first place. "Coffee makes me sneeze anyway."

"Right. Well, can we go now?"

"Yes, but I have to warn you, lunch is on you. I'm broke."

I'd agreed to an hour of study, not lunch. The girl was impossible. "Fine," I surrendered. "I know a place close by."

* * *

Billet-doux wasn't really Trieste's scene. "I thought you said this place was great," she whispered, leaning across the table.

I continued reading through her essay, paying her next to no attention. "It is great."

"It's empty, Adam. Perhaps they have issues with the health department."

I looked up. Trieste was glancing at the floor, perhaps looking for signs of vermin.

"It's closed, Trieste. I thought it would be a quiet place to study."

She looked embarrassed. "Oh. I just thought the service was terrible."

I laughed blackly. "Don't let my brother hear you say that."

"Does he work here?"

"Sometimes." I turned my attention back to the papers in my hand.

Trieste managed to keep quiet until I'd finished reading. Once I was done, I straightened them and handed them back.

"Well?" she asked, pushing her glasses up her nose.

"It's fantastic," I said truthfully. "I would be proud to submit that kind of work."

She grinned and leaned back. "I know."

"Trieste, if you knew it was good, why did you drag me out to read it?"

"I just wanted you to see how good it was."

"Humble, aren't you?"

"No," she replied. "Not really. Can we eat now?"

Trieste Kincaid grows on you – like a flesh-eating virus. As much as she annoyed me, I was warming to her. I was feeling no urge to ditch her and make a run for it so I headed to the empty kitchen to see what I could rustle up for lunch. Left-over pasta was the best I could do. I microwaved it half to death, piled it onto a couple of plates and made my way back to front of house.

Trieste was standing near the far wall, studying Charli's canvas prints.

"These are very good," she said, glancing back at me.

I set the plates down on the table. "They are."

"I like this one the best." The canvas she was pointing at was very familiar. It was a picture of the cliffs at Pipers Cove – the very same picture that had led me to Charli in the first place.

I stood beside her, studying it as intently as she did. "It's my favourite too."

* * *

We'd almost finished lunch when Ryan strutted through the front door. The smart comments started immediately. "Cute place for a first date, Adam," he taunted, walking toward our table. "Your wife's restaurant."

I took the high road, because I almost always do where he's concerned. "Ryan, this is Trieste Kincaid."

She held out her hand. "Hi."

Ryan grinned as he met her handshake. "Hello, Trieste. Nice ears."

She took no offense at all. "Thanks," she replied, running her hands over the top of her beanie.

"Trieste is in her first year of law at Columbia. She's also looking for a job," I explained.

"Great," replied Ryan, walking toward the kitchen. "Good luck with your search."

I called out to him. "I think you should hire her."

He didn't even slow his walk. "No."

I turned my attention back to Trieste. "You can start Monday."

Ryan spun around and stalked back to the table, looking seriously pissed. "We're not hiring."

I ignored him and winked at her. "Monday."

She smiled.

My brother looked like he was in danger of exploding right out of his pretentious suit. "No. Trieste, I'm sorry. My brother is a little out of line. We're not hiring."

I leaned back in my chair, grinning at him. "Three words for you, Ryan. Power. Of. Attorney."

A look of pure anger swamped him. "What are you talking about?"

Trieste cleared her throat before interjecting. "Power of attorney is the authority to act for another person in legal or financial matters."

I laughed. Ryan didn't see the funny side.

"Yes, thank you, Miss First Year Law," he said sarcastically before turning to me. "Why didn't you tell me Charli gave you power of attorney? I just sent her a heap of papers to sign. You could've saved me the headache and signed them yourself."

I shrugged. "Hire Trieste and I'll consider it for next time."

He caved instantly. "Trieste, you start Monday. Lose the ears."

As soon as Ryan was gone, Trieste thanked me. "No big deal," I replied. "Just don't sneeze in the coffee."

I wasn't entirely sure that my gesture was an honourable one. Trieste had told me she was desperate to find a job. I figured giving her one would keep her out of my hair. She was an excellent student. She didn't need mentoring any more than I needed her calling me at dawn on the weekends.

* * *

Considering it was a Saturday night, I was surprised that Ryan was home when I got there. He seemed surprised to see me too. The massive canvas print I was dragging through the door might have had something to do with it.

Instantly, he knew I'd swiped it from Billet-doux.

41

"Great," he muttered. "First you're getting me to hire staff against my will and now you're stealing artwork."

He might've been pissed but at least he held the door open while I carried it inside.

"I want to hang it here." I crossed the room and leaned the canvas against the far wall.

Ryan stared at the picture. "As a reminder of your tragic loss?"

I scowled. "She's not dead, idiot."

"I like the Manhattan skyline ones better. The Brooklyn ones are good too. Pick one of those."

"No, I like this one." It was *my* picture. As far as I was concerned, it was her best work.

"Where was it taken?" asked Ryan.

"Pipers Cove."

"Never Never Land," he snorted. "That's where I sent her mail."

"Let's hope for your sake that's where she is then."

His focus shifted from the picture to me. "Why?"

"Because you need her to sign it. I lied when I said I had power of attorney. I just wanted you to give Trieste a job."

He punched me in the arm, sending me staggering to the side. "You are such a dick."

December 23
Charli

Living with Gabi and Alex wasn't working out. The house was just too small for the three of us. Besides, the Parisienne was driving me crazy. I used to be able to read her perfectly. She was notoriously pushy, uptight and chatty. Although still uptight, she was now quiet and absent a lot of the time. I couldn't stand the shift.

Something was definitely going on. I questioned Alex a few times but he brushed it off as her having a bad day. Gabrielle seemed to have a lot of bad days. I was beginning to think my return to town had something to do with it.

I waited until Alex had left for his morning surf, cornered her in the kitchen and tried to brighten her mood.

"Gabi, I've been thinking," I began. "Do you think it would be alright if I moved into the cottage?"

She left me hanging, waiting until she'd poured her tea before answering.

"Why would you choose to live alone?"

"I just miss having my own space. Besides, most of my stuff is there anyway."

She nodded but her expression remained blank. "Your father won't be pleased."

"I can handle Alex. I'm asking if you'd be okay with it."

She brought her mug to her lips, blowing a long breath to cool her tea. "I think it's a fine idea. But you can tell your father."

* * *

I agreed with Gabrielle's prediction that Alex wouldn't be thrilled with the new living arrangements, which is exactly why I made a bolt for the cottage before he got back from the beach.

Bouncing between Décarie real estate was something I'd become accustomed to. And just like the last time, I only had one suitcase of belongings to unpack when I got there. The first thing I did when I got inside was draw back the sheer curtains in every room. There really wasn't anything else to do. The cottage was fully furnished, spotlessly clean and gloriously quiet.

It didn't take Alex long to catch up with me. The grumbly red ute pulled onto the driveway an hour after I'd arrived. I met him at the door.

"Hi." He seemed a little apprehensive.

"Hi."

I held the screen door open but he made no attempt to come inside. "Do you want to walk for a minute?" he asked, giving an upward nod toward the yard.

I trailed behind him as he ventured into the garden. Most of the flowers had ended their spring run of blooms but pink peonies and plenty of lavender kept the rockeries colourful and bright. It was a glorious scene and I still couldn't grasp that Gabrielle had given it up.

Alex stopped and turned to face me. "Do you really want to move in here, Charli?" he asked, getting straight to the point. Perhaps he thought Gabrielle was pushing me out the door.

"Yes. I really do."

"I'd rather you stay with me," he said quietly. "I'd worry less."

"Oh, come on, Alex, I've been on my own for a while now. I can't stay with you and Gabrielle. I don't think she's happy having me there."

His face twisted. "It's nothing to do with you, Charli."

"So what then?" I pressed. "I know something's going on."

I could tell by the tortured look on his face that an explanation was going to be awkward for him. And like crazy and crying, my father did not do awkward.

"Gabs wants to have a baby."

I ducked my head, chasing his eyes. "*Gabi* wants to have a baby?"

"*We* want to have a baby," he amended, sounder much surer. "And it's proving trickier than anticipated."

"Um, is there a problem?" I had no clue how else to word it.

Alex dropped his head and kicked at the lawn. "No. There's no medical reason why she can't conceive. We know that because we've both been prodded and poked by every specialist in Hobart."

"Both of you?" My voice was high with surprise. Surely Alex's fertility wasn't in question. I was living proof that all his parts were in perfect working order.

For some reason, he laughed. "It's been twenty years since I fathered my first child. I suppose a lot can happen in twenty years. We just needed to be sure that –"

"That you're not too old?"

"Yes, because thirty-seven is positively ancient," he replied.

I laughed. He managed a coy smile.

"No wonder she's so uptight."

"Just go easy on her, Charli. Gabi has a lot on her mind."

I nodded. "I hope it works out for you."

He shrugged. "Of course it will. I keep reminding her that I make beautiful, clever children and it will be worth the wait. There's another kid out there for me. One came much earlier than expected and the other is taking a little longer, that's all."

I stepped forward and wrapped my arms around his middle. He leaned down and kissed the top of my head. Nothing else needed to be said.

* * *

Alex was furious when he found out I'd been travelling without a phone. I drowned out most of the lecture but I recall the terms 'serial killer' and 'shallow grave' being bounced around a couple of times.

Before he left the cottage, he presented me with a new one. "Don't lose it," he warned.

I stayed in the garden long after Alex left, sitting at the weather-beaten picnic table enjoying the summer sun on my back. I toyed with the idea of breaking in the new phone by calling Adam. Then I calculated the time difference and realised it was after one in the morning in New York. I also remembered that we weren't together any more. We weren't supposed to have anything to say to each other.

I put my phone to another use and emailed Bente. Through all the craziness, we'd kept in touch in the few months since she'd left New York with Lucas, her wannabe rock star boyfriend.

As it turned out, life on the road was not for Bente. Nor was Lucas. They'd only made it as far as Boston when she realised that she liked her men a little more clean cut – a little more Décarie-esque perhaps. Within a week she'd landed a job reporting for a small community newspaper, found an apartment, and was happier than ever.

In my last email, I'd told her that I'd left Adam and travelled the long way home via Africa.

I told you he was a frog, she'd emailed. *I'm glad you came to your senses*. I couldn't help smiling.

I composed my reply, defending my frog for a few lines before taunting her with mention of the glorious summer weather. I'd just hit the send button when someone called my name. I looked up to see Flynn Davis leaning against the low wooden fence that separated the cottage's yard from the property next door.

"Flynn, hi," I said, surprised. "What are you doing here?"

"I live here," he replied, thumb pointing at the house behind him. "What are you doing here?"

"Not breaking and entering, if that's what you're thinking. I'm staying here for a while."

"I wasn't thinking that for a second," he replied, laughing. "It'll be good to have you around, Charli."

I smiled. "Thanks. I think it's going to be good being around."

* * *

Using his key to get in, Alex woke me at a ridiculously early hour the next morning. "Charli, you have to get up."

It wasn't even light. I groaned but it did little to save me from the infantile man in the doorway flicking the light switch on and off.

"Alex, I'm tired. Go away."

"No chance of that, Charli. We're going to the beach," he said, far too enthusiastically. "A bit of fresh air will do you good."

"No, sleep will do me good. Take Gabrielle to the beach."

"Gabs doesn't do the beach at dawn. You do."

He tugged my blankets. I gripped the top of my bedding, fighting to stay covered. "No," I protested. "Go home."

"No chance. We're driving down to Cobb."

Cobb beach was south of the Cove. Alex surfed there because he had skill. The waves were huge because they were only a metre or two above a jagged reef. I didn't surf there because I liked the idea of living to see my thirties.

"I don't do Cobb, Alex." The words came out in a growl.

"You don't need to go in the water. You can sit in the sand and watch me in awe."

Fabulous.

"You're not going to leave me be, are you?"

I lost my grip on the blankets as he gave one last tug. "Nope. Now get up."

* * *

It was my first excursion to the beach since I'd been home and – not that I'd ever admit it to Alex – it was worth getting out of bed for. As soon as I got out of the ute I realised I'd missed everything about it. The mild December morning was crisp. The overcast sky and dark ocean was the biggest reminder of all that I was home.

I followed Alex down the sandy trail that cut through the heavily vegetated dune, stopping to pick a few long reeds. Alex was already dragging on his wetsuit by the time I caught up. I looked out to sea and felt a pang of jealousy. Huge waves thundered to shore, pounding onto the sand. I desperately wished I could follow him out there.

"Don't even think about it," he warned.

I waved the reed at him. "Did you drag me down here to taunt me?"

He laughed, a wonderful deep sound that I hadn't even realised I'd missed until I heard it. "Do you wish I'd left you in bed?"

"No," I conceded. "This is where I'm supposed to be this morning."

He began digging a groove in the sand with his foot. "Is today going to be difficult for you, Charli?" he asked gently. My mind spun as I tried to figure out what he was talking about. "I thought bringing you down here for an hour or two might take your mind off things."

"I don't know what you mean."

"Oh." His face brightened, instantly relieved by my indifference. "Okay then. Well, if you need me, I'll be out there." He pointed out to sea.

I rolled my eyes at him. "Just go." I zipped my hoodie all the way up to my neck, wrapped myself in Alex's towel and slumped down in the cool sand. I watched him jog down to the waterline, shift the board from under his arm and barrel into the waves in one fluid motion, showing no hesitation whatsoever.

We were wired exactly the same way. At times my father was just as mercurial and extreme as I was. Ironically, those were the traits that made him worry incessantly about me.

Jumbled daydreaming kept me occupied for a long time. As the morning progressed, a few other diehard surfers joined Alex out on the break while people on their morning walk began strolling the length of the beach. One of the walkers was Meredith Tate, the Beautifuls' mother. I recognised Nancy the half-bald Pomeranian first. The ugly little beast obviously hadn't conquered her eczema problem.

I stayed put, rugged up in the sand at the base of the dunes, looking enough like a vagabond that with luck she'd steer clear of me. I didn't want to talk to her. I knew she'd quiz me about Mitchell. He'd made a vague promise that he'd be home for Christmas and I didn't want to be the one to break it to her that he had no intention of following through. I took my phone out of my pocket and checked the date on the screen, wondering how many days Mitchell had before he'd break his mother's heart.

In an instant, the reason for Alex's offer to take my mind off things became clear. It was Christmas Eve. It had been a year to the day since I'd married the man who, despite everything, I wholeheartedly loved.

It seemed a shame to let the occasion pass without acknowledgement. I grabbed my phone and snapped a quick picture of the sea. I scrolled through to Adam's number and hit send, praying I wouldn't regret it.

December 23
Adam

The weather that evening was horrendous. The snowstorm outside kept Ryan and me holed up in the apartment. He was probably there against his will. I had nowhere to be anyway.

Ryan likes to cook when he's bored. It's his thing. He's like a mad professor in the kitchen, turning simple recipes into science experiments. Tonight's effort was some sort of cake.

He kicked my feet off the coffee table and set his masterpiece down. I think that was the moment I was supposed to tell him how amazing it looked.

"Well?" he prompted.

I shrugged. "It's a pink cake."

"Yes," he said seriously. "It's a pink cake. I think I used too much beet juice. What do you think?"

"I think you're a girl."

The only thing that saved me from wearing the cake was my phone beeping. I picked it up. I didn't recognise the number and there was no message, but I recognised the picture instantly. It was a beach at Pipers Cove. I should've guessed that's where Charli would go. All roads lead to Alex. It was the first rule of La La Land.

"It's from Charli, isn't it?" Ryan guessed. "Tell her to sign my papers."

"No. I don't care about your papers. I doubt she does either."

"What does she want?" I ignored him, leaving him to jump to his own conclusions. "She's joined a clan of travelling Peruvian basket weavers, hasn't she?"

"No. She sent me a picture." I could feel myself grinning. "Tonight the universe doesn't completely suck."

To anyone else the gesture would've seemed tiny, but in my mind she'd thrown me a lifeline. I'd spent days worrying that she'd never speak to me again.

I typed and deleted my reply fifty times before giving up and dropping my phone on the table. A text just wasn't going to cut it.

"What are you doing, Adam?" Ryan grumbled. "Let it go."

"I have the next two weeks off," I said, thinking out loud. "Now that I know where she is, I could spend it with her."

He let out a long sigh. "You're just setting yourself up for another fall."

I didn't care. As long as every ending we suffered brought on a new beginning, it would be worth it. "I'm going to do this," I told him, jumping to my feet. "I want to see her."

He called out as I got to the doorway. "Can I give you a bit of advice before you go?"

Nothing he said could blacken my mood. "Sure."

"If she lets you in the door, don't ruin it," he said flatly. "She's much smarter than you, which means you're not going to get too many more chances where Charli's concerned. Don't tell her you'd do anything for her. She knows it's not true."

For once he was right. I vowed not to promise her anything. I'd done enough damage that way already.

December 25
Charli

I'd assumed that being slapped in the face was as bad as a Christmas Day could get. I was wrong.

Having lunch at Floss and Norm Davis's was a given. It was a tradition that had been in place since I was four years old. As much as Alex and I loved their company, Floss's vegan fare left a lot to be desired.

The guest list was as dodgy as the menu this year, thanks to the sudden influx of Davises in town. Policeman Flynn and his big brother Wade made the list – along with Wade's plus one, his delightful fiancée, Jasmine Tate.

I trudged up to the steps of the Davis's front porch, trailing behind Alex and Gabrielle reluctantly. Floss met us at the door with outstretched arms and a huge grin on her ruby red lips. One by one she pulled us into a tight hug before allowing us to file through the door. "Welcome home, my darling," she crooned, smooshing me against her chest. "You look beautiful."

I smiled. "Thanks Floss, so do you."

Floss looked very…festive. Gingerbread and candy cane brooches jazzed up her green tent-like dress and she wore a gold tinsel headband in her curly red hair.

Alex moved straight to the kitchen. Gabrielle made a beeline for the Christmas tree to add our gifts to the pile. I wasn't quite sure how to busy myself. After shifting a sleeping cat, I sat on one of the velvet recliners.

"Where is everyone, Floss?"

"They'll be here, Lovie," she replied, shifting the lace curtain aside to peer out. "Any minute now."

Alex and Norm came back a moment later, beers in hand, debating the riveting topic of how best to change the blades on a lawnmower. Gabrielle shifted a cat and sat on the chair next to mine. "You spent Christmas with Jean-Luc and Fiona last year, didn't you?" she asked, leaning over to whisper the question.

"Yes."

"Did they have a lovely tree?" She stared at the Christmas tree in the corner of the room and sighed heavily. "They always have an outstanding tree."

Floss's tree would never have been described as outstanding. The top half of the plastic green branches displayed chintzy coloured baubles. I wondered aloud why the bottom half was bare.

Floss chimed in. "The cats attack it." She picked up a floppy grey cat and cradled it like a baby. "Prevention is better than cure."

Flynn Davis arrived next. After being swamped by one of his grandma's hugs, he made it in the door. He looked different without the starchy police uniform, but nervous and ill at ease. His powder blue-and-white plaid shirt was tucked into his dark blue jeans. His brown belt matched his brown boots. All that was missing was a cowboy hat. Floss proudly introduced him to the room.

"You remember Gabi and Alex," she crooned. Alex stood and shook his hand. Gabrielle gave a smile and little wave. "And this is little Charli. She's all grown up now."

Flynn smiled at me. "Good to see you again, Charli. Are you feeling better?"

"Much, thank you," I mumbled. Alex frowned. "Flynn busted me for speeding on the way into town."

Alex's frown intensified.

"And Charli nearly spewed on my shoes," added Flynn, still grinning. "She wasn't feeling well."

Floss and Norm cackled as if he'd told the funniest joke in history. I didn't find it particularly funny. Neither did Alex or Gabrielle. Both of them remained stone-faced, and I quickly changed the subject. "Lunch smells good, Floss."

"It's a fabulous spread this year," she announced proudly. "Orange glazed beets, sautéed red cabbage, lentil and mushroom pie…"

"Sounds great," gushed Alex insincerely. Gabrielle took a gulp of wine before dishonestly agreeing.

It was a long day made impossibly longer by the arrival of Wade Davis and his sparkly plus one. Jasmine tottered up the path singing. "Merry Christmas to me! Merry Christmas to me!" She hadn't changed one bit. Her long blonde hair, over-processed and straggly at the ends, was pulled into a loose ponytail. I couldn't quite make out the sparkly motif on her white T-shirt, but it perfectly matched her gold sling-back pumps. Wade ambled behind her, carrying an armful of gifts. I used the time it took him to get to the porch to check him out.

He was a monstrously huge man – without an ounce of fat on his body. He was like a beefed-up Ken doll, which made him a perfect match for sparkly tramp Barbie who was now pounding on the door.

Floss jumped up to greet them.

"Granny Floss!" Jasmine beamed, hugging her tightly. "Merry Christmas!"

"To you too, Lovie," crooned Floss.

Jasmine broke their embrace, leaned back and tugged at her shirt. "Look at this. It's a cat!"

Floss broke into a hearty chuckle. "Oh, so it is! You have a glittery kitty on your shirt."

"I knew you'd like it," replied Jasmine, breaking into a giggle of her own.

I'd stepped into some sort of alien universe. Who was this moron, and what had she done with that bitch Jasmine Tate? I glanced at Alex, perhaps seeking reassurance. He winked at me and stifled a grin.

Wade fell through the door a second later, dumping the stack of presents on the floor. Jasmine slapped his beefy arm. "They're breakable, babe," she chided. He kissed her cheek by way of apology.

"That's enough of that, you two." Floss pointed at us all. "We have guests."

Jasmine gasped as if she'd only just realised we were in the room. "Alex," she greeted with a nod of her head.

"Hi Jasmine," he replied.

Jasmine nodded again, stiffly. "Mademoiselle Décarie."

I bit my lip, trying desperately hard not to laugh. Jasmine might have turned over the biggest leaf in the forest but Gabrielle had cut her no slack whatsoever. And Jasmine was still addressing her like an authoritative high school French teacher because of it.

"And Charli." She purred my name as she tottered toward me, arms outstretched.

I stood up, bracing myself for an artificial hug. Instead she grabbed my hands and held them away from my body while she gave me the once-over. "You look so pretty. Still no fashion sense, though."

Said the girl with a sequined cat on her shirt. My mouth fell open but I said nothing. She dropped my hands and leaned in to whisper. "White isn't your colour."

Floss worked quickly to smooth things over. "Wade," she said, tapping him on the chest. "You remember Alex's daughter, Charli. She was just a wee mite last time you saw her."

A huge grin swept beefy Wade's face. "How are you, Charli?" He spoke as if I was still a wee mite. "You probably don't remember me."

I shook my head. "No. I'm sorry."

"I'm Jasmine's fiancée." He actually sounded proud of it.

"Lucky guy," I praised, forcing a smile.

* * *

Dinner was every bit the ordeal I expected it to be. Worse than the sautéed cabbage was the ridiculous toast that Wade insisted on making. He stood, puffed out his already mammoth chest and charged his glass.

"I'd just like to make a toast to my fiancée, Jasmine," he declared, gazing at her. He cleared his throat. "You are the wind underneath my wings and the flesh overneath my bones."

I nearly choked on a glazed beet.

As soon as I could escape without being considered rude, I excused myself and slipped out to the back yard. The Davis's yard was as cluttered as the house. The grass was in desperate need of cutting. Old wheelbarrows and car tyres had been recycled into pots that housed mostly dead plants. Everywhere I looked, a garden gnome stared back at me. In the far corner was *La Coccinelle*, parked up on a boat trailer. Part of me felt as if I was seeing an old friend. A bigger part of me felt a little wounded by her presence.

I stood on the patio, staring at the boat for a long time. The tinkle of three different wind chimes clashing in the breeze was downright irritating – but less irritating than watching Wade and Jasmine's public display of affection at the dinner table.

"Nice boat, don't you think?" came a voice from behind.

I spun around to see Flynn.

"Very nice," I agreed, turning my attention back to the boat. "She hasn't always looked that good."

Flynn moved to stand beside me. "Really? I can't imagine it."

"She used to be a pile of junk. Adam spent hours bringing her back to life."

"Adam?"

"My husband," I explained, inadequately.

"Oh." He sounded surprised. "Does he restore boats professionally?"

I glanced at Flynn, trying to work out whether he was fishing for information or genuinely clueless. "No. He's almost an attorney."

He laughed. "Almost?"

"He'll have his degree in a few months."

"I see. Will he be joining you here then?"

"You're not very subtle when it comes to playing detective, Constable."

"I'm sorry." He actually blushed. "I don't mean to pry."

That was a lie. That's exactly what he meant to do. He just wasn't very good at being sly about it.

"Your grandma knows everything about everyone, Flynn. I'm sure she'd fill you in on all the gaps." He glanced at me, flashing a quick half smile, but I could see the pity in his blue eyes. I shook my head. "There's no story here, Flynn."

"Ooh, I'm sure there is," crowed Jasmine, appearing out of thin air. "And I want to know everything!"

Turning the tables was the only chance I had of escape. "I want to know about you and Wade," I told her. "He seems lovely."

It was a less than honest assessment. Wade was all brawn and absolutely no brain.

"He's gorgeous, isn't he?" asked Jasmine lovingly.

I nodded, told her how lucky she was to have found him and asked how they'd met, managing to sound interested. Flynn bowed out, making an excuse about wanting another drink. After he'd gone, Jasmine grabbed two plastic chairs from the corner of the patio. She sat on one and pointed to the other.

The story of Wade and Jasmine was hardly spellbinding. They'd met when her father embarked on a fitness kick and decided to hire a personal trainer. Beefy Wade got the job – and the girl.

I had to concede that Wade Davis might be good for Jasmine. Somewhere along the line she'd lost the caustic personality that I despised so much. I still didn't like her, but I wasn't feeling any urge to dye her hands orange either. Besides, Floss had warmed to her. That had to count for something.

"Well, I'm sure you'll be very happy together."

"Thanks, Charli," she crowed. "I'm really glad you're back in town for a while. Will Adam be here soon?"

For once in his life, Alex's timing was impeccable. "Charli," he called, stepping out. "Are you ready to go?"

I jumped out of my seat. "Yeah." I turned back to face the chief Beautiful. "I'll see you later."

"Yes. We'll do lunch or something. We have a lot of catching up to do."

I doubt she meant to sound threatening. I forced a smile and rushed toward Alex, who was holding the door for me.

"I hope you've been playing nicely," he whispered as I passed. I went into the house without answering him.

December 26
Adam

Travelling over the Christmas period isn't ideal. It's supposed to be the season of goodwill and cheer, but everybody I saw looked miserable.

JFK airport was bedlam but LAX was worse. By the time I finally arrived in Melbourne I wasn't sure what day it was. When I got to Hobart three hours after that, I wasn't even sure what my name was. I was exhausted. Just after midnight I picked up a rental car and began the hour-long drive to the Cove.

As desperate as I was to see Charli, I wasn't an idiot. Given the latest turn of events, turning up at Alex's door at one in the morning would be detrimental to my health. I had no idea what Charli's explanation for returning home alone had been. The truth was bad enough.

I decided to head to the cottage and wait until morning. I knew it was empty. I hoped that the spare key was still under the doormat.

The street was in darkness. There weren't even streetlights. A full moon guided me fumbling up to the porch. I finally found the key and made my way inside.

And the ambush began. A tangle of long blonde hair rushed at me through the darkness. I knew it was Charli, because she came out swinging. It was hardly a hardcore attack. Whatever she was whacking me with only registered as irritating because I was so tired.

"Charli, stop!"

She didn't stop.

I threw her over my shoulder and dumped her on the couch as gently as I could considering she was still whaling at me.

I flicked on the light and stared at my beautiful, crazy wife.

"Adam!" She rushed out my name. "I thought you were a burglar."

"So what was your plan, Charlotte?" I asked. "Beat me to death with a plastic spatula?"

She looked at the utensil in her hand and dropped it. "What are you doing here?"

"I'm here to see you."

Charli took a long time to process my words before jumping up and leaping at me. The hold I had on her kept her feet off the floor. Her hands held my face in place while she kissed me over and over. The reunion was going well until she stopped kissing me, leaned her head back and pinched my cheek, Grandma Nellie style.

"Ow! What was that for?"

"I was just checking that I'm awake. It'd suck if I was dreaming right now."

I dropped my head, smiling into the curve of her shoulder. "You're supposed to pinch yourself, not me."

"Oh."

I lifted my head and was met by the gorgeous smile I'd missed so much. "I want to tell you why I'm here," I murmured.

"You chased me," she said smugly. "That's why you're here."

I needed to set the record straight. She needed to know that nothing had changed. I hadn't figured a way out of the mess we were in. We were still stuck in limbo and I was still a selfish ass. I was just a selfish ass who couldn't stay away from her.

I lowered her to her feet. If flee-itis kicked in, she'd thank me for it.

"I just needed to see you. I have a few weeks off so I –"

She put a finger to my lips. "I'm not stupid, Adam. There's no Disney movie playing in my head. You're on Christmas break, right?"

I nodded and she dropped her hand. "I've got two weeks."

"Okay. Two weeks." She calculated. "We'll just have to make the most of it."

I grabbed her waist and jerked her forward. "Do you have something in mind?"

Before I'd even got the question out, she was unbuttoning my shirt.

"No," she mumbled. "Nothing."

I gripped her T-shirt, yanked it over her head and dropped it to the floor. I then dropped Charlotte to the floor, impatient to feel her body against mine. "Disney would never approve of this," I murmured, closing my eyes as my lips touched her warm skin.

I felt her hold on me tighten as she shuddered. "I never liked the Disney version anyway," she breathed.

* * *

I woke early the next morning feeling cold and disoriented. Even in summer, Tasmanian mornings are cold. My neck was stiff and I regretted the decision to fall asleep on the living room floor. The rug did nothing to cushion us.

Charli looked completely content. She was beside me, covered by the throw from the couch, sleeping like the dead. I stroked her cheek. She didn't stir.

"Charli," I whispered. I kissed her shoulder, marvelling at how incredibly warm she felt. "Time for bed."

She groaned but didn't move. Somehow I got her off the floor and down to the bedroom. I laid her on the bed, covered her up and swept her hair off her face. She was asleep again in seconds.

* * *

It was really early. I stood at the back windows watching the first hint of daylight crack above the horizon. The dark ocean lightened as daylight took hold, revealing pounding waves that raged against the shore. It truly was a beautiful place. The only thing that would've made the setting more perfect was a decent cup of coffee. I wasn't going to get one in the cottage – I couldn't even find a jar of instant coffee. Plenty of cereal though.

Gabrielle made great coffee. As soon as I thought it was a respectable enough hour to be visiting, I left Charli a note and slipped out the door.

I didn't make it as far as the house. Alex was in the shed. Sneaking past was impossible. He would've seen me coming the second I pulled onto the long driveway. I had no choice but to front him. All I could do was hope that Gabrielle had also seen me arrive as I was probably going to need medical attention at some point.

He barely looked up as I got to the door. As a precautionary measure, I went no further than the doorway.

"Adam," he said ominously. "Gabs is still in bed. It's early."

It *was* freakishly early, barely after seven. And if she was still in bed, I was on my own.

"I'll come back later then." I replied, making no attempt to leave.

Alex continued scrubbing a block of wax across his surfboard, which was laid out on the workbench. "When did you get here?" he asked.

"Last night."

"I knew you'd show up sooner or later," he said. "I was just hoping it would be later – when she'd come to her senses and forgotten your name."

His attitude was nothing less than I expected or deserved. I wasn't even going to try defending myself.

"Are you going to try talking Charli into going back to New York?" he asked. "Is that why you're here?"

"No. I wouldn't do that. I have a couple of weeks off. I just wanted to see her."

Alex didn't reply. In fact he didn't say anything. I almost wished he'd just thump me and get it over with.

"What do you know about surfing, Adam?" he asked finally.

"Not a whole lot."

He glanced up at me and smiled – and not in a good way. "Maybe it's time you learned."

"I've seen the size of the waves this morning," I replied. "I came here for coffee, not a near death experience."

"Relax, Boy Wonder," he taunted. "I won't let you die."

Nothing about him sounded believable.

Abandoning the board, he grabbed one of the wetsuits hanging from the rack behind him and thrust it at me. "How tall are you?" he asked sizing me up with his eyes.

"Six, two."

He turned to the wall and grabbed a board. The thing was huge – at least eight foot.

"I know it looks big but it'll float," he explained. "Even if you don't." He followed up with another evil smile.

"This wasn't what I had in mind when I came here."

"I know that, Adam. But things don't always work out as you plan, do they?"

* * *

We left my car at the house and took Alex's ute. At least I'd left evidence of my last known whereabouts. We ended up at the beach below the cottage. We were the only ones there. I wasn't sure if that was a good or bad sign. Alex had hardly said two words since we'd left the house. I didn't know if that was good or bad either. He became a little chattier when he hit the sand, but only to bark instructions.

"This is a long board," he said pointing at it. "That means you can't cut through a wave. If you think you're going to have trouble getting over it, turtle roll."

He'd already lost me and he knew it. "Grab the rails and flip it over," he elaborated.

"The rails?" The man was speaking a different language.

"The edges."

"Okay."

"Paddle straight into it. If you approach at an angle, you're going to roll. Rolling is bad. Stay perpendicular to the oncoming wave, then turtle roll if you need to."

"You just said rolling was bad."

"Rolling *is* bad."

Unless there's a turtle involved. This was going to end in tragedy, but I figured he knew that already.

"What happens if I wipe out?"

He dropped his head and laughed blackly. "Oh, you're going to get massacred, Adam. No doubt about it."

"Great." I drew out the word. "Any advice that will keep me alive would be appreciated."

He looked pensively out to sea. "If you wipe out, relax and let yourself sink. Waves are powerful, but they don't have nearly as much pull below the surface. Just let yourself sink and you'll pass safely underneath it."

I glared at him, horrified. "This is what you do for fun?"

He turned his head, looking straight at me. "Every day of my life."

The instructions didn't stop once we were in the water. Somehow I managed to paddle out past the breaking waves. Alex was already there, sitting on his board, rolling over the oncoming waves as he waited.

"You look forward, I'll look back," he told me. "When I tell you to go, go. Paddle hard. Don't try and get up, stay on your belly and just coast in. Got it?"

"Yeah." *No.*

I kept my focus on the beach ahead, wondering how many pieces I'd be in when I reached the shore. It was like waiting to be struck by a train. I felt the dips as we rolled over the top of three more waves before he spoke again.

"Get ready," he warned. There was nothing I could do but listen to him. "Go, Adam! Go! Go! Go!"

I paddled hard. The wave rolled under me and I went nowhere. That happened more than once. I was hoping Alex would lose patience and give up, but he didn't. He was determined to kill me.

"Try again. Next one's the charm," he told me.

After my millionth attempt, something incredible happened. I actually caught a wave. I paddled hard until the force of the water took over. From there, I just hung on for dear life – and felt the absolute rush of my life.

As soon as I was through it, I wanted to go again. Alex stayed out past the breaking waves, waiting for me to paddle all the way out again, which seemed to take forever.

"That was freaking awesome!" I yelled, long before I could be sure he'd hear me.

He laughed. "What did I tell you?"

"I want to go again."

"Yeah, I figured you might."

I knew that forcing me into the water that day wasn't a bonding exercise. Alex was a grown-up version of Charli. There was a deeper meaning to it, I just wasn't privy to it yet.

"Why are we out here, Alex?"

He grabbed the nose of my board to stop me drifting away. My board wasn't sleek, short and pretty like his, but it did float better. He was half submerged.

"I just want you to understand it," he replied. "It's one of the many reasons why my kid doesn't belong in a big city. I made her that way."

He made it sound like the greatest thing he'd ever accomplished. I wasn't about to argue the point. As long as I was floating on a piece of fibreglass hundreds of yards from shore, my life was in his hands.

"I get it. And for the record, I already knew that your daughter doesn't belong in a big city."

"That creates a bit of a problem for you, doesn't it?"

"Not really," I mumbled. "We'll work it out."

"She doesn't need you, Adam," he told me. "Sometimes she just thinks she does."

"You might be right," I agreed, "but I need her."

"From what she's told me, you don't deserve her."

"You might be right about that too," I conceded.

Giving me an unsympathetic grin, he shoved the nose of my board, widening the distance between us. "Ready to go again?"

"Yeah. Let's go." I sounded much surer this time round, but my confidence turned out to be a little premature. It was hard to pinpoint the moment it went bad. One minute I was on top of the whole world, coasting through the water. The next minute I was under it, thrashing around, trying to stay alive.

I should've heeded the warning to relax and let myself sink, but the urge to get to the surface took over. I fought the water the whole way in and came out second best, eventually surfacing in knee-deep water near the shore. I staggered onto the dry sand and collapsed in a heap, coughing like a pack-a-day-smoker.

Alex appeared a few minutes later. It was too much to think he'd come in to check on my welfare. He walked up to the beach to retrieve the board that had washed up after me.

"Not too bad," he said examining it. "Nothing I can't fix."

"Oh my God!" screamed a familiar voice in the distance. "Alex, you've killed him!"

A tad dramatic maybe, but at least she was concerned.

"He's not dead, Charli," scoffed Alex. "He's probably feeling more alive than he ever has."

She knelt beside me and pulled my head onto her lap. "Are you okay?"

I squinted, focusing on her lovely, worried face. "Charli," I muttered. "How did you know I was here?"

"I was watching from the house. I knew the only idiot stupid enough to be out this morning was Alex. I grabbed the binoculars to see who the other idiot was and saw it was you!"

"It was freaking amazing, Charlotte," I muttered, brushing her hair from my face.

She glared at her father, who was somewhere behind me chuckling.

"Oh great. He's delirious," she growled. "Alex, what were you thinking? He could've drowned."

"Lighten up, Charli," he replied. "Boy Wonder actually has skill. He managed to stay alive, didn't he?"

"No thanks to you!"

He laughed, and for some reason I did too, even though it hurt. Charli wasn't impressed. She stood up, letting my head thump on the sand, and uselessly tried pulling me to a sitting position.

"Get up," she ordered, turning her wrath on me. "You're as foolish as he is."

* * *

A long hot shower brought me back to life. Once I was able to convince Charli that I wasn't on the verge of death, her mood lifted.

"You're sure you're okay?" she asked, handing me a towel.

"Better than okay," I told her. "It was awesome."

"Great. So now you're a convert, you can move here and surf all day. We'll grow dope and buy a Kombi van."

I swiped the towel down my face, laughing into it. "Nice plan, Coccinelle." I wrapped the towel around my waist, grabbed her hips and pulled her forward.

"It really was a rush," I told her, pressing up against her. "Scary and unpredictable. A bit like being married to you."

"I knew you were going to get thrashed. I was halfway down the trail to the beach before you even got to shore."

It was fair to assume there was a something lacking in my technique, but I was still curious. "How did you know?"

She put her finger on my chest, drawing an invisible diagram. "You caught it at an odd angle. You were always going to roll, especially on that big clunker board," she explained. "I'm glad you lived through it though."

I leaned down and kissed the wry grin off her face. "Me too."

* * *

After all I'd endured that morning, getting a caffeine hit became a matter of survival. I was prepared to head out to see Gabrielle again but Charli talked me out of it. "You need a bit of a heads-up where the Parisienne's concerned," she hinted. "We'll go to the café instead."

"Wait," I caught her hand as she passed me. "I want to know about Gabi. What's going on?"

"I'll tell you on the way," she promised. "I'll tell you *everything* along the way.

* * *

I could've negotiated the streets of Pipers Cove blindfolded – all eleven of them. And we drove down just about every one, buying time while Charli brought me up to speed on all the small town news.

I wasn't all that interested in hearing that Jasmine Tate had finally secured a man, or that my Audi now looked like a souped-up mess. Hearing of Gabrielle's fragile state did concern me, though.

"So are we supposed to mention it or not?" I asked.

She shook her head. "I don't think so. She'll tell us if she wants us to know. Alex only told me because I gave him no choice."

"It'll work out for them," I assured her, reaching over to muss her hair. "And when it does, you'll be a big sister."

She pushed my hand away, chuckling. "Wise guy."

By the time we pulled up at the café, Charlotte was all talked out. As I reached the door, she grabbed my arm. "There's one more thing you should know."

"Good or bad?"

"Horrendous. Nicole is back in town – working here."

"Alex took her back?"

"Alex doesn't know the whole story."

I wasn't sure how this was going to play out. Charli certainly wasn't showing any sign of forgiveness. I could see the tension on her face.

"Do you want to go somewhere else?"

She shook her head. "No. I haven't done anything wrong."

I don't know what sort of reaction I was expecting from Nicole when we walked in. Her cheeks went beet red at the sight of us – hardly the sign of a career criminal.

"Hi," she meekly greeted.

I smiled but said nothing, leaving it to Charli to set the mood.

"Hi," she said coldly.

Probably realising that was all she was going to get from her, Nicole turned her attention to me. "How are you, Adam?"

"Good, thank you."

"How long are you in town for?"

I opened my mouth but Charli chimed in. "Stop talking, Nic."

And that was the end of that. Charli walked around the counter and made me a world-class coffee in record time. Nicole stood frozen, looking close to tears. I wandered around the café, trying to look occupied. And no one said a word.

Charlotte marched us out the door the second she handed me the cup.

"Well, that wasn't awkward," I mocked as we walked back to the car.

"I have nothing to say to her, and nor do you. Stay away from her," she ordered.

"Yes Ma'am."

Charli spun to face me. "I can't forgive her, Adam." She'd obviously been struggling with the notion. "I don't have it in me."

"You forgave me," I reminded her. I'd put her through a whole lot more than thirteen grand's worth of pain.

She looked at me, slowly shaking her head. "I didn't forgive you. I left you."

My straight-talking wife had a way with words. Whether she realised it or not, she'd bitten me hard.

"Moved on without me, huh?" I teased, trying to deflect the sting.

The corner of her mouth lifted as she fought against smiling. "Leaps and bounds." She threw out her arms. "Didn't look back once."

I set my coffee on the roof of the car before pulling her against me. Her body went limp as I dipped her backwards. "You forgot about me?"

"Yes," she breathed. "Three short weeks and you're nothing more than a cute bloke in a car park."

"You're a cold woman, Charlotte Décarie," I declared, leaning in closer. "Let me refresh your memory."

I pressed my lips to the side of her neck, deciding she was anything but cold. I might never have let her go if we hadn't been interrupted by the sound of a car braking hard on the gravel.

I righted Charli and turned to see something that vaguely resembled the Audi I used to own. It was trashed – completely and utterly wrecked. Even the back bumper was held on with wire.

"You weren't kidding," I mumbled. "They've killed my car."

Charlotte muffled her laughter by burying her face in my sleeve.

"Adam!" screeched Jasmine, messily exiting the driver's side. "Fancy seeing you here!"

I reached for Charli's hand. "Yeah," I replied dully. "Fancy." I tried hard not to look her up and down but it was impossible not to. Jasmine hadn't changed much. She still looked like a two-dollar hooker.

"We all thought you'd broken up." She alternated her finger between the two of us. "That's the word around town anyway."

"Two guesses where the word came from," Charli muttered. I squeezed her fingers, silently promising her a quick getaway.

"Well, it's nice to see you again, Jasmine," I said politely, edging away from her.

"Wait, wait!" She lurched forward, thrusting her left hand in front of my face. "Did you hear my news? I'm engaged."

I ducked out of the way of her hand and opened the passenger door of the car. "Great. Congratulations."

"Aw, thanks, Adam. I knew you'd be thrilled for me."

"Thrilled," I listlessly confirmed.

Charli grabbed my coffee off the roof and got in the car. Jasmine followed me to the driver's side, cornering me like a lipstick-wearing rottweiler.

"His name's Wade. He's a personal trainer. You should meet him."

"I look forward to it."

"Great. We'll have dinner tonight. Just the four of us. My parents have opened up a restaurant at the vineyard. Say, eight o'clock?"

I hadn't seen it coming, nor could I think quickly enough to get out of it. My head involuntarily nodded.

"Fab," she crowed, slapping my arm. "We'll see you then."

At the first chance of escape, I got in the car and slunk down in the seat. "Charlotte, what's the current status of your relationship with Jasmine Tate?"

She giggled. "Put it this way: if she was on fire, and I had water, I'd drink it."

"That's what I thought," I mumbled. "I might have just given you grounds for divorce."

"What did you do?"

I couldn't look at her. "I just accepted a dinner invitation for tonight. Apparently they've opened up a restaurant at the vineyard."

"Why would you do that?" She sounded utterly appalled.

I glanced at her from the corner of my eye. "I didn't know what to say."

"Latin, French and English." She ticked the words off on her fingers. "You're fluent in all of them. You couldn't think of anything?"

I grabbed my phone from the console. "Give me her number. I'll call and cancel."

She snatched it out of my hand. "Oh no you don't, Boy Wonder. You're going to suffer through it. That's your punishment for being a wuss."

I grinned at her. "You're so lovely when you're mad. I like it."

She grinned back. "Keep making dates with the enemy and you'll see a lot more of it."

* * *

Knowing we only had two weeks together should've been accompanied by the awful feeling of being on borrowed time. But I wasn't feeling it. We seemed to have fallen back into place as if we'd never been apart. I wasn't going to waste time trying to figure it out. I just wanted to enjoy being with her.

I was also enjoying the quiet pace of life in a country town.

It wasn't a total escape. My mother had been blowing up my phone since I'd left New York. I'd expected to be in trouble for bailing on Christmas with the family; that's why I'd left Ryan to break the news.

I stood on the veranda, checking my voicemails while I watched Charli in the yard. I was listening to a demon woman giving me marriage advice while watching an angel woman wander around the garden. Choosing between the two wasn't difficult. I deleted the demon mid-message – just as she got the part about marriage being forever. I focused on the angel instead, who was snipping at flowers with a pair of scissors.

Charli suddenly stopped dead, standing completely still with her arms by her sides.

"Charli?" I called. "Are you okay?"

She turned and flashed me her loveliest smile.

"Yeah. There's a bee."

"Are you trying to get stung or not get stung?" I couldn't be sure. If I remembered correctly, it was number eighty-something on her never-done list.

Ignoring the threat of the bee, she walked over to me. I reached for her hand and helped her onto the veranda.

"I don't want to get stung today," she replied. "I'm busy this afternoon."

"Doing what?"

"I thought I might go and see Gabrielle. I want to take her some lavender." She waved the bunch at me. "You probably want to catch up with her too, right? We can pick up your car while we're there."

"Okay." I frowned. "Odd gift, though."

She shrugged. "Not really. It's baby bait."

"There's a story here, isn't there?" It was one of my dumber questions. I already knew the answer.

"Not unless you want to hear it."

She knew very well that I wanted to hear it. The question was whether Gabrielle was going to want to hear it. I'd never known Gabi to be particularly interested in La La Land. On the other hand, if she was as desperate in her quest to have a baby as Charli seemed to think she was, she might be prepared to entertain anything.

December 26
Charli

Dealing with Gabrielle was hard work. Alex had made me promise not to rattle her cage, but the truth was it didn't take much to wind her up these days. Every time I saw her, she looked like she was about to burst into tears.

Adam followed me as I walked up the path to the house, carrying my little bunch of lavender with both hands like a nervous bridesmaid. Gabrielle was on the veranda in front of an easel, stabbing at it with a brush. She usually favoured pretty pastel landscapes. From where I stood, it looked as if she was trying to murder the canvas.

"Hello Gabi," said Adam, stepping forward to kiss her cheek.

"Oh, Adam," she beamed. "I was so excited when Alex told me you were here. I'm sorry I missed you this morning."

"It was early."

"I hope Alex went easy on you." The Parisienne wasn't renowned for sly smiles. She surprised me by pulling one off perfectly.

"I survived." He pointed at the canvas. "What are you working on?"

I couldn't see the painting from where I stood, but Adam's frown spoke volumes. "What's it supposed to be?" he asked.

"Nothing. Just colour. Do you like it?"

"Sure," he replied, not very sincerely.

The Parisienne dropped the brush into a jar of turpentine. I got the impression she didn't particularly like it either.

Adam sat down on a wicker chair near the door. I glanced at him in time to see him motion with his head for me to give up the lavender.

I thrust it at Gabrielle as she reached for the screen door handle.

"For me?" she asked.

I felt like a primary school kid giving the teacher flowers. "Yeah, but there's a reason."

She eyed me suspiciously. "Did you do something?"

That is precisely why I hate being gifted flowers. Every bunch I ever got was by way of apology, usually from Fiona and sometimes from Ryan. They're nothing more than a big fat sorry wrapped in a bow.

I shook my head. "No. Nothing. I just…" I straightened up and with a nod of encouragement from Adam, found my voice.

"Aed fairies, they're Estonian," I told her. "Unborn babies supposedly take the form of Aed fairies. They hang out in the garden because they love to play."

She blinked at me a few hundred times, but didn't speak. I took it as an invitation to continue.

"The problem is, when it's time to come into the house and take the form of an actual human child, they get side-tracked because they love the garden so much. That's where the lavender comes in." I pointed at the bunch in her hand. "Sewing sprigs of lavender into the hem of the curtains helps them find their way inside. The wind blows the scent into the home. They follow the fragrance of the garden."

Gabrielle looked down at the lavender in her hands. I couldn't be sure what was going to happen next. As far as she knew, I didn't know a thing about her fertility problems. Not only had I called her out on it, I'd sold Alex out too. She now knew he'd told me.

"And you believe this will help?" she asked.

I shrugged. "The way I see it, if your baby is an Aed fairy right now, he probably just needs a bit of direction. This is Alex's kid we're talking about. I'm Alex's kid too. We like to play outdoors."

Her next move astounded me. She threw her arms around me and drew me into a tight hug. "*Tu es bien la fille de ton père*," she whispered.

I looked quizzically at Adam over her shoulder. He winked at me and smiled.

Gabrielle released me and headed into the house, mumbling something about making a pot of tea. I walked to Adam and he reached for my hand, pulling me into his lap.

"I think she appreciated that."

"What did she say?" I asked curiously.

"She said you're your father's daughter."

Her strange sentence stuck with me. Just as we were leaving, I snuck down to their bedroom. I don't know what made me check but I walked over to the window, immediately noticing two sprigs of lavender pinned to the lightweight curtain. Alex had beaten me to it. He'd already told her about Aed fairies. I *am* my father's daughter, and if things worked out how they were supposed to, I'd soon be sharing him.

* * *

There was a time when going to dinner with the sparkly couple would've had me cowering in the corner. Those days were over. After what I'd endured in the past year, it would be a walk in the park.

That didn't mean I couldn't stir the pot a little. Jasmine Tate was Pipers Cove's self-proclaimed supreme fashionista. I dug through the packing boxes in the spare room, found a gorgeous dress that Ivy had made for me and matched it with a pair of heels that were worth more than the Audi – the Audi in its current state at least.

"What do you think?" I asked, doing a twirl as I walked into the lounge.

Adam stared, wide-eyed. "I think we should stay in for the night."

"I've been playing in the dress-up box." I fanned out the bottom of my dress. "I'm going to give Miss Tate a run for her money."

He flashed me a half-dimpled smile. "I think you'd do that regardless of how you were dressed, Charli."

I walked over and straightened his already-straight collar. "You might struggle, though," I teased. "I don't want you to be jealous of Wade when you meet him. No tears before dessert, okay?"

His sexy smile matched my sexy black dress perfectly.

"I'll try not to be too intimidated," he promised.

"Good man." I patted his chest. "Let's go."

* * *

The restaurant at the Tate vineyard exceeded my expectations. The converted barrel room had undergone some changes since the twins' infamous twenty-first birthday party. It was now a quaint restaurant. It wouldn't have given Billet-doux a run for its money but it was nice – more country chic than Manhattan chic. And thanks to the peak tourist season, it was almost a full house.

There were about fifteen tables, a large stone fireplace and dark wooden furniture. The white linens and tableware brightened the small space, making it seem larger than it was. Ryan would've been impressed.

Adam seemed impressed too. Like me, he'd been expecting shagpile carpet and disco balls hanging from the ceiling. We'd laughed about it on the drive out there.

We arrived before our companions. It was only half a reprieve though. Lily met us at the door and showed us to our table. "It's so great to see you again, Adam," she chirped, weaving between tables. "We all thought you'd split up and sent Charli packing."

Nothing Lily ever said seemed to damage me. It was as if she had no filter. Whatever popped into her head is what she said. I couldn't hold stupidity against her. Adam wasn't as forgiving where the Beautifuls were concerned so I jumped in before he had a chance to reply. "Are you working here, Lily?"

"Three nights a week," she confirmed. "Sometimes I think my parents only opened it so I'd have a job. It gives me something to do."

I shot Adam a smirk. It was a modus operandi I was familiar with. I'd become part owner in Billet-doux for the very same reason. He pulled a face at me.

Lily seated us at a table in the back corner. It dashed any hope of making a quick escape if we needed to, but on the plus side it lowered the chances of anyone I knew seeing me socialising with the Beautifuls.

Jasmine traipsed through the door a minute later. Adam stood as she approached because he was polite. I remained seated because I wasn't. She leapt at him and kissed both cheeks. "Aww, you came," she said, whacking him in the arm with her little sequined clutch bag.

"Of course we came," I chimed, trying to rescue him by diverting her attention.

Jasmine gave me the once-over. "Nice dress. You scrub up alright."

There hadn't been any scrubbing involved. I was dressed and good to go in ten minutes. I suspected it had taken her a lot longer to get her sparkly-slut Barbie look happening.

"Where's Wayne?" asked Adam.

"Wade," she corrected. "Parking the car. It's a bit tricky in the dark. Only one of the headlights is working."

Adam nodded, stupefied. His look became even more stunned when Wade made his appearance, wearing a ridiculously tight T-shirt with a glittery tiger on the front. I must've missed the memo about sparkly animal motifs being in vogue this year. He also wore sunglasses, which probably added to his troubles when it came to parking at night.

Jasmine screeched his name as he walked in, making every diner look toward the door. "Over here," she called, waving.

He took the glasses off and hooked them on the neck of his shirt. "G'day," he crowed, approaching the table.

"Adam, meet Wade Davis. My fiancée," Jasmine announced proudly.

Adam stood again and held out his hand. "Adam Décarie."

Wade's next move beggared belief. "None of that formal stuff here, mate," he said, right before he hugged my poor terrified husband and belted him on the back. "Good to meet you."

"You too," choked Adam, wrestling free.

Jasmine clicked her fingers, beckoning Lily. She rushed over with menus. I quickly scanned mine, trying to work out what would take the least amount of time to prepare so we could get the hell out of there.

"Not bad digs, eh Adam?" Wade asked, peeking at him over the top of the menu.

"Very nice," he replied, still sounding traumatised.

"The food is great too. They do amazing dolphin potatoes."

From the corner of my eye I could see Adam's expression change as confusion set in. I should've forewarned him that he'd be taking a crash course in Wade-speak.

"Dauphinoise potatoes?" he asked.

Wade stared blankly across the table at him. "That's what I said."

I squeezed Adam's knee under the table as I spoke. "Adam's French is a little rusty, Wade."

"No worries." He grinned. "It's a complicated word to pronounce."

Adam took a long sip of water that I was fairly sure he didn't need.

"Your family is in the restaurant business too, right, Adam?" asked Jasmine.

In a million years, I'd never understand how they got their information. I thought Bente was good. Her journalism skills had nothing on the residents of Pipers Cove.

"My brother is, yes," he confirmed.

"What about you, Adam?" asked Wade. "What do you do?"

Jasmine reached over and slapped his chest. "I told you," she snapped. "He's nearly a lawyer."

"And you, Charli?" asked Wade, quickly recovering from the whack. I suspect he was used to it.

"Charli doesn't need to work. Adam is loaded," said Jasmine answering for me.

Adam took offense, as I knew he would. "Charlotte is an accomplished photographer," he defended. "Her pictures are on display in Manhattan."

The man had a way with words. Hanging my prints on the walls of Billet-doux hardly qualified me as accomplished.

"Really?" drawled Jasmine, widening her kohl-heavy eyes. "I should get you to take some pictures for my salon. I have my own salon now. Did you know?"

"No, I hadn't heard. I assumed you still worked for Carol."

Wade's hand flew up, making me jerk back. "We don't mention Carol Lawson. She's the devil."

Jasmine dropped her head, leaning down to hiss. "She wasn't happy that I branched out."

I actually wanted to hear the story but decided against asking her.

"Envy-ness," scoffed moronic Wade. "That's all it is."

Adam glanced at me, silently willing me to get him out of there. I tried to make it as painless as possible. I switched the topic of conversation to their wedding plans – and that's where it stayed for the next two hours.

The Beautifuls were at their best when talking about themselves. We were at our best when we weren't answering intrusive questions; so it was a ploy that benefited all of us. We managed to finally escape after dessert, relatively unharmed and with all our wits about us.

As we got to the car, I stepped in front of Adam blocking his path. "Put your hand to your heart and repeat after me," I demanded.

He did as he was told.

"I, Adam Décarie, solemnly vow never to accept dinner invitations from Beautifuls again."

Grinning, he repeated the statement.

"Good. Well done." I stepped aside and he opened the door for me.

"I think you enjoyed it," he teased. "You seemed very interested in the discussion about chocolate fountains and ice sculptures."

I slipped into the seat. "I was trying to be nice."

"I've never known you to be nice where Jasmine's concerned."

"What can I say? I'm over drama."

I'd seen enough of it to last me a lifetime.

December 26
Adam

The drive home from the vineyard was mostly silent. Charli was in a world of her own unless I asked her a question.

"It's a full moon," I noted, dipping my head to look up through the windshield. "My dad used to tell us that a man lived on the moon."

"Jean-Luc told you that?" she asked, surprised.

I glanced across at her and smiled. "Yes, Ma'am."

"Hmm," she replied. "It's a nice story, but not true."

"Charlotte!" I tried to sound shocked. "Are you telling me there is no man on the moon?"

She shook her head. "Nope. Your dad suckered you."

"I'm so disappointed."

"You should be. He got the tale totally wrong. A woman lives on the moon. Her name is Clotilde. She's a French fairy.

I smiled ahead through the windshield. "I like her already."

"I thought you might." She giggled. "It's her job to guide lost mortals to their happiness," she explained. "If you look up at the full moon and ask her nicely, she'll hook you up with your bliss. She drops *La clé de la vie* down to you."

"The key of life," I translated.

"Your French has improved since dinner, Monsieur," she praised, making me laugh. "Not all shooting stars are stars. Sometimes they're just *La clé de la vie* dropping to earth."

"So what do you do with the key?"

"You have to find the gate it opens. And when you do, you find your bliss."

"Have you ever been tempted to call on Clotilde, Charlotte?"

"Not since I met you," she replied. "I'd be too worried that the key she dropped me wouldn't fit your gate."

* * *

I think I enjoyed Charlotte most when she was on home turf. She was calmer, happier and far more settled. She also liked to sleep late.

I decided against waking her that morning and opted for a run along the beach instead. Getting to the trail by cutting through the back yard of the house next door was something I'd done a hundred times. It was vacant the last time I'd been there so no one minded.

It wasn't vacant any more. I was embarrassed, but the policeman who was standing there as I broke through the bushes, just looked confused.

I came to a stop and ripped my headphones from my ears. "Hello."

"G'day."

"I'm Adam." I pointed behind me. "From next door."

He frowned. "I'm Flynn. I live here. Charli never mentioned you were coming."

"Was she supposed to?"

He shrugged. "None of my business. How long are you in town for?"

That was none of his business either. "A while," I muttered unwillingly.

"Charli's a good girl," he announced, frowning at me. "She doesn't deserve a hard time." He sounded like a poor imitation of her father – someone who actually had the right to try menacing me. I had no idea what he was accusing me of, so I said nothing. "Where is she this morning?" he asked, craning his neck as he looked past me.

"Asleep."

Constable creepy stared at me for a long time, leaving it up to me to speak again.

"Okay then. Well, I'm heading to the beach." I pointed to the trail. "I won't cut through again. This house was vacant last time I was here." With a bit of luck, it would be vacant next time too.

"Are you planning to visit often?" he asked.

Who was this dick? "Over and over again, Flynn."

I don't know if he said anything else. I put my headphones back in my ears and made a run for the trail.

* * *

I got home an hour later, showered and had breakfast before returning to the bedroom. Charli's position hadn't changed. I looked down at my creature of mayhem and felt like the luckiest man on earth, for no other reason than I loved her. Life without Charli was structured, organised and dull. Any normal man would've been thrilled to give it up for her. I was beginning to realise that there was something really wrong with me.

I lightly traced the arch of the tan lines where her panties rode up, making her stir but not wake up. I made my own line up her back, kissing my way up to her shoulders. Finally, she woke. She turned over and I fell down beside her on the bed.

"Sorry," I whispered insincerely. "Didn't mean to wake you."

"What time is it?" she mumbled, grabbing my arm to check my watch.

"Not too late. Go back to sleep if you want to."

"And what are you going to do?"

"Watch you some more," I replied unashamedly.

She breathed out a quiet giggle. "That's wrong on so many levels, Adam."

"Au contraire, Coccinelle. I find it fascinating."

"Really?" she asked dryly.

I skimmed my finger over the white line on her hip. "Strange things happen when you escape Manhattan."

"Like?"

"Like, you get these cute little tan lines," I replied, grabbing her.

"I do," she agreed, wriggling. "Sunshine will do that to you."

I picked up a wisp of her hair and twisted it around my finger. "Your hair gets lighter too."

"Sun, and probably salt."

"You're happy here, aren't you?"

"I belong here, or somewhere like it," she confirmed. "I also belong with you, which is a problem."

"Not for me," I replied, moving to kiss her. "I'll just keep coming back here, or somewhere like it."

As things stood, I was prepared to bounce back to her indefinitely. That was my plan. I wondered what hers was.

"Charlotte," I murmured, "what are you going to do while you're here?"

"I don't know," she said vaguely. "Maybe I'll take on some shifts at the café or something. What do you think?"

My head fell back on the pillow. "I think it's a waste of a beautiful mind."

She should've been shooting higher.

"Do you think Alex wasted his mind when he opted for a quiet life at the beach?"

"It's different, Charli."

"No, it's not. Life here isn't inferior to the one you've chosen. It's just different. It's quiet. I want quiet."

"I wasn't passing judgement. Live your quiet life."

"I will. I think I deserve it after…" Her voice trailed off and she looked away from me, but I pieced the rest of her sentence together without trouble.

I brought her hand to my mouth and kissed her fingers. "I will tell you every day how sorry I am if you want. I can't change what happened."

"Stop talking, Adam," she muttered, looking to the ceiling. "It gets us nowhere."

I wanted to talk. We *needed* to talk. I put my hand on her cheek, turning her face toward me. "Please, talk to me."

"You might not like what you hear."

"Try me."

She pulled in a long breath, preparing to thrash me with an invisible stick. "I hate the damage you do to me, Adam. It's a physical injury this time around. Like jetlag but worse. That's what you left me with." It didn't seem like a good time to remind her that she was the one who left me. "There's only so many times I can endure it before I drop dead."

"Charlotte, I won't let it happen again. That's all I can promise for now."

"I'd rather you didn't make promises," she said quietly. "You're not good at keeping them."

The stick had suddenly become a sword. I vowed to do better, but only in my head. Saying it out loud would've sounded like another promise begging to be broken.

December 30
Charli

I loved waking up next to Adam. I just hadn't managed to achieve it since he'd been back in the Cove. We seemed to be running on different clocks. He was on New York time, and I was stuck somewhere over the Indian Ocean. He'd been up for hours before waking me. By the time I showered and dressed, it felt as if half the day was gone.

I walked into the kitchen and he handed me a mug of warm tea and an even warmer kiss. "Gabi's on her way over."

"Why?"

"I don't know. She just called and said she was on her way over."

A hint of panic set in. It was probably an impromptu rent inspection. My eyes darted around the room, trying to judge whether it was tidy enough.

Too bad if it wasn't. She appeared at the door only a minute later. Adam let her in, greeting her with the Décarie double-kiss routine.

"Is Charli here?" she asked. I was standing in plain view. Maybe she'd missed me while scanning for dust.

"I'm here," I called from the kitchen.

"Hi," she said quietly. "I have a favour to ask."

"I'll leave you two to it," said Adam, making a quick exit.

Gabrielle sat at the table.

"Do you know Edna Wilson?" she asked, completely out of left field.

"Crazy Edna?" Everyone knew her. Children in town grew up fearing Crazy Edna – me included. When I was nine, Mitchell told me that she

86

used to capture little girls and cut off their hair. I'd been terrified of her ever since.

"She's supposedly psychic," said Gabrielle, nodding.

I walked over and joined her at the table. "Gabi, she eats small children and boils their bones."

She half smiled. "You know this to be true?"

"Of course." I nodded. "Everybody knows it's true."

"Well, Floss told me she was very gifted. I thought I might pay her a visit. I was hoping you'd come with me."

I widened my eyes, shocked. "You want to get your fortune read?"

She cringed a little. Even she realised how absurd it was. "Yes."

"Gabrielle, you're a Décarie," I reminded. "As far as fortunes go, you're good."

She looked embarrassed now. "I'm getting desperate, Charli. What if Edna can give me some insight into my family situation? It might give me some hope if I know there's something good on the way for us."

"Look," I said gently, "I'm all for fae and fate but I'm not sure how I feel about psychics, least of all one who eats children."

"Will you come or not?"

"What did Alex say when you told him?"

She looked away. "I didn't tell him."

I wouldn't have told him either. He would've flipped his lid. When I'd asked him if the hair-cutting rumour was true, his answer hadn't exactly put my nine-year-old mind at ease: "Probably," he'd replied. "You should wear your hair up to be safe."

I sighed heavily, gearing up to do something foolish. "I'll come with you. But if you tell anyone we were at Crazy Edna's, I'll deny it."

She looked relieved. "Thank you, Charli. "

I slipped away to the bedroom. When Adam came in, I laid out Gabrielle's plan in a muted whisper.

As expected, he found it ridiculous. "You're not seriously going?"

"I can't let her go alone," I replied, crouching to tie my shoes. "I couldn't live with myself if she ended up having her bones boiled."

He stared at me, puzzled. I didn't have time to elaborate. I straightened up and kissed him chastely. "I'll tell you all about it when I get home."

I felt sad that Gabrielle's quest to have a baby had pushed her to such extremes. I also felt strangely protective of her, which is the only explanation I had for the nonsense I was about to partake in.

We stepped onto the porch of Edna's rundown cottage, dodging the holes where planks of decking were missing. I left it to Gabrielle to knock on the door.

Crazy Edna kept us waiting a ridiculously long time. When she finally answered, I realised it had probably taken her the full five minutes to get there.

"Welcome," she greeted us theatrically.

I'd never been that close to Edna before. She was tiny, made even shorter by her hunched posture. She had wild grey hair that was pinned back from her face with a plastic red rose hairclip. I had no idea how old she was. She had supposedly been a hundred and fifty when I was a kid. Her small hands shook, which probably explained why her red lipstick was smudged. She didn't look like someone who ate small children. I actually felt a bit disappointed.

She showed us through to a small room at the front of the house and then disappeared. It gave us time to check out the room. It wasn't witchy and dark like I expected it to be; it was decked out in a tacky nautical theme. I could overlook the ceramic dolphins and big seashells that took pride of place on the mantelpiece. Even the dried starfish nailed to the walls didn't bother me. What was a little freaky was the fact that she had most of my Pipers Cove postcards displayed on a pinup board.

"Look," I whispered, pointing. "How weird is that?"

"They're all over town, Charli," Gabrielle reasoned. "It's not that odd."

Edna shuffled into the room, killing the conversation.

"Sit down, girls," she instructed in a voice as shaky as her hands.

I glanced across at Gabrielle as we sat down at the small table in the centre of the room. She didn't look anywhere near as freaked out as she should've. If anything, she looked excited to be there.

Edna sat opposite us and things began to take a turn for the weird. She reached for a jar of sand from the shelf behind her and poured it onto the table.

"Sand is from the earth," she explained. "I use it to talk to the earth."

The sceptic in me wanted to grab a dustpan and sweep it up. The bohemian fairy in my head talked me out of it.

We sat silently as the old woman spread sand across the table with both hands.

"Touch the sand," invited Edna. "Make a slow circular motion and think of a question in your heart."

Gabrielle nudged me with her shoulder.

"No chance," I muttered, nudging her back. "You do it."

Gabrielle's hand was shaking as much as Edna's as she ploughed through the pile on the table.

"I want to know if I'm going to have a baby." Her voice was tiny.

"Nice one, Gabs," I chided. "You just gave her everything she needs."

"The sand gives me what I need," corrected Edna, frowning at me. "All the answers are in the sand."

I stared at the old woman, eventually deciding that she probably wasn't a con artist, just delusional. Alex would describe her as being a few feathers short of a whole duck. "So what's the answer?" I asked.

The old woman turned her attention to the sand, drawing a strange set of symbols in it with her crooked old-lady fingers.

"There is already a child here," she replied.

"No." Gabrielle shook her head. "I have no children."

"There is already a child here," repeated Edna, more forcefully this time.

I leaned across to whisper to Gabrielle. "Maybe you're pregnant."

She glanced across at me. "Maybe. How exciting!"

"*Procella* child," warbled Edna.

"What does that mean?"

Edna didn't answer.

"Okay, Gabrielle," I whispered from the corner of my mouth. "She's speaking in tongues. Can we leave now?"

The Parisienne stood up. Edna raised her voice, ordering her to sit back down. Perhaps too scared to defy her, Gabrielle did as she was told.

Both of us sat silently as she began raking through the sand again.

"This child brings a break – a disconnection." Things were getting creepy now. "Much unease and big changes," she added.

It wasn't sounding like the perfect family setting was on its way. In fact, it was nothing more than a forecast of doom and gloom.

"Okay, we're done. Let's go." I stood up and tried pulling Gabrielle to her feet. She stayed put, giving me no choice but to sit back down. Edna continued sifting through the sand as if my attempt to make a break for it hadn't happened.

"You." She pointed her shaky hand at me. "You should know something."

"What?" I asked, truly terrified.

"You're going to run out of time," she announced.

How the heck did this become about me? I didn't invite the old woman to read my sand. I hadn't even touched it, for crying out loud. I folded my arms across my chest, shaking my head in protest.

"Can we get back to the baby now, Edna?" asked Gabrielle. The old woman began stirring the pile again, concentrating hard. "I'm telling you, *Procella* child is already here."

Gabrielle straightened up in her seat, looking too damned excited by Edna's ramblings. I had to get her out of there.

"Let's go, Gabrielle."

The second she stood up I began steering her toward the door.

"The earth talks," called Edna. "You should listen."

I quickened my pace, roughly pushing Gabrielle to the door.

I don't think I took another breath until we were out of the house. Clearly I was the only one showing signs of trauma. The Parisienne hooked her arm through mine as we walked to the car like we were taking a leisurely stroll.

"Do you think she might be right?" she asked. "I'll be able to find out in a few days. Wouldn't it be wonderful if I am pregnant?"

I didn't want to be the one to burst her bubble, but I didn't want her hinging her entire happiness on the ramblings of a crazy lady either.

"What about her prediction of a disconnection?" I asked. "That wasn't exactly heart-warming."

"I wasn't listening to that part," she replied.

"You shouldn't have been listening to any of it. She was talking rubbish, Gabi. We don't know anything more than we did an hour ago. She's off her rocker."

"I hope not," replied Gabrielle. "I want that *procella* baby."

"What the heck is a prosciutto baby anyway?" I asked.

Gabrielle laughed. "Nothing to do with deli meat, I hope."

* * *

I called Adam on the way home, mainly to reassure him that our bones hadn't been boiled. To my surprise he was hanging out with Alex, helping him stack the last of the chopped wood.

There had been a big shift in the relationship between Boy Wonder and my father since their morning in the surf. Alex was impressed that Adam had given it a crack, and Adam was impressed that my father hadn't killed him.

All the wood was neatly stacked by the garage when we got there. Gabrielle made a beeline for the house. I went to the shed, following the sound of the blaring stereo. I hung back in the doorway and spied for a moment. Alex was holding two planks in place while Adam hammered nails into it.

"What are you building?" I yelled over the music.

Both of them grinned like a couple of naughty schoolboys.

The explanation came from Alex. He'd run out of wood to smash so they'd come up with the bright idea of smashing golf balls instead. "We're building a platform so we've got a flat surface to launch from."

"We're going to stand at the top of the hill and whack them into the field," added Adam, moving to turn down the music.

"Can't you just go to a golf course like normal people?"

Alex grinned at me. "Where's the fun in that?"

Alex's history of smashing inanimate objects was long. Adam had a history of playing in sheds and working with wood. Both of them liked loud music.

It was a match made in heaven.

* * *

Gabrielle and I sat on the veranda, watching as the golf game got under way. It was hardly a professional setup. Alex only had one golf club – and I doubt he'd ever used it to play golf.

They took turns whacking balls into the paddock. Within minutes, they were all out.

"They obviously didn't think that one through," murmured Gabrielle.

Their chances of finding the balls in the long grass were slim to none. Undeterred, Alex picked up a gumnut off the ground and lined it up. The hard seedpod made such a crack as he hit it that Gabrielle flinched, nearly spilling her mug of tea. The nut didn't go nearly as far as the balls but it amused them enough to want to do it again. Gathering fallen gumnuts and belting them into a paddock with a golf club was about as far removed from his New York life as Adam could get. I wished I could keep him there forever.

Gabrielle finally put a stop to the game when they ran out of nuts and began discussing climbing the eucalyptus tree to get more. "Enough, Alex," she scolded. "Please come inside now. You can help me make lunch."

You can take the Parisienne out of school but you can't take the schoolteacher out of the Parisienne.

Alex dutifully followed her into the house. Adam stepped onto the veranda, handing me a gumnut.

"Thank you," I crooned, taking it from him.

He held the golf club out. "I saved the last shot for you."

I followed him down to the wooden platform. Adam stood behind me, positioning my arms as I held the club. When he took a step back, I took my hardest swing – and managed to knock it just a few metres from where we stood.

"Okay," he said laughing, "so you're not a golfer."

"No," I agreed, turning to face him. "Bogan golf has never rated highly on my list of skills to master."

He frowned a little. "What's a bogan?"

"A redneck," I replied. "Face it, Adam. You're a bogan. You'll be wearing plaid shirts next."

His arm swooped around my middle and I dropped the club on the ground.

"At least I managed to hit the ball," he murmured, pressing his lips to the side of my neck.

December 31
Adam

We didn't exactly have good memories of our last New Year's Eve together so I was hoping to make this one a little more memorable. New Year's Eve in New York is a big deal. New Year's Eve in Pipers Cove is not.

It had been a quiet day so far. We'd been laid out on a blanket in the yard since mid-morning. Charli was enjoying the sun and I was enjoying her.

"How are we going to ring in the New Year, Charlotte?" I asked.

She turned onto her stomach and propped herself up on her elbows. "Well, we were invited to Jasmine's beach party. That might be fun."

I put my hand to her forehead. "You've had too much sun," I teased. "Get in the house."

"It's fancy dress." She flashed a cheeky grin. "Ten bucks says Jasmine and Wade go as Barbie and Ken."

"I don't plan on being there to find out. I was hoping we could find something more interesting to do."

"What do you suggest?" She wiggled her eyebrows, looking more crooked than sultry.

"We're in La La Land, Charli. Can't you conjure up a little magic?" I trailed my fingertips down the length of her arm.

"Like what?"

"How about a fairy soiree?" I teased. "There's been a lot of fairy talk over the past few days. I've still never seen one, and to be honest, there's a chance I'm becoming a non-believer."

She pouted a little, looking so lovely that I wanted to lurch forward and kiss her. "Say it isn't so," she drawled.

I draped my arm across her back. "I'm afraid so, Coccinelle."

"Well, that just won't do. You'll get your wish, Boy Wonder. We'll party into the New Year with the fairies."

"You're all talk."

"I'm not. You want fairies, you'll get fairies," she said.

I grabbed my phone off the edge of the blanket and held it out to her. "Do you need to call them? It seems rude to just show up unannounced."

She pushed my hand away. "They'll be expecting us."

"You are so full of baloney." I swept my hand through the hair covering her face and tucked it behind her ear. "Beautiful, but full of baloney."

"I'm not," she whispered. "I'll take you to meet the fairies. But we have to get a few supplies first."

I was more than happy to play along because this was Charlotte at her very best. "Like?"

"We need dark clothing and some red cellophane."

I frowned, clueless. "Okay."

"And a torch. We'll need a torch."

"Charli, I said fairies, not witches." I'm American. In my mind, I was picturing a wooden pole with a flaming pitch-soaked rag at the top. Then I remembered that she's Australian, and she meant a flashlight.

"We'll go to Alex's," she continued. "He'll have everything we need."

I wondered if she planned to tell her father about her fairy visit, then wondered what his take on it would be. A normal person would be alarmed. But Alex wasn't normal. He was the sole reason Charli was planning to spend New Year's Eve with fairies in the first place.

We stood up and Charli scooped the blanket off the lawn.

"Hello, Charli," called a voice behind us. "How are you?"

We spun around to see Flynn leaning on the side fence.

"Fine thank you," she replied politely.

"Catching some sun?"

"Yeah."

"Nice day for it."

"Yeah," she repeated.

Something about Flynn Davis didn't sit right with me, but I was prepared to give him the benefit of the doubt. I took a step closer to Charli. Maybe he hadn't seen me standing there while he was making small talk with my wife.

"Are you going to Jasmine's party?" he asked, still ignoring me.

"No, we have plans."

"Oh, that's too bad. I was looking forward to seeing you there."

What a tool. "Let's go, Charlotte," I muttered quietly.

Charli gave him a weak wave and headed to the house. I stared him down for a few seconds before following her.

"He's weird, Charli," I told her as I walked in.

"I think he has a crush on me," she admitted.

I looped my arm around her waist drawing her closer. "Understandable, but completely and utterly futile. Maybe I should tell him that."

She rolled her eyes at me. "He knows, Adam."

"Can't say I blame him for trying, though," I muttered, making her smile. "You are gorgeous."

* * *

Alex and Gabrielle were standing on the veranda in a huddle when we arrived. The conversation looked intense and Gabrielle looked upset. It was a far cry from the relaxed bogan-golf mood of the day before.

Neither of us made any attempt to get out of the car. "What do you think that's about?" I asked.

Charli undid her seatbelt. "I have a fair idea."

"Tell me."

"Gabrielle's not pregnant," she said bleakly. "Crazy Edna is a crock."

I'd suspected as much when she'd relayed the story to me the night before.

I looked across at the unhappy couple. "Should we go home?"

"No. Just give them a minute."

It seemed a long time before Alex finally released his hold on her. Gabrielle slipped into the house, leaving him standing there. Just as we were getting out of the car, she flew out again, hurled something on the lawn and stormed back inside.

Both of us slowed as we walked up the path, checking to see what she'd thrown. It was Charli's bunch of lavender.

I took a long stride forward and grabbed Charli's hand.

"Poor Gabi," she whispered. "I feel terrible."

"It's not your fault," I murmured.

We stepped onto the veranda. "Hi Dad," muttered Charli.

She only ever called him dad when he looked like he needed it. Today, I think he needed it.

"Hey," he replied.

"Is Gabi okay?" asked Charli.

"Charli, what were you thinking taking her to Edna Wilson's?" he asked.

She shook her head. "I didn't. I just went with her for moral support. I tried talking her out of it."

He nodded, immediately accepting that for once, the harebrained idea hadn't come from Charli. "It kind of backfired on her."

"Is she okay?" I asked.

"She will be." He looked down at the banished lavender on the lawn. "She's having a rough day."

We'd already guessed why. No one needed the agony of hearing about it. Charli moved quickly to change the subject. "Do you have a torch we can borrow? We're going to see the fairies."

I watched Alex's expression closely, expecting him to melt down at any second. He was being bombarded by craziness from all angles – first Gabrielle's not-so psychic visit and now Charli's fairy adventures. But he replied casually, as if there wasn't a scrap of madness in her words. "Yeah. There's one in shed."

"Alex." I spoke very slowly, leaving no room for misinterpretation. "We're going to visit *fairies*."

His smile looked more like a smirk. "I heard. You're going to see the fairies."

I shook my head in disbelief.

"What about red cellophane?" asked Charli. "Do you have any?"

Alex shook his head, still unperturbed. "You won't need it. I've got a torch with a red lens."

Her grin brightened to stellar level. "Thank you." She grabbed my hand and dragged me down the steps, toward the shed.

I turned as we got to the door, in time to see Alex pick up the lavender and walk into the house.

* * *

Fairy get-togethers are not black tie affairs. Charli made us dress like a couple of criminals in dark hoodies and jeans.

"Is this necessary?"

"Yes, it's cold out. Stop complaining." She grabbed the flashlight. "Are we good to go?"

"It's only five o'clock."

She pulled me toward the door. "Party starts at dusk, Adam. Let's go."

* * *

We drove further south than I'd ever been before. The weather got cooler and Charli got warmer. I held her hand just to keep her from bouncing around the interior of the car.

"I'm so excited to show you the fairies," she beamed. "You're going to love them."

I couldn't begin to imagine how she was going to pull this one off. Part of me was worried about it. This was extreme La La'ing at its finest.

I'd learned my lesson after my last visit and wisely rented an SUV this time round. It held up well when we pulled off the highway and drove down the crude gravel track.

The scrubby bush hid the ocean from view, but I could hear it. Maybe we were visiting water fairies. I spent the trek to the beach trying to remember the name of the fairies that burn men's skin and dissolve into puddles. Then I began to worry that I was going a little mad.

As we neared the beach, Charli stopped. "We have to be really quiet now," she instructed. "And move slowly." I must've looked nervous. She hooked her arm through mine. "Don't be scared," she said darkly. "I won't let them get you."

She was enjoying this way too much.

We broke through the bush to the open sand but went no further. Charlotte sat at the edge of the reeds and patted the sand beside her.

"Can't we sit on the beach?" I asked. If there was even a slight chance that this fairy nonsense was real, I wanted to be able to see them coming at me.

She shook her head. "Sit."

She reached into her bag and handed the flashlight to me. Next came the camera. It wasn't the one she usually used. This one looked antiquated and clunky. I'd never seen it before.

"Is that a fairy camera, Charlotte?" I was only half joking.

"It's a Polaroid camera." She snapped the film cartridge into place as if loading a gun. "I wanted to capture the moment for you."

Something told me I was going to remember it forever, whether I had the photographic evidence or not.

"Polaroid is magic," she added. "I love the instant gratification of watching the picture develop before your eyes."

I was constantly in awe of this girl. I always had been. "Show me," I ordered.

She leaned in close, held the big box camera out with both hands and pressed the button. A white card ejected from the bottom, and she held it in front of me.

"See?" she marvelled. "Instant selfie, old school style."

I watched the cloudy picture of the two of us come to life – like magic.

"Your talent is wasted here, Charlotte," I murmured. "You're the biggest small town girl I know."

The light got dimmer and the temperature dropped as the day slipped away. I inched closer to her to keep warm. We'd been there nearly half an hour and hadn't spotted a single fairy. It was time to call her out on it.

"Looks like they're a no-show. We could probably still make Jasmine's party." I breathed the words into her ear.

"No need," she said smugly. "They're here."

I straightened up, looking in all directions, mentally slating myself for being gullible. I saw nothing.

"That way, Adam." She pointed to the ocean.

I followed her finger and squinted at the shoreline and noticed the most spectacular thing I'd ever seen. Little penguins, no more than a foot tall, wandered out of the surf and made their way up the beach toward us.

"Meet the fairy penguins," she whispered. "Sit still and be quiet."

Little did she know, I wasn't capable of moving or talking at that point.

She turned on the flashlight and pointed it at the penguins waddling through the sand. They continued on their way, unperturbed by the red light.

One by one they disappeared into the scrub behind us, heading for their burrows.

I had never seen anything like it, and probably never would again. "I love you," I whispered. "So freaking much."

Her giggle came out in a quiet breath. "I know."

We didn't move for a long time, until all the penguins were out of sight. Charli turned off the flashlight and the scene became even more perfect.

The moon was large, casting a silver glow though the cloudless sky, and Peter Pan would've been impressed by the number of stars on show. All I could hear was the calm ocean rolling into shore. And at that moment, I swear life was perfect.

"I told you I knew some fairies," she gloated.

"Is that really what they're called, Charlotte?" I asked sceptically.

"They're actually called Eudyptula minor. It's Greek, I think," she explained. "It means 'good little diver'. Australians call them fairy penguins, because that's how we roll."

The darkness hid none of her smile.

"Why are they coming ashore?" I asked.

"They're hanging out with their chicks. When the hatchlings are big enough, they'll move out to sea."

I swept my hand under the fall of her hair, resting it on the back of her neck. "Why do they all come in at the same time?"

"Because there's safety in numbers. They've got to get all the way from their beach to their rookery and hope that nothing eats them along the way."

"You're like a penguin aficionada, aren't you?"

She laughed. "Not really. I just grew up with Alex for a father."

* * *

One lifetime was not going to be enough with this girl, especially considering we were living it five minutes at a time.

We were back at the cottage and headed to bed before ten. I couldn't think of a better way to see in the New Year. I switched off the lamp, plunging the room into pitch black.

"Adam, how long are you going to keep bouncing back to me?" Charli asked. Her hand found my face and I turned to kiss her palm.

"Forever."

"That's a big ask."

"Let me worry about the details," I said quietly. "I'm sure we're not the first couple to have a long-distance relationship."

She knotted her hands through my hair and craned her neck as I kissed her throat.

"Nope. Our penguin friends do it all the time," she replied a little breathlessly. "Not fairy penguins, Adelie penguins. They mate for life – totally monogamous. They spend the winter hanging out in the southern hemisphere before making their way down to Antarctica. That's when the fun begins."

"I like fun," I murmured, lowering my head to kiss my way down her body.

"The males are big show-offs," she continued. "They strut and parade around trying to catch the attention of the females."

"Do I have your attention, Charlotte?" I asked, kissing a line across her warm stomach.

"You have everything of mine," she breathed.

I smiled against her skin. "What happens next?"

She put her hands on the side of my head, guiding me back to her face. "Well, when a special penguin catches his eye, he presents her with a precious stone foraged from the frozen ground. If she accepts the stone, they start a bond for life. Each year he returns and they find each other again, and another stone is presented as a token of affection. They use the stones to build their nest."

"So there's hope for us yet." I kissed the corner of her mouth. "All I have to do is keep coming back with rocks."

"There's always hope for us, Adam," she said seriously. "No matter what."

January 2
Charli

The supermarket in Pipers Cove is the social hub of the town. I usually avoided it at all costs, but Adam objected to living on cereal.

Our quick trip to buy a few groceries turned in to a half-day event by the time I'd finished talking to everyone who stopped me. I recounted the last two years of my life and introduced Adam a hundred times. Ever polite, he pretended to be happy to meet every one of them.

"You're quite the celebrity," he whispered as we escaped Floss's next-door neighbour, Mrs Simpson.

"They're just nosy."

Alex had obviously told them nothing about my time away. He had epic skill when it came to deflecting gossip.

"Can we get coffee here?" asked Adam hopefully.

I stopped, halting both of us. "You should make a New Year's resolution, Adam," I suggested, drumming my finger into his chest.

"I don't make New Year's resolutions, Charlotte," he scoffed. Perhaps that was because his whole life was one big resolution.

"You should give up coffee."

He looked at me as if I'd lost my mind. "And what will you give up? Make it painful. It has to be something you'll miss."

"You," I said miserably. "In about a week from now."

He grabbed the trolley and began pushing it forward again. "We should be enjoying this week," he said. "Don't put a dampener on things."

It was impossible not to. Mitchell's ninth wave analogy sprung to mind. The feeling of being hit by my rogue wave was getting stronger every day. I couldn't understand why the despair wasn't crushing him. "I hate that you function so well without me," I grumbled. "It doesn't seem fair."

Adam turned to look at me. "Is that what you think? I'm miserable without you, Charli. There are words I don't even say when you're not around. They're meaningless," he rambled. "Everything becomes meaningless. It's a pathetic existence."

I smiled wryly. "I feel so much better now."

He smiled back. "I'm glad you can take comfort in my misery."

I giggled. "It's a mutual predicament, Adam."

* * *

We were loading groceries into the car when I spotted the one person I was actually keen to talk to. Crazy Edna was ambling up the footpath at a snail's pace.

"Mrs Wilson," I called. The old woman looked up.

"Who's that?" asked Adam.

"Crazy Edna."

Adam grabbed a handful of my sleeve to stop me approaching her. Perhaps he knew how angry I was. I had a major bone to pick with the witchy old shyster. Edna approached us instead and Adam tightened his grip.

"Hello, dear."

"You've caused a lot of trouble in my family, Mrs Wilson."

"How?" She had the nerve to sound surprised.

"Gabrielle is heartbroken because you told her she was pregnant. She's not pregnant. Your prediction was wrong."

The old lady seemed completely unaffected by my lecture.

"I never said she was pregnant."

"You did!"

She shook her head. "I said I could *see* a child," she told me. "I stand by that claim."

She looked at Adam, and had the nerve to smile at him. He was in danger of ripping the sleeve off my shirt now.

"In future, please keep your visions to yourself," I muttered, making a grab for the last bag of shopping in the trolley.

"The earth talks to me," insisted Edna, reverting back to her warbly theatrical voice. "It's my duty to listen. The child I see isn't the French girl's." She leaned forward, speaking to Adam. "It's yours."

January 2
Adam

The slow pace of life in Pipers Cove evaporated in an instant. I was now running at full tilt trying to keep up. One minute we were grocery shopping, the next minute we were being thrown for a loop by a crazy old lady in a parking lot.

"Get in the car, Charlotte," I ordered, determined to put an end to it.

She seemed to have lost the ability to walk.

"You're a nasty, crazy old woman," Charli shouted.

Edna barely reacted. I expect that was because she'd heard it before. She pointed at me. "You're going to run out of time."

"What is that supposed to mean?" barked Charli, throwing her hands in the air. "You said the same thing to me the other day. At least be original in your ramblings."

I wasn't prepared to let Edna answer. I'd heard enough. I practically forced Charli into the car. As soon as we were on the road I glanced across at her. She was staring out the window. I grabbed her hand, squeezing her fingers. "Say something, please."

"What if she's right?"

"Please tell me you're not buying into this mumbo jumbo." She shrugged, giving me no reassurance whatsoever. "Charli, I think you'd know if she was right, wouldn't you?"

Sometimes I adored Charlotte's take on the world. It was ethereal and enchanting. Other times it was just plain ridiculous – like now. I could deal with fairies and La La Land, not this.

"I don't know what to think," she said. "But I know weird things have been happening to me lately."

"Like?"

She held her hand up. "My curly fry rings fit me. They never used to."

"You grew into them," I reasoned. "Give me something a little less La La."

She frowned. "I'm tired all the time."

"Jetlag."

"I've been home for weeks, Adam. I don't think it's jetlag any more."

"Maybe you're sick."

"Would you prefer it if I was?"

I answered with a disapproving look.

"My period's late."

"How late?"

"Late, late."

I wasn't sure what late, late meant, but it didn't sound good. "Charli, how have you not told me this before?"

She shrugged. She actually shrugged. We might as well have been discussing the weather.

"I wanted to wait and see what happens."

"A freaking baby is what's going to happen if you're pregnant." I thumped the heel of my hand on the steering wheel, totally frustrated with her.

"It's probably nothing," she muttered. "I wish I hadn't told you."

"Well, we need to find out one way or another. I'm not taking a crazy woman's word for it. We'll get one of those test thingies."

She shook her head. "I can't just walk in to a shop and buy a pregnancy test. Floss Davis will be knitting booties before we get out the door."

"Fine. We'll drive to Hobart. And if that's not far enough we'll go to Launceston."

"Stop it, Adam," she snapped. "Just give me a minute to think."

It was a long minute. Charli didn't say another word in the next half hour. I just kept driving, sticking with my Hobart plan.

"Charli, I need to know." I sounded desperate. "*We* need to know."

"Okay. I have a plan," she announced. "We're going to steal a test."

I wasn't outraged. The only plans Charli ever made were of the criminal variety.

"We're going to break into my dad's house," she continued. "Gabrielle keeps heaps of them in the bathroom cabinet. I've seen them. She'll never notice one missing."

"What if they're there?" I asked.

"They're not there. Alex is at the café and Gabrielle is teaching an art class at the community hall until four." She waved her phone. "I just texted them both to double check."

I didn't question her sketchy plan. I just changed direction and headed for the house.

As expected, no one was there, but it still felt shady.

"Don't look so panicked, Adam," said Charli. "A little illegal activity is good for the soul."

I glanced at her and was met with a smile. "You know, I should be concerned by your enthusiasm," I told her. "If you pull a balaclava out of your bag, I'm leaving."

She reached into her bag, wiggling her eyebrows at me. I breathed a small sigh of relief when she produced a set of keys.

"You have keys," I said, stating the obvious.

"Of course I have keys. It's my dad's house. You're the only person who doesn't have keys to their parents' house."

"My parents probably don't even have keys to their house. We don't need keys."

"No, you don't," she agreed. "You use a Mrs Brown to get in."

"Get out of the car, Charlotte," I muttered making her laugh.

We made a dash for the bathroom the second we were in the door. Charli opened the cabinet, and a heap of boxes crashed into the sink.

"I told you," she said, trying to restack them. "Hundreds of the bloody things."

"Just pick one and let's go," I ordered, keeping watch at the door.

"Relax, Adam. You make a terrible thief. You're so antsy."

"Charlotte," I groaned, "can we take this seriously please?"

She picked up a box and began reading the instructions. "I'll just do it here."

It occurred to me that I didn't really know what 'it' was. "What do we have to do?"

"You've probably done enough." She tore the wrapper off a white plastic stick and waved it around. "I have to pee on this."

"So do it," I said urgently.

She blinked at me a few times. "Are you planning to watch?"

"No, of course not." I stepped into the hall and pulled the door closed, wishing I were anywhere but in that house. After a long minute, she called me back in.

"Well?"

"I don't know yet. We have to wait a few minutes."

Determined not to wait a second longer than necessary, I set the timer on my phone. We said absolutely nothing as the seconds ticked past like hours. We just stared at each other. Every possible scenario played out in my mind – and none of them were particularly good. Charli looked perfectly calm. I had a sinking feeling that she was already picking out names.

"Are you okay?" she asked.

"Fine."

"You don't look fine."

"What do you want me to say, Charli?"

"Are you mad?"

"No. It's just unexpected. I thought we were careful."

She cocked an eyebrow. "You don't even sound like you believe that."

I had to concede that she was right. I am sensible and cautious in every aspect of my life, except all things Charlotte. "We've had the odd moment, I guess."

She stepped forward and whispered. "Like your parent's downstairs powder room at Thanksgiving?"

"A few moments then," I amended.

"Or the wine cellar at Billet-doux?"

I grinned, because her cheeky expression gave me no choice. "That didn't count."

"Oh, it totally counted, Adam."

My phone beeped, announcing the possible end of life as we knew it. We stared at the white stick on the counter.

"You look at it," Charli ordered.

I picked it up and studied the result. I couldn't even pretend to know what it meant. "There are two pink lines. One is pretty faint though."

Charli re-read the instructions. "Faint counts, Adam."

"Counts as what?"

"A positive result," she said flatly.

I learned something that day. Tipping the stick upside down does not make the second line disappear, nor does running it under water. Hiding it in your pocket does, but only until you take it out again.

Charli stared at me while I futilely tried rewinding the last two minutes of our lives. "Can we go home now, Einstein?" she asked finally.

Her sarcasm was warranted. My brain was mincemeat.

"Yeah. Let's go."

We wandered back to the car like a couple of stunned sheep.

Charli spoke first. "Do you remember the time I told you that I wanted to have ten of your babies?"

"Yeah."

"I don't really."

Thank God!

"But one might be lovely," she added.

It wasn't the direction I was hoping she'd want to go. Nothing about going through with it seemed right. I just couldn't think of a tactful way to say so.

I glanced at her only briefly, because I was a coward. "I think we need to talk about it. We've got choices, Charli."

"You said you weren't mad."

"I'm not. I just want to be sure we explore every avenue."

I winced as I said it. Even to me I came across sounding like a cold-hearted jerk.

"What are your concerns?" she asked, matching my mechanical phrasing.

I looked at her as I mapped out the answer in my head. I didn't want a baby. We were too young. We lived on opposite sides of the world. We were a scattered mess. I really, *really* didn't want a baby.

I decided to put the least damaging reason into words. "We're not ready."

She unclipped her seat belt and angled toward me. "How do people know when they're ready, Adam?"

"They plan it. They talk about it and prepare for it and generally make sure their lives are in order."

"Don't you think some things are just meant to be?"

I shook my head. I refused to let La La Land even rate a mention. I wasn't interested in hearing how my stupid carelessness resulted in a gift from the fairy realm.

She slumped back, resting her head on the headrest. "It doesn't seem fair, does it? Gabi and Alex would kill to be in our position. We've just stolen their most longed-for wish."

"Charli, stop it," I muttered. "One has nothing to do with the other."

"Nothing happens without reason, Adam." She turned to look at me. "If I lose faith in that, then nothing in my life makes sense."

I wanted to kiss and scream at her simultaneously, but wasn't capable of either. All my concentration needed to be spent reasoning with her.

"How are we supposed to tie this all together? We can't keep ourselves together. Bouncing a child back and forth between nations is not –"

She cut me off with a desperate offer. "I'll come back to New York."

It didn't feel the least bit honest. How I handled that would determine what sort of man I was.

"Really?" I asked.

"Yes."

"And you'd settle?"

"Yes."

I found myself agreeing to her absurd offer.

I was a dick. A selfish, dishonest dick.

January 2
Charli

The only thing worse than being backed into a corner is realising that you put yourself there. Going back to New York was a dumb idea and I couldn't understand why I'd suggested it.

It didn't take a genius to tell that Adam wasn't thrilled to be having a baby. Trying to wash the positive result off the test was a sure-fire sign that parenthood was not a road he was ready to travel.

I wasn't entirely sure how I felt, mainly because I didn't feel any different than I had three hours earlier, when I was late, late and not pregnant. At that moment the white stick didn't seem any more credible than Crazy Edna.

"I should probably see a doctor," I said, thinking out loud. "Just in case the test was wrong."

"Do you think it could be?"

I shouldn't have said anything. I'd just given him hope. "Probably not. I think they're fairly accurate."

His head lolled back as he closed his eyes and let out a long breath. I could hear his mind ticking over. When things don't go to plan, Adam comes up with new ones. It's how he's programmed to function.

"We're going to work this out, Charli," he promised.

As far as I was concerned, there wasn't anything to work out. It was a done deal. I just wanted him to find the joy in it.

"Well, let me know when you've come up with a plan," I said sarcastically.

He turned his head, looking positively wounded. "Charli, I –"

"Stop talking, Adam." I threw open the car door. "It gets us nowhere."

If he spoke again, I was too far away to hear. I marched to the house without looking back. Looking back was pointless. Standing still wasn't an option either. Life was now rushing forward at a terrifying pace and I had a terrible feeling that Adam wasn't going to be able to keep up.

January 3
Adam

Going for a run that morning was less about exercise and more about punishing myself. I figured I deserved a little pain at that point.

The topic of returning to New York hadn't rated a mention since the night before, which proved something that I already knew. It wasn't something Charli was looking forward to. It was something she was going to go through with because she felt it was the only option she had.

If I were a good man, or even a slightly better man, I would've talked her out of it. But I'm not particularly good. I loved her. It was the only excuse I came up with for being so unreasonable.

The base of the cliffs put a stop to my run. I literally ran out of beach. As I turned to head back I noticed Nicole coming down the beach toward me. She saw me too – and hightailed it up the trail to the parking lot. I called out and she stopped, but didn't turn back.

"Are you avoiding me, Nic?" I asked, jogging toward her.

"Maybe," she confessed. "You're supposed to hate me."

I smiled. "Yeah, I've been warned not to talk to you."

"Look, Adam," she could hardly look at me, "I don't want to cause any problems."

"You don't have that kind of power, Nicole."

"I owe you a lot of money," she said regretfully.

"I'd settle for an apology."

Finally she glanced my way. "I *am* sorry. Things just got out of hand. I've tried to talk to Charli but she's not interested in anything I've got to say."

"Can you blame her? It was a terrible thing to do."

"I know." Her frown was one of total agony. "Do you think she'll ever forgive me?"

I shrugged. "I don't really know."

"Maybe you could put in a good word for me?"

I had no intention of doing any such thing. "Just give her a bit of time. She never sold you out. I think that counts for something," I told her.

"What do you mean?"

"She never sold you out. Charli never told anyone that you stole her money. She could've destroyed you, Nicole. But she didn't."

She looked surprised and I wondered if I'd given her too much information.

I didn't hate Nicole for what she'd done, but I wasn't going to put in a good word for her with Charli, either. We had enough on our plates without throwing Nicole Lawson into the mix.

I made an excuse to leave and left her on the beach, accompanied by the knowledge that Charli was ten times the woman she'd ever be.

* * *

I arrived home to an empty house. I had no idea where Charli was and, true to form, she'd left no note telling me.

It shouldn't have worried me. It wasn't anything she hadn't done before, but this time felt different. Everything was beginning to feel different. We were back to hanging on by a thread. I hated the shift between us – and more tellingly, I resented the reason behind it.

When she did finally walk through the door a couple of hours later, I made it my mission to let her know exactly how much I loved her. It was pretty much the only truth we had left. I pulled her into my arms the second she was in reach and kissed her, really kissed her.

"What was that for?" she asked wriggling free.

"Because I love you." She walked further into the room and dropped her purse on the couch, leaving me hanging. "Where have you been?"

"I went to the doctor."

"Without me?"

She answered with a small nod.

"What did he say?"

"I'm ten weeks pregnant," she said matter-of-factly. "I'm due on August first."

I slumped on the couch. My head was spinning. "Ten weeks? We still have options then."

It was something I shouldn't have said out loud – or at least worded better. My career as an insensitive asshole was an accomplished one.

January 6
Charli

The next few days were fairly miserable for us. Whenever our lives started going haywire, dishonesty crept in. It was our thing.

I kept Adam in the dark about everything I was feeling on the off-chance he got brave and returned the favour. As a result, we were hardly talking. It was an absolute waste of the short amount of time we had together.

He killed time hanging out with Alex. Bogan-golf, surfing and playing in the shed kept him away from me for hours at a time. I suspect that was because the man who who'd mastered three languages was incapable of putting his feelings into words when it came to dealing with me.

I was putting more and more thought into the idea of having a baby. The joyful part of me imagined a cute, perfect child with her father's good looks. The old-fashioned part of me imagined a happy nuclear family far different from anything I'd ever known. The realistic part of me foresaw a much bleaker picture. Living in New York was no guarantee that I'd get my happy family. New York Adam could be a selfish jerk. I wasn't naïve enough to think a baby was going to make him change his ways, especially knowing he didn't want it in the first place.

I decided to take a shot at changing his mind.

Thanks to our recent grocery run, I was able to put together a decent meal. Adam arrived home just after six, and for a fleeting moment it was just like old times.

"Hey." He leaned down to kiss the top of my head. "How are you feeling?"

I'd heard that question a few times lately. It was his way of gauging my mood, not my physical state. "I'm good. I cooked dinner."

He lifted the lid on the pan, perhaps doubting me. It was the first meal I'd cooked since he'd been there.

"Looks good."

I shrugged, confident that the dish was at least edible. "I was hoping we could talk." My voice was unfairly small. I wanted to demand that we talk. I should've screamed it at him.

"Me too," he replied, just as weakly.

Dinner was almost done before the baby rated a mention, and it was left to me to bring it up. "I want to know what you want to do."

He glanced at me only briefly. "Are you asking me because I have a choice?"

I set my fork down and leaned back, refusing to let him avoid my stare. "Tell me something true, Adam. Tell me anything, as long as it's true."

He locked eyes with me. "I love you, Charlotte."

"I know," I replied flatly. "That's all I've ever known. Tell me something else that's true."

Adam spoke slowly, and very precisely. "We're not ready for this and I don't want to drag you back to New York. I don't want to have a baby. I think going through with it is a mistake."

I put great effort into not appearing as gutted as I felt. His way of thinking was completely one track, and it had always been that way.

"I know it might put a dent in your plans, but –"

"A baby we're not ready for isn't a dent, Charli. It's a massive crater," he corrected. "It's not even about my plans. What about your plans? You still have no idea what you want to do. Having a kid is going to narrow your choices."

I leaned forward, gripping the edge of the table with both hands. "Haven't you ever changed course just a little bit, Adam?"

"No, Charli," he said regretfully. "I've always manipulated you into changing yours."

His sad eyes spoke ten times louder than his voice. It made looking at him difficult. I straightened up and pulled in a long breath. "Well, this honesty thing is a barrel of laughs, isn't it?"

He reached for my hand but I pulled away. "You asked me to be honest, Charli."

"I did," I shakily agreed. "What will happen if I decide to keep it?"

He was quiet for a while but still came up blank, even with the extra thinking time. "I don't know."

"Don't you think you'd be a good father?"

"I'm a twenty-three-year-old self important jerk, Charli. I suck as a husband. I'd suck even more as a father. We're just not ready for this."

"*You're* not ready for this," I clarified.

"And you are?"

I shrugged apathetically. "I'm adaptable."

"Well, we both know I'm not."

"Let's cut to the chase, Adam," I said coolly. "You want me to end it."

He stared at me for a long time, probably trying to come up with a way of softening the blow.

"Yes, Charlotte. I want you to end it."

He failed. And it killed me.

He reached for my hand again. This time I didn't pull away. "When we're ready, we can have plenty of kids."

Just not the one we'd already made.

I don't know what he said after that. I completely shut down. He was being logical and sensible – because that's how Adam thinks. The problem was, I didn't want logical and sensible. I wanted hope and excitement, not damage control. Realising I wasn't ever going to get it, I stood up, dumped our half-eaten plates in the sink and went to bed.

January 6
Adam

I didn't know whether to follow her or not – so I didn't. I cleaned up the kitchen, had a shower and wasted another hour pretending to watch TV. When I was fairly certain she was asleep, I crept into the bedroom.

I could tell sleep hadn't come easily. Charli was tangled around the sheets as if she'd been tossing and turning.

I gently moved the bedding, trying not to wake her as I straightened it up. Barely touching her, I splayed my hand across her bare stomach. Her skin felt so warm lately. Maybe that was another symptom we'd missed. I tried my hardest to feel some connection to the baby growing inside her but couldn't seem to link my brain to my heart. There just wasn't any happiness to be found. I said a silent apology to the child I didn't want, covered Charli over and switched off the light.

* * *

Charlotte's side of the bed was empty next morning. I figured she'd headed to the beach for some time alone.

I still wasn't overly concerned when I noticed that my car wasn't on the driveway, but my calm resolve started to wear thin by late afternoon. I was about to start calling around when she finally walked through the door just after four.

She looked terrible – pale, and dressed far too warmly for the summer afternoon.

"Where have you been?" My voice sounded strange so I cleared my throat and repeated the question.

"Hobart," she replied.

"I was worried about you. Is everything alright?"

She walked past me and sat down on the couch. "It is now. Everything's back to normal."

Dread flooded my body in the form of heat. "What did you do?" It came out sounding like I was accusing her of something terrible.

She slowly shook her head, ignoring the tears that had begun spilling down her pale cheeks. "I did exactly what you wanted me to do."

I had no clue what to say. I had no idea what to do.

"I didn't want you to go through it alone, Charli. I would've come with you."

I didn't even know what *it* was. Disgracefully, I had no idea what she'd endured that day.

"Don't pretend you're not relieved, Adam," she muttered.

I was relieved – and appalled and sad and consumed by self-loathing. Breaking Charli's heart was the worst kind of pain I could inflict, and despite my promises not to, I did it over and over again.

"I'm so sorry." It was the best I could come up with.

She stared at me, emotionless. Her brown eyes looked wooden, vacant and dead. "Don't you dare say that to me. You're not sorry." She sounded dead too. "You can't tell me you don't want to do this and then be sorry that I ended it." I crouched in front of her, resting my elbows on her knees. I put my hands on hers, taking no solace when she didn't pull away. "You're never going to change, Adam," she whispered. "You're never going to be able to give me what I want, no matter how much you love me."

The lump in my throat was getting harder to swallow away. I dropped my head. "Neither of us know what the future holds, Charli."

"Yesterday our future included a family. We were right there, on the very edge of something really special – and you still couldn't give in and surrender to it."

"I can't –"

"You can't. I know," she said flatly. "You have a plan and you're sticking to it."

The truth hurt, but I wasn't going to deny it. Denying it would mean lying to her. I'd had my fill of lying to her.

I lifted my head to look at her. "The timing was terrible, Charli."

"I get it, I do," she uttered. "And now it's over. Happy days."

I tightened my grip on her hands. "Let me go," she ordered, snatching her hands free. She stood and walked around the couch to get away from me.

"I love you, Charli."

Agony and frustration flashed across her face before she recovered, straightened up and wiped her eyes with the cuff of her sleeves.

"It doesn't mean a thing any more. I give up everything for you – even the things I don't want to. What do you give me?"

Nothing was the answer. I'd held this girl on an invisible string for a long time. I'd promised her a happy ending a million times, never having a clue how to deliver. There just wasn't any happy medium for us. We were either supremely happy or painfully miserable – sometimes on the same day. That's what I gave her.

I walked around the couch, wanting nothing more than to wrap my arms around her. But I reached for her hands instead, again too tightly.

"Let me go," she demanded, trying to pull away.

"Please, Charli," I begged. "Just listen."

Her hands relaxed, giving me the slightest hope that she was at least prepared to hear me out, but she wasn't.

"I want you to let me go, Adam," she said eerily calmly. "Then I'll let you go."

I knew what was coming. I could feel it. "You should leave." She pulled away and pointed at the door. "Everything ended today."

"Charli –"

"Get out, Adam."

"No. I'm not going anywhere."

The sound that escaped her lips was nothing I'd heard from her before. It sounded like a humourless laugh caught in a sob. "For how long? You're leaving tomorrow anyway. Go now."

I took a step toward her. She stepped back so I went no further. "No."

The stand I was making did me no favours. "Get out!" she yelled. "I don't want you here!"

I stayed put, doing nothing to calm her down. She continued screaming at me to leave. The next thing I knew, Flynn Davis was pounding on the screen door, probably thinking I was murdering her.

"Charli?" he called. "Is everything okay?"

She rushed to let him in.

Flynn stalked through the door in full policeman mode. He had the blue uniform and one hand on his holstered gun to prove it.

"I want him gone," said Charli. "Make him leave."

"Charlotte." I choked out her name. "Seriously?"

"I want you to get out of my house!" She picked up a cushion and hurled it at me. I blocked it with my arm.

Flynn looked at me. "You heard her, mate. It's time to leave."

He'd probably been dreaming of a moment like this since he first laid eyes on me. Finally, he had his chance to swoop in and save her.

"I'm not going anywhere," I replied.

"Then I'll arrest you for trespass," he said smugly.

I looked at Charli and was struck by the determination on her face. She was actually prepared to let that happen. I took one more shot at making her see reason.

"I don't know how we'd find our way back from there," I told her. "Please don't do this."

"I'm tired of going back, Adam." Her face was sad but her voice was calm and the rage had gone. "We only go back because we can't go forward. Just let me go."

"That's what you want?"

"Yes," she replied, choking back a cry.

I stared at her for a long moment, trying to make sense of the last few days. Charli wasn't trying to make sense of anything. Charli was done. Charli was long gone.

"Let's go, mate," said Flynn, giving an upward nod.

"I am not your mate. And I'm not leaving." I growled, making one final stand. "You'll have to arrest me."

* * *

Of all the things I'd hoped to achieve in life, being holed up in a foreign jail wasn't one of them. Not that it was exactly hardcore. It was a windowless room with a cheap desk, a schoolroom chair and an anti-drug poster on the wall.

"Just cool off in here for a while. Someone will be in shortly," instructed Flynn, pulling the door closed.

I couldn't even be certain that the door was locked. I was just about to stand up and check when it opened and a female officer appeared.

"Time to go," she said, way too cheerily.

I'd only been incarcerated an hour. The Australian legal system obviously worked quickly.

I remained seated. "What am I being charged with?" I needed to know. It would be the first thing Ryan would ask me when I called him to make bail – after he stopped laughing, of course.

"No charges," she said. "You're free to go. Your ride is here."

I expected to see Charli in the reception area. I used the time it took to walk down the corridor to work out what I'd say to her. I wasn't angry with her, just confused and desperate to make things right.

Charli wasn't my ride. I rounded the corner and came face-to-face with Alex.

"This day just couldn't get any worse, could it?" I mumbled.

"Oh, I don't know," he replied. "Things can always get worse, Adam."

* * *

Alex didn't take me back to the cottage. We ended up at his house, on the golf course.

"I made a brilliant discovery yesterday," he said, handing me a bucket full of golf balls. "Biodegradable golf balls," he announced. "So it doesn't matter if we lose them."

I couldn't have cared less about losing golf balls. I was in the midst of losing something much more important.

"I'm not really up for it today," I muttered, setting the bucket on the ground.

"Today is a great day for golf, Adam. There's nothing like beating the crap out of something when you're pissed." He handed me a club. "And considering I just picked you up from the lockup, I imagine you're pissed."

It didn't take me long to work out that Alex was absolutely clueless when it came to the events of that day. Charli had called him to bail me out and told him nothing else. If she had, he would've been beating the crap out of me.

"Not a touchy feely person, are you, Alex? Most people like to talk about their problems."

He picked up his club. "Not me. Especially when the problems involve Charli. I just hit things – wood, golf balls, the ocean. I'm not fussy."

He sounded collected, but the curiosity must've been killing him.

I knew I had to tell him everything. I was selfish but not a selfish coward. "I have to tell you something," I said gravely.

He lined up a ball on the platform. "I'm listening."

I took a long moment to plan the conversation in my head. Trying to explain that his twenty-year-old daughter had just had an abortion at my insistence was like trying to put a positive spin on a fatal car crash.

After hearing the details, he didn't say anything for a long time – but the next three golf balls were smashed down into the field with sickening force.

"Do you two have to attend every act of stupidity that you're invited to?" he asked finally.

"Apparently."

"You're supposed to be smart, Adam." He tapped his temple. "That's why we call you Boy Wonder." He still sounded perfectly calm, which confused me. If ever he had reason to tear me apart, this was it.

"I'm not smart where Charli's concerned."

"You dumb each other down." He took another swing, sending the ball so far into the field that I didn't see where it landed. "I raised a strong, independent kid. The girl who came home was neither of those things." He pointed the club at me. "That's the effect you have on her."

"I know," I said regretfully.

"I thought the worst I was going to have to deal with was you showing up and convincing her to go back to New York."

"I told you I wouldn't do that."

I held off telling him she'd suggested it anyway. He had a golf club in his hand.

"Yeah, you did. You just convinced her to do something much worse instead."

"Charli made up her own mind."

"I'm having trouble believing she got there on her own," he replied, shaking his head. "It doesn't really seem like Charli's style."

I'd had the same ugly thought more than once in the last few hours. As much as I believed ending it was the right decision, I'd pressured her into it and I knew it. I took a shot at defending myself anyway. "She didn't even tell me until it was over and done with. I would never have let her go through that alone."

He lined up another ball. "Yeah, you're a real stand-up bloke."

I waited until he swung before speaking again. "I love her, Alex. I could've left town tomorrow without telling you any of this, but I didn't. I'm worried about her and I wanted you to know everything."

"You don't need to worry about Charli," muttered Alex. "I'll take care of Charli."

It brought no comfort. I wanted to be the one to take care of her. I just had no idea how. I doubt I ever did.

"She's done with me," I told him.

"I wish I could be certain of that."

"She had me arrested to get me out of the house," I said bitterly. "Trust me, she's done."

He looked straight at me. "Eventually she's going to get over you, Adam."

I nodded. "I want her to be happy."

"Look," he said, showing a hint of empathy. "I'm not going to give you a pep talk. I can't parent you. At times like this, I'm not old enough to parent my own kid. But I want you to both find what you're looking for. You just need to learn how to leave each other alone."

* * *

I spent my last miserable night in town at Alex and Gabrielle's house. Gabi didn't ask why I was there and I didn't tell her. Considering her current frame of mind, that was a task best left to Alex.

We spent the evening dodging the huge elephant in the room. Gabrielle was a smart woman. She knew something major had happened, and I didn't want to be in the same country as her when she found out what it was. Gabrielle wouldn't take too kindly to the news that we'd ended the one thing she was desperately hoping for.

By morning I was anxious to get out of there. I made one last trip to the cottage on my way out of town. The time I spent planning what I'd say to Charli during the drive there was all for nothing.

She wasn't there.

If that wasn't a strong indication that she was firm in her decision to cut me loose, the fact that my luggage was sitting on the porch was. I walked slowly to the car, hopeful that she'd come bursting out of the door at the last second, but it didn't happen.

Ryan had said it best. Charli was much smarter than me. She'd finally woken up to the fact that she deserved better than anything I had to offer.

January 7
Charli

An expression of relief is as easy to read as a smile or a frown. And when I saw relief flash across Adam's face when I told him he was off the hook, I knew letting him go was the right decision.

Unlike relief, deception can be carried out with a completely straight face. Perhaps that's why he didn't pick up on the fact that I was lying through my teeth when I told him I'd ended the pregnancy. In truth, the only thing I'd terminated was us.

I knew from the beginning that deciding to keep the baby would mean losing Adam. He'd been devastatingly honest with me. A child was something he wasn't ready for. He was stubborn, selfish and one-track, but I could accept it because hidden behind his relief was sadness in its purest form. It gave me hope that one day, he'd figure out why he felt that way. I would never give up on him. But for now, I was on my own.

I spent the morning at the beach. I didn't want to be anywhere near the cottage when Adam turned up. I knew his flight was at one. When I was sure he'd be well on the way to Hobart, I went home.

Alex turned up at my door soon after, armed with a chocolate cake that I prayed he hadn't cooked himself.

"How are you feeling?" he asked.

I was between a rock and a hard place. I had no idea how much Adam had told him, if anything. I wasn't sure how to answer him.

"Okay."

He set the cake down on the table before turning back to face me. "So are we going to talk or are we going to pointlessly dance around the subject, then talk?"

I couldn't find the words to speak.

"You might as well tell me, Charli," he urged. "I already got the story from Adam."

My heart began thumping at an alarming rate. "What did he tell you?"

"Everything." He threw out his arms. "Sang like a bird."

Something was off. If Adam had told him everything, my father would've been bouncing off the walls – either furious with me or hopelessly concerned. I wasn't getting either vibe from him.

"He told you about the baby?" It was the scariest question I'd ever asked him.

"Yes – and that you'd had a termination."

I winced as he said it. It was such a horrid word. Alex turned away and began pacing the room, probably trying to escape the awful conversation.

"What was your first thought when you found out, Charli?" he asked.

I didn't hesitate. "I wanted to have it."

Alex stood on the other side of the room with his arms tightly folded. I had no idea what he was thinking. It made plotting my next move impossible.

"I've only ever known you to go with the first thought, Charlotte." He'd used my full name. That wasn't good. "A girl who chances her entire existence to fate isn't going to terminate a baby. She's going to go with the first thought."

"She is," I confessed in a tiny voice. "It's a one-shot deal."

"That's what I thought," he said smugly.

"I couldn't end it."

"That's okay. It's your choice."

I growled in total frustration. "Why can't he just be who I need him to be, Alex?"

The look he gave was one of sheer pity. "He just might not be that guy, Charli."

"He is that guy," I insisted. "But I can't wait around for him to grow up and catch up."

I'd never felt as if I had a choice when it came to loving Adam. I did, however, have a choice on how it played out.

Alex walked over and kissed my forehead before whispering his next sentence. "It had to happen sooner or later, Charli. You've finally found something that you want more than him. Good for you."

He turned around and began walking toward the door. "Enjoy your cake. It should be edible. Gabrielle made it."

"That's it?" I asked. "Where are you going?"

"Have you seen the water today? It's magnificent."

I chased him onto the veranda. "You've just found out that I'm going to make you a grandad at thirty-seven, Alex. Thirty-freaking-seven! Don't you want to yell at me for a while?"

He didn't turn back and he didn't reply. I had no idea what to make of it but I didn't ponder it for long. I grabbed my gear and followed him to the beach.

* * *

No amount of sleep seemed to be enough to get me through the day lately. At least I now knew why. By the time I paddled out to Alex I was ready to lay my head on my board and go to sleep.

"I'm so tired," I groaned, dropping my head.

"You should have stayed home with your cake then," he teased.

I dragged my arm through the water, splashing him. "I want to talk to you."

He spread his arms wide. "Step into my office."

I took a long look around, soaking up my surroundings. The ocean in Pipers Cove wasn't the bluest of blue. It was navy and dark, which was a perfect match for the craggy backdrop of the cliffs. The sand was bright white, painting a neat stripe between the rocks and the water. I'd spent most of my life dreaming of escape. Ironically, now I just wanted to bunker down and stay.

"I'm so glad to be home," I told him. "This is where I'm supposed to be."

"It all comes down to how you like your chickens," he replied.

I turned in time to see a hint of a smile ghost across his face.

"Chickens?"

"Kids are just like chickens, Charli. You can raise them free-range or in cages. I prefer mine free-range."

"Alex, all this salt water is muddling your brain."

"You muddle my brain," he corrected, flicking water at me.

"Are you upset with me?" I asked.

"I think you've chosen a tough road. It's not what I wanted for you," he replied. "I'm worried about you."

I could accept that. I was worried about me too.

"Did you give Adam a hard time?"

Alex hadn't shown me a hint of anger at the news. It made me worry that Adam had borne the brunt of it.

"Boy Wonder was honest with me. I appreciated that," he told me. "I don't always get honesty from you."

I dragged my arms through the water, keeping my board close to his. "I've jumped out of a tall tree this time, Alex," I muttered.

He smiled, though it had a rueful tinge. "I'm at the bottom, Charli. You'll be fine."

He'd just made paddling a hundred metres off shore totally worth it. It was exactly what I needed to hear.

"Can we please just keep this to ourselves for a while?"

He grimaced as if I'd asked him to do something illegal. "Adam needs to know, Charli. Sooner rather than later."

"I'm going to tell him."

"Yes you are," he replied. "I'm going to make sure of it. Keeping his child from him isn't going to be the big get-even for being a jerk, okay?"

"Okay."

"I'll give you a bit of time, but Gabs isn't going to be very sympathetic. She won't keep quiet for you."

I wasn't stupid enough to think I could keep the baby a secret forever. Gabrielle and Adam were cousins. It might make their family reunions a little awkward. "I'll figure it out," I muttered. "How do you think she'll cope with the news?"

"I really don't know," he said softly. "You know how desperately she wants a baby of her own."

"I think the universe screwed up, Alex. They sent the baby to the wrong address."

My father smiled. "The universe doesn't make clerical errors, Charli. Everything is exactly how it's supposed to be."

January 9
Adam

I'd arrived back in New York two days earlier than scheduled. I'd neglected to warn Ryan. That made finding a mystery blonde wandering around the apartment inevitable.

"Hello." I greeted, pulling my luggage through the door.

"Hi there," she replied, tilting her head to the side.

"Where's my brother?"

"I'm not sure." She sounded confused. "Who's your brother?"

I frowned. "Ryan. The guy who lives here."

"Oh." She snorted out a loud giggle. "He's in the shower."

"Alone?" I felt it important to ask. It *was* Ryan we were talking about.

She nodded and I walked out of the room, leaving her taking up space and oxygen on my couch.

I didn't knock on the bathroom door. I just barged in. Ryan didn't flinch at the intrusion. It was probably something he dealt with often.

"You're back," he exclaimed, clearing a patch on the glass.

"Yeah. Who's in the lounge?"

"Candice. She's a graphic artist."

"I'm sure Candice is *very* graphic. Send her home."

He turned off the water. "In fairness Adam, I didn't know you were coming home. If you'd called ahead, graphic Candice wouldn't be here." I felt my shoulders slump. I had no reason to be giving him attitude. Ryan looked at me for a long moment. "How was the trip?"

"Eventful."

134

"Do you want to talk about it?"

"Not really."

"You don't look good."

"I'm fine," I said wearily. "I'm going to bed. Just get rid of Candice, okay?"

* * *

I didn't surface until late the next morning. Candice was gone. Ryan was not. He was standing at the counter, thumbing through a newspaper.

"Aren't you working today?" I asked.

He folded the newspaper and thumped it down on the counter. "Later. I wanted to see how you were first."

I'd never known Ryan to be concerned. I must have really looked bad the night before.

"I'm okay."

"How's Charli?"

I poured myself a cup of coffee, immediately noticing that he'd brewed the one I like, as opposed to the mud he prefers. I'd never known him to be considerate either.

"Charli's fine. I'm fine. We're both fine. We're just going to be fine separately from now on."

Ryan wasn't buying my indifference, which was unfortunate because I wasn't sure I'd live through explaining it to him.

"Tell me what happened," he demanded.

I stared at him, still stirring my coffee. "It started great. I went surfing with her father, who hates me. He nearly drowned me. He started to warm to me a little after that. We mended our differences and played golf. I fell in love with my wife for the hundredth time after she showed me fairies. Then a crazy old woman read a pile of sand and predicted that Charli was pregnant. It was all downhill from there."

Ryan remained stone-faced but his eyes were wide. "You knocked her up?"

That was all he'd managed to pull from my rant.

"Momentarily," I replied bitterly. "We ended it."

He looked away from me. "Oh. I'm sorry."

I set the mug down, shaking my head. I didn't know what to say. I wasn't sorry. I was relieved. I'd also never hated myself more in my life. I didn't quite know what to make of it.

"So what happens now?" he asked.

"Charlotte's done with me." I sounded totally disconnected from the drama. "I'm going to file for divorce and leave her alone."

"Are you sure that's what you want?"

I'd put a lot of thought into it on the long trip home. Charli had made herself perfectly clear. She wanted me to let her go. A divorce definitely constituted letting her go.

"I just want her to be happy, Ryan. I can't do that. I just keep screwing things up."

"*C'est la vie*, huh?"

"Yeah," I muttered. "Something like that."

February 3
Charli

I'd done a lot of ducking and weaving over the past few weeks. The Beautifuls were trying hard to recruit me. Jasmine had turned up at my door more than once, extending the manicured hand of friendship.

"We're here for you, Charli," she told me. "We know you're down on your luck since Adam dumped you."

Adam's desertion had been a whispered topic around town since the day he left. Thankfully, his arrest hadn't made the headlines. I was glad Flynn had shown some discretion. Ordinarily, the gossip would've destroyed me, but my mind was on keeping much bigger news a secret. I was fourteen weeks pregnant, and apart from Alex – and possibly Crazy Edna – not a soul knew.

Nicole Lawson was also on the list of people I avoided. Every time I went to the café, she'd bail me up to apologise for being a thieving snake. It hadn't meant anything to me the first time I heard it. A hundred apologies later, it meant even less.

Alex was unhappy with my decision to keep punishing her. Every time I'd cut her down for trying to make amends, he'd corner me later and chastise me for it. "You could do with a friend right now."

No one needed a friend like Nicole, least of all me.

Flynn Davis was the last member of my duck and weave list – and the hardest to avoid. I saw him every single day. Sometimes it would be as subtle as a wave across the fence and others it was a full-blown ambush. Once Adam left, he made no secret of the fact that he had designs on me –

something I'd suspected since Christmas. Usually I only had to decline dinner invitations. Today's suggestion was a little more bizarre. He turned up at my door to invite me out for a sail on his grandad's boat.

"*La Coccinelle?*" I asked in disbelief.

"Yes. She's beautiful when she's in full sail."

"Flynn, my husband restored that boat," I reminded. "Don't you find that weird?"

"I can overlook it." He shrugged. "It's not like you're together."

There was no point denying it. He'd witnessed our spectacular crash and burn first hand.

"Look, I'm not trying to hurt your feelings, Flynn, but you're just not getting it," I said gently. "I'm not interested."

Flynn was like a skittish, enthusiastic puppy. Just in case he wasn't house trained, I never let him into the cottage.

"Charli, some things take time," he said smiling. "I'll wait."

Getting rid of him was easy as shutting the door. "Bye Flynn."

Most people would've been appalled by my rudeness. Not Flynn Davis. "Bye, Charli. See you later," he called through the closed door.

I peeked through the curtain at him as he strolled back to his house, promising myself that there would be no more letting him down gently. The next time he cracked on to me, I vowed to drop him from a great height.

February 4
Adam

I held off consulting a lawyer for nearly a month. If there was even a slight chance that Charli was having second thoughts, I would've called the whole thing off. The problem I faced was that she never had second thoughts. I tried my luck by calling her anyway. I stood on the steps outside my father's office, braving the icy February weather and an icier Charli.

"Hello?" she answered groggily.

I'd woken her. I checked my watch and worked out the time difference – something I should've done before calling.

"Hey, it's me," I replied sheepishly.

"Adam, it's the middle of the night."

"I know. I'm sorry."

"You shouldn't be calling me." Her voice was colder than the air temperature. It made me turn the collar up on my coat.

"Please, just listen for a second," I pleaded. "Remember the story you told me about the Adelie penguins?"

"Of course," she said quietly.

"Well, I want to know something. What if the male penguin was a dick?"

"What do you mean?"

"What if he didn't know how to forage for rocks? Let's say he was absolutely clueless," I elaborated. "Would the female give him time to learn or would she kick him straight to the iceberg curb?"

There was silence for a long time. I busied myself by kicking at a spot of gum on the pavement. Finally she spoke.

"She wouldn't have a nest, Adam," she replied. "She uses the rocks he gives her to make a nest. She needs them. If he can't give her what she needs, she has nothing. Why would she wait for him if he can't give her what she needs?"

"She wouldn't," I replied, defeated. "He'd have to let her go. I get it. Charlotte, I'm sorry I woke you up."

I quickly ended the call; mainly to stop myself from telling her I loved her. I didn't think she'd appreciate hearing it.

* * *

Ryan had offered to come with me to my father's office. Moral support wasn't his motive. He was more interested in hearing the details of the divorce settlement.

"You should retain Billet-doux," he'd told me. "Then I don't have to deal with Tinker Bell either."

He made it too easy for me. "I'm thinking of giving her Nellie's too," I replied.

At that point he demanded he be at the meeting. I didn't care either way. I just wanted it over and done with. He was sitting in the reception area when I stepped out of the elevator.

My father's PA, whose name I couldn't remember, sauntered toward us. Ryan straightened in his chair. "Tenille, sweetheart. How are you?"

Tenille. Her name was Tenille.

"Fine, Ryan." She was having trouble looking at him – probably because her eyelashes were longer than her skirt. "Mr Décarie should be free shortly. Would you like coffee while you wait?"

"No thank you, sweetheart," he replied, granting her a sordid smile.

I waited until she was out of earshot before speaking. "You slept with her didn't you?" I muttered from the corner of my mouth.

"Twice," he confirmed, unrepentant.

I didn't get a chance to call him out on his whorish ways. Tenille announced that the king was ready to see us.

* * *

Our father barely glanced at us as we walked in. "Hi boys, take a seat."

We did as we were told. My father pushed a stack of papers across his desk at me.

"Adam, I've put together a file for you. Someone from this office will call you in a day or two to sort out the details," he said, getting straight down to it. "I expect that it will be fairly cut and dried. I want it sewn up quickly."

"So do I. Why did *you* put a file together?" I was annoyed. I was perfectly capable of working out the details.

My dad locked eyes with me. "There's no prenuptial agreement. You've paved the way for a glut of problems in the future. I want it dealt with properly."

I was shaking my head before he'd even finished speaking. The notion that Charli would ever make a grab for my family's money was ludicrous.

"Charli couldn't care less about money."

My dad leaned back. I leaned forward, resting my elbows on his desk.

"Son, you cannot predict what will happen in the future. There is an extraordinary amount of money at stake, and as it stands your wife could make a claim for a substantial amount of it."

I didn't know how to win this argument. I looked to my brother for help.

"Charli wouldn't go after money, Dad," Ryan defended. "Glitter isn't expensive."

"I'm very fond of Charli," insisted my father. "I'm truly sorry things haven't worked out. But it's time to put an end to the unfortunate episode and move on. You have a busy year ahead."

He spoke as if my union with Charli was nothing more than a blip on my radar. I felt sorry for him, and then felt lucky for knowing better. I remembered the five-minute rule. Five minutes of something amazing would forever trump a lifetime of nothing special.

February 15
Charli

I went for a long walk that morning, ending up so far down the coast that I ran out of beach. At the base of the cliffs I took the trail up to the road, ending up in the car park opposite the café.

"Hello, my first born," crooned Alex from behind the counter. "How are you feeling?"

"Hi. Shattered. I walked here."

"All that way?" Even he sounded impressed.

I walked to the fridge and grabbed a bottle of water. "Can you please drive me home?"

"I can't right now. I'm the only one here."

I batted my eyes and pouted a little, to no avail, so I pulled out a stool at the counter and settled in for the morning.

Nicole walked through the front door a few minutes later, and looked horrified to see me. I liked that I had that affect on her.

"Hi," she said timidly.

"Hey, Nic," replied Alex.

I purposefully said nothing, making her even more nervous.

"Ah, I just collected the mail from the post office," said Nicole, waving a stack of envelopes in Alex's direction. "Sorry I took so long. There was a queue."

"Were you worried that he'd think you'd done a runner?"

"Charli," chided Alex, taking the mail.

I felt no remorse. If she was embarrassed, it was because she deserved to be. Finally, her eyes drifted upward. "Are you always going to hate me, Charli?"

I'd almost forgotten how brash Nicole could be. It was impossible not to be impressed.

"I haven't decided yet."

Alex thumbed through the mail, eventually handing me a big white envelope addressed to Charlotte Décarie. Ryan had struck again.

"Nic, do you think you could drive Charli back to the cottage?" he asked. That was my punishment for being a bitch to her.

I glared at him, then across at Nicole. He looked fed up. She looked petrified. "Sure," she replied, sounding like it was the last thing on earth she wanted to do.

"Great." I tucked my mail under my arm. "Let's go."

* * *

The distance from the café to the cottage was short by car – no more than five minutes. Neither of us said a word. I grabbed my mail and clambered out of her car as soon as it stopped. Nicole didn't take the opportunity to make a quick getaway. Instead, she turned off the ignition. I didn't slow to ask why. I kept walking to the house.

"Aren't you lonely, Charli?" she called.

I stopped and slowly turned back. Nicole stood leaning on the open door. "What are you talking about?" I asked roughly. "Why are you even talking at all?"

"Be honest," she pressed. "Both of us have ended up back in the Cove because things didn't work out. Neither of us would ever have come back here otherwise. I'm really lonely here, Charli. I just wondered if you felt the same."

I'd realised weeks ago that life in Pipers Cove was going to be undeniably quiet. Refuting it was pointless, so I avoided the question altogether. "What do you want from me, Nic?" I asked angrily. "I'm not going to invite you in for coffee and tell you all my troubles."

"Yeah, well, you probably should cut back on caffeine while you're pregnant anyway."

I gasped, stunned. "Who told you?"

"I can see it, stupid." She tried a twisted laugh. "If it's supposed to be a secret, you might want to invest in some Spanx."

"You can't see a thing!" I yelled, putting my hand to my stomach. "Who told you?"

"Settle down. I overheard you talking to Alex. I'm happy for you. Why are you keeping it a secret?"

"It's no one's business," I said sourly. "Including yours."

I stepped onto the porch. Nicole called out again as I jammed the key in the lock.

"Charli, where's Adam?"

I practically yelled my snippy response. "I don't know, Nicole. Where's Ethan?"

"Invite me in and I'll tell you everything," she offered. "You know you want to hear it."

I should've ordered her off the property. But I couldn't. As much as I hated to admit it, she was right. I'd been dying to hear her story since I'd found out she was back in town.

* * *

We sat drinking tea at the dining table. Neither of us seemed particularly comfortable with the grown-up setting. Back in the day, our deep and meaningful conversations generally took place in her cluttered bedroom while we listened to loud music and ate copious amounts of chocolate. It was a lifetime ago.

"So? What happened?" I asked.

"What do you want to know?"

"Hmm, let's see." I drew out the words theatrically. "I'd like to know what possessed you to betray your lifelong best friend for the sake of a bit of money and a loser boyfriend."

Nicole shook her head, making her brown ponytail swish behind her. "It was never about the money."

"So it was about Ethan. Was he worth it, Nicole?"

Her lips pressed into a tight line as she stared into her mug.

"My punishment for betraying you was dished out early, Charli." Her voice faltered as she fought back tears. "Being with Ethan was a nightmare."

I didn't want her to cry. I wanted her to be unrepentant and proud of her criminal ways. It would have made hating so much easier to do.

"Tell me what happened," I pushed.

"Well, the beginning was pretty great. He filled the void of losing my best friend to the American tourist." She smiled crookedly and I scowled, refusing to let her put any of the blame on me. "He said all the right things and promised the earth. I tried to keep it casual but I guess he suckered me in."

I couldn't quite believe that that was all it took for her to cross to the dark side, especially considering she'd been successfully warding off the advances of Ethan Williams since primary school.

"So how long before it turned bad?"

She shifted in the seat and let out a long sigh. "As soon as we left town I knew it was a mistake." A hard laugh escaped me. "I'm glad you find it funny."

I shook my head. "Nicole, I'm genuinely sorry that your decision to skip town with a bad boy resulted in you being treated badly."

She dropped her head and began to cry, which is something I'd only ever seen her do a few times. I had no idea how to comfort her, or even if I wanted to.

"Look, just tell me what happened," I urged.

Nicole composed herself as best she could and launched headlong into the whole sorry saga.

As it turned out, life on the run wasn't such a great gig. Nicole and Ethan spent an entire month holed up in a dodgy backpacker's hostel in Melbourne because he was too paranoid to leave the country.

"Ethan was worried that the police were involved," she explained, grimacing. "He was convinced that if we left the hostel, we'd be picked up. It was ridiculous."

I shook my head, frowning at her. "I didn't call the police."

I should've called the police.

"Ethan wasn't worried about you," she mumbled. "He was worried that Adam had caught wind of it. He actually made me call him to find out if he knew anything. Adam was totally oblivious, of course."

I'd long considered that phone call to be her biggest betrayal of all. It hurt to even think about it.

"You told him I'd done a runner with Mitchell," I growled, drumming my finger on the table. "You screwed me over all over again."

"I had to tell him something, Charli," she replied, clearly ashamed. "I had no real reason to be calling him in the first place."

"You should never have called Adam."

"Of course I shouldn't. I did a lot of things I shouldn't have done."

I frowned. "Why didn't you just ditch him? You could have come home."

The look she gave me was one of the strangest I'd ever seen. "I just couldn't." She shuddered then, reliving a memory that didn't seem pleasant. "He kept the money, my passport, everything."

She smoothed back her hair, composing herself. "Eventually, he figured out that no one was coming for us so we jumped on a plane and went to Fiji. And that's as far as we got."

Nicole spent a year and a half in a small resort town, working two jobs to support her surfer bum boyfriend. Inexplicably, their bounty of stolen money ran out within weeks.

"You had thirteen thousand dollars!" I cried in disbelief. "Where did it all go?"

She scowled down at her now cold cup of tea. "Ethan likes the good life. We were always broke. I cleaned rooms at two different hotels to keep him cashed up. It was a vicious cycle. I couldn't even scrape together the money for a ticket home," she said bitterly. "But Ethan lived like a king, full of drinking, surfing and women. I guess I got what I deserved."

I'd wished the worst on Nicole more than once in the past two years. But in my mind, the worst entailed getting stung by jellyfish or losing her luggage. It didn't feel good knowing that things had gone so awry for her.

"One day we got into a terrible fight. I can't even remember what it was about. Ethan was raging drunk. "

I wasn't sure I wanted to hear the rest, but something in Nicole's expression made me listen.

"He hit me." She paused, steadying herself by drawing in a breath. "I knew that had to be the end. It could only get worse. I called Mum that night. She sent me a plane ticket so I could come home."

I remembered how distraught Carol had been when Nicole had taken off. "She must have been so thrilled to have you home," I said quietly.

Nicole smiled for the first time since the conversation had begun. "She howled when she saw me. I looked completely down and out."

I'd always known Ethan was a controlling pig but I never suspected he was a thug. "Are you still afraid of him?"

A pained frown flashed across her face. "When I got home, I took out a restraining order. Even if he does follow me back, he can't come near me."

I stared at her for a long time, weighing up my options. There were two. I could forgive her and move on, or continue being infuriated by her betrayal. Perhaps she'd been punished enough.

"I'm sorry for what you went through," I murmured. "But I'm having trouble forgiving you."

Her shoulders sagged. "I hate what I did but I can't take it back," she said shakily. "It's been miserable here without you."

I picked up the cold cups of tea and carried them to the kitchen. "Why haven't you been hanging out with the Beautifuls? I hear they're recruiting," I asked, lightening the conversation considerably.

Nicole groaned. "I couldn't stand it. They'd probably grant me membership, though. They're down on numbers now that Lisa's gone."

I poured both cups of tea down the sink. "Yes. Where is Lisa?" I hadn't given Lisa Reynolds a single thought until that moment. I felt a little bad about that. She'd always been a key member of the Beautifuls.

"Well, it turns out that Lisa actually has a brain. She's attending university on the mainland. Engineering, I think."

"Wow," I marvelled. "Who knew?"

"I know, right? I thought she'd end up working at Jasmine's salon. Have you been there yet?"

"Hardly," I scoffed.

"Her daddy bankrolled it," she explained. "It's three doors down from Mum's salon. You can imagine how that went down."

It would have been World War Three. I was almost sorry that I hadn't been around to witness it. Then I imagined Carol and Jasmine going at it on the main street. It would have been a blur of fake tan and sequins. I shuddered, relieved that I was on the other side of the world at the time.

Conversation remained light while I made more tea. The scene had been set. It was my turn to be interrogated.

"So, what's your story, Charli? What brought you home?"

My story paled in comparison to hers, especially considering I only gave her minor details, starting with the year I spent with Mitchell. "Mauritius, Madagascar, South Africa and then I made my way to New York," I explained, ticking the list of destinations off on my fingers. "We had a great time."

She nodded, but seemed uninterested. "I want to hear about Adam."

I was unwilling to give her details. "It didn't work out. He came here and we tried again, but it didn't work."

She nodded. "How does he feel about the baby?"

I sucked in a long breath, debating whether to lie or tell the truth. Honesty won out. "He doesn't know."

Her eyes widened and she leaned back. "Are you going to tell him?"

"When I'm ready." My tone instantly took on a dark edge. "*I* have to be the one to tell him, Nicole. If he finds out before I'm ready, I'm going to know it was you who sold me out."

Her hands flew up in the air as if I'd threatened her at gunpoint. "I'd never do that, never."

I didn't trust Nicole one iota. She'd had no problem screwing me over in the past.

The heavy turn in conversation wasn't welcomed by either of us. Nicole glanced at her watch and made an excuse to leave. I was happy to let her go.

* * *

It had been a long day. After a lazy dinner that consisted of a handful of almonds and a sandwich, I headed to my room with my Billet-doux mail and a pen, preparing to spend the next twenty minutes signing my name. I settled in bed and tore the strip off the top of the envelope.

It wasn't paperwork pertaining to Billet-doux. It was something much more serious.

I'd been served divorce papers.

My first inclination was to bury myself in the covers and cry, but I willed myself to take a more grown-up approach. I'd demanded that Adam let me go. He was doing it in spectacular fashion.

I began reading through the twenty-three page document, distancing myself as if I was interpreting how someone else's life was being broken down in dollars and cents. I was actually quite curious to see what an errant Décarie wife was worth.

From what I could tell, Adam was playing extraordinarily fair. I'd retain co-ownership of Billet-doux and all my personal possessions. At first it seemed like a silly clause to include, but then I remembered the clothes and shoes that were still boxed up in the spare room. I had a wardrobe worth literally thousands of dollars.

My eyes drifted to my left hand. The curly fry rings glittered under the low light of the bedside lamp, reminding me that they were also worth a small fortune. I glossed over the part pertaining to 'an adequate cash settlement.' It made me feel like a whore.

I forced myself to keep reading.

According to the documents on my lap, Adam owned four properties in New York City. I'd only ever known about the apartment he shared with Ryan. It highlighted the fact that I was clueless when it came to his finances. It made me wonder what else he hadn't told me.

In fairness, I couldn't exactly take the moral high ground. I had a contraband baby growing inside me and, he knew nothing about her.

I bundled the papers together, stuffed them back in the envelope and cried myself to sleep.

* * *

My father always seemed to know when things weren't right. I didn't think my demeanour was any different than normal, but within ten minutes of being in the cottage his interrogation began.

"What's going on, Charli?"

"Why would you ask me that? What do you think is going on?"

"You're fidgeting and you haven't touched your food. If I'm going to bring you breakfast, the least you can do it eat it."

I slunk down in my chair, looking at the spread on the table. Alex had gone all out that morning, appearing at my door with enough food to feed the whole Cove.

"There is something going on," I volunteered.

I stood and picked the envelope of doom off the coffee table. I didn't want to explain it to him. I didn't even want to talk about it. I handed it to him, demanding that he read it for himself, which he did with the slow speed of a first-grader.

"I'm sorry," he said finally. "But he's only doing what you asked him to."

"I didn't ask him to divorce me!"

"Charli, you had him arrested to get him out of here. That seems pretty final."

"If I sign those papers, it's all over," I said sadly.

Alex's face twisted into a frown. I knew that look. It was the one he gave just before launching into a conversation he didn't want to have. "You know it might never be completely over, right?"

"He doesn't want the baby." He didn't even want *me* any more.

Alex brought both hands to his face and let out a long moan. "You don't know that. You haven't given him the opportunity to decide whether or not he wants to be involved. As far as he knows, there is no baby. You might have written him off too early."

"I don't think I did."

He shook his head. "You didn't give him time to think it through, Charli. Adam doesn't go with the first thought, like you. He probably constructs pie graphs and flow charts, analyses them and then makes a decision." He smiled wryly. "That's why he's Boy Wonder."

I began clearing the table, busying myself so I wouldn't have to look at him. "What if I decide not to tell him?"

It was an idea I'd been toying with since I woke that morning. I just wasn't sure how I'd pull it off. It didn't matter, anyway. Alex wasn't going to let it get that far. His hand gripped my wrist.

"Sit down, Charlotte," he ordered. "We're going to have a little chat."

A chat implied something light-hearted and pleasant. Alex's idea of a chat was neither of those things. It was harsh and borderline mean.

"Your child deserves to have her father in her life. If there's even a chance that he wants to be involved, you have to make sure that happens."

"I had no mother. You did okay."

His body tensed but his voice stayed calm. "Olivia made a conscious decision not to be involved in your life. If she had changed her mind at any stage, I would've made allowances for that."

"But she didn't, did she?" I asked acidly.

"No, she didn't. I don't know why some people can walk away and others can't, Charli. It's just the way of the world. You have to at least give Adam the choice, and then you've done your part. It's up to him from there."

He walked into the kitchen and snatched the calendar from beneath a fridge magnet.

"What are you doing?"

"Pulling rank," he said coolly, dropping the calendar down in front of me. "Pick a date. Any date between now and, say, the beginning of July."

"Why?"

"Because that will be the date you tell him," he ordered. "That will give you a few more months of being Adam-free and easy. After that, you put your big girl pants on and deal with him."

I stared at the calendar, pondering my lack of choices. If I refused, he'd tell him anyway. "The third," I volunteered listlessly. "My big girl pants will be huge by then."

Alex wrote it in. "It's the right thing to do Charli."

February 19
Adam

My demons were huge – the kind that jolt you awake at four in the morning. The lack of sleep and constant bad mood wasn't working for me. I was more of an ass than usual and had developed a low tolerance for idiots.

My circle of friends was very small because of it.

I'd ignored Parker's many attempts to make peace. I did enjoy his efforts though. I usually let him get through his whole speech before cutting him down. Kinsey skipped town some time after Christmas, humiliated and destroyed by her so-called boyfriend's indiscretions. Kinsey and I had never been close so I was glad not to have to deal with her, but I still felt terrible. No one deserved that kind of treatment. I remained civil to Whitney, taking heart in the fact that running into her was always a million times more uncomfortable for her than me. She was the one person I was overly nice to. It seemed to intensify the awkwardness. She'd bumble her way through a few minutes of strained conversation and then practically run away.

That left Sera and Jeremy. I was lucky to have them. Every time I came close to claiming hermit status, they'd call me up and drag me out. I wasn't very good company, even on my best day. But they persevered, and I was grateful for it.

Trieste Kincaid was persistent too. She was also funny, intelligent and forgiving. I needed her to be forgiving because I often behaved badly. It wasn't unusual for me to cancel pre-planned study sessions with her – or worse, just not show up. I found it to be a pointless exercise, especially when I was busy with my own study. Trieste was a brilliant student. There was nothing I could help her with.

She also turned out to be a fairly decent server. I'd expected Ryan to fire her the minute I left town, but he hadn't. In the few weeks that I was away she'd proven herself quite an asset to Billet-doux. Impressing Ryan was no mean feat. When I'd asked him how her job was working out, his answer surprised me.

"She's quick, polite, and can add without a calculator. The girl's a machine." That was as close as he ever came to complimenting one of his members of staff.

* * *

Despite the bleak February weather, I made good on my plans to meet Trieste in the park that morning for coffee.

"I thought you'd stood me up again, Adam," she scolded, handing me a cup that was barely warm. "This coffee cost me five bucks."

"I'll pay you back."

"Why are you so late?"

I sat beside her.

"I got side-tracked." That was the best I was going to give her.

She cocked an eyebrow. "By your own dark thoughts?"

Trieste read me pretty well. She also didn't judge me. Perhaps that's why I'd confessed just about all of my Charli-related sins to her in the weeks since I'd been home. Beside Ryan, she was the only person who knew the whole story.

Maybe I'd been subconsciously expecting her to run away in disgust upon hearing it. She didn't, though. Trieste continued calling me at seven in the morning to invite me out for coffee and study.

"What are you working on at the moment?" I asked, changing the subject.

"Property law. What about you? What are you working on? Obviously not yourself."

"Do I look that bad?"

"Yes," she confirmed. "You look really sad."

I took a sip of the cold coffee. "I like being sad."

"Well, you do it well. Sad likes you too."

Trieste and I made an unlikely duo. Beside school, the only thing we had in common was that we were social misfits. I was unpopular because I was a jerk who couldn't be bothered with people. Trieste had very few friends because she was odd. Her motor mouth and strange fashion sense were only the surface of her strange quirks. But I liked her. And for some unknown reason, she liked me.

"You should come to Billet-doux for lunch today," she announced, tossing her cup in the trash. "I'm working the lunch shift. I'll get you discount on your meal."

I laughed humourlessly. "That's very generous of you."

"What can I say?" She shrugged. "You're a fabulous tipper. It's a win-win."

* * *

I went to Billet-doux for lunch, mainly because I had nowhere else to be. Charlotte always maintained that lone diners cut a pathetic figure. I wondered what she would've made of me sitting at a table by the window by myself. Perhaps noticing how dismal I looked, Trieste stole a few minutes with me while I ate.

"See that guy over there?" she asked with an upward nod.

I looked past her. "The guy behind the bar?"

"Yes. His name is Felix. I think he's dreamy," she said wistfully.

I grinned at her juvenile choice of words. "Dreamy?"

"Yes, dreamy. He's twenty-one. He doesn't have a girlfriend. He has a dog called Windsor and he lives with his brother."

I set my fork down. "Don't go there, Trieste," I teased. "Any guy that lives with his brother is a loser."

She giggled, a loud cackle that I'd become used to. "I think he's cute."

I took another look past her, studying the dreamy Felix. I couldn't really see the attraction. Felix was average looking, short, and trying very hard to grow a moustache.

"Are you going to make a move?"

Her eyes widened. "No! Of course not."

I picked my fork up and began pushing food around my plate. "Why not?"

She shrugged. "I wouldn't know how."

"Well, how do you normally approach a guy you like?"

"I never have. I've never even been on a date."

She wasn't the least bit embarrassed by her admission. I, on the other hand, could feel the heat in my face.

"You should put yourself out there, Trieste," I told her.

"I'm waiting for the right one," she replied.

I half-smiled. "Do you think Felix might be it?"

She stood up, preparing to get back to work. "You never know your luck in a big city, Adam."

February 21
Charli

Shopping had never been a favourite pastime of mine, but the Parisienne could be very persuasive. She won me over by inviting me to dinner afterwards. Gabrielle was a spectacular cook, and lately I had become a spectacular eater. We ended up in Hobart, wandering around Salamanca Place, a lovely precinct made up of rows of old sandstone buildings that are almost as old as Australia.

It was market day, which meant Gabi could get lost for hours checking out the arty wares on offer at the stalls. At least it wasn't clothes shopping. Fiona Décarie had permanently scarred me with all-day dress shopping expeditions.

By late afternoon I was getting tired and trying not to let it show. I'd been trying not to let a lot of things show lately, and had resorted to wearing ugly oversized hoodies to hide my little pot belly.

"Oh, look at this," crowed Gabrielle, fanning out a dress hanging on a rack. "This would be perfect for you."

In another lifetime. The pale pink chiffon dress was lovely, but the waist looked tiny.

"I don't think so."

"Nonsense." She thrust it at me. "Try it on."

The lady manning the stall pointed to a curtain. "Go behind there. There's a mirror."

Gabrielle nudged me toward the makeshift changing room, leaving me with little choice.

I put the dress on as best I could, reappearing a minute later holding the side of it to hide the fact that I couldn't do the zip up. Gabrielle took one look and pulled a face. "No. That won't do."

I could've told her that without trying it on. "Can we go now?" I begged.

She nodded, frowning at me. "Yes. Let's go."

* * *

We arrived back at the house, exhausted and famished – at least that's how I was feeling. Gabrielle had a little more energy. She headed straight for the kitchen and set about rustling up a meal.

Alex was in the shed. I didn't quite know what to do with myself. I was tired enough to sleep the rest of the day away but hungry enough to wait for whatever Gabrielle was concocting.

"What are you cooking?" I asked, venturing into the kitchen.

"Chicken," she replied brusquely. "I shall make extra."

I sat at the table, a little afraid of her sudden mood swing. The Parisienne was not to be underestimated when angry and wielding cooking implements.

"Why are you making extra?"

She took a pan out of the cupboard and slammed it down on the stove, making me jump. "Because I am astutely perceptive," she barked, waving a big spoon at me. "And I've realised that you are now eating for two."

My heart dropped. My secret was out, and she wasn't exactly jumping for joy at the news.

"Calm down, Gabi," I muttered.

She continued waving the spoon. "Alex will hit the roof!"

"He already knows."

"Your father knows?" She pulled out a chair, laid the spoon on the table and buried her face in her hands. "Of course your father knows. Of course you would have told him."

I wanted to run from the room. Gabrielle was truly distraught. When she finally moved her hands from her face, angry tears rolled down her porcelain cheeks. "You have no business having a child!" she yelled. "You can barely look after yourself. What were you thinking?"

I didn't respond. She stood up, slamming both palms on the table. I shrugged, incensing her even more. Her fist smashed on the laminate, making me jump. "How does Adam feel about it?"

"Adam doesn't feel anything about it. Adam doesn't know yet."

"Unforgivable!" I didn't even know she was capable of yelling that loudly. "That child is a Décarie!"

"What does that have to do with anything?" As far as I knew, Décarie babies weren't born with superpowers – unless being obscenely good looking was considered a superpower.

Gabrielle marched across the room, ripped the phone from its cradle and thrust it at me. "You call him right now. You tell him everything."

I had no idea how to handle her. She was under the assumption that I was doing Adam a disservice by keeping him in the dark. How was I supposed to explain that he would want no part of it anyway?

"I'll call him when I'm ready," I said calmly. "He doesn't need to know yet."

Gabrielle smashed the phone on the table, which worked in my favour. The chances of getting a dial tone now that it was in three pieces were slim. "That child has a birthright beyond anything you can imagine, Charli."

My temper finally gave way. I stood up, shoving the broken phone at her. "Despite what you all might think, you're not freaking royalty, Gabrielle. This kid is a Blake."

The conversation was way off track now, and I wasn't sure how we'd got there.

Alex rounded the doorway so quickly that he practically skidded to a stop. "What the hell is going on? I can hear you from the shed."

"Your daughter is with child," hissed Gabrielle, like a seventeenth century witch.

"I know," he admitted.

"I know you know," she said, slumping into her chair. "What is shameful is that Adam doesn't know."

Alex grimaced. "She'll tell him when she's ready. It's early days."

Gabrielle punched out a sarcastic laugh that I hadn't heard before. "Early days? I can *see* that she's pregnant." She pointed at me but looked at Alex. "It's hardly early days." As suspected, the pink chiffon dress had been my undoing.

"Getting upset isn't helping," said Alex gently.

"I shall tell Adam myself," announced the Parisienne, trying to piece the phone back together. She'd begun sobbing again, which killed Alex. He took the broken phone from her and held her hands. "You're not going to call him, Gabrielle. Adam won't hear about this from you. Do you understand?" His voice was gentle but there was seriousness in his tone. He was ordering her to keep quiet. "We'll talk about it later. Now isn't the time."

Gabrielle caved instantly, pressing her head against his chest. "This is most unfair," she whispered between sobs.

He swept his free hand through her auburn hair, trying to soothe her.

I felt terrible. I also felt guilty. I had stumbled headlong onto the path of motherhood, neither planning nor preparing for it. For me it had been a simple and careless process, which was clearly the crux of Gabrielle's distress.

There was nothing left for me to say. I slipped out the door without another word.

* * *

I thought I'd have a few days' grace when it came to dealing with the Parisienne, but she tracked me down at the beach the next morning. It was the first time I could remember seeing her there, and she wasn't handling the sand well.

I halted my walk and watched as she staggered toward me. I considered making a run for it. I didn't want to be around to see something wound as tight as Gabrielle unravel again. When she got closer and I could see that she didn't look too distraught, I relaxed a little.

"Can we sit?" she asked, sounding breathy and worn out. "Please?"

We walked up to the dry sand. She crumpled as if she'd lost the use of her legs.

"Are you going to yell at me again?" I asked. "Because I really don't need it right now."

"No," she replied. "I just want to talk. Yesterday was terrible."

I had to bite my tongue to stop myself apologising to her. I had nothing to be sorry for. When all was said and done, her anguish had nothing to do with me.

"I didn't set out to hurt you, Gabi. Obviously I didn't plan this," I began. "But I'm happy. I want you to be happy too."

She brought her knees to her chin and wrapped her arms around her legs. It was a move I was jealous of. I couldn't have copied her if I tried.

"I am happy for you. I just don't understand why you would cut Adam out of the picture. Why haven't you told him? I think it's most unfair."

Gabrielle's loyalties were with Adam, and it had always been that way. It came as no surprise that she was so quick to defend him. It left me with no choice but to tell her the whole sorry tale. True to form, Alex had told her nothing, which was no mean feat. It would've been World War Three in their house after I'd left the day before. Once I explained that Adam wanted a termination, she backed down.

"I gave him an out, and he took it." I spoke far more casually than a statement like that deserved.

"I know Adam," she said strongly. "If he'd known the truth, he would have done the right thing."

I shook my head, reliving the misery all over again. "And what's the right thing, Gabi? Living a miserable life he doesn't want?"

Better than anyone, I knew how awful that felt. I just couldn't do it to him – or myself.

"He has a responsibility to –"

"I'm not holding him to anything, Gabrielle." I could feel frustration setting in. She just wasn't getting it. "For a long time I thought I needed Adam. I realise now that I don't."

Her eyes drifted away to the rough ocean ahead. "You no longer love him?"

I picked up a handful of sand and sifted it through my fingers. "I'm always going to love him. I'm just not prepared to keep giving in to him. Things are better this way, for both of us."

She looked across at me, resting her cheek on her knees. "He's going to have to know."

"I realise that."

"What does he have to do to make it right?" she asked.

Turn up at my door, I answered silently. Saying it out loud would've sounded weak, which would've made convincing her that I had it all together impossible.

"Adam hasn't done anything wrong," I told her. "We just want different things. I'm not going to punish him for that. He's free to live his life."

"And what are you going to do?"

I looked out at the ocean, imagining every possibility. "I'm going to raise my chicken free-range. She's going to be my happy ending."

"A chicken?" She sounded confused. "A girl chicken?"

I glanced across at her, smiling. "I'm sure it's a girl. I've thought that from the beginning."

"Are you going to find out for certain?"

"I don't need to. I know she's a girl and I know she's perfect."

Gabrielle stretched her hand toward me. "The universe told you?"

I shrugged. "Maybe."

She put her hand to my stomach. The look on her face was one of sheer wonderment. "I envy you so much."

"I'm going to need help, Gabi." I wasn't trying to make her feel better. I was speaking the absolute truth. I had no clue what I was doing and wasn't stubborn enough to pretend otherwise.

"We're going to be here for you, Charli," she promised in a tiny voice. "All babies are blessings."

* * *

"Earth to Charli," called Nicole, waving her hand in front of my face.

"Did you say something?" I asked, snapping out of my daydream.

"I asked you if you want a cup of coffee," she repeated.

I'd spent quite a bit of time at the café lately. Being with Nicole gave me a chance to test the friendship waters. I wasn't entirely sure that there was a place for my traitor ex-best friend in my life, but after all she'd been through I felt as if I at least owed her a chance.

"No, she doesn't want any coffee," chimed Alex, jingling his car keys as he headed toward the door. "It's not good for the baby. I'll see you in an hour or two... maybe three."

Alex wasn't quite the workhorse he used to be. Nicole practically ran the place, which I think suited them both. She ran things her way and he cut out to go surfing whenever he pleased.

"He disappears all the time," grumbled Nicole as soon as he walked out the door. Her annoyance didn't seem genuine. Being left to her own devices was hardly a bad thing.

"Do you still have a thing for him?" I teased. "Do you miss him when he's gone?"

Nicole swiped a cloth along the countertop, pretending to clean it. "Alex is hot, Charli. Too bad he's your daddy."

It felt so good to laugh. Staying happy was a coup, because after signing divorce papers, I wasn't at all hopeful any more.

I'd received another sign that morning that led me to think my happy ending was slipping out of reach. The rings I'd finally grown into were now getting tight and uncomfortable to wear.

"It's probably just temporary," reasoned Nicole. "You have lots of changes going on in your body right now."

I slipped the rings into my pocket and rubbed the red mark on my finger.

"We'll see," I mumbled.

* * *

The bell at the top of the door jingled and Wade Davis strutted in, breathing heavily like he'd run all the way from Hobart.

"Forty-three minutes and twelve seconds," he announced, pressing a button on his watch.

"Nice work Wado," praised Nicole. "That's a record, isn't it?"

"What's going on?" I whispered from the corner of my mouth.

"Wade and Jasmine run ten kilometres every morning. They're quite the fitness freaks," explained Nicole, winking at me.

Madness, I thought. I twisted on the stool to get a better look at Wade – and turned back quickly before I permanently damaged my eyesight. He was bobbing up and down in a strange squatting motion, warming down after his run.

"Gross," I mouthed, wide eyed and repulsed out by his red spandex shorts.

"Wait until you see Jasmine," whispered Nicole, grinning.

I didn't have to wait long. Jasmine staggered into the café soon after, doubled over and gasping for breath.

"Well done, babes!" boomed Wade. "Forty-three minutes and fifty-eight seconds."

Jasmine's melodramatic panting sounded positively obscene. "Water, get me water." Nicole grabbed two bottles of water out of the glass fridge and handed them to the sparkly athletes. "Thank you," wheezed Jasmine.

"Do you do this every day?" I asked, too curious for my own good.

"Beauty is pain, Charli," explained Wade, raising his left arm and kissing his bicep.

I covered my mouth to stop myself giggling – or vomiting. I hadn't decided which. Jasmine pulled out the nearest chair and slumped on it in an unladylike pose. "We're trying to get super fit before the wedding. We want to look our best."

"Of course," I agreed.

At that moment Jasmine looked far from her best. Embarking on a long distance run while wearing a full face of makeup didn't work for her. She looked like a hot, sweaty panda.

"Adam likes to jog, doesn't he Charli?" she asked, looking at me through black-rimmed eyes.

"Yeah," I replied, unaffected by her intel gathering. "Except in winter. He goes to the gym in winter."

"You should think about taking up jogging," she noted, still a little breathless. "You're way out of shape these days. It's sad to see you let yourself go like that."

Nicole laughed. I scowled at her but it had no effect.

"You know, Charli," began Wade, sauntering toward me. "I can help you out with the few extra kilos you're carrying. Never misunderestimate the power of exercise."

I cleared my throat. "Ah, that's a very generous offer but I'm going to have to turn you down. I'm enjoying being fat."

"Oh I see." He had the good grace to look embarrassed. "Good for you."

Jasmine fervently shook her head. "Well I'm sorry, Charli, but you're out of the wedding. I can't possibly have a fat bridesmaid. The photos would be horrible."

Nicole returned to the business side of the counter, cackling the whole way. "Were you going to ask Charli to be a bridesmaid? Seriously?"

Her incredulity was warranted. Jasmine had been my mortal enemy for as long as I could remember. Being an attendant at her wedding beggared belief.

"Jasmine wants the whole bridal party to be blonde," interjected Wade. "They'll match the pink dresses better." The staid expression on his sweaty face led me to believe he was deadly serious.

"That's right," agreed Jasmine, rolling the lid of her bottle of water between her fingers. "It doesn't matter, though. I was thinking of asking Penny. Remember her?" I could only think of one girl named Penny. If memory served me correctly, her high school career had been as miserable as ours, thanks to the Beautifuls. "She works at the bait and tackle shop now," she added. "I love her hair. She has ghastly skin but I think I can work with her."

"Doesn't Penny hate you?" asked Nicole.

"Why would she hate me?"

"Er, because you were a bitch to her in school?" Nicole suggested. "You used to call her Pensioner Penny."

"She wore corduroy!" snapped Jasmine. "No one wears corduroy!"

"Calm down, babes. You'll get frown lines." Wade put a protective arm around her.

A chuckle escaped me, which I masked with a cough. I didn't dare glance at Nicole. One smirk from her would have had me on the floor in hysterics.

"Anyway, I've changed, Nicole," spat Jasmine, holding her left hand in the air and pointing at her ring. "I'm freaking engaged now."

And to Jasmine Tate, that meant everything. Finding a man who believed she was worthy of marrying was her idea of success. It was that small town mentality that I'd spent a lifetime running from.

Some days, the decision to come back to Pipers Cove made no sense at all.

February 23
Adam

With the exception of Ryan and the hot little blonde that turned up at our door looking for him, I hadn't spoken to a real person in two days – and I'm not sure that she counted. I was beginning to think I was going mad. I had to get out of the apartment.

I spent the next few hours torturing myself with a run through the park. The freezing air burned my lungs, but it was a good kind of pain, far different from the pining-to-death agony I normally suffered from. I was at the top of the Wollman rink, adjusting the cleats on my shoes, when someone screeched my name.

I spun to see Bente's sister barrelling toward me. I used the time it took her to reach me to try and remember her name. I came up blank so I greeted her little girl instead. Fabergé wasn't an easy name to forget.

"I'm getting ice-cream," announced Fabergé.

"Great," I replied, working hard to smile.

"No, she's not," said her mother.

Fabergé let out a scream that made me flinch. It ended when her mother put her hand over her mouth. I almost thanked her for it.

"You look like crap," said the woman, looking me up and down.

"I've been running," I defended. "No one looks good when they're running."

"No, it's more than that," she countered. "The single life isn't treating you well. You look heartbroken."

I wondered what heartbreak looked like. My condition was much more severe – possibly even terminal. I was suffering full mind and body break. I probably looked like death.

"So, how have you been?" I asked, shifting the conversation.

"So-so." She moved her hand away from Faberge's mouth and patted her stomach. "It's not easy being pregnant when you have a four-year-old running around."

I hadn't even noticed until she pointed it out. Once she had, I couldn't help staring at her stomach.

"Well, congratulations," I offered.

"Thanks."

A strange feeling of sadness gripped me as I stole another glance at her belly. I tortured myself trying to imagine how Charli would've looked pregnant – and then wondered why.

"Ah, I have to go," I stammered.

"Okay," she said nodding. "Take care of yourself, Adam."

I said goodbye to Fabergé and took off running.

* * *

I was in a complete funk. I'd given up everything I loved for a life that was now strangling me. I had no idea what to do about it.

I must've been completely downtrodden because I found myself confiding in my brother while he was preparing dinner.

"What's Bente's sister's name?" I asked, pulling up a stool at the island counter.

"Ivy." He spat out her name. "She hates me."

"I saw her today. She's pregnant."

Ryan took a break from chopping vegetables to look at me and smirk. "That might calm her down a bit."

"I think about it a lot," I said randomly. "Charli, I mean."

Ryan grimaced. "Why would you even go there?"

I absently twisted my wedding ring off my finger and spun it on the counter. "What if we made a mistake?"

168

It was unfair to imply that both of us had got it wrong. Charlotte had done her very best to change my mind a hundred times. I was to blame for the loss, not her.

He groaned as if I'd said something ridiculous. "You can't go back. You're going to have to find a way of getting past this."

I slipped the ring back on my finger. "I hate myself, Ryan," I admitted. "So freaking much."

My brother set the knife on the counter, staring at me for an uncomfortably long time. "I know."

I don't cry. I'm not a crier, but at that point total despair consumed me. My chest constantly ached and I could barely think straight. It was an incredible release to actually let my guard down, hang my head and fall apart. "I've lost everything."

Ryan walked around the counter. "I'm not going to tell you that it's going to get easier," he said, kneading the nape of my neck, "but eventually, you'll get better at dealing with it."

I wanted nothing more than to believe him, but at that moment, recovery seemed impossible. The only thing worse than the damage I'd done to myself was the thought of what I'd done to Charli.

It was a pain I deserved to suffer for the rest of my existence.

February 24
Charli

Inviting Gabrielle to accompany me to the doctor's office that morning was purely tactical. Alex had begged me to cut her some slack. If it made living with her more bearable, I was happy to help him out. "She's just trying to find her place, Charli," he told me. "She's not sure where she fits in with all of this."

I really couldn't blame her. I wasn't entirely sure where she fit in either. The step-grandmother of my kid was also her first cousin once removed.

Visits to the doctor were a necessary evil. Being poked and prodded was invasive and sometimes cringeworthy. Having Gabrielle there didn't help.

"Your body is on loan, Charli," she told me over and over. "Do the best for your baby."

"I am," I replied.

"You eat cereal for dinner!"

Usually I'd bite back, but pregnancy had gifted me a skill that had eluded me my whole life. I was a lot more even-tempered and level-headed these days.

Gabrielle declined my offer to come inside when she dropped me back at the cottage. When I heard a knock at the door just a few minutes later, I thought she'd changed her mind. I quickly gave the dining table a wipe over with my sleeve and made my way to the door.

It wasn't the Parisienne. It was Flynn Davis.

"Hello, Charli," he said meekly. "How are you?"

I knew the upcoming conversation by heart.

"Fine, thanks. How are you?"

"Good. I'm good. Do you like fish, Charli?"

I was impressed. He'd changed his game plan. He'd never used the fish angle to ask me out on a date before.

"Yes, I love fish. It's brain food," I replied.

"I just picked up some beautiful salmon from my Grandpa this morning. There's far too much for one person. I thought maybe we could split it."

I have no explanation for the next words out of my mouth. "How about you come for dinner and let me cook it for you?" I offered.

He nearly fell over. "I'd really like that. Does tonight suit you?"

"Ah, sure," I stammered, a little off-guard. "Tonight will be fine."

I wanted to set ground rules. I wanted to him to be clear that I was offering him dinner and nothing more, but there was no kind way of putting it into words.

When Alex turned up later that afternoon, I considered sending him next door to play the heavy-handed father. If anyone could let Flynn know exactly where he stood, it was Alex. But of course I didn't. True to form, I didn't mention it.

* * *

Flynn arrived right on time, with a plate of fresh salmon in one hand and a bottle of wine in the other. He made me laugh by thrusting both at me as soon as I opened the door, which did nothing to quell his skittishness.

"Smooth, Flynn," he muttered, chastising himself.

"Come in, please." I held the door open with my foot.

"I hope the wine's okay," he said, following me through to the kitchen. "Jasmine assured me that this is the best pinot noir they've produced in years."

"I'm sure it's lovely." I pretended to study the label. "I'm not much of a wine buff, though."

"Oh. You don't like wine?"

I shook my head falsely. Ordinarily, I had no problem with wine. The prospect of foetal alcohol syndrome was the problem.

"Oh, I'm so sorry. I should've brought something different."

I found Flynn's tendency to apologise for every little thing annoying. His impeccably neat, perfectly pressed clothes also grated. It was most unfair. Flynn had never been anything but super nice to me. Perhaps that was the problem.

I grabbed a corkscrew and handed it to him. "I'll let you do the honours. If I do it, you'll spend the evening picking bits of cork out of your glass."

"It seems a shame to open it if I'm the only one drinking."

"I'm sure Jasmine can get her hands on more."

"You don't like her much, do you?" he asked.

"We have a long and colourful history," I replied, more than willing to leave it at that. "How do you feel about her marrying your brother?"

Flynn shrugged. "He loves her. They're similar creatures, a good match."

My giggle sounded positively wicked. "How very diplomatic of you."

He pulled the cork and I slid a glass along the counter.

I was glad Flynn had brought wine. After a few glasses he loosened up, which made conversation easier. I kept the focus on him, unwilling to let him know too much about me. Keeping my distance was important. I'd spent weeks keeping him at bay. The last thing I wanted was to appear interested in anything more than a casual dinner.

I managed to do Norm's salmon justice by poaching it to perfection, and the company was surprisingly good. Hosting dinner parties had never been my forte but I pulled it off.

Partying into the night had never been my forte either, especially lately. By ten o'clock, feeling absolutely shattered, I was ushering Flynn and a plate over leftover fish out the door.

* * *

Clearing the air with Nicole was good for my soul, and my social life. When she called me the next morning to suggest hanging out for the day, I jumped at the chance. I was bustling around, still getting ready when she arrived.

"Hello," she called, through the mesh of the screen door.

"Hey."

She walked in, carrying a massive floral arrangement. "I've brought you a present."

"Flowers?" Coming from her, I thought it was bizarre.

She walked over to the table and set the flowers down. "Relax, they're not from me. They were on the doorstep. Maybe they're from Adam." Adam would never send me flowers. He knew better. I began fossicking through the bunch looking for a card. "It's here," said Nicole, plucking it out of the centre.

"They're from Flynn." I tossed the card on the table.

Nicole lurched forward and picked it up, taking it upon herself to read it out loud. "Because I woke up thinking of you," she read, making me cringe. "Wow. That's a bit full on, isn't it?"

I wholeheartedly agreed. I thought I'd set very clear boundaries where Flynn was concerned. "What do I do about this?"

"Just talk to him. Tell him you're not interested."

"I thought I'd already done that," I mumbled.

Getting out of the house for the day took on a new urgency. I didn't want to be there in case Flynn came knocking. I put on my black oversized bump-hiding jacket and headed for the door.

Nicole called me back. "Don't you want to see the present I brought you?" She was waving a tote bag I hadn't noticed before.

"What is it?"

She upended a pile of clothes onto the couch. "I thought you might be able to get some use out of these, unless you prefer looking like a frumpy emo kid."

I took no offence because she'd described my current wardrobe to a T. I was alternating between black and grey hoodies that I'd swiped from Alex, both at least five sizes too big.

She held up a purple hoodie. "I know it's not exactly stylish, but it's an improvement – a little bit girly and only a size or two too big."

Grateful, I swapped jackets immediately. "What do you think?" I asked, zipping it all the way up and settling both hands in the front pocket.

A tiny smile crossed her lips as she looked me up and down. "I think you've got no reason to be hiding anything in the first place. You're having a baby, Charli, not harbouring a criminal."

It was a secret I just wasn't ready to let go of yet, and Nicole knew me well enough to know why. I felt the need to explain anyway. "I don't want people talking about me. I don't want to be that stupid girl who's come back to town knocked up and alone."

"I came back here with a nastier tale of woe than you did. You've nothing to be ashamed of. If anyone should be living the life of a recluse, it's me."

I couldn't refute what she'd said. Nor could I defend her. Nicole had done some truly wicked things in the past.

"They can only hear about it once, Charli. People can only be appalled and disgusted once and then they have to get over it. If they can't, it becomes their problem."

* * *

We weren't looking for trouble, but choosing Jasmine's salon for a manicure instead of Carol Lawson's made it inevitable. Carol would flip out if she knew we were fraternising with the enemy.

It was a complex, covert operation. We parked much further up the street than we needed to and walked down to the salon. We didn't want Nicole's mother to see us from her shop, just twenty metres further down the road.

Neither of us even wanted a manicure. We were just being nosy.

Nicole set the scene as we walked down the street. "She has massive pictures of herself all over the place."

"What did she call her salon?" I quizzed.

Nicole grabbed my hand, pulling to me an abrupt halt. "See for yourself," she said, pointing to the shop window beside me.

I read out loud. "The Best Salon In The Cove."

It was too stupid for words. If I hadn't seen the pink sign with silver lettering for myself, I'd never have believed it. I was too stunned to even laugh, which was probably a good thing because Jasmine came barrelling out of the shop to greet us.

"Hello, girls!" she squealed. "What can I do for you today?"

I couldn't answer. I was too focused on her outfit. The tight dress with the zipper at the front looked like a nurse's uniform – except it was hot pink. She was now Sparkly-nurse-tramp Barbie.

"How about a manicure?" asked Nicole. "Do you have time?"

Jasmine pretended to think about it. "Come inside. I'll check the appointment book." Foolishly, we did as she asked.

The inside of Jasmine's salon proved something I'd known for a long time: money can't buy style. It was plain to see that a small fortune had been spent making The Best Salon In The Cove look the tackiest. Lime green walls, purple vinyl chairs and plenty of chrome and glass dominated the small space. Four blue monochromatic pictures hung on the walls, all of the owner. There was something quite disturbing about seeing Jasmine's face staring at me from every direction.

"You're in luck." Jasmine flicked through the appointment book too quickly to convince anyone that she was actually checking it. "I can fit you in now. Come and sit at the nail station."

We did as we were told, taking seats at the small glass-topped nail desk at the back of the shop. Jasmine produced a small bowl, squirted it full of clear liquid and plunged my hands into it.

"Where are your pretty rings?" she asked, tapping my bare finger.

Jasmine Tate was a bowerbird, attracted to glittery objects. She hadn't noticed the baby in my belly but had immediately noticed my missing bling.

"I'm not wearing them," I said, stating the obvious.

"Aww," she crowed. "Bad memories?"

Nicole wiggled her fingers. "We're here for a manicure, Jasmine."

"Yes, and I'm very honoured," announced the chief Beautiful. She ferociously took to Nicole's left hand with a file, as if trying to saw her fingers off. "It's nice to know who my true friends are."

"Oh, has something happened?" Nicole's concern sounded very convincing. "You seem a little upset."

Jasmine stopped filing. "You're not going to believe it."

"Try us," I urged, making Nicole hide a smile.

"Pensioner Penny turned me down," hissed Jasmine, beyond incredulous. "Can you believe it?"

We shook our heads, tutting in outrage.

"I told her she had a chance to be part of the society wedding of the century. All she had to do in return was commit to a four-month fitness regime and undergo a series of skin treatments. I even offered her discount on the treatments!"

"Wow," muttered Nicole. "And she turned you down? That's too bad."

"Too bad for her," snapped Jasmine, pointing the file like a knife. "I'll find someone else."

"That shouldn't be too hard," consoled Nicole. "You know everyone in town."

Jasmine's problem was, everyone in town knew *her*. I couldn't think of a single person who hadn't been tormented by the Beautifuls in one way or another.

She sighed. "It's a shame you're such a bitch, Nic, I would've asked you otherwise. You're cute as a blonde." She bored into me with a look of sheer pity. "And you're just so out of shape. It's a shame. I thought living in the fashion hub of the world would've inspired you to grow some style."

Nicole brought her hand to her mouth to stifle her giggle.

"Yeah," I said wistfully. "Shame."

My thoughts turned to the cache of designer clothing that I had boxed up in the cottage – and the girl who used to wear them. Charlotte Décarie had had impeccable style, but she'd almost sold her soul to get it. Charli Blake had no intention of growing some style. She was too busy growing a baby.

The conversation was absurd but relatively harmless and moderately entertaining. And as much as I hated to admit it, Jasmine's manicuring skills were as good as I'd ever seen. We slipped out of the salon two hours later as stealthily as we'd arrived, leaving Carol Lawson none the wiser that we'd ever crossed enemy lines.

* * *

For a few short hours I'd managed to forget my worries. Nicole drove me back to the cottage and we made a loose arrangement to meet the next day. I felt happy and relaxed until I walked into the house. The flowers were still sitting on the table where we'd left them. I felt tension flooding my bones.

I read the card one more time before tearing it in two. I didn't want Flynn waking up thinking of me. I didn't want Flynn Davis thinking about me at all. The gesture of giving me flowers was inappropriate.

Calling to thank him anyway would've been good manners, but I couldn't bring myself to do it. Instead, I pulled out every bloom that symbolised anything grander than friendship and threw them in the bin.

I must've felt some guilt in doing it, because the sound of my phone ringing startled me half to death. I grabbed it from the front pocket of my jacket, vowing never to carry it in there again. If I had jumped, the baby had probably somersaulted. I didn't recognise the international number that lit the screen.

I made a deal with myself. If it was Adam, I'd tell him everything and let the cards fall where they may.

It was impossible to dwell on the past when I had something amazing just on the horizon. Thoughts of Adam fell under the category of dwelling. He wasn't there on the night I first felt her flutter inside me because he chose not to be. The loss was his, not mine – and that's what I kept telling myself.

I answered the phone as casually as my thumping heart would allow and headed outside, desperate for sunshine. "Hello?"

"Mrs Décarie, my name is Michael Fontaine. I work for Décarie, Fontaine and Associates." He spoke painfully slowly as if reading from an unrehearsed script. I managed to walk all the way across the yard to the picnic table before he finished his introduction. "I have been retained by your husband, Adam Décarie. I am representing him during your divorce proceedings."

"What can I do for you, Mr Fontaine?" The superior tone came remarkably easy because I felt no pressure whatsoever. I wasn't speaking to the Mr Fontaine who partnered a law firm with Jean-Luc. I was speaking to his son. I had never met Michael, but knew a little about him thanks to Fiona Décarie's wretched fondness for gossip. I recalled a conversation where she'd described him as a mousy, inept, daddy's boy. At the time, she'd been furious with Adam's decision not to join his father's firm after graduation. "Imagine Jean-Luc's displeasure," she'd said sourly. "Both of his sons refuse the position, paving the way for an imbecile like Michael Fontaine. According to Ryan, he barely passed the bar. He's only there because of his father."

I'd ignored the hypocrisy. I was just thrilled that Adam had turned it down in favour of travelling the world with me. In actuality, his plans were much more conservative. He'd already accepted a clerkship with another firm.

Just thinking about it infuriated me, which was mighty unfortunate for mousy Michael Fontaine.

"The reason for my call is to ascertain the contact details of your legal council. He or she is yet to make contact with us."

It was one of the most convoluted sentences I'd heard in a long time.

I sat down at the picnic table. "I'm not sure what you mean," I said vaguely, admiring how perfect and smooth my manicure looked against the weathered wooden table. "What is it that you want, Mr Fontaine? I signed the papers."

A long pause followed and I could hear the rustling of paper.

"You signed the papers incorrectly. Ah, if you're having a problem understanding them I could explain them to you," he offered, sounding too flustered to explain anything. "Better still, your attorney could do it. Have you retained an attorney, Mrs Décarie?"

He was making it too easy for me. "I managed to retain one for almost a year, but I had to let him go," I said wistfully. "Things didn't work out."

"Err, Charlotte," he stammered, obviously reading my name off a page. "May I call you Charlotte?"

"Sure," I quipped. "Can I call you Mick?"

"Michael, yes."

"Mike?"

"It's Michael. I sent you another copy. Have you received it yet?" He lowered his tone and slowed his speech, perhaps to compensate for my apparent lack of brain cells but making himself sound damaged instead.

"Nope."

"Do you check your mail regularly?"

I sighed for effect. "I try to, Mick, but we have a real problem with the kangaroos."

"Kangaroos?"

"Yeah, most days those big suckers just snatch the mail right out of the box."

For some reason, the paper rustling ceased immediately.

"I can send you another copy, perhaps via courier this time," he offered, sounding a little frightened.

"I'll tell you what, Michael," I began, preparing to put an end to the nonsense. "How about you just save yourself the trouble? I did get the paperwork and you can tell my husband that I have no intention of signing it correctly any time soon."

The petition had included a standard clause stating that Adam and I had no children together. I couldn't sign it. It was a big fat lie, and I didn't know what the legal ramifications of telling big fat lies would be.

"Mrs Décarie, Charlotte, I implore you to reconsider," he begged. "The terms of the settlement are very reasonable."

Adam clearly wanted this wrapped up. And for some stupid reason he'd hired mousy Mick to do it. I almost felt sorry for him.

"I'm sure it's very reasonable, but I'm not signing off on it," I repeated.

"If that's the case, I shall have no choice but to advise my client to file for divorce in absentia," he said, finally sounding like a lawyer. "It will proceed with or without your signature."

I didn't really mean it when I told Michael to have a nice day as I ended the call. I did, however, mean to hurt my phone when I threw it on the ground. And I definitely meant for it to get wet when I marched to the edge of the yard and tossed it to the rocks below. I wasn't just throwing my phone away; I was letting go of all hope.

I marched back into the house. The damn flowers were still on the table. Continuing with my psychotic tantrum, I tossed them in the bin. Obviously my new-found even temperament had been fleeting.

Charli Blake was clearing house.

* * *

I knew I'd come to regret destroying my phone. I just wasn't expecting it to happen so soon. When my power went out later that night, calling Alex to come and fix it wasn't an option. I grabbed a torch and headed to the fuse box.

"Need a hand?" asked a voice from behind.

I squinted through the low light to see Flynn strolling across the dark yard.

The lid of the fuse box clapped loudly as I dropped it shut, making it sound like I'd slammed it on purpose. If he thought I was being bad tempered, he overlooked it.

"I looked over and saw the house in darkness," he explained, stepping onto the veranda. "It's probably just a fuse."

Looked over from where? I wondered. I studied the house next door, concentrating on the positioning of the windows. It was the first time I'd noticed the break in the trees along the fence line. It gave him an uninterrupted view of the cottage from his kitchen window.

I suddenly felt a little unnerved. Exactly how much time did Flynn spend looking at my house from his? I pushed the ugly thought aside. "I was going to call Alex but I lost my phone today."

Flynn smiled like he knew differently. "There's no point calling your dad when I'm just next door. I'll have it sorted in a minute."

True to his word, he fixed the problem, pushed the ancient ceramic fuse back into place, and brought the house back to light.

"Thank you," I mumbled.

"You're welcome." He switched off the torch and handed it to me. "So, did you get my flowers?"

His smile made me feel guilty. I prayed he wouldn't ask to see them. If he did, I'd have to point him in the direction of the wheelie bin on the verge.

"Flynn, about the flowers –"

He cut me off. "I enjoyed our dinner, Charli. Perhaps we could do it again."

I was shaking my head before he'd even finished speaking. "I don't think so. I have a lot going on." I began edging toward the front door. As I made a grab for the handle he spoke again. "By a lot, you mean the baby?" he asked.

I was horror-struck. He'd cottoned on that I was pregnant and he was still interested in dating me.

"Yes." I choked out the word.

"He's not here for you, Charli, but I could be. There's nothing wrong with moving on – before you forget what it's like to be happy."

His comment was rude and out of order. Things were becoming borderline creepy. "I think you should go."

Flynn stepped off the porch. "Good night, Charli," he said simply. I said nothing. He disappeared into the dark garden that separated our houses. I headed inside and locked the door.

February 25
Adam

Michael Fontaine is a dick. His father is one of the partners at Dad's law firm, which is the sole reason he managed to land a job. He passed the bar the same year as Ryan – after failing twice. Last I heard he was sharpening pencils and making coffee from an office in the basement, so when he called to let me know he was handling my divorce, I was a little shocked.

"Perhaps we could meet and discuss the fine details?" he suggested.

There were no fine details, let alone ones that needed discussing. "I'm pretty busy, Michael," I replied, gearing up to end the call.

"Your wife signed the papers but there's an issue with her signature."

He suddenly had my full attention. "What issue?"

"If you have the time, I'd rather discuss it in person."

This was going to be good. I glanced at my watch, calculated how long it would take me to get there and arranged to meet him within the hour.

Michael Fontaine must've done some serious ass kissing of late. When I got there, Tennille showed me through to the swank office next door to my father's. Michael sat at the huge mahogany desk looking like a preschooler on a take-your-son-to-work day.

As soon as I walked in, he started shuffling paper around. I couldn't work out if he was looking for something or trying to look important. If importance was the look he was shooting for, he should've reconsidered wearing a polyester suit.

I leaned across the desk and shook his hand, trying not to appear grossed out by his sweaty palms. "How are you Michael?"

"A little under the pump, actually," he stammered.

I sat opposite him and settled back. "Busy, huh? How many cases are you handling these days?" I was curious to know what sort of caseload warranted a prime office with views.

"Ah, just yours. It's proving to be quite complex." I must've stared at him for too long. A sheen of sweat appeared on his forehead. "Can I be frank with you, Adam?"

I shrugged. "Sure."

"Your wife is a nightmare to deal with." He sounded relieved to get the words out. Charlotte must have done a real number on him.

"What did she do?"

I tried to keep my expression straight as he described the phone conference, but cracked when he got to the part about the mail-stealing kangaroos.

"This is her signed documentation." He pushed it across the desk at me. "As you can see, it's worthless."

I thumbed through the documents to get to the last page. "Ah, that's not her signature."

It wasn't even her name.

"No, I checked," he replied solemnly. "Charlotte Elisabeth Décarie has never gone by the alias Adele E. Penguin."

Inappropriately, I laughed.

"I'm not sure how to proceed from here," he told me.

I shrugged. "Me neither."

"I have a lot riding on this case, Adam," he said nervously. "I'm hoping to be able to prove myself to the partners. If I can't wrap this up, I've got no chance of getting my own office."

I glanced around. "What's wrong with this one?"

"This is my father's."

Of course. I should've realised that the nameplate on the door was Michael senior's.

"Look, Michael," I began. "Just send them to her again and –"

"I already have. Twice. We could file in absentia."

"No. Charli's not absent. She just doesn't want to sign."

And I loved her for it. I didn't know what to make of it – but I loved her for it. It went a tiny way toward healing me.

"With all due respect, Adam, that's hardly relevant."

It was very relevant. I didn't want her to sign either.

I was done with Michael Fontaine. I picked up the documents and made a beeline for the door.

"So what do you want me to do?" he called.

I turned back, grinning. "Absolutely nothing."

February 26
Charli

I woke late the next morning feeling unfairly exhausted. My fatigue was purely cerebral. I'd been dealing with too many idiots lately and it was starting to wear me down.

The only remedy I could think of was time at the beach. A long walk seemed even more inviting when I realised it would be low tide. If I could muster the energy, perhaps I'd look for my phone– if only to make sure it didn't end up choking a defenceless seal.

The weather was superb. It was sunny, bright and still. The ocean was as calm as a millpond, which made running into Alex there almost shocking.

"What are you doing here?" I asked as soon as he was within earshot. "I thought you'd be at work."

He flashed me a wily smile and I knew the answer would be good.

"I'm not going anywhere near that café this morning," he told me, mussing his wet hair with a towel. "Jasmine and her crew have hijacked it. They're discussing her wedding plans over coffee." He shuddered, but I suspected it had nothing to do with being cold.

"Nice." I grinned. "So who's going to be there?"

Alex pulled a face like he'd just tasted something horrid. "All of them. Her mother, the groom, Floss, Lily, all of them."

"And you left Nicole to deal with it?"

"She's way tougher than me," replied Alex through the T-shirt he was dragging over his head.

I couldn't help laughing. "Maybe I'll go and keep her company."

"Why on earth would you do that?" He sounded appalled. "You're better off hiding out down here."

I'd come to the decision that there was no point trying to keep my pregnancy under wraps any more. One by one, people were realising the reason for my sudden weight problem and bad fashion sense. If I let it go on much longer, it would become a game of Chinese whispers. I didn't want to hear on the grapevine that I was pregnant with triplets by multiple fathers.

"I think I'm done hiding," I replied. "Maybe it's time to just put it all out there."

Unexpectedly, Alex lurched forward, taking my face in his cold hands, grinning like an idiot. "I'm so proud of you," he said, exaggerating the declaration by gritting his teeth.

I giggled and he released me. "It might not end well," I warned, smiling. "No matter how big my belly gets, Jasmine will always find room to eat me alive."

"She'll have to go through me first," he said, sounding almost scary. "If anyone gives you a hard time, come to me."

That should've been the moment that I mentioned my overzealous neighbour. My father could talk sense into him, or knock sense into him if talking didn't work.

Instead, I asked him to organise an electrician to check out the wiring at the cottage.

* * *

I sat in the car park for a long time, working up the courage to go inside. I knew that once I went in there would be no going back.

I'd ditched the oversized bulky jacket in favour of a pink camisole top that hid nothing. Although tight, the black shorts I wore still fit me – if I wore them low on my hips. I bravely had at least two inches of bared belly on display for the world to see. And at the moment, the whole world was in the café discussing the wedding of the year.

I slipped in so quietly that the bell on the door barely tinkled. At first my presence didn't rate a glance. I suspect it was because the wedding party was in the midst of a fierce discussion about sugared almond bonbonnieres.

I glanced at Nicole who was behind the counter, grinning. She put her forefinger to her temple like a gun. I wanted to tell her that being there couldn't be that bad. Then I looked at the wedding planners from hell and realised it could.

Floss noticed me first. She stood and very slowly shuffled toward me. Her already big brown eyes were the size of saucers by the time she reached me.

She pointed at my stomach. "Charli, Lovie, are you..." Her voice trailed off.

"Having a baby, yes," I replied, finishing her sentence.

It took a great deal of effort not to cover myself up, possibly because I knew it was hopeless.

Never one to hold back, Floss threw her arms around me, squealing and crying tears that I hoped were joyful.

"How wonderful," she beamed, releasing me just enough to plant her hand on my bump. "And what a pretty baby it will be. Adam must be over the moon."

"Yeah."

I didn't have time to dwell on the lie because Meredith Tate piped up. "How does your father feel about it, Charli?"

I looked at the mother of the Beautifuls and suddenly felt a little intimidated. Meredith Tate was the sort of woman who commanded respect but gave very little in return. Like her eldest daughter, she was tanned, bleached, sparkly – and judgemental. And *she* thought *I* was trash. It was an opinion she'd held since my brief tryst with Mitchell, her only son, almost four years earlier. Judging by the look on her heavily made-up face, nothing had changed.

Meredith twisted to get a better look at me. It was a hard position to keep polite considering her short skirt. Fortunately, she kept her legs tightly crossed as she bounced her foot up and down, making her gold anklet jingle.

Who wore anklets these days, for crying out loud? They hadn't been chic since Pensioner Penny's corduroys were in fashion.

"My father is – and always has been – very supportive of me," I replied in the strongest tone I could muster.

Her smirk was borderline cruel. "Of course."

"Well," interjected Wade, slamming his hand on the table. "What a revolution."

"Revelation, Wade," corrected Meredith dully. Perhaps she was getting bored by his idiocy.

"You'll be a wonderful mother, Charli," said Lily. "Congratulations."

I smiled at her appreciatively. "Thanks, Lil."

Four down, one to go, I thought. At the end of the day, only Jasmine's reaction really mattered. She was the only person in the room that I felt could truly destroy me – even after all I'd been through.

Ignoring Meredith's baleful glare, I looked at the chief Beautiful, who seemed to be taking forever to process the news. After what seemed an eternity, she jumped out of her chair and stalked toward me. "Oh my God!" she screeched, pointing at me.

I put my hand to my stomach, instinctively bracing for the worst. I expected a nasty told-you-so lecture, just like old times. I'd never given her a better reason to mock me.

"Oh my God!" she repeated, this time pointing at my shoes. "Are those Louboutins?"

I looked at my feet. "Ah, yeah. They're last season's, though."

Last season's? I couldn't believe I'd said it.

"I love them," she said admiringly. "I want a silver pair for the wedding." I'd just fed her the gossip of the century and she was more interested in my sandals. "I love them," she repeated. "Oh, and good news about the baby. Glad you're not just fat."

Nicole burst into giggles. Floss shushed her. Wade and Lily picked up the sugared almond conversation from where they'd left off. Meredith told them both to shut up. Jasmine continued to stare at my shoes.

I couldn't have wished for a better outcome.

* * *

I'd spent a lot of time home alone, even when I lived with Adam. Walking into an empty house had never bothered me, but today something seemed off. I wandered from room to room trying to find reason for the creeped-out vibe I was getting. Nothing looked out of place until I got to my bedroom.

The top drawer of the dresser was half open.

I spent a few minutes reasoning with myself. Logic told me I'd left it open myself. My pregnant mind was like a sieve – I'd been guilty of putting the milk in the pantry more than once in the past few weeks. But logic had never been my strong suit, and darker thoughts took over. What if someone had been in my house? I thought back to the uneasy conversation I'd had with Flynn on my porch, feeling the same level of panic as I'd had then.

I slammed the drawer shut, went to the lounge and locked the screen door. I'd never been fastidious when it came to security, even when I lived in New York.

Locking the door was so out of character that poor Alex nearly head butted the mesh as he tried to open the door. I raced to unlock it. "Sorry," I mumbled, twisting the key to let him in.

"Everything okay?"

"You tell me. What did the electrician say?"

Alex walked in but didn't venture past the doorway.

"It was a just a dodgy fuse. He replaced a few of them."

"Did he come in the house, Alex?"

"No, why?"

I shook my head. "No reason."

"Listen," he said gently, "if you're nervous about being here, come home."

"I'm not nervous. I'm staying here."

"Here," he said, holding out a phone. "Gabrielle had a spare one. Use it until you find yours."

I felt bad about the story I'd spun about losing my phone, but it didn't seem like a good time to confess that it was swimming with the fishes.

"Thanks. And thank Gabi for me."

"I will," he said, making his way to the door. "And if you need me, call me. Or Flynn, you can call Flynn," he suggested. "You can't get much safer than having a policeman next door, right?"

I forced a tight smile. "Right."

May 24
Adam

I'd done it. I officially had a law degree. I didn't have a wife, any semblance of a social life or much else going on, but I did have a law degree.

My mother organised a ridiculous, over-the-top party to mark my graduation. When she'd first mentioned it, I insisted that she scale down her plans. Her idea of scaling down was hosting the party as Nellie's rather than Billet-doux.

Enduring the event might have been easier if not for the fact that the purple circle made the guest list, along with seventy other people I didn't give a damn about. Parker hunted me down as soon as he walked in the door, coming at me as if we were long lost friends.

"Congrats, man." He slapped me on the back.

"You too," I muttered unenthusiastically.

We'd both graduated. Law school was a journey we'd started together. We'd been best friends since we were nine. I felt a twinge of sadness that things had gone so far off track.

Parker obviously felt it too. He spent the next few minutes trying hard to make small talk – so hard that he actually broke a sweat. I put him out of his misery early.

"Parker, let's get something straight," I began. "I didn't invite you here tonight. My mother invited you."

He actually had the nerve to look hurt. "I don't know what else I can do to make it up to you, Adam. I'm sorry for what happened."

I shook my head. "There's nothing to make up. You're a dick. We're not friends and we're never going to be again." I pointed at him as I backed away into the sea of guests. "That's on you."

Kinsey was my next opponent. I hadn't seen her since before Christmas and probably wouldn't have recognised her if she hadn't tapped me on the shoulder.

She looked better than I'd ever seen her – at least twenty pounds heavier and nowhere near as fragile. She'd cut her blonde hair shorter and her pale skin had a bit of colour to it.

"Kins. How are you?"

She stretched up, kissed both my cheeks and hit me with a stun gun smile. "I'm great. Really wonderful."

"You look gorgeous." It was a compliment I'd never imagined paying her.

Kinsey spent the next few minutes filling me in on the last few months. Desperate to get out of town, she'd taken off to Florida to spend time with her sister. "Amazing things happen when you get out of this place." She winked at me. "There's a big world out there."

I smiled. "Absolutely." A few months in Sarasota hardly qualified as exploring the big wide world but she definitely seemed to have benefited from it.

"I needed to get away," she said, glancing venomously in Parker's direction.

I knew exactly what she meant. She wasn't the only one who'd had an escape plan after Parker-Gate exploded.

"I'm glad you're happy, Kinsey."

She touched my arm, batting her eyes at me. "What about you?" she asked.

"I'm great."

I could tell she was desperate to broach the subject of Charli. Thankfully, she decided against it.

"You're a lawyer now," she announced, throwing her arms out wide.

"Nearly. I still have to sit the bar exam in July."

"You'll ace it," she said.

After a few more minutes of banter, I told her to enjoy the party, excused myself and slipped into the crowd.

* * *

The night went on forever. My mother paraded me around the room a hundred times like some prize. I shook hands with guests of her choosing, smiling until my face ached.

Ryan and I had borne her wrath before the party even started. She'd turned up at our apartment at six o'clock, raided our wardrobes and laid out our clothes as if we were kids.

"For goodness sake, snap out of it," she'd barked, noticing my lack of enthusiasm. "This is supposed to be a joyous occasion."

"For you or me, Mom?" That comment resulted in her nearly strangling me with the tie she'd chosen.

Ryan wasn't such a pushover. He chose his own tie and ordered her out. "We're grown men, Mom," he told her. "Go home."

As it turned out, he wasn't entirely grown. He ended up wearing the shirt she'd picked out for him.

* * *

I finally managed to escape the party by sneaking up to the empty mezzanine, but the peace was short-lived.

"Hiding out?"

Whitney stood at the top of the stairs. I hadn't seen her coming. If I had, I might've hurled myself over the balustrade.

"Whitney Vaughn." I dragged out her name.

"How are you, Adam?" she asked, sauntering toward me.

I shrugged but said nothing.

Whitney pulled out a chair and sat down. "Your mom is looking for you."

"Is she?"

"She is. Your father was too, earlier. He was talking to Judge Lassiter. You start your clerkship with her soon, right?"

"Yup."

"It was nice of her to come to your party."

"It was," I agreed.

I shouldn't have been surprised to learn that my father knew Judge Lassiter. I'd been deliberately secretive when applying for my clerkship. I wanted to do it off my own bat, without using his influence to gain any favours. Seeing him downstairs, chatting with her as if they were old friends, made me wonder if it had been such a coup after all. Chances were he'd pulled strings anyway.

"I thought you'd be more excited about it, Adam," said Whitney. "This is everything you've ever wanted."

"How do you know I haven't changed my mind?"

"Have you?" she asked softly.

I stared down at the party below. "A career in law," I announced resentfully. "That's my calling, right? I've had my eye on the prize since I was ten. My whole life has led to this moment."

She stared at me, chewing her bottom lip. "You've always been ambitious."

She was right. I was hardly multi-faceted. I'd been focused on that one goal my whole life. Nothing had stood in my way – not even Charli. Now I'd achieved it, the cost of what I'd lost was finally starting to sink in, and I'd become a miserable human being because of it.

"I'm probably not good company right now, Whit," I told her.

"I've dealt with worse."

I had a long history with Whitney Vaughn. At one point I thought I loved her. Then I met Charli and realised I'd never even come close. Whitney didn't challenge me. I'd lived my life and she'd lived hers. We'd met in the middle when it was convenient.

"Have you ever been in love, Whitney?" I asked curiously.

She shook her head. "No."

At least the mediocrity had been mutual. For some reason, I smiled at her. "You should stop wasting time with assholes. Find someone who's going to be good to you."

"You weren't always an ass, Adam. You have a good heart." Whitney reached out and fussed with the corner of my collar. "We were good for each other once."

I let out a slow groan of disapproval. "What are you doing, Whit?"

She smiled in reply, giving me her best flirty look. It had been a long time since I'd been on the receiving end of a Whitney charm offensive. It wasn't awful. It was just pedestrian and did nothing for me, which made my next move absolutely unfathomable. It also obliterated my good-heart status.

"Do you want to get out of here?" I leaned in close and whispered the question, expecting to be struck down by lightning at any second.

With a tiny smile, she slowly nodded and the soulless deal was complete.

We left via the service stairs at the back, leaving any sense of decency and the last bit of my conscience behind.

* * *

I hailed a cab and took Whitney back to the apartment. I knew Ryan wouldn't be home early. He was too much of a control freak to let my mother take his restaurant over, and would probably be the last to leave Nellie's because of it.

"You've redecorated," she noted, wandering around the living room.

"Ryan's domain," I replied, searching the fridge for a bottle of water. "I just sleep here."

Whitney stopped pacing to study the Pipers Cove canvas on the wall. "Is this one of Charli's?"

I cringed at the mention of her name. The whole exercise of bringing Whitney home was a ploy to get my mind as far away from Charlotte as possible. "Yes," I confirmed. "That picture was the very beginning."

Whitney frowned, having no idea what I meant. I didn't explain.

"Did she take a picture of the ending too?"

I wondered what it would look like if she had. I didn't answer. I offered her a bottle of water instead.

Whitney walked around the counter at a ridiculously slow speed. I used the time to figure out what the hell I was doing. One-night stands had never been my forte. They just weren't my thing. And yet here I was, on the very edge of a new all-time low.

Whitney set the bottle of water down, linked her arms around my neck and pressed herself against me.

I didn't move.

Whitney was pretty – an elegant, well-put-together brunette with doe-eyes that were anything but. But it wasn't enough for me. My mind was on a blonde whose beauty extended far beyond pouty looks and flirty innuendos. There weren't words to describe how lovely Charli was. I'd never even tried. She was sunshine and warmth. She was my heart. And she was gone.

Coming to my senses happened quickly. I broke Whitney's lock on my neck with both hands. "Whit, I shouldn't have brought you here. You need to leave." I felt appalled with myself and embarrassed for her. "I'm so sorry."

She pulled in a breath and frowned. "Is it because of Parker?" she asked quietly. "That's over now. It has been for a while."

I shook my head, taking a step back. "No. It's because of Charli. That will never be over, no matter much I want it to be."

She stepped forward, and as she reached for me I grabbed her wrist to keep her at a distance.

"It doesn't have to mean anything, Adam," she said softly.

I released her and walked to the living room to get her out of my space. "That's the whole point, Whit," I said, turning back. "It wouldn't mean a damn thing to me, which means I am really not what you need right now. I've done enough damage lately."

I just wanted her gone. I did the kindest thing I could think of. I called a cab and got her out of my apartment.

Desperate to put an end to the day, I fell into bed as soon as she left. I couldn't even be bothered turning the light off. I turned my head on the pillow, immediately noticing the photo on the nightstand. I stared at the Polaroid picture for a long time, studying the couple smiling back at me. It was the picture Charli had taken of us on New Year's Eve – one of the last good nights we'd had before everything went to hell. Until then, I hadn't realised how symbolic it was.

"She did photograph the ending," I muttered aloud.

* * *

Ryan surfaced before me the next morning. He was sitting at the table poring over paperwork when I got to the kitchen.

"Hard night?"

"Nope. I came home early."

He looked at me, smiling wryly. "With who?"

I poured myself a cup of coffee. "No one."

"Liar."

Ryan pointed to the couch. A blue shawl thing was draped over the back of it. I'd paid so little attention to Whitney that I wasn't even sure it was hers.

I had no choice but to explain the sorry events of the night before, purely to stop Ryan jumping to conclusions. "I'm glad your brain kicked into gear," he muttered. "The last thing you need is that level of guilt."

He was right.

I pulled out a chair and joined him. "What are you doing?"

He shuffled papers. "Your errant little wife has left me with one hell of a mess," he grumbled. "She hasn't returned any mail in weeks. You should've done me a favour and retained Billet-doux in the divorce."

"It wouldn't have made any difference. She didn't sign off on the divorce."

"Really," he drawled, sounding too interested. "Holding out for more glitter money?"

"No, she just didn't want to sign."

"So where does that leave you?"

I shrugged. "Married, I guess."

He pulled a face. "You two are ridiculous, her especially." Charli was turning into a giant pain in Ryan's ass. Her lack of aptitude when it came to Billet-doux was letting the side down and he was close to breaking point. "I think it might be time that I paid her a little visit." He sounded like an assassin gearing up for his next hit. He gathered his papers. "I haven't had a vacation in a long time. I could visit Never Never Land, buy her out of my business and be back by the end of the week."

He'd made it sound so simple. Life in Pipers Cove didn't run that way, but I was prepared to let him find that out for himself, mainly because it would benefit me too. I wanted to know if Charli was okay, and wasn't above sending a spy to find out.

The only plan more flawed than Ryan's idea of a quick visit to Pipers Cove was the one he came up with of me overseeing his restaurants while he was out of town.

"No way," I protested.

"It's the only way it can work, Adam. It's not like you have anything else going on at the moment."

Sadly, he was right. I still had over a month to go before the start of my clerkship. I had no real excuse not to help out.

"Fine," I relented, after just a few seconds. "I'll do it."

"Right." He leaned back, resting his hands behind his head. "Well, it looks like I'm bound for Never Never Land. I should call the travel agent and book. What's the quickest way? Through LA?"

Peter Pan flooded my head. "Second star on the right, and straight on 'til morning."

May 27
Charli

Just like my waistline, the secret of my pregnancy was well and truly busted. The news that Alex Blake's wayward daughter had returned to the Cove pregnant and alone spread like wildfire. No one ever asked me about Adam, but I suspect his name was constantly being bounced around town. For the most part, I didn't care what was said behind my back. People were respectful enough to be kind to my face.

Once the secret was out, my body responded accordingly. By the time I reached the thirty-one week mark, I looked like I'd swallowed a beach ball.

Floss Davis had become my one-woman fan club. Every week she presented me with a new gift. The latest was a pair of hand-knitted booties. She took great pleasure in informing me that they were made from organic wool. I tried hard not to appear confused. Wasn't wool a natural fibre anyway?

Nicole's mother, Carol, was also an unlikely supporter – sort of. "I'll cut your hair short for you," she offered. "Once the baby comes you won't have time to shower, let alone wash and style your hair. You'll be a mess."

According to her, I was destined to become an exhausted, unkempt new mother. I was also set for a lifetime of stretch marks and very little sleep.

"Mum!" scolded Nicole, mortified. "Leave her alone. We came here for a pedicure, not a lecture."

"I'm educating her, Nicole," hissed Carol, dismissing her with a flick of her head. "Someone needs to offer Charli some guidance. God knows her father isn't able to do it."

Carol Lawson's lack of tact wasn't intentional. It was just her way. The cringeworthy *educational* chats she used to subject Nicole and me to when we were younger had scarred us for life. Until then I'd never heard anyone say the word *noo-noo*. Funnily enough, I'd never heard anyone other than Carol say it since.

Filling my days with shifts at the café, taking pictures or getting obligatory pedicures wasn't exactly enthralling but it kept me out of the house – and away from my neighbour. In fairness, I hadn't seen much of Flynn lately. Maybe my belly made the prospect of dating me unappealing. Whatever the reason, I was glad he was over me.

* * *

Some days I had no choice but to stay in – usually when I ran out of things to wear. I looked at the mountain of clothes on the laundry floor and groaned, resigned to the fact that I'd found my calling for the day.

I was bundling a load into the machine when someone started beating at my screen door. The urgent pounding frightened me half to death. Through the weave of the mesh screen I got a perfect view of my caller. And it was the last person I expected it to be.

"Open the door, Tinker Bell," Ryan demanded, like the egotistical jerk he was.

The full gamut of emotions surged through me. I was excited to see him and yet I was fighting the urge to close the curtains and pretend I wasn't home. I was feeling like a cornered felon. The minute Ryan Décarie laid eyes on me, my life on the lam would be over.

"Hurry up, Charli. I know you're in there!" He pounded harder.

Abandoning my hiding spot in the laundry, I ambled to the door, but it did nothing to stop his impatient hammering. It occurred to me that he couldn't see through the privacy mesh. It allowed me a few more minutes to keep my secret.

"I'm here." He jumped at the sound of my voice. "Stop bashing my door."

Ryan put his too-handsome face up to the mesh, trying to see inside. "Well, open it then," he purred menacingly.

"Why are you here, Ryan?" I did my best to sound annoyed – or at the very least, inconvenienced.

He took a step back, arms outstretched.

"I've just spent twenty-something hours in the air and you're seriously going to converse with me through a closed door?"

"Answer my question."

Ryan groaned. "I'm sleep deprived and off my game. What was your question?"

"Why. Are. You. Here?"

"Charli, as much as it pains me, we are business partners," he said. "It's not working out is it?"

I agreed wholeheartedly, but my response didn't suggest it. "I guess not."

"All you had to do to keep things running smoothly was keep up with the paperwork. I keep sending it to you but get nothing back."

I felt a little bad. After the phone call from Michael Fontaine, I'd stopped opening my mail. Poor Ryan was paying the price.

"So you came all this way to get me to sign some papers?"

"Yeah, because that's entirely logical. I'll just fly to the end of the earth once a month to make sure you're doing your homework."

I couldn't blame him for the sarcasm. To Ryan, his businesses were everything. He'd travelled to the other side of the world because I'd dropped the ball. He had every right to be annoyed.

"I'll sign whatever you want me to."

"It's gone beyond that, sweetheart," he said in his usual patronising tone. "I'm here to make you an offer. I think it's time we put this to bed and I just buy you out. Agreed?"

I didn't even hesitate. "Agreed."

I would have heard his sigh of relief from across town. "Brilliant. So are you going to let me in or would you like me to just write you a cheque and slip it under the door?"

"I'll let you in."

"Today?" he asked, rattling the door handle.

I'd reached the end of the line. Ryan was three seconds always from seeing my belly. I made one last-ditch effort to retain control. "You have to promise me something first."

Perhaps thinking that negotiations might be ongoing for a while, he grabbed a deck chair and sat down. "Why are you such a damned child?"

"Please, Ryan. This is important."

Probably too exhausted to fight me, he caved in. "Fine." He slapped his hands on his knees. "Cross my heart, hope to die, wish upon a star, whatever you need."

"You won't contact Adam while you're here," I demanded.

Far from outraged, he punched out a hard laugh. "Look, I know you and Adam are not in a good place right now –"

"He's trying to divorce me."

"Trying being the operative word," he noted. I breathed in deep, determined to keep my wits. Ryan seemed to take pity on me. "I'm not here to do my brother's bidding, Charli," he said, dropping the choler. "I have no interest in whether or not you play nice in your divorce. I just want you out of my business."

Ryan leaned back, stretched out his legs and folded his arms. I hoped he wasn't about to go to sleep. I wasn't anywhere near finished with him.

"You promise not to call him, no matter what?"

"Yes. Do you want me to put it in writing?"

I unlocked the door and stepped out. The weary traveller didn't move a muscle. Fearing I'd shocked him to death, I nudged his foot with mine. "Wake up," I ordered, realising his eyes were closed.

"I'm not asleep."

"Open your eyes then."

Ryan cocked his head and looked up at me, squinting as if focusing took effort. His pose didn't waver but a slow smile crept across his face. I truly had no idea which way the conversation was going to go. "Well, well, well," he drawled, stretching out the words. "Isn't this a game changer?"

I put my hands over my stomach as if that was all it would take to keep her out of view. "Please don't call Adam." I spoke in a strange tone reminiscent of someone trying to talk a jumper down from a rooftop. "I'll let him know in plenty of time."

My father would make sure of that.

"What are you waiting for, Charli? A sign? When the moon ducks lay their eggs at sunrise, you'll tell him? When the pixies get permission from the high elf, you'll tell him?"

I didn't kick up at his stupid comment. "What's a moon duck?"

"I have no freaking idea," he muttered.

Ryan hoisted himself out of the chair like a tired old man, and dragged another chair across for me. We sat side by side for a long time while he processed the news.

"You stupid girl," he finally grumbled. "The child will be taken care of, Charli. He or she is a Décarie."

He'd announced it with the same reverence as Gabrielle. And it was just as maddening hearing it the second time around. "She's a Blake," I snapped. "She's going to grow up here and be grounded and normal. She's going to be free-range."

"Normal?" he scoffed. "What could you possibly know about being normal? And free-range. Like the moon ducks?"

"Yes," I replied bleakly. "I imagine moon ducks are free-range."

"Peachy. Adam will be so proud. Décarie babies aren't free-range, Charlotte. Their lives are privileged and structured." Probably wishing he'd missed his flight, Ryan leaned forward, and buried his face in his hands. "You've created one hell of a mess."

I let it go. This was a battle for her father, not her uncle. "What's going to happen when he finds out?"

He lifted his head. "What do you want to happen?"

I wasn't about to humiliate myself by telling him about the small part of my heart that was still hoping for a fairy-tale ending. "I don't know."

"I don't think that's true," he accused. "You want him to be thrilled by the idea of having the kid that you told him was gone, come to this godforsaken hick town, build you a picket fence and live happily ever after."

When he stopped for breath I cut in sourly. "I didn't ask you what you think I want."

"Look at me, Charli." It was a softly spoken demand – but a demand nonetheless. I did as I was told. "I'm *always* going to tell you the truth. You know that, right?"

I nodded, bracing for the very worst. His answer was going to hurt. "Adam hasn't been coping very well. When he finds out that all the guilt has been for nothing, he's going to be really upset. I don't know what's going to happen, but don't go making picket fence plans."

To hide the fact that he'd just delivered a perfect coup de grâce, I closed my eyes and settled back in my chair. The lovely warmth of the sun on my belly was a welcome distraction from the trauma shaking my already battered heart.

When Ryan finally spoke again, I realised he'd been using the time to come up with a game plan. He asked when the baby was due.

"The first of August."

He nodded. "Hold off telling Adam a little while longer," he suggested. "He has his exam coming up soon. Once that's out of the way, hit him with it."

"Yes," I agreed. "Must not disturb the study."

Ryan chuckled darkly. "Lighten up, fairy pants. He's going to need to pass. He has a baby on the way."

* * *

Ryan Décarie was not renowned for uplifting, morale-building conversations, which was fine because that wasn't what I needed. All I wished for was direction and a clear head. Without realising it, his brand of no-nonsense straight talking had been exactly what I was looking for. I was ecstatic that he was there.

"Where are you staying?" I asked.

He didn't open his eyes. "I'll find a hotel."

"Not in this town." I snickered. "There are no hotels."

He turned his head, glaring across at me like I'd just ruined his entire trip. "Awesome news. We really are in the boondocks, aren't we?"

I could've directed him to at least ten bed-and-breakfasts, but I knew Ryan too well. As much as I'd enjoy hearing him whine about shared bathrooms and lace curtains, I couldn't do it to him. "Stay with me," I offered.

His eyes flitted in every direction, quickly surveying the property. "Here?" He sounded appalled.

"It's not that bad. Just remember to keep the doors and windows closed at night so the snakes don't get in."

"Snakes?"

"And spiders, but we don't need to go there," I reached across and patted his arm. "Don't make eye contact with the possums and remember that we can only flush the toilet when it's high tide."

It was impossible to keep a straight face, which blew my charade in an instant.

He exhaled a long breath of relief, ruffling both hands through his already messy dark hair. "You're lying."

"Yes," I admitted. "You make it so easy."

He restudied his surroundings.

"Why on earth would you want to raise a baby here, Charli?"

I looked at the infinite blue ocean in the distance. He'd picked a picture-perfect day to show up on my doorstep.

"Stay a while," I suggested. "You'll figure it out."

* * *

Ryan needed sleep, which was perfect because I still had a mountain of laundry to contend with. I made up the bed in the spare room while he brought his luggage in from the ridiculously self-indulgent Mercedes he'd hired. He appeared in the doorway, black Vuitton suitcase in hand.

"I'm sorry about the boxes," I said, pointing to the untidy heap of FedEx clutter. "I haven't unpacked properly yet."

"It's fine, Charli," he replied tiredly. "I won't tell my mother that her meticulous packing ended up in a messy pile on the floor."

"Fiona packed them?"

Ryan moved to the window. "She insisted on doing it herself." He held the sheer curtain aside and peered out. "Mom hasn't taken your departure well."

Better than anyone, I knew the wrath of Fiona Décarie was not to be underestimated. After all that had happened, I was undoubtedly back on the top of her hit list.

"She must hate me." I fluffed up a pillow and dropped it on the bed. "I didn't even say goodbye."

"She's not upset with you, Charli," he said, turning back. "Her anger is reserved entirely for Adam. It's quite amusing really. I'm enjoying being the favourite son, regardless of how short-lived it may be."

"She's angry with Adam?"

He smiled at me with tired eyes. "Furious. The queen is convinced that he should've tried harder to make it work. She cried for a week when he told her he'd filed for divorce. It was as if you'd died."

I sat on the edge of the bed, trying to make sense of this. I was not expecting to hear that she blamed her precious boy for anything. It was a strange turn of events that went a tiny way toward lightening my heavy heart.

"I'm so glad you're here," I told him, picking one of the many random thoughts in my mind. "And for what it's worth, I'm sorry I let you down with Billet-doux."

"Later. Right now I need to sleep."

I walked to the door. "Sleep well, Ryan. And watch out for the snakes."

I pulled the door closed just before the pillow thudded against it.

* * *

My father stopped by the cottage on his way home from the café to carry out a welfare check, because he hadn't seen me all day. "Everything okay?" he asked, breezing through the door.

I was sprawled on the couch, exhausted by the tonne of housework I'd done while Ryan slept off the jetlag.

"Everything's good," I told him, and rattled off the list of boring accomplishments I'd achieved that day.

Alex placed his hand on my forehead, frowning. "You need to take it easy."

I brushed his hand away. "I'm pregnant, not sick."

"What do you have planned for dinner?" he asked, changing the subject. "Come home with me. Gabi is cooking coq au vin."

"Tempting but no. I have a house guest." I spoke with too much jubilance.

"Who?" Alex asked, gripping the arm of the chair. "No, don't answer. I already know." He was about to jump to a big conclusion. I kept quiet because I relished the thought of setting him straight. "I thought that the flash car parked on the street belonged to one of the neighbours. But it doesn't, does it?" he asked glumly.

I shook my head, grinning errantly.

Alex sank into the chair and let out a sigh. "You look too happy, Charlotte. I don't want to hear that you've worked it all out in a couple of hours. Be a smart girl."

He rattled off the lecture like a well planned speech. I got the impression he'd had it in his head for weeks and was glad to be rid of it.

"Do you have anything else to crush my spirit with today?"

Alex locked his hazel eyes with mine. "Only more of the truth. Don't get me wrong; I'm happy that Adam made the pilgrimage. It was the honourable thing to do. But you have a lot to work out. Whatever problems you had are still there." Speech over, he released me and began glancing around the room. "Where is Boy Wonder anyway?"

"In New York I expect," chimed a voice from behind us. "Hanging out with Batman and the rest of the crew."

I twisted around to look at Ryan. He leaned against the doorway, arms folded and smirking.

My head snapped back to Alex. He should've been embarrassed by what Ryan had heard. But he wasn't. He was Alex. He stood and held out his hand, looking as self-righteous as I'd ever seen him. "I'm Alex. Charli's father."

Ryan crossed the room to meet his handshake. "Ryan Décarie. Boy Wonder's brother."

I anticipated fireworks. Alex thought of Adam as cocky and hubristic, and here he was shaking hands with a bigger, badder version.

"Apologise, Alex," I demanded.

"I don't need to apologise, Charli," he said, reclaiming his position on the armchair. "I've never said anything about Adam that I'm not prepared to say to his face."

My father was behaving like an unadulterated brat.

"I like to call it as I see it too," replied Ryan, taking the last spare chair. "I'm not offended by your father's assessment, Charli. I don't think it differs that much from mine."

Alex chuckled blackly. I scowled at him and glared at Ryan.

"Don't act so surprised," chided Ryan, grinning. "I'm not going to sugar-coat it for you."

"You should be defending your brother," I said crossly, "not agreeing with Alex."

His smile didn't slip. Nor did his trademark condescension. "In order to do that, I'd have to point out your shortcomings. You're not blameless, Tinker Bell."

Ryan wasn't telling me anything I hadn't heard before. I just couldn't believe he had the chutzpah to say it in front of my father. Even more bewildering was that Alex wasn't jumping to my defence – or questioning why he'd referred to me as Tinker Bell. Instead, he changed the subject.

"So what brings you here, Ryan?"

"Well," Ryan began, "I'm in the unenviable position of having your daughter as a business partner. I'd like to get off that ride now. I'm here to persuade her to sell her half of our restaurant to me. As soon as we can negotiate a price, we'll draw up the paper work and call it quits."

"No negotiating, Ryan," I snapped. "You can take my share for free."

"And that is exactly why you're a terrible business woman. Great at keeping secrets, though – or lying, depending on how you look at it."

"Or *who's* looking at it," added Alex.

"Adam will be looking at it," I growled, surprised by the tag team assault being unleashed on me. "I'll tell him about her soon."

"You keep saying 'her'. Do you know for sure it's a girl?" Ryan asked, putting a halt to the imminent row.

"*I* know for sure. Others aren't convinced," I muttered, glancing at Alex.

Alex threw both hands in the air. "I believe in your hunch. It's Gabrielle who's uncertain."

Ryan grimaced at the mention of her name and I pounced, acutely aware of the dislike he held for her.

"Ryan's looking forward to spending some time with the Parisienne while he's here," I said. "Maybe we should come for dinner tonight after all."

"Parisiennes are from Paris," muttered Ryan. "Gabi is from Marseille."

"Tinker Bells are from Never Never Land," I shot back. "I'm from Pipers Cove."

He acknowledged my point with a nod. "Touché, Charlotte from Pipers Cove."

I turned to Alex. "Oh, we're *definitely* coming for dinner."

* * *

Bullying Ryan into going to Gabrielle and Alex's for dinner took no effort at all.

"I might as well get it out of the way," he said, opening door of the pretentious silver Mercedes for me. "If I came all this way and didn't visit her, my mother would hang me."

I slipped into the too-low leather seat as gracefully as I could and used the time it took him to walk around the car to smooth my dress and pull myself together. My growing paunch was beginning to curse me with the posture and stance of a long-haul truck driver.

"How long since you've seen Gabi?" I asked as he got in.

"Not since her wild New York days," he replied, wiggling his eyebrows.

"I doubt she's ever been wild."

"Sure she has," he drawled. "I heard that she once put her paintbrushes away without cleaning them properly."

Ryan started the car and pulled out onto the street. It had been a long time since I'd played tour guide. I pointed out a few unimpressive landmarks as we coasted through town, including the famous lighthouse-that-never-was sign.

"I just can't see the charm" Ryan allowed his eyes to wander from the road for too long while he checked out the scenery. "Living here would be my idea of hell."

I gazed out the window impassively. I'd felt the exact same way for most of my life, but for the time being I was exactly where I was supposed to be.

We arrived at the house just on dusk. A yellow glow from the lights filtered through the open windows, setting a warm and inviting scene, but it wasn't enough to motivate Ryan.

"Cheer up," I teased, noticing his expression. "Gabrielle's cooking coq au vin. It's to die for."

He glanced across, smiling crookedly. "You're such a simple creature at times."

Alex met us at the door. Gabrielle interrupted the idle greeting by bounding out of the kitchen and launching herself at Ryan. I wasn't sure what I was expecting but overenthusiastic hugging wasn't it. Ryan reciprocated, breaking her hold only to do the Décarie double-kiss routine.

"It's been such a long time," she crowed, grabbing his hands and pushing him to arm's length while she looked him up and down. "You haven't changed one bit."

"You have," he noted, smiling. "You used to be blonde, back in the day.

She put a finger to her lips. "Shush."

"Blonde, eh?" teased Alex. "Who knew?"

"Oh yeah," purred Ryan, swinging her hand. "She was a rebel."

* * *

Dinner was divine. Unexpectedly, the company was too. Gabrielle and Ryan chatted, laughed and reminisced like old friends rather than two cousins who didn't particularly like each other. I was beginning to wonder if Ryan had embellished the animosity between them.

Alex seemed to be enjoying himself too, mainly because he learned a few things about his arty French beauty queen that night. If not for Ryan spilling the beans, he'd probably have never found out about the thick glasses she wore as a child or her short-lived foray into modelling as a teen.

The embarrassing revelations weren't one-sided. Thanks to Gabrielle, I found out about Ryan's brief high school obsession with techno music and baggy clothes. I tried to picture it in my mind. I couldn't do it. The man wore tailored shirts, for crying out loud.

Ryan mistook my thoughtful stare for fatigue. "Are you tired, Charli?" He downed the last mouthful of wine in his glass. "We can go if you want to."

It was after eleven. I hadn't managed to stay awake that late at night for weeks. "A little."

Ryan smiled. "Comes with the territory, I expect."

"Yes, of course," concurred Gabrielle. She began clearing the table. "You need your rest, Charli."

I suddenly felt older than my years. Confusingly, I also felt like a child being dismissed from the table because it was time for bed.

"There's plenty of time to catch up," agreed Alex, pushing his chair back. "How long did you say you're in town for?"

Ryan followed his lead and stood. "I'm hoping to be out of here by the end of the week, depending on how acquiescent your daughter is to my not-so-hostile takeover."

I glowered. "I told you, just give me the papers and I'll sign it over."

"Maybe I'll give her an extra few days to come to her senses," suggested Ryan, transferring his smirk to Alex. "Her negotiating skills are a little off."

Alex chuckled, but the Parisienne was determined to put her two cents in. "You do need to put some thought into this, Charli," she urged. "You have a child to support now."

It was too much to think that Alex hadn't told Gabrielle all about the Billet-doux situation. Her input annoyed me because she had to know her concern was a crock. I'd married very well and I was on the cusp of divorcing even better. The reality was, if I never managed to get my act together it would make no difference to the financial support of my child. I was loaded.

"You're absolutely right." I thumped my hand on the table, making the setting rattle. "You can buy me out for two million dollars."

He didn't bat an eyelid. "Now I definitely need to give you a few days to come to your senses. You're delusional."

* * *

The ride back to the cottage quickly turned into an inquisition.

"I thought you couldn't stand Gabrielle," I accused. "You looked pretty chummy tonight."

Ryan flashed me a puzzled sideward glance. "I haven't seen her in years. Were you hoping for a brawl?"

"No, of course not. I just wasn't expecting you to be so friendly."

"She hasn't had a chance to aggravate me. I'm sure if I was subjected to her company for any length of time, the affability would wane."

I laughed out loud at his convoluted words. "You're such a dick."

"I try my best," he retorted, grinning.

* * *

Waking up the next morning knowing that I wasn't alone in the house was a joyous feeling. But I knew it would be short-lived. Ryan had made it clear that as soon as the Billet-doux affair was wrapped up, he'd be on the first flight to New York. I expected him to hit me with his buyout offer over breakfast, but he never mentioned it. Perhaps the salt air was slowing him down.

The man opposite me looked nothing like the jetlagged Manhattanite pounding on my door the day before. He looked relaxed dressed in faded jeans, grey T-shirt and bare feet.

"I stole something from your father's house last night," he announced.

I didn't buy it. I continued eating my cereal as if he hadn't spoken. I did smile though, giving him licence to continue the nonsense.

"C'mon, Charli," he goaded, leaning across the table. "Don't you want to know what it is?"

"No."

He leaned back. "You used to be one of the best crooks around," he reminisced. "Motherhood is making you soft."

I rolled my eyes. "Oh for goodness sake. Tell me."

Ryan reached into the pocket of his jeans and pulled out – of all things – a cork. He placed it reverently on the table.

"And you think *I'm* a simple creature?"

His smile brightened to Décarie level. "That pinot we had last night was outstanding."

"I wouldn't know," I muttered, taking my bowl to the sink. "I didn't have any."

"It got me thinking. If that's the calibre of wines in this region, I should meet with the supplier, buy a few cases and have it shipped home for the restaurants. What do you think?"

Why did he care what I thought? I rinsed my bowl and returned to the table on the pretence of mulling it over. I picked up the cork and rolled it between my fingers, reading the winery name on the side. It was from the Tate estate.

"In theory, I think it's a great idea." I tossed the cork at him. He surprised me by catching it. "In practice, it might be the worst business decision of your career."

As far as I knew, the Tate's wine sales were the domain of Meredith. Even Ryan would find it challenging to deal with her.

"Why?"

"They're… difficult to deal with," I replied cryptically.

"You know them?" I tilted my head to one side, silently answering his question. "Of course you know them. You probably know everyone in this backwater town. You can set up a meeting for me."

"Why would I help you do that? I can't stand them." I spoke with absolute contempt. "If you want to go making deals with the Beautifuls, on your own head be it."

"Who are the Beautifuls?"

I had a good mind to march him down to Jasmine's salon and feed him to her.

"The Beautifuls are the daughters of your winemakers. It's a small town and word gets round. One way or another, you'll have to go through them to get to the pinot."

His crafty smile proved that whatever he was thinking was positively obscene. "Relax, Casanova. Only one of them is single and neither of them are beautiful. One is the proverbial mean girl –"

"And the other?" he pressed, cutting me off before I had a chance to tell him.

I sighed, picturing Lily in my mind. "Dumb as a stump."

Ryan chuckled down at the table. "Sounds challenging."

"Leave it alone, Ryan," I warned. "After years of making my life a misery, things have finally settled down. I don't want you causing trouble."

"I find it hard to believe that anyone could get the better of you," he mocked. "Besides, I happen to have a way with mean girls."

"And dumb girls."

He smirked at me. "Why do they hate you so much?"

I snatched up his half-full coffee mug and marched it to the sink. "Probably because I slept with their brother and dyed their hands orange."

Ryan burst into a roar of laughter that showed no sign of ending any time soon. I walked out and left him to it.

May 29
Adam

I didn't need to spend much time at Nellie's. Paolo ran it with an iron fist and I was happy to leave him to it. Billet-doux was a little more my speed. It was calmer and quieter. And best of all, the place pretty much ran itself.

I had no idea what I was supposed to be doing. Even Trieste wasn't really sure.

"Ryan just hovers and then disappears into his office for a while." She wiggled her fingers in the direction of the diners. "Just mingle."

I'd never been one for mingling, even when I was sane. I choose to hang back and observe from a distance instead.

Billet-doux was far more up-market than Nellie's. The lunch crowd was mainly businessmen and groups of women who had a fondness for big jewellery and little dogs. The staff were much more interesting to watch. Everyone seemed to get along, and from what I could tell Ryan was a good boss. No one had a bad word to say about him, which could only mean that none of them knew him well. His no-screwing-the-staff rule obviously still stood.

Trieste still jabbered incessantly about Felix, but had never made a move. He seemed oblivious to her hardcore attempts at flirting. She stopped at the bar to chat and bat her eyes a hundred times a day. Wondering if he was as inept at the dating scene as Trieste, I decided to give him a bit of a push. I waited until things had quietened down after the lunch rush. He greeted me with a wide smile.

"It's Felix, right?" I asked, pretending to be unsure.

"That's right."

"Felix, what do you think of Trieste?" I leaned my elbow on the bar, looking back at Trieste as she cleared tables.

I glanced at him. He looked scared, as if he didn't know the right answer. "I like her?"

"Great," I said, ignoring his terror. "She likes you too. You should ask her out."

Felix looked across at her. "No, I don't think so." He didn't sound scared any more.

"Why not?"

"She's not my type."

I believed him but persevered anyway – showing scary Fiona Décarie tendencies.

"Why not? She –"

He cut me off. "She has blue stripes in her hair."

I looked at her. "Yes, today she does."

"She's just not for me," he said apologetically.

I should've left it at that, but for some reason I didn't. "What would it take for you to change your mind?"

His answer – and the speed in which it came – astounded me.

"Two hundred dollars. And you pay for the date."

Hiding my disgust was nearly impossible, but considering I'd started the conversation, I decided to back out of it quietly.

"You're right," I said, straightening my pose and backing away. "She's not your type."

June 3
Charli

Alex called me asking me to cover Nicole's morning shift at the café. "Please Charli," he begged. "Apparently she has a last-minute appointment in the city. She's really left me in the lurch."

I really didn't mind helping him out but was curious to know why he couldn't just cover her shift himself.

"*I* can't do it." He spoke as if the whole idea was preposterous. "Look at the water. The waves are outstanding."

Nicole was pacing around the café when I arrived, antsy and eager to leave.

"Sorry I'm a bit late. I got here as soon as I could."

That was lie. I'd showered, dried my hair and spent ten minutes drawing Ryan a mud map of how to get to the Tate vineyard.

"It's fine. No problem," she replied, grabbing her bag. "I should be back in a couple of hours." I wanted to know where she was going but didn't ask. Our renewed friendship was in its infancy. As a rule, that made sticky-beaking a no-no.

Business that morning was painfully slow. I put it down to the glorious weather. No one in their right mind would choose coffee and cake over sun and sand, including the café's proprietor.

Reading every magazine on the rack killed a bit of time. So did chipping the nail polish off my recently manicured fingers. Not only was I bored out of my skull, but I was getting uncomfortable too. Perched on a stool is not an easy position to maintain for hours on end when seven months pregnant. I felt mildly depressed at the realisation that Gabrielle had been right. My body was on loan. And unlike Ryan's Billet-doux buyout, this was a hostile takeover.

I got more edgy as the minutes ticked by. I would have been grateful to see anyone walk through the door, except Flynn.

I'd been at the café for over two hours when Lily flounced through the door. It was the only time I could ever remember being happy to see her.

"Hey," she trilled. "What are you doing here?"

"Just filling in for Nicole for a couple of hours," I explained. "What are you doing here?"

She leaned across the counter to whisper her reply. "I'm buying a coffee."

I laughed at the theatrics. She'd made it sound as if we were doing a drug deal. "As far as I'm aware, buying coffee isn't a crime."

"It is if you're one of Jasmine's bridesmaids. We're on a strict diet."

I'd always felt a little sorry for the junior Beautiful. She'd lived her whole life under her older sister's maniacal rule. I wondered if that might change once Jasmine got married. Maybe she'd be content just to rule Wade's roost instead of the whole henhouse.

"Wade seems like a nice guy." It was all I could think of to keep her talking.

Lily rolled her eyes, pulled out a stool and sat down. "He's not very smart, is he?" she asked, scrunching up her nose. "I used to think *I* was stupid until Jasmine brought him home."

I burst into giggles. The junior Beautiful laughed too, but I wasn't certain that she knew why.

Hanging out with Lily wasn't as bad as I'd remembered. Perhaps we'd all done a little growing up in the past few years. We spent the next half hour catching up, mostly about her brother. "Mitchell hardly ever calls," she revealed. "Mum was furious that he didn't come home for Christmas. Do you think he'll ever come home, Charli?"

My thoughts turned to the beach bum in question. Mitchell was the happiest, most content person I knew. It was a frame of mind that most people spend their entire lives in search of. And he'd found it by living in a run-down old shack on a quiet stretch of beach in Africa. No, I didn't think he was ever coming back.

"One day, I'm sure," I fibbed.

She smiled, satisfied by my answer. "I wish I was like him sometimes," she breathed. "Free and easy."

I sighed. "Me too, Lil. Me too."

The coffee I made her was a faultless piece of art, right up until she unloaded six packets of sugar into it. I expected her to fall into a coma at any minute. If that were to happen, I'd be back to being bored and alone. Thankfully, it wasn't to be. Nicole showed up a few minutes later, only half an hour later than promised. She moved to the business side of the counter and made herself a cup of coffee. I was itching to ask her where she'd been but managed not to.

"Been busy?" she asked.

"Run off my feet," I lied.

"Things are about to pick up," she told me, taking a rushed sip. "A Merc just pulled into the car park. You ought to see the guy driving it. Freaking gorgeous."

Lily ran to the window to catch a glimpse of the mystery man.

As expected, Ryan strolled through the door. He looked only at me with an expression darker than thunder.

"What's the matter?" I asked.

"Who knew making a simple business transaction in this town would be so difficult?"

I grinned. "I knew. I told you, too."

I had a whole range of scenarios playing out in my head. Maybe he turned up to buy his wine and Meredith ambushed him, Mrs Robinson style. Or perhaps she'd taken note of the ridiculously decadent car he was driving and inflated the price of the wine. But Ryan was no fool. He wouldn't pay a cent more than he thought it was worth.

"Driving all the way out there was a monumental waste of my time," he grumbled, either oblivious or unconcerned by the two drooling women hanging on his every word.

"Why?"

"It was closed."

"That's it?" I couldn't hide my disappointment. "That's the story?"

"Hi," said Nicole, picking her moment to break into the conversation. "I'm Nicole."

Ryan politely extended his hand across the counter. "Ryan Décarie. Pleased to meet you."

"Oh my God," muttered Lily, still standing near the window. "There are two of them?"

Ryan spun around at the sound of her voice. He clearly hadn't noticed her on the way in. Lily walked toward him, looking a little awestruck. It was too much to hope that he hadn't noticed.

Ryan held out his hand. "Adam is my brother. And you are?"

"Lily Tate," she replied, having no clue that her surname was Ryan's magic word of the week.

"Oh," he drawled, holding her hand longer than necessary. "You're the vintner's daughter?"

I glanced at Nicole, silently apologising for him.

"Oh, no. My parents grow grapes."

Nicole dropped her head, trying to bury her giggle. I kicked her foot.

"Ryan is trying to buy some Tate wine to take back to the States, Lily," I explained. I gave her the condensed version because at that moment, as she gazed into the prince of darkness's eyes, I doubt she could've coped with anything more in depth. "He owns a couple of restaurants in New York."

Lily frowned, shaking her head. "The vineyard is only open to the public on the weekends."

"That's too bad," drawled Ryan, finally releasing her hand. "I was hoping to spend a great deal of money there."

He was losing his edge. Lily didn't give a damn how much money he intended to spend on their wine. All she wanted to know was if he was single and how long he was in town for.

Perhaps taking pity on her, Nicole took over. "So, are you planning to stay a while?"

"A week or so."

"Adam came for a week and stayed for months," recalled Nicole.

Abandoning Lily, Ryan ambled toward the counter. He smiled at Nicole, recognising that unlike the Beautiful, she was playing with a full deck.

"My brother's reason for staying wasn't business related." I pulled a face at him. "I'm not that easily distracted. As soon as my business affairs are wrapped up, I'll be out of here."

"It's a long way to come for wine," suggested Nicole, still digging for information.

He smiled, undoubtedly impressed by her doggedness. "No place is too far to travel for good wine, Nicole."

* * *

Now that Nicole was back to hold the fort, I had no reason to stay at the café. Once Ryan had extracted Meredith's phone number from Lily, he didn't either.

We stood in the car park discussing plans for the rest of the afternoon. Mine were simple. I'd whittle away the rest of the daylight hours at the beach; possibly taking pictures to compensate for the fact that surfing was off the agenda. Ryan's plans were a little more hardcore. "I'm going to cut down some trees with your dad." He spoke like an amped-up teenage boy, thrilled by the prospect of doing some damage.

I wasn't quite sure what to make of Alex and Ryan's budding bromance.

"Have you ever actually used a chainsaw before?"

His enthusiasm was contagious. "No, but I'm a fast learner."

I tried to imagine Ryan wearing chequered flannelette. It was an unfair thought. Alex cut wood all the time and didn't own a single flannelette shirt.

"You like Alex, don't you?"

"I feel sorry for your father," he retorted. "He's surrounded by needy women. His daughter is a nutcase and he's shacked up with an imperious French princess. He deserves a bit of manly downtime."

* * *

I didn't make it to the beach. When I got home, I flopped on the couch feeling tired, slightly unwell and huge. If I continued to grow at my current speed, I'd have to start borrowing Floss's tent dresses to see me through the next few months.

Nicole arrived on my doorstep just after four. I wasn't surprised; I knew she'd come for the lowdown on Ryan. Too lazy to answer the door, I called her in from the couch.

"What a day," she announced wearily, flopping beside me.

I picked that moment to quiz her about her appointment in the city that morning. I wasn't entirely hopeful of getting an honest answer. It highlighted the fact that I still didn't trust her.

"I've been taking steps to keep the wolf at bay," she said, making no sense whatsoever.

"What does that mean?"

"The restraining order I took out on Ethan expired. I needed to renew it."

I felt slightly bad for Nicole. The whole Ethan saga had been an ordeal that never seemed to end.

"You'll get through it, Nic. You're tough."

"I know I will." She picked my phone off the coffee table. "New phone?"

"Not exactly. Gabrielle lent it to me."

"Ooh," crowed Nicole, swiping her finger across the screen to unlock it. "Maybe we can still check her emails."

I settled back into the couch. "No, I've already tried."

"Shame," she huffed. "We'll just have to Google ourselves then."

I dreaded to think what might show up if Nicole Lawson Googled herself. 'Lying, treacherous thief on the run' came to mind.

"Oh my God, Charli!" She lurched forward on the couch, displacing me. "There are heaps of search results for you!"

I struggled to dig myself out of the cushions while Nicole read the page she'd opened.

"Adam Décarie and his wife, Charlotte, dressed in vintage Balenciaga," she read in an over-the-top posh accent. "Ooh, there's a picture."

I wasn't the least bit surprised by what she'd found. I'd attended a hundred boring functions with Adam. The level of tedium could always be determined by the number of times we were photographed at the door.

"Let me see," I grumbled, levering myself forward enough to make a grab for the phone. I examined the picture closely. I felt so far removed from that life that I barely recognised the couple looking back at me.

Nicole shamelessly snatched the phone back. "God, you're both so pretty," she purred, scrutinising the small photo. "You look perfect together."

"Too bad we broke up then, huh?"

Her hand went limp, angling the phone so the picture was out of sight.

"I'm sorry. I didn't mean to make you sad."

I shrugged. "I'll recover."

"Do you miss him, Charli?"

I put my hand on my belly. "Of course I do. I love him."

"How can you love him after all that's happened?" she asked sourly. "He broke your heart."

"There's still hope," I muttered.

"You'd take him back, just like that?" She clicked her fingers.

She didn't understand. No one did.

There weren't words that defined the way I felt about Adam. I loved him no less than I did when we were together and happy. If he had walked through the door at that very minute, I would've grabbed him and gladly taken another five minutes.

"True love is still true, even if you can't live it the way you want to," I told her.

"Why don't you just call him and tell him about the baby?" she asked. "He's going to have to know soon anyway."

The thoughts I had of Adam rushing back to the Cove at news of the baby were slipping away by the day. Ryan didn't seem to think he was going to take it well. Alex was a little more positive, but preparing me for the worst anyway. I didn't even know what the worst was – and that was the most frightening part.

"I've put it off for too long. I'm scared to tell him now," I admitted.

"I can understand that," she said casually. "He could make things really difficult for you."

"How?"

"Well, his family are loaded and they're all lawyers. You duped him. If he decides to play nasty, you might have a fight on your hands."

That was one scenario I'd never even considered. I was appalled by the idea. "Adam would never do that."

"How do you know?" she asked. "You don't know what he's going to want to do." I could feel my expression crumple and Nicole worked quickly to smooth things over. "Look, all I'm saying is you need to be prepared for anything. Chances are, he's going to be majorly pissed that you lied to him."

I was now fighting back tears. Nicole didn't notice. She brought the phone back to her face and continued checking out the pictures she'd found. "I love that dress. It's just gorgeous," she said.

"You can have it if you want," I blurted, putting no thought whatsoever into my offer.

Her brown eyes widened. "Oh, no. That's not what –"

"It's in one of the boxes in the spare room." I levered myself off the couch. "I'll get it for you."

I slipped down the hall, needing a minute alone. Fortunately, I found the dress in the first box I searched. I fanned it out on the floor. The vintage ivory satin gown with black lace overlay was stunning. I had no qualms about giving it to Nicole. It looked tiny. I couldn't ever imagine fitting into the dress, or any other part of that life, ever again – and selfishly, I didn't want my kid anywhere near it either.

* * *

"Look what else I found," said Nicole, briefly glancing back at me as I walked back in. "Adam Décarie – fresh from his doomed union with the Australian – was back in wonderful form while celebrating the twenty-third birthday of Seraphina Sawyer in uptown Manhattan on Saturday night. There's a picture if you want to see it."

"No, I don't want to see it!" I couldn't trust myself not to scroll down in search of other photographic proof that Adam's life got wonderful after we split.

"Of course not. Sorry. That's really rough reporting." She managed to sound contrite and outraged at the same time. "Who would write something like that?"

I didn't have to check the website to know. "Her name is Tilly Roberge. She writes a malicious little blog about the goings on in her wicked little neighbourhood." Dress in arms, I sat on the edge of the couch, mindful of sinking too far back into the cushion if I leaned back. "She's a whole bag of nasty."

"Who is?" asked Ryan, injecting himself into the conversation as he strutted through the door.

"Tilly Roberge," I explained.

"Tilly Roberge." He dragged out her name, making it sound practically pornographic.

I rolled my eyes at his shameless reminiscing, making Nicole laugh.

"Ignore him," I urged. I bundled up the dress in my lap and dumped it on hers, far less gently than the three-thousand-dollar gown deserved. "Do you like it?"

She dropped the phone in favour of the dress, holding it out in front of her. "It's so beautiful," she crooned, smoothing her hand over the intricate lacework. "Are you sure you want me to have it?"

Ryan answered for me. "Someone might as well get some wear out of it. I don't think Tinker Bell is going to need it for a while."

"Don't you have something better to do?" I snapped, whipping my head around to glare at him.

"Yes I do," he replied, throwing both hands in the air and backing out of the room. "I'm going to take a shower."

* * *

By the time Ryan waltzed back in, Nicole had gone. I was still doing my best slob impression on the couch.

"How was the beach?" he asked, flopping down beside me.

"I didn't go. How was the tree felling?"

"Alex is my new hero," he beamed, leaning forward in his chair. "He chops wood for fun, Charli. *For fun.*"

I was astounded by his enthusiasm. I'd never known Ryan to get excited over anything, let alone something as mundane as replenishing Alex's wood heap.

I allowed him to go on with his tale uninterrupted. "He cut it down with a chainsaw – making it fall exactly where he wanted it to – genius!"

I grinned. "He's had a bit of practice."

"Did you know that he uses an axe to chop it up for firewood?"

I snickered, amused by his naivety. "What else is he supposed to use?"

"But an *axe*, Charli. Old school." He spoke as if the whole concept was alien.

"I'm happy you had fun," I said.

Ryan ruffled both hands through his damp hair. "It was fun, right up until the drive home. I got pulled over for speeding."

"Were you speeding?"

"Possibly." He shrugged. "Obviously that's a huge crime in this town. I thought the cop was going to lynch me."

"Don't take it personally," I consoled him. "Constable Davis isn't happy with me at the moment."

"Why? Did you sleep with his brother and dye his hands orange too?"

A picture of Wade Davis flashed through my mind. "Ugh! No. He has a bit of a crush on me. I shut him down."

"A *recent* crush, Charli?" I nodded. "You're pregnant."

I couldn't blame him for the disgusted tone. I thought the whole notion was distasteful too.

"Yeah. But I think I finally got through to him. I've hardly seen him lately, which is impressive considering he lives next door."

"What a creep. Maybe I should go over and have a quiet word."

"Or maybe you should settle your bad Armani self down and forget about it," I suggested. "I don't need the drama."

* * *

As much as Ryan enjoyed his newfound hobbies, he had one more thing on his Pipers Cove bucket list. He wanted to go fishing, and much to his surprise, Alex had refused to take him.

"Alex isn't into fishing," I told him. "Alex is friends with the fish. They watch him surf."

"Okay, you can take me fishing then."

I stared at him as if it was the most ludicrous idea on earth – and considering I was seven months pregnant and in a constant state of exhaustion, it probably was. "You're such a bossy jerk," I grumbled.

Ryan gave me weird puppy-dog eyes that made him look damaged. "Pretty please, Charlotte?"

"And what are you going to do if you actually manage to catch a fish?"

"You can skin it and cook it for me, wench."

I gave him a shove, but it was a weak protest. An hour later, we were in my father's shed, rifling around for a fishing rod.

"What sort of fish will we catch?" he asked.

I could've told him we'd be fishing for two-headed purple tiger fish and he would have believed me. "Bream, probably."

"What do we use for bait?"

The man was absolutely clueless, and I could feel the wickedness creeping in. It had been a long while since I'd had fun tormenting someone, and Ryan was the perfect mark. "Behind the house, at the top of the paddock, there's a creek," I explained. "The best bait for catching Bream is little heebie fish. The creek is full of them."

"Do we catch them with this?" He thrust a fishing rod at me.

"No, just a net will do. They're only small."

Alex appeared in the doorway and asked us what we were doing. Ryan was so ramped up that he laid out the plan in ten seconds flat.

Alex looked at me in a way that immediately made Ryan question why. "Is there a problem?"

Ryan couldn't tell that he was battling to keep a straight face, but I could. "No problem," he said, taking the net from me. "But you'll need a smaller net. Heebie fish are tiny." He hung the net back on the wall and grabbed one with a smaller weave.

"This is what we need?" asked Ryan sceptically, swatting it through the air like a tennis racquet.

I couldn't blame him for being unsure. The small net hadn't seen the light of day since my butterfly hunting days when I was ten. "It's perfect," I told him.

* * *

Just on dusk we walked up the dirt track toward the creek armed with a bucket, a butterfly net and a torch. Ryan might as well have been on a trip to the moon.

"Do I just scoop them out of the water?" he asked.

"Yes."

"How will I see them? It's getting dark."

"You'll see them," I assured him.

After twenty more questions, we reached the creek. The water was barely knee deep at its highest, but Ryan looked nervous. I couldn't blame him: daylight was almost gone and the dark bush behind the creek made for an eerie scene. The wind made the thick bracken rustle. It wasn't a familiar sound to Ryan. He kept staring at the bush as if waiting for something to leap out at him.

I sat on a big rock near the edge of the water and ordered him into the creek. He rolled up his jeans, pulled on a pair of gumboots and waded in, net at the ready.

"It's cold," he complained. That was an understatement. It would've been bloody freezing.

"Such a brave little soldier," I mocked.

"Now what do I do?"

"Start scooping heebies."

His back to me, he dutifully scooped the net through the water. I used the time to gather a handful of rocks.

"Like this?" he asked after a few seconds.

"Perfect," I praised.

Just as he was getting into it, I tossed a small rock into the bush on the other side of the creek. Ryan straightened at the sound and stared into the endless dark bush.

"What was that?" he hissed.

I managed to keep my voice straight. "Nothing. A possum maybe."

Satisfied with my answer, he went back to scooping water – and I went back to tormenting him.

"Have you ever heard of a fairy called Eolande, Ryan?"

"Of course I haven't," he replied, only half paying attention.

"She's Scottish," I explained. "A beautiful female fairy that likes to capture fishermen."

"Really?" he said dryly. "Do tell me more."

"She appears in flowing water, like rivers and creeks."

I pegged another rock into the bush while his back was turned. Ryan's head snapped up following the sound and my hand flew over my mouth to muffle my laugh.

"There's something out there." He punched out the words.

"No there's not." I shone the torch into the bush to prove it. "You're imagining things. Do you want to hear my story or not?"

He waded closer to the bank, and closer to me.

"Tell me the stupid story," he demanded, failing miserably at downplaying his terror.

"Well, she attracts men with her sad moaning and wailing. Thinking she needs rescuing, the fisherman follow the sound of her cries," I explained. "When she lures him to the water's edge, she leaps out of the creek and grabs him."

Ryan looked at the water, blackened by the low light. "What happens next?"

"She loves him to death. She has her way with him over and over until he dies of exhaustion. Then she moves on and finds another victim."

He took a moment to process this before returning to the task of heebie catching. His mind was clearly elsewhere. He hadn't even questioned why his net was coming up empty.

As soon as he was occupied, I threw my third rock.

Ryan tossed the net on the bank and scrambled out of the water. "That's it," he declared, pulling off his boots. "We're done."

He scooped up the empty bucket and walked away, leaving me to fend for myself. He was at the edge of the track before I even managed to stand.

"Wait for me," I called between giggles. "I can't move that fast any more."

He barely slowed. "You should've thought of that before you brought me to the haunted woods."

I was laughing so hard now that my belly hurt.

"Move, Charlotte," he ordered. "I'm not waiting for you. Whatever's in the forest can have you."

He was well on the way to the house before he stopped to let me catch up. It was then that the penny dropped.

"Heebie fish," he said thoughtfully.

"What about them?"

"Are they any relation to the heebie jeebies, Charli?"

"Oh, you've heard of them?"

Even in the darkness, I read his expression perfectly. He'd been had, and he knew it. He shook his head, muttering down at the ground. "I can't believe I fell for that."

"Me neither, you big baby."

"Your father was in on it too, wasn't he?"

"Of course he was," I confirmed. "You don't learn wickedness. It's generally inherited."

He pointed at my belly. "We've so much to look forward to, haven't we?"

"I'll teach her everything I know," I declared, putting my hand to my stomach.

"I've missed your evil ways," he told me, slinging his arm around my shoulder as we walked. "It's surprisingly good to have you back."

"Thank you very much," I replied, doing my best Elvis impression. "It's good to be back."

June 15
Adam

I wasn't overly surprised that Ryan had changed his plan of getting in and out of the Cove in less than a week. Nothing in that town moves quickly, including Charli.

She'd agreed to the buyout, as I knew she would. It was up to him to work out the details, which he hadn't got around to because he was caught up in extracurricular activities like buying cases of wine and cutting down trees with Alex.

I was totally jealous.

I had only spoken to him a couple of times since he'd left, and only asked about Charlotte once.

"She's doing fine," he promised me. "I'll tell you all about it when I get home."

He'd given me nothing, but that was okay. Any mention of Charli was a double-edged sword. I wanted to know how she was, but feared hearing the answer. Either way, I was left feeling as if I'd been stabbed.

* * *

Considering my list of friends was down to extremely low single digits and my brother was out of town, my phone should've been quiet. But it wasn't.

I'd been taking calls from Judge Lassiter's office every other day. I was now on a first-name basis with Laura, the judge's PA. She kept contacting me with an offer of starting my clerkship early – an offer that I politely declined over and over again.

Anyone would've thought I was an accomplished attorney in high demand rather than a recent graduate who hadn't even sat the bar yet.

I knew my father was behind it. I didn't want to confront him about it, so when I was summoned to my parent's house for dinner that night, I left it him to mention it.

The queen spent the evening fussing over me. My father spent the night lecturing me, as I knew he would.

"A clerkship is an important first step in your career. I don't understand why you're delaying."

"I'm not delaying," I defended. "I start in mid-July. That's always been the arrangement."

"Procrastination is unbecoming," he growled.

I kept eating, paving the way for my mom to jump to my defence. "He deserves a break, Jean-Luc. He's worked his tail off up to this point."

"The hard work hasn't even begun yet," he scoffed.

"I'm holding down the fort at the restaurants until Ryan gets home," I muttered. "I'm not procrastinating."

People who attain law degrees at twenty-three are not procrastinators. It was almost unheard of, but not spectacular enough to satisfy my father. My brother and I had been pushed into every accelerated program available, taken extra classes and maintained near-perfect grades since we were kids. Instead of folding under the pressure, we'd both worked incredibly hard. When Ryan opted out of a career in law, our dad nearly lost the plot. I was his last hope, and his desperation was beginning to show.

I moved to change the subject. I picked up my wine glass, holding it up to the light. "Mom, do you know why they cut patterns into crystal glassware?" I asked.

"I imagine it's for decorative purposes," she replied.

"Not originally." I rolled the stem of the glass between my fingers. "It was a tradition started by a Scandinavian couple, Geirvé and Hersir."

"Really?" The scepticism in her voice made me smile.

"Yes. They were madly in love. He was a prince and Geirvé was a pauper girl."

"Oh," crowed my mother putting her hand to her heart. "Like you and Charli."

I rejected the absurd comparison. "Charlotte is not a pauper and I'm not a prince."

"You're my prince," she beamed.

"Do you want to hear the story or not?"

My father chimed in. "No. Enough nonsense. We were discussing your future."

"No, *you* were discussing my future, Dad," I corrected. "Mom and I were discussing fairy-tales."

"Let him speak, Jean-Luc," insisted my mother, flicking her napkin at him.

He groaned but complied.

"Geirvé worked in the kitchen of the castle. She wasn't allowed to speak to Hersir so they used to meet in secret," I explained. "Whenever she wanted to arrange a meeting, she'd cut a mark in of the crystal glasses just before serving his meal, letting Hersir know that she would be waiting for him later that evening. Over time, all the glasses in the castle ended up looking like this." I held up the glass. "The king thought they looked great. He had no idea they represented secret booty calls."

My mother must have been taken with the tale. She overlooked my choice of word. "Oh, how romantic."

"Absolute nonsense," barked Dad.

I ignored him. So did my mother. "It didn't end romantically," I said gravely. "Geirvé found out he was seeing other women and vowed to get revenge for breaking her heart. She spent hours grinding one of the glasses into tiny shards and hid it in his food."

My mother gasped. "What a wretched, wicked girl!"

I smiled down at the table. "He deserved it, Mom. He was an ass."

"Did he forgive her?" she asked.

"No. He died," I replied. "A slow painful death. That was his punishment for breaking her heart."

"What a terrible story, Adam."

"Not all fairy-tales have happy endings, Mom."

I knew that better than anyone.

"It showcases his mindset," scoffed my father. "Charli's nonsense has damaged him. *Charli* has damaged him."

Charli's stories hadn't damaged me. They'd captivated and enchanted me. The lack of ambition and bad attitude I'd recently acquired was entirely my own doing. It was my dose of crushed glass. It was *my* punishment for breaking her heart.

"Charlotte is a good girl," defended my mother. "Eventually they'll sort out their differences."

I didn't have the heart to tell her otherwise.

"I'd prefer that our son just sort himself out," he barked. "He should be focusing on his career."

Décaries have a long history of overachieving. When you're born into money, you tend to spend the rest of your life trying to prove that you deserve it. Both Ryan and my father would've been independently wealthy without their inheritances. Following in their footsteps had always been the plan – only now, the plan sucked. I'd lost things along the way that no amount of money or success could replace. And I got the distinct feeling that it was all downhill from here.

"I'm going to organise a social get-together with Judge Lassiter," said my father, brainstorming. "Perhaps dinner."

"I'm sure you'll enjoy it," I muttered, toying with my food again.

He slammed his hand on the table. It was his version of a cease and desist order. "You will be there too," he declared. "I'd like to prove that you're not a complete ingrate."

I wasn't conforming when I agreed to attend. I just couldn't be bothered arguing. I left straight after dinner, making no excuse for my early departure. I was close to saying something I would regret, and as much as my father deserved it, my mother did not.

* * *

The last thing I was expecting was to find Trieste on my doorstep when I got home. As I got out of the elevator, she jumped to her feet.

"What's the matter?" I asked. I expected to hear something terrible. She'd never shown up at my apartment before.

"Where have you been?" she asked. "I've been waiting here for over an hour."

I twisted the key in the lock. "Dinner at my parents' house." The door opened and I ushered her in ahead of me.

"I was worried about you," she said, flustered. "I thought you'd be home. You're always home. You have no life."

I couldn't deny it. It was true.

"Why are you really here, Trieste?"

"I wanted to talk to you about something." I pointed her in the direction of the couch. Conversations with Trieste were notoriously long. I was probably going to need to be seated to hear it.

She sat, picked up a cushion and gripped it to her chest. "It's about Felix."

I groaned, flopping on the couch opposite her. "What about him?"

"I'm having trouble talking to him," she revealed. "We don't seem to have a whole lot in common."

"Don't you have a girl friend you can discuss this with?" I asked, desperate for an out.

"Not really. Besides, a boy's point of view might be more relevant in a situation like this."

As far as I knew, there was no situation. Felix wasn't into Trieste, which was fine by me because he was a douchebag of epic proportions. I just didn't want to be the one to tell her.

"Look," I began. "If he's not interested, he's not interesting. Let it go."

"I like him."

I swiped both hands down my face, groaning. "Trieste, you're impossible."

"Adam, you're a terrible friend," she shot back. "You're supposed to be encouraging and supportive."

Did she know me at all?

"What about hobbies? Find some common ground," I suggested.

"Do you think it'll work?"

No. I didn't think it would work. Even if Felix did see the light, it would be a recipe for disaster. Two people with nothing in common had absolutely no hope of holding it together. I'd been there.

"Sure." I lied like I meant it.

She tossed the cushion aside and leaned back, thinking hard. "He likes liqueurs – the fancy ones. He talks about that a lot."

"And you like liqueurs?" I quizzed sceptically. "That's your common interest?"

She straightened up the ears on her beanie. "No. I don't know anything about them," she admitted. "I did try some champagne at my cousin's wedding once, though."

I smiled at her naivety. "Great. What else have you got to work with?" A relationship based on a mutual love of alcohol didn't seem exactly spellbinding.

"Nothing. Let's stick with the liqueur angle. I'm a quick learner." She sat forward in the seat. "You could teach me all about them. That way, I'll have something to talk to him about."

I was shaking my head in protest before she'd even finished laying out her plan. "That's the dumbest thing I've ever heard."

She widened her eyes. "Truly?"

I stared at her for a long moment. "No," I conceded, "but close."

* * *

I had no idea why Trieste always seemed to get the better of me. I gave in to her stupid suggestion and raided Ryan's liquor cabinet.

I drew the line at letting her taste test the whole collection. I picked four of his best bottles and told her to make do. I lined up some shot glasses on the coffee table and poured a miniscule amount of cognac into one of the glasses. Trieste was hard to cope with sober. I didn't want to see her smashed.

"What is it?" she asked, holding up the glass. "I like the colour. It looks like caramel."

"Grand Opus Cognac," I replied, double-checking the label.

She brought the glass to her lips and took a small sip.

"It's strong," she choked.

"They're all strong," I told her. "That's the point."

After half an hour and a dozen or so sips, she'd picked her favourite – Revolution Brandy, because she liked the colour. The taste seemed to be wasted on her. She described it as being warm.

It was then that I realised Trieste was a lightweight. The girl who usually talked a mile a minute was now three sheets to the wind, slurring her words and constantly pulling at the ears on her beanie. Despite her protests, I insisted she stay the night and sleep it off.

It was a momentous occasion. Trieste Kincaid became the first woman in history to actually sleep in Ryan's bed.

* * *

She was gone the next morning. I found a note sitting on the pile of sheets she'd stripped from Ryan's bed.

Unbelievably, the girl jabbered as much in print as she did in speech.

These are top quality sheets. If you wash them using an extra rinse cycle, you'll remove all of the detergent residue. See you at Billet-doux this afternoon. Don't be late.

Love,
Trieste Kincaid.

Trieste was special. That's the only word to describe a girl who leaves a note like that and signs her full name.

I hadn't had any intention of going to Billet-doux that day but followed her orders and turned up anyway – on time, which impressed her no end.

"You came," she beamed, rushing me at the door.

"Didn't you think I would?"

"I wasn't sure. I read somewhere that alcohol can act as a depressant. I was worried that you would wake up even grumpier than usual. I left the number for the suicide hotline on your fridge just in case."

I dipped my head to mutter my reply. "Thank you for your concern, but I didn't actually drink anything."

She widened her eyes. "Really? I was drinking alone? That's so sad."

Trieste sounded so appalled that I couldn't help laughing. "I've heard that alcohol can act as a depressant," I told her, leaning down to speak quietly.

* * *

I didn't think Trieste would remember much of the liqueur lesson from the night before, but getting wasted hadn't dented her memory at all. Not only had she remembered, she must've left my apartment, gone to the nearest liquor store and researched some more.

I stood just out of sight and listened as Trieste gave Felix her best spiel. He didn't exactly seem enamoured. He continued polishing glasses and nodding every time she paused to take a breath. Maybe I should've reminded her that less is more. When she started rattling off the alcohol content of everything on the top shelf of the bar, I was ready to run over and shut her down myself. Then I remembered that Felix was shady, and I didn't want him to be enamoured by her in any way, shape or form.

* * *

It turned out to be a busy night at Billet-doux. I ended up staying until the end of dinner service, doing nothing more important than being present. After I'd secured the night's takings in the safe, I made my way back to front of house, preparing to leave.

When I heard voices coming from the staff cloakroom as I passed, I stopped to listen – perhaps because it was Felix talking.

"She's been all over me for weeks," I heard him say.

I recognised the guy he was talking to as one of the kitchen staff. "What are you going to do about it?" he asked.

"Give her what she wants," replied Felix, like the smarmy douche that he was.

"She's weird, dude."

"Weird but willing," said Felix, making kitchen guy chuckle.

The rat I'd always smelled where Felix was concerned was now beginning to stink. Kitchen guy continued laughing as Felix tore Trieste to shreds.

I hung behind the partially open door until I couldn't take it any more. Once he mentioned his plan of getting her into bed, I drew the line.

I pushed the door all the way open, making them both jump.

"Hey, Adam."

I swear I saw his almost-moustache twitch.

Kitchen guy bolted past me as quickly as he could without running.

"We were just talking about Trieste," volunteered Felix. "I've asked her out on a date."

He'd made it sound so innocent, as if he'd suddenly seen the light and realised how great she was. I wanted to smack him.

I pointed toward the door. "And now you can go out there and tell her that you've changed your mind," I ordered.

He shook his head. "Why would I want to do that?"

"A few reasons. Firstly, date rape is illegal. That's the plan, right? Get her smashed and get her back to your place?" He didn't answer me so I continued. "Secondly, I think you like working here. If you want to keep working here, you're going to cancel and you're going to leave Trieste alone."

The idiot actually thought about it for a second before calling my bluff.

"You can't fire me."

"You want to try me?"

After a long moment of deliberation, he pushed past and skulked out to front of house.

Trieste was on the far side of the room, straightening tables, too far away for me to hear the conversation. I saw her nodding as he broke it to her.

Trieste was a tall girl. She seemed to shrink before my very eyes as her shoulders slumped. She looked devastated.

If I was a good friend I would've gone out there to comfort her, but somewhere along the line I'd lost the ability to deal with anyone I cared about – and I truly did care for Trieste. She'd seen me through some pretty dark days lately. A good friend would've returned the favour.

Unfortunately, I wasn't a good friend. I was the kind of friend who snuck out the kitchen door so he didn't have to deal with her.

June 26
Charli

It took a couple of weeks for Ryan to pull together his wine deal, and as much as he insisted he got a bargain, it still cost him plenty. Apart from dealing nonstop with Meredith Tate, he'd also taken Lily out for dinner in the hope of getting a better deal. Hearing the gruesome details over breakfast the next morning was the highlight of my week.

"It was excruciating, Charli," he complained. "I endured an hour long car ride to Hobart with the girl. She never shut up. By the time we got there, I practically had nothing to live for."

I was laughing so hard it became soundless. "I did warn you."

He shoved the last piece of toast into his mouth. "No amount of prior warning could've prepared me for that."

"Are you going to see her again?" I asked, trying to compose myself.

Ryan took his plate to the sink. "Not if I live to be a hundred."

The only sure-fire way of not seeing Lily again was to get out of town, but his initial plan of buying me out and getting back to New York as soon as possible seemed to have gone awry. I liked having Ryan around so I never questioned why. He'd hardly mentioned Billet-doux lately, let alone presented me with his buyout offer. I never questioned that either.

I began clearing the table. "Do you have plans today?"

I had to ask. Thanks to his bromance with Alex, his social schedule was busy. They were constantly chopping wood, pulling cars apart in the shed or surfing. To clarify, Alex surfed. Ryan fluffed around in the low-breaking waves trying to find his balance on a mini-mal board that Alex had been storing in the shed for a hundred years.

Having fun was a concept that eluded Ryan most of the time. The uptight, suit-wearing New Yorker had crossed over to the dark side by becoming a laid-back country hick, if only temporarily.

"I have nothing planned. Why? Do you have something in mind?"

I finally felt ready to make a start on the nursery. Alex and Gabrielle had offered to help me clear out the spare room and paint plenty of times, but like all things important, I'd been putting it off.

"Will you help me paint the baby's room?"

Judging by his expression, the mere suggestion had caused him pain. "You should probably know, I've never painted a wall in my life."

"That's because you've always paid someone to do it. You'd never chopped wood or worked on cars until you got here either," I reminded.

He smiled brightly, proud of his boondock accomplishments. "I suppose not."

* * *

Ryan's promise of ignoring Flynn only held until he saw him. As we were leaving to head to the hardware store, Flynn appeared on his front porch. He glanced at us but kept walking to his car.

It was the big mouth New Yorker who spoke first. "Hello, Officer Davis."

"Ryan, shut up," I hissed.

Flynn changed course. "Hello. How are you?"

"Fine." Ryan glanced back at me.

Flynn turned his attention to me. "How are you, Charli? You look lovely."

"Doesn't she?" gushed Ryan. "Her husband is a lucky man."

The look of fury I directed at him was wasted. His back was turned.

Thankfully, Flynn took the high road. He made polite excuses and left quickly.

"Why did you do that?" I hissed, as soon as he was out of earshot.

"No reason."

"Get in the car, Ryan," I told him.

* * *

The aisles of Norm's hardware store seemed narrower than I remembered, perhaps because I was wider. Ryan followed me to the back, righting a broom as I knocked it over and shifting a display of gardening gloves out of my way.

"You're like a human bulldozer," he muttered.

I pointed at the paint selection chart on the back wall. "Shut up and pick a colour."

Ryan pretended to study the chart. "Don't you already have something in mind?"

"Yes, purple."

He clapped his hands. "Purple it is. Choose your tint and let's get out of here." Something about my expression as I glanced at him made him groan out loud. "It's not that simple is it? You're going to give me a big crock of fairy stories, aren't you?"

I shook my head. "Not if you choose the right colour."

Ryan turned his attention to the chart. "Well, I like that one." He pointed at a deep purple square. "It's the same colour as five-hundred-dollar poker chips."

It was truly a horrible shade, and far too dark for a nursery.

I dismissed his idea instantly. "How about lilac?" I suggested. "Lilac represents the purest form of love. The sincere kind, where nothing is expected in return."

"It's not bad," he conceded, "but very boring and pastel. How about something a bit brighter and more lively?" He pointed out another poker chip purple.

I scrunched up my nose. "Nothing about violet is lively."

"Why not? It's bright."

"It symbolises meekness and humility. Violets are shy flowers. They hide under their leaves."

He looked across at me, frowning. "You are so full of baloney."

"It's the truth, Ryan," I insisted. "Where do you think the term 'shrinking violet' comes from? I don't want my kid to be a shrinking violet."

"I sincerely doubt that's a possibility, Charli," he retorted. "She has you for a mother."

* * *

I didn't feel up to making small talk with Norm while he mixed my paint. We decided to take a walk down the main street while we waited. As expected, Ryan was unimpressed by Pipers Cove's shopping hub.

"At least each store is exclusive," he teased.

"Not quite. We have two beauty salons." I pointed down the street toward Jasmine's salon.

Ryan read the sparkly sign. "I take it that is the best one?"

I muffled my laugh with my hand, unwilling to draw the attention of the sparkly Barbie lurking inside. As we passed, I peeked through the front window and spotted Wade at the counter. He saw me too. I probably could've gotten away with a quick wave, but I was in the mood for tormenting Ryan. I grabbed him by the elbow and dragged him inside.

"Hi, Wade," I beamed. "Are you manning the salon today?"

"Just for a minute. Jasmine stepped out to get some lunch."

"Oh, I see."

Ryan cleared his throat, either prompting me to introduce him or hurry up and get him out of there.

"Who's your friend?" asked Wade, making the call for me.

I patted Ryan's arm. "Oh, he's not my friend. He's my brother-in-law. This is Ryan."

"Oh, right, the wine bloke. You're Lily's new flame."

"No," snapped Ryan. "That flame was extinguished early, Wayne."

"Wade," he corrected. "I think you'd better set things straight with Lil. I don't think you've distinguished anything."

I made a polite excuse to leave and nudged Ryan toward the door.

"Wait," called Wade, stepping out from behind the counter. "Aren't you going to buy something, Charli? You're the first customer we've had all day."

At a loss, I glanced around the salon. "Ah, I don't think I need anything."

"How about some shampoo?" he suggested. "We have a strawberry one."

He snatched a bottle off the shelf and waved it at me. Nothing about smelling like a punnet of fruit appealed, but I felt sympathetic enough to let him continue his pitch. "We have vanilla too, but I have to be honest, it doesn't taste anywhere near as good as it smells."

"What about something more spicy, Wade?" I asked, trying to divert his attention from Ryan, whose body was shaking with silent chuckles. "How about something like sandalwood or patchouli?"

He pointed at me as he backed away. "Don't go anywhere. I'll check out the back."

When he was gone, I picked up the fruity shampoo, unscrewed the lid and sniffed it. Ryan whispered, "How does it taste, Charli?"

I elbowed him in the ribs. "Shut up."

"We could make a run for it while he's gone." He gave an upward nod toward the door.

I smirked. "I can't run very fast these days."

"I'll carry you."

I stepped away in case he decided to throw me over his shoulder. "Just be nice. Maybe you could use your fabulous business acumen to argue the price of shampoo with him. Get me a good deal."

"I'm not going to argue anything with him," he replied. "I refuse to have a battle of wits with an unarmed opponent."

I was keen to get out of there too, before Jasmine returned. We walked out of the salon with two bottles of shampoo purchased out of pity, and headed back to the hardware store to collect our paint.

* * *

By the time we got back to the cottage, I was too tired to paint. Ryan didn't try talking me round – it was a job he hadn't been looking forward to in the first place.

"You should sleep," he told me. "You don't look good."

Looking good wasn't achievable these days, so I took no offense. I nodded and staggered toward my room.

Something caught my eye as I passed Ryan's room. The window was wide open and the lightweight curtains were flapping in the breeze.

I called Ryan in. "Did you leave the window open?"

He slammed it shut. "I don't think so," he replied casually. "Maybe I did."

I didn't feel right. "Remember what I told you about snakes?"

I'd made a joke of it but it wasn't funny. It was getting harder to put the strange goings-on in the cottage down to forgetfulness. It unnerved me.

"I'll make sure it's locked in future." He studied me. "Are you sure you're okay?"

"Yeah. Just tired."

* * *

I still felt a little off the next day, but I wasn't expecting to feel a hundred percent until I could see my toes again. Figuring I was as recharged as I could be, we made a start on the nursery.

Painting walls with Ryan was akin to doing a craft activity with a preschooler. When he'd told me he had no idea what he was doing, he truly meant it. "So what am I supposed to do with this?" he asked, waving the paint-loaded roller at me.

"Roll it on the wall," I said, slowly and carefully.

He glided the roller down the wall, leaving a patchy lilac streak. "Oh, look at that," he marvelled. "It's like magic."

"You're hopeless," I teased. "Adam would've finished that wall by now."

Ryan grinned at me. "I'd be perfectly happy to call him in to finish the job. I'd love to step aside."

It dawned on me that he was talking about something much more important than the wall.

"That's why you're still here, isn't it?" I asked, thinking out loud. "Because he's not."

Ryan placed the roller in the tray on the floor, picked up a rag and began wiping his hands. "He would want me to make sure you're looked after."

A sarcastic laugh tumbled out of my mouth. "Have you met Alex? Trust me, I'm well taken care of. You're free to go any time."

"Charli," he pointed at my belly, "when I first found out about this, I thought it was madness – a ridiculous life-altering mess you'd created."

His words caused physical pain. I could feel a headache coming on. I put my hands to the side of my head, massaging my temples.

"But I get it now," he continued. "And I'm enjoying being here, for both of you."

"So stay," I muttered.

"It's not that simple. I'm not supposed to be the one experiencing this. Adam should be here. I shouldn't be the one painting his kid's nursery. Don't you see how wrong that is?"

I'd reached the end of the line where Ryan was concerned. He wasn't prepared to keep my secret any longer.

"You're going to tell him, aren't you?"

"Yes." He didn't look the least bit apologetic.

"When?" I whispered out the question and continued rubbing my temple.

"I booked my flight this morning," he told me. "I leave the day after tomorrow, which gives you a day or two to call him. If he doesn't know by the time I get home, I'm going to tell him everything."

"An ultimatum, Ryan?" I asked acidly. "You're really going to do that to me?"

"He needs to know, Charli. Every single day that passes is another day he misses out on."

I didn't have the strength to argue with him. I was having trouble finding the strength to remain standing. "I need to sit down," I mumbled.

Ryan lurched forward, making a grab for me. "What's the matter?"

"I don't feel well."

"Come, sit," he said, guiding me out of the room to the couch. "What do you need?" he asked.

"Nothing."

"Are you mad at me?"

I huffed out an almost-laugh. "Since when have you cared whether I'm mad at you or not?"

A smile crept across his face. "Since never," he conceded. "But I don't want you to be upset about this. Adam is my brother. I want him to know, and I think now is the time."

I nodded, admitting defeat. There was nothing I could say to change his mind – and I wasn't sure I wanted to. No good can come from keeping secrets, especially the one I was holding.

June 27
Adam

I didn't hear from Trieste for over a week. I'd held off calling her because I had no idea what to say, and I'd stayed away from Billet-doux for the same reason. When she finally did call me, I was over the moon.

"Can you meet me in the park at ten?" It sounded more like a demand than a request.

"Of course." I would've agreed to meet her anywhere.

"Don't be late, Adam," she warned. "If you're one minute late, I'm leaving."

"I'll be there," I promised.

I got there half an hour early, armed with coffee. Trieste wasn't impressed. She stomped down the sidewalk in her Doc Martin boots like she was heading to a fight.

"Do you come in peace?" I asked.

"I'm so mad at you right now," she growled. "How dare you threaten Felix like that?"

I thought back to my conversation with the jerk in question. I didn't remember threatening him but couldn't rule out that I had.

She flopped beside me on the bench, folding her arms. I tried to butter her up by offering her a now cold cup of coffee. She shook her head. "Come on, Trieste," I urged. "It cost me five bucks."

She took the cup. "Why did you do it? You knew how much I liked him. Ryan doesn't care if his employees date each other."

I'd wondered what excuse Felix had spun her. He'd obviously decided against the date-rape-is-illegal angle and gone with blaming me instead.

"He's a fool, Trieste."

"Well, I'll never get a chance to find that out for myself now, will I?"

"I didn't make him call it off because you're co-workers," I explained. "In the beginning, I was all for him taking you out. I even asked him to. It wasn't until he wanted me to pay him to do it that I realised he was a dick. When I heard that he'd asked you out anyway, I knew his intentions weren't good. I don't want you to get hurt."

"Pay him?" she gasped, horrified.

Obviously that was too much information. Whoever said that honesty was the best policy had never dealt with Trieste.

"I refused."

"Oh," she snarled, slapping a hand on her knee. "That makes all the difference."

"I'm sorry," I said.

"You're an idiot!" The words roared out of her. A couple passing by spun back to look at us – so did the Shih Tzu they were walking. "You actually asked him to take me out?"

"As soon as he mentioned money I backed off. It was a stupid idea."

She pointed at me. "You had no business interfering. What is it that makes you think you can manipulate a situation to make it go your way?"

It was probably the most vicious question I'd ever been asked – and it proved that Trieste had me completely figured out. Manipulation was my preferred approach when it came to getting my own way. Trying to convince Felix to date her was only a small example. I'd done far worse in the past, and Charli had borne the brunt of it.

I could look back now and see that it had all been for nothing. I'd won nothing other than a life that I no longer wanted.

"You should be focusing on your own life, which at the moment is a complete wreck," she barked.

"I know that," I mumbled.

There was no denying it. My current life sucked. If I died and went to hell, it would take me a week to realise I was there.

"You're the worst friend I've ever had," she complained.

I folded my arms and leaned back, feigning indifference. "In fairness, I never claimed to be a good one."

My bad attitude tore open a floodgate. Every little bit of frustration I'd subjected her to over the months came rushing out. "Some days I have no idea why I bother with you." She held out her hand and started ticking off on her fingers. "You're mean. You're unreliable. You're arrogant –"

"Okay, okay. I get it," I interrupted. "I have nothing going for me."

"You always smell good," she grumbled. "That's about it."

"Thanks, I think."

Trieste twisted on the seat, angling toward me. "You have a disease, Adam. You're an ass."

"Being an ass is a disease?" I asked.

"Being an ass is a symptom. Regret is the disease."

"Thank you, Doctor Kincaid," I muttered.

She softened only slightly. "I'm sure you weren't always this way, Adam. You need to find a way of turning things around."

I couldn't refute a single word she'd said. I hadn't always been this way, but feared I was too far gone to find my way back.

"This is it for me, Trieste." I waved my arms around. "This is what I chose."

"Then you chose wrong, didn't you?"

"Yes," I agreed.

I'd known it for a long time but you reap what you sow.

"You're a recent law graduate with a judicial clerkship lined up. You're supposed to be flying high right now. Why do you keep delaying your clerkship?"

I stared at her for a long time before answering. "Because I'm not sure I want it."

"Your heart's not in it any more, dummy." She tapped the side of her head. "Where is your heart?"

"With Charlotte." That answer came much easier.

"Right. So what are you going to do about it?" I couldn't have answered if I wanted to. She jumped in again. "You're going to go to her and beg for forgiveness."

"It's not that simple."

"Go to her, stupid," she growled. "At least give it a shot. The way I see it, you've got nothing to lose."

I shook my head at the hopelessness of it all. "I talked Charli into doing something irreversible. How will telling her that I regret it serve as anything other than another kick in the head?"

Trieste thumped my arm. "You're looking for excuses not to man-up and go. You're such a loser, Adam."

"I am." I puffed out a quick laugh, leaned over and planted a kiss on her cheek. "I'm sorry for being such a stupid-dummy-idiot-loser."

"Get your act together and sort yourself out," she instructed. "Then we'll talk forgiveness."

* * *

I parted ways with Trieste at the entrance to the park and walked the short journey home. I'd just arrived when I received a call from my father's PA. Tennille instructed me to be at my parents' house no later than eight the next evening. He'd teed up dinner with Judge Lassiter, just as he'd threatened to.

"Mr Décarie has requested that you make sure you're on time and come without attitude." It sounded like she was reading off a list. Jean-Luc's instructions were very clear. It pissed me off that he hadn't taken the time to call and tell me them himself.

"I'll keep it in mind," I said dully. "Thanks Tennille." I hung up on her then, Ryan style.

Another call came a few minutes later. When I read the number on the screen, I considered letting it go to voicemail. But ignoring her was pointless. She'd only keep calling until I answered.

"Hello mother."

"Darling, how are you?"

She didn't give me a chance to reply. She launched into her list of instructions for the upcoming dinner, as if I needed coaching on how to behave. At least she'd taken the time to call me herself. I paced the living room, grunting in acknowledgement every time she paused for breath.

Ridiculously, it might have been the first time I realised just how under the thumb I was. Epic organisation and structure had played a huge part in my life for as long as I could remember. The only time that ever changed was when Charli was around.

Something in my thick head finally clicked. I'd been desperately unhappy for a long time, accepting the misery because I was hell-bent on punishing myself. If I continued to do what I'd always done, I was only ever going to get what I always got.

I was just about to grow a spine and tell my mother of my epiphany when the universe threw me a sign that I was on the right track. I turned around just in time to see the Pipers Cove canvas fall off the wall and crash to the floor. If Ryan had hung it, I would've put it down to shoddy workmanship – but I'd hung it, so I put it down to magic.

I stood with the phone to my ear, staring at the blank wall.

"Adam? Are you still there? Adam? Hello?"

"I'm here, Mom." I muttered. "I'll call you back."

I dropped the phone on the couch and stood staring at the wall, weighing up my options.

I only had one.

I had to get out of New York. I was done with mediocrity. I was going to follow my heart, and she lived in the tiny Tasmanian town that had just crashed to the floor.

* * *

Charli once told me that getting out of Dodge is an act that must be done quickly. I ran around the apartment like a lunatic, packing.

I couldn't explain the urgency. I just had an overwhelming belief that I needed to get out quickly, which was strange considering I'd spent months having trouble getting out of bed in the morning.

I booked a ticket online, hailed a cab and made a detour to my parents' place on the way to the airport. I wasn't planning on coming back any time soon. The least I could do was tell them.

As luck would have it, Mom was arriving home just as I got there. I didn't even need to go upstairs. I told the driver to wait and called out to her as she got to the door.

"Darling!" She looked surprised. "What are you doing here?"

"I need to talk to you," I said. I took her bags and led her to the small sofa near the elevator.

"What is it?" she repeated, catching my urgency.

I sat down beside her and grabbed her hand, just in case she freaked out and decided to take a swipe at me, then laid out my half-baked plan.

"We have dinner plans tomorrow night," she reminded me.

"Mom, did you hear anything I just said?"

"Yes of course."

"I'm not coming back," I reiterated.

"I'm thrilled that you're willing to work things out with Charli, but you must prioritise," she said gently. "You're due to sit your exam soon. Perhaps you should delay your trip until then. Charli will understand."

I was shaking my head before she'd even finished speaking. "I'm not sitting the exam, Mom."

"This will kill your father, Adam," she warned, finally showing a hint of displeasure.

"He'll get over it," I promised.

"But you've worked so hard."

Arguing the point wasn't difficult. "I've worked hard for years on the wrong thing. If I'd put the same effort into my life with Charli, things would've been so much different for us," I explained. "We're owed a happy ending. I'm not going to find it here."

"You're going to give up everything you've worked for?" she asked dubiously.

I grinned at her. "She's my other half, Ma. No matter what I have or what I do, if she's not with me, I have nothing."

Every bit of concern left my mother's expression. She looked as calm as I'd ever seen her. Confident that she wouldn't smack me, I let go of her hand.

She reached across, taking my face in her hands. "Then you should go," she encouraged, smiling at me.

Her about-face astounded me. I wasn't actually sure I trusted it.

"Really? What about Dad?"

She dropped her hands to her lap. "I'll tell Jean-Luc," she promised. "I'll make him understand."

"Will you do one more thing for me? Will you pack the rest of my things and courier them to Gabrielle's cottage in Pipers Cove? It has to be done today."

"Alright, but what's the hurry?"

I had no idea. All I knew is that it had to be done that day. "Please. Today."

"I'll go to the apartment and do it now."

"Thank you," I breathed.

She took my hand. "You're a good man, my son," she said in French.

"I will be," I replied confidently.

* * *

I had no qualms about leaving New York. For the first time in a long time, I felt excited, hopeful and free.

After checking my luggage and making my way to the departure lounge, I called Trieste to let her know my plans.

"Finally," she groaned. "I'm glad you're not a complete loser."

"Thanks," I said sincerely. "I'll keep in touch, okay?"

"No, you won't," she shot back. "But that's alright. That's how I'll know you're doing okay."

"You're wonderful, Trieste. I might not have told you that before."

"No, you haven't – because you're a dick. But I forgive you."

I rushed out a bray of relieved laughter. "Thank you."

The phone call was short and worthwhile, much like our friendship. I owed Trieste Kincaid a huge debt of gratitude. I doubt I would've made it through the past few months without her. She'd pulled me from the wreckage of my life and done her level best to keep me in line. I would never forget it.

June 29
Charli

The weather was wicked. It was dark, windy and threatening rain at any second. I didn't envy Ryan. I would've been terrified at the prospect of getting on a plane that morning, but it didn't seem to faze him. He was back in New York mode – with a few minor adjustments.

"If you need anything, call me," he instructed, tossing his suitcase into the boot of the Mercedes. "And please don't name her something stupid. I don't want to hear that you've called her Periwinkle or Sugarplum."

I laughed but he was serious.

"I'm glad you came, Ryan," I said, winding my hair around my hand to stop it lashing my face.

He finally smiled. "So am I," he conceded. "Maybe you can visit us next time. The rest of the family will be thrilled to meet the mini Tink."

"We'll see what happens," I replied vaguely.

"No matter what happens, she has family, Charli. We're all family. Don't ever forget that."

I'm sure he meant to sound encouraging, but I couldn't help feeling slightly threatened as I remembered Nicole's worst-case scenario.

"You'd better go," I said, taking a step back and looking at the sky. "You'll miss your plane."

Ryan kissed both my cheeks. "Call him, Charli."

"I will."

I could tell he didn't believe me but he let it go. "I'll see you soon."

I stood on the driveway, watching until the silver Mercedes was out of sight. That was the moment I realised that he'd never presented me with his buy-out offer. Somehow, I didn't think it mattered any more.

June 29
Adam

I'm not a nervous flyer but I was so relieved when the plane touched down in Hobart that I could've kissed the ground. The weather had made for the hairiest landing I'd ever endured. I grabbed my luggage and made a run for the car rental desk, hoping to get to the Cove before the rain hit.

I still wasn't used to everything in the rental car being on the wrong side, but it was a little easier this time round; I suspected it was the same SUV I'd rented the last time I was here.

I synced my phone with the Bluetooth, pulled out of the parking lot and tried calling Ryan. It went straight to voicemail, which was unusual. Ryan always picked up, even if just for the joy of hanging up on his caller a second later. Perhaps time in Pipers Cove had mellowed him.

I was looking forward to seeing him. No doubt he'd be furious with me for leaving his restaurants unattended, but that would only last until he found out what a half-assed job I'd done while I was there.

I was looking forward to seeing Charlotte even more.

I had no idea what sort of reception I'd receive. I knew that proving I'd changed my ways was going to be a hard sell. But it was important that she knew I'd finally woken up to myself. All I could do was hope she'd believe me.

I got within twenty kilometres of town just after ten o'clock. Already out of whack from the change in time zones, I found the strange weather was playing tricks on my mind. The gloomy sky made it seem much later in the day. Just staying on the road took effort. The wild wind thrashed the car, and the trees beside the road were bending at impossible angles. I felt the full ton weight of the black sky. I'd never seen weather like it.

When my phone rang a short while later, I assumed it was Ryan calling me back. I hit the answer button on the steering wheel.

"Not even picking up the phone, you dick?"

"Adam?"

I wanted to fade away at the sound of Charli's voice.

"Charli," I choked. "I'm sorry. I thought you were Ryan returning my call."

"It's okay," she replied. "He might not call back for a few days. He's travelling. He left this morning."

"Oh."

I'd probably passed him on the highway. I felt disappointed that I'd missed him – until Charli spoke again and I forgot I had a brother.

"I was hoping we could talk for a minute."

Just hearing her voice filled me with joy. Having her tell me that she wanted to talk catapulted me to the point of rapture.

I played it cool. "Sure."

"I know things haven't been great between us for a while but –"

"Charli, listen." I cut her off. I didn't want to go over old ground. I wanted to run in a completely new direction for a change. "I love you. No matter what, you must know that."

"It's getting harder to believe since you tried divorcing me," she replied, sounding a little shaky.

I couldn't help smiling. "You're a difficult woman to divorce, Charlotte Décarie."

"Yeah, well, I don't go down without a fight."

I couldn't pick the emotion in her voice. Her words were casual, yet she sounded stressed out. I didn't know what to make of it.

"I thought that's what you wanted."

"You thought wrong."

"I've made some terrible choices lately, Charli," I admitted. "I pushed you into going along with them. I'm not even going to say sorry because it wouldn't hold any meaning, would it? You've heard it from me too often."

"So what are you saying then?" she asked.

I worked hard to think quickly. An apology was hard to articulate now the word 'sorry' was off the table.

"I regret everything, Charlotte," I confessed. "If I could turn back time, things would be different right now. There'd be a baby on the way for us. No divorce, no doubts, no selfishness. Just plenty of foraging for rocks."

Mentioning the baby was insensitive and idiotic. I'd inadvertently delivered the kick in the head I was trying to avoid. I slammed my hand on the steering wheel, cursing my stupid mouth as the sound of her crying filtered through the car.

"Don't cry, please," I begged.

"I'm okay," she sniffed. "Talk to me about something else for a minute."

It was a strange request, but if it meant she'd stay on the line I was happy.

I slowed the car and looked to my left. The first glimpses of the Cove showed just how nasty the weather was. Massive black clouds swirled in from the sea like toxic smoke.

"There's a storm coming," I said. "A big one, I think."

"Really?" she asked. "Here too. I'm watching it roll in. The sky is so dark and the windows are rattling. What does yours look like?"

"It's the same sky, Charli. I'm watching it come in over the Cove too."

"What?" she gasped. "Where are you?"

"About two minutes away from you."

"You're here? Who called you?"

"No one. Why would anyone call me?"

She started sobbing again, louder than before. I had no idea how to calm her. I wasn't even sure what had upset her in the first place.

"You have to tell me why you're here." She'd made it sound as if knowing meant the difference between life and death.

"For you, Coccinelle," I said with reverence. "I finally worked it out. You said everything happens for a reason, right?"

Her breath caught as she sucked in a sharp sniff. I took it as a yes.

"I'm looking at things with fresh eyes. It took me months to get to this point. I'm done trying to make my plans work for me. I want to make better ones. I don't care what they are, just as long as you're part of them."

I turned into her street at a slow crawl, which was odd considering I was desperate to get to her. "Are you still there?"

"I'm here," she said quietly. "Where are you?"

"I'm on the driveway." I turned off the ignition.

I sat for a moment, staring at the little white car she'd been renting since Christmas. I was already making plans in my head. As far as I was concerned, we were done with temporary arrangements. No more renting cars and squatting in other people's houses. We were going to lay down roots and be normal – at least as normal as any couple in La La Land could be.

"Do you believe in second chances, Adam?" asked Charli.

I smiled at the question, took the phone off speaker and held it to my ear.

"*Deuxièmes chances?* I wish I someone would throw a few my way, yes."

"What would you do with them?"

I got out of the car and fought the wind all the way up to the house, stopping half way to shove back a bush that had blown across the path.

"I'd go back to January and be brave enough see things through."

"I'm really glad you said that," she whispered.

I stepped onto the veranda and made my way to the door. "Why, Charlotte?"

Just as I made a grab for the handle, the door swung open. Charli stood in front of me, holding her phone to her ear. "Because my waters have just broken."

June 29
Charli

Adam's phone hit the deck. Then Adam hit the deck, dropping to his knees as if he'd just been hobbled. I let him fall apart. It was the least I could do.

"Are you okay?" I finally asked.

He sort of nodded, which gave me hope he wasn't comatose. Adam reached forward and lifted my shirt. I could feel his confusion as he stared at my stomach. After a long moment, his hands gripped my hips and his head fell forward. I ran my fingers through his hair while he rested his cheek on my belly. I usually hate people touching my stomach, but considering he put her there, and they were meeting for the first time, I let him have that moment too.

All I could hear was the howling wind and the rattling of the dodgy old windows. I wasn't in any pain, nor was I feeling panicked or hurried. All I could feel was Adam's relief and total calm.

Finally, he stood, taking my face in his trembling hands.

"I want you to know," he struggled to get the words out, "I –"

"Shush." I cut him off. "There's nothing I need to hear right now."

I wasn't up to listening. And despite the fact I had a million things to say, I wasn't up to talking either. I kissed him instead, covering all bases. It was a welcome-back and a glad-you-came-to-your-senses and an apology all rolled into one. I considered it a brave move on my part. I had no idea how he'd react, but when I felt his body relax against mine I knew that for now, it was enough.

Feeling the first twinge in my belly, I broke free. "Can you get something for me?"

He swiped his hands down his face, pulling himself together. "Anything. What do you need?"

"A shovel."

He looked at me quizzically and put his hand to my forehead. It was a familiar gesture that I'd missed terribly. Checking for a temperature was common practice when crazy kicked in.

"There's one in the garage," I added.

"I'm fairly sure you're not going to need a shovel, Charli," he said, sounding more like himself. "And if you do, the hospital probably has one of their own."

He spotted my overnight bag on the floor and leaned down to pick it up.

"Please, Adam. Just work with me here."

He slung the bag over his shoulder and reached for my hand. "I am going to work with you for the rest of my life."

"I appreciate that. Now get me a shovel."

* * *

Adam dutifully loaded my bag, the shovel and me into his car. Once we were on the road, I laid out my plan.

"We have to stop at Alex's house."

"Can't we just call him?"

"No." I shook my head. "I don't think they're home anyway. I just need to pick something up."

Adam took his eyes off the road for longer than he should have, but didn't question me. He was outwardly calm. The only hint that we were in a hurry was the fact that we got to Alex's in record time. He jumped out of the car and ran to open my door.

"Do you have your key?"

"We don't need to go in. Grab the shovel."

"We're digging?" He sounded appalled.

"Don't sound so surprised, Adam. What else would we need a shovel for?"

"We're digging?" he repeated.

"*You're* digging," I clarified, patting his chest. "I might sit this one out if that's okay."

I'd spent fifteen years debating how to spend the box of wishes that I'd buried. I'd come close to digging it up a couple of times, but always managed to talk myself out of it. Today seemed like the perfect day to unearth it – if only I could remember where it was buried.

I didn't have the heart to tell Adam that I wasn't exactly sure where it was, but after digging the third hole and coming up empty, I think he cottoned on.

"This is ridiculous," he complained, sounding more worried than irate.

"Please. Try there." I pointed to his left, in between two geranium bushes.

"Last hole," he warned, looking up at the angry sky. "The baby's coming, the rain's coming, and this is getting us nowhere."

"Let me call Alex." I grabbed my phone out of my pocket and swiped the screen. "Please pick up, please pick up," I whispered, walking back to the car.

"Charlotte Blake," crooned my father after the third ring. "What can I do for you today?"

I cut to the chase. "Alex, where's my box buried?"

"The box of wishes?"

He knew exactly what I was talking about, which proved something I'd known for a very long time. My dad was all shades of awesome.

"Yes."

"You're digging it up today? I would've liked to have been there for that." He actually sounded disappointed. "What's the occasion?"

"I'm having a baby today."

I probably should've worded it better. Alex freaked out. I couldn't make much sense of the orders he was barking at me because my focus was on Adam, who'd just dug up my box.

"Is this it?" he called, holding up a dirty parcel wrapped in plastic.

I nodded, moving the phone away from my ear to dull the sound of my father's rant.

"Alex, listen," I urged, putting the phone back to my ear.

"No, you listen. Where are you, my house or yours? I'll come and get you."

"No need," I replied, watching Adam walk toward me, box in hand. "Adam is here. He just found my box."

"Oh," he replied, instantly mollified. "Good. That's good news. You won't need me then."

"I'm always going to need you, Dad," I promised. "Just not at this very minute."

"I love you, Charli," he told me. "Good luck with your chicken."

I ended the call as Adam reached me. Just as he handed me the box, a whole world of pain raged through me. He somehow managed to catch me and the box as I doubled over.

"Please, please, please can we go now?" he begged, opening the car door. "Sit."

I shook my head, fobbing him off. I didn't want to sit. I didn't want to stand either. I had no clue what I wanted to do, but thankfully the pain passed and I didn't have to decide. I turned my attention back to the box, taking it from Adam and tearing the wrapping off.

He was curious enough to wait, but indignation set in the second I lifted the broken lid. "Shells and toys?" His voice was calm but frustration was evident. "Charli, I've just spent twenty minutes digging up shells and toys?"

I closed the broken lid as best I could. "Every wish I saved until I was five is in this box. I might need them today."

He stared at me, nervously chewing his bottom lip while he thought it through. "Okay," he said finally. "Can we go now, please?"

"Finally," I huffed cheekily. "I've been waiting on you for a really long time."

June 29
Adam

We were half way to Hobart when the next contraction hit. The rain started at the same time, which meant I had no choice but to slow down. It was a manoeuvre that didn't impress Charli.

"Let me drive," she growled through gritted teeth.

"I don't think that's a good idea," I told her, reaching over to put my hand on her stomach.

She slapped me away. "Don't touch me. You can't ever touch me. Never, ever, ever."

"Okay," I agreed, holding my hand up in surrender. "I'll keep a safe distance." I glanced across. She'd tightened her grip on the box in her lap.

"Tell me about the box, Charli." It was a desperate attempt to take her mind off the pain. "Tell me about the stuff in it."

She flipped the lid open. "I don't remember most of the things in here. Just the shells."

"Tell me about them."

Her explanation was understandably short and fractured but I managed to piece together the gist. Every ounce of faith Charli possessed was contained in a broken wooden box. I didn't necessarily believe in it, but I understood.

"So each shell represents two wishes?" She nodded, pursing her lips as she blew out a hard breath. I glanced into the box. "You're loaded, Charli. Totally wish rich."

She managed a laugh and her breathing evened out. "I'll share them with you," she offered.

I didn't need them. I couldn't wish for more than I'd been given in the last hour. I was no longer standing on the edge of La La Land looking in; I was right in the middle of it, looking out, and I was finally beginning to realise what a prime position it was.

* * *

We were quiet for a while. Charli seemed distracted by the teeming rain and flashes of lightning. I had a million thoughts running through my mind to keep me occupied. I was sure I'd stumbled across an emotion that no man had ever felt before. I'd monumentally screwed up and selfishly thrown away everything that meant anything – only to have it all handed back to me in an instant. I could barely make sense of it.

"She's early, Adam," said Charli, snapping me back to the moment.

I glanced at her. "A month, right?"

"Four weeks, four days, to be exact."

I worked hard to come up with something encouraging to say. I had no clue whether to be worried or not. I was winging it. We both were.

"Maybe she's big," I suggested. It may have been the dumbest thing I'd ever said to her.

Charli practically lost the plot. "Yes. She's probably huge," she wailed, throwing out her arms. "You're fifteen feet tall and I'm tiny. She's going to take after you. This is never going to work. They're going to have to saw me in half to get her out. There's going to be blood and guts everywhere."

I quickly backpedalled. "No, no, no. I won't let that happen. I swear."

"Shut up, Adam. You suck," she sobbed.

I wasn't game enough to speak again.

Nothing else was said until we pulled up at the emergency entrance of the hospital. Charli tried her best to strike a deal with me. "Take me home," she blurted, grabbing my hand. "If you take me home, I promise I'll come back tomorrow and do this."

I bit my bottom lip, trying really hard not to smile. Smiling would've gotten me killed at that point.

I moved my free hand to the side of her face. I couldn't work out which one of us was trembling. "We're going to do this and then we're going to have a wonderful life here, just the three of us."

Her lovely brown eyes widened as she thought it through. "You're staying here?"

"If you'll have me."

"What about your job?"

"Charli, we have all the time in the world to talk about this. Let's just focus on –"

She pulled away and gripped the dashboard with both hands, cutting me off with a terrible pained moan. I couldn't stand it. I practically fell out of the car and rushed to help her out.

"Get my stuff," she wailed, falling into my arms as I opened her door.

"I'll come back for it," I assured.

"Okay," she whimpered, clinging to me. "But leave the shovel. We don't need the shovel."

* * *

The adage about the calm coming before the storm didn't apply to us. The storm came first, and four hours later I was in the unbelievably calm position of holding my tiny daughter in my arms.

Despite being a few weeks early, she was perfect – just small and in a hurry, much like her mother. I thought she looked like her mother too, which suited me fine. My tiny girl had an angelic little face, lips shaped like a kiss and a killer frown when unhappy. She also had Charli's cheeks, which made her exceptionally perfect. There was no dimple in sight, which meant she'd be spared a lifetime of cheek poking at the hands of her mama.

Everything had gone exactly according to plan, which was phenomenal considering there wasn't one. If living in the moment meant having more days like this, I was content to never make another plan in my life.

Charli slept. Part of me wanted to shake her awake and tell her how truly amazing I thought she was. A bigger part of me wanted to live to see another day so I left her alone. I spent time getting to know our new baby instead.

I paced the quiet room holding the weightless bundle in my arms. There was so much I wanted to tell her and I found myself absently drifting between two languages as I spoke.

Promising her the world wasn't difficult. I meant every word of it. My daughter didn't care what a jerk I could be, or how I'd come dangerously close to missing out on her. When her dark blue eyes locked on mine for the first time, with a look reserved just for me, I was done. I was already a better man than I'd ever been before.

"Show-off," mumbled Charli. "She's probably not impressed by your accent at all, you know."

I turned, not even trying to dull the idiotic grin on my face. "You didn't sleep for long."

"I'm not tired."

Despite the obvious lie, I lowered the sleeping baby into her arms.

"She suits you, Charlotte," I said, sweeping my hand through her tangled hair.

She grinned at me, and at that moment she'd never looked more beautiful. She was sunshine and warmth, my heart and the mother of my child.

"She suits you too," she replied.

I half smiled but couldn't find the words to speak. It was a terrible reaction. It made me seem unsure.

Charlotte looked down at the tiny bundle, cradling the top of her head with her palm. "Did you mean it when you said you'd stay, Adam?" she asked quietly. "It's okay if you didn't. We can work something out. I'm sure I said a hundred things I don't mean in the last few hours."

I pulled a chair close to the bed. "So you didn't really mean it when you said you were going to sue me for physical and emotional distress?"

She cringed at the unwanted reminder. "No, probably not."

I sighed, feigning relief. "Well, that's good news. You had me worried for a moment."

"I'm sorry I didn't tell you sooner," she whispered.

I'd put a lot of thought into it over the past few hours. I felt sad that I'd missed so much, but knew I had no one to blame but myself. I felt frustrated that Ryan hadn't told me weeks ago, but understood why he'd kept quiet. The only person I had to be angry with was me – and I was too freaking smitten with my daughter to be angry.

"I never gave you a reason to tell me." She deserved to know I wasn't mad at her. "I was a jerk. I'm not upset."

"No?" She sounded surprised.

"No, Charli," I confirmed, smiling at her. "I'm counting my lucky stars right now. You've given me everything."

"What happens now?"

I put my hand on top of hers, leaned across and kissed her. "I'm going to spend the rest of my life giving you both everything."

June 29
Charli

In the mayhem of that day, there was one thing I knew for certain. My baby was the prettiest baby in the history of all babies. Perhaps that's why I couldn't sleep for looking at her.

Adam spent time getting to know her. I already knew her. I'd felt her every move for months. She even looked like I imagined she would – a perfect mix of the two of us, with her father's dark blue eyes.

I held her until I couldn't. I could feel my eyes closing and my arms slipping. Adam noticed and took the baby from me, lowering her into the crib by the bed.

"I hate that crib," I mumbled. "It looks like a plastic bucket."

"It's not that bad," he replied, peering at the baby. "She seems to like it."

"Do you think they'll let us go home now?" I asked, mid-yawn.

Adam gently pushed the crib aside. "No. They're not going to let you go anywhere until you get some sleep." He made a half-hearted attempt at fluffing my pillow, and fussed with the blankets.

"Are you tucking me up, Adam?" I teased.

He grinned at me. "Be quiet and go to sleep." He sat beside me and brought my hand to his lips.

"I don't think I can," I told him.

"Do you want me to tell you a bedtime story?"

"No. But I could tell you one."

His smile started slipping. "You are so beautiful. I've missed your stories so much."

I moved my hand to the side of his face, settling my thumb in the deep dimple before it disappeared. "I've missed the hole in your cheek."

He laughed, making me realise I'd missed that too. "Just sleep," he whispered.

The ease of being with him was astonishing. There was no awkwardness or unfamiliarity. We could be apart for months at a time and just click back into place. The reason why was a simple one. I loved him, and I'd never forgotten that he loved me with all he had, even when it wasn't enough.

"Don't you want to hear my story?" I mumbled.

"Yes; then rest, okay?"

I nodded weakly. "It's about a fairy called Alouette."

"Why are so many of your fairies French?" he asked, reaching across to tuck my hair behind my ear.

"They're not *my* fairies. We belong to them, not the other way around."

"My mistake." He smiled. "What's so special about Alouette?" He said her name perfectly, putting his usual sexy spin on the pronunciation.

"She's not actually French. She hangs out in the Aleutian Islands."

"Alaska?"

"Yes."

"Go on."

"Well, she's like a rock star in the fairy realm – highly revered. She has one of the most important jobs of all, and she does it all by herself."

"No help from the grizzly bears, then?"

"None. It's her job to deliver the souls of babies to their fathers, just before they're born." I could feel my eyes closing. "The father carries it with him for safekeeping, then hands it over to the child when it's born."

"How?" he asked.

"I don't know," I mumbled.

"Well, how do you know when Alouette delivers the soul?"

"She gives you a sign." I wondered if he'd received a sign. I still had no idea why he'd chosen that particular morning to show up at my door. My money was on magic, but I expected a more logical explanation from Adam. I would've asked him about it but sleep took over, putting an end to the very best few hours of my existence.

June 29
Adam

Charli managed to get a few hours' sleep before Alex and Gabrielle arrived. They'd been held back by the horrible weather, and Gabrielle hadn't handled the delay well. She was so keyed up that Alex had to keep a grip on her hand to settle her. I was relieved to see her so excited, but there was an air of awkwardness. I felt like I'd stolen something from her.

At first I could barely look at her. She picked up on it immediately, inciting a very short but direct conversation in French. Neither Alex nor Charli demanded a translation. They were totally absorbed in the little person in Alex's arms.

"All babies are blessings, Adam," Gabi whispered. "Even ones that are not mine."

I nodded stiffly. "I'm glad you're here, Gabrielle."

She pulled me into a brief, tight hug. "There is no place I would rather be."

"Thank you," I whispered.

"You've been given a wonderful gift, Adam," she added. "If you mess this up, I shall hunt you down and kill you myself."

Gabi was done with me after that. In fact, Gabi was done in general. She only had eyes for the little baby she'd been waiting months to meet. Alex seemed reluctant to give her up, but she gave him no choice, all but wrestling her from his arms. He gave in and turned his attention to Charlotte, who didn't seem to have benefited at all from the two hours of sleep she'd just had.

"I have something for the baby," he told her, "but Gabs made me leave it in the car."

"Ridiculous," mumbled Gabrielle, unimpressed. "A ridiculous gift."

I would have loved to know what it was but was too afraid to ask.

He turned to me. "I have something for you too, Adam."

"Is it going to hurt?" I asked, only half jokingly.

Charli burst into a quick fit of giggles.

"Ignore him, Adam," said Gabrielle, still fixed on the baby. "He's not going to do you any harm. He's a mild-mannered grandfather now."

"Yes, he is," agreed Charli, grinning at her father. "So what would you like her to call you? Gramps?"

"More importantly," Alex began, pulling a face, "what are we going to call her? What's her name?"

Charli turned to me. I was actually relieved by the clueless look on her face. It meant I wasn't going to have to spend days talking her out of some weird bohemian name that she had her heart set on.

"We don't have a name," she replied.

"Oh, you must think of something quickly," ordered Gabrielle. "How about a family name?"

"No kid of mine is being named after spider," scoffed Charli, making Alex chuckle.

"How about a Décarie family name?" Gabi suggested. "Something French." She gazed down at the baby in her arms. "We have a great aunt called Hortense."

I shuddered. We'd been terrified of grand-tante Hortense as children. She had a five o'clock shadow and smelled of camphor balls. "That's a terrible name," I told her.

Charli was more diplomatic. "It's not for us."

Alex stood next to Gabrielle. "Well, you've got to call her something," he insisted, lightly touching the baby's head. "She's too pretty not to have a name."

"We'll work on it," Charli promised.

Working on it happened as soon as the conversation turned to the vicious weather.

"Power lines and trees are down all over the place," explained Gabrielle.

"And we have no driveway," added Alex. "There's a big crater where the water washed the track away. I'm going to have to bring in a truckload of gravel just to bridge it."

Charli whipped her head in my direction, grinning. "Adam, what do you think?"

I'd taken a crash course in La La that day. Perhaps that explained why I understood exactly what she was asking me. I was the only one who did, though.

"Think about what?" demanded Gabrielle.

"Alex just came up with the perfect name for her," I said, returning Charli's smile.

Alex looked confused, even after taking a few seconds to think it through. "Gravel?" he asked. "I prefer Hortense."

"Bridget," corrected Charli, meeting my smile. "We're going to call her Bridget."

Gabrielle carefully transferred the baby to Alex, too excited to hold her any longer. "Fabulous! I think it is a beautiful French name," she crowed.

I studied Alex as he walked to the window, wondering if my hold on her would ever look that relaxed. He didn't hold the baby cautiously like the rest of us. He had an expert technique that could only have come with practice.

"Welcome, Bridget," he whispered to the bundle in his arms. "You're going to love it here, I promise."

* * *

It took a long time for Alex to convince Gabrielle that it was time to leave. If she could've hidden the baby in her bag and taken her home, I'm sure she would have.

I was looking forward to spending some quiet time with Charli, but moments after Gabi and Alex left, a crotchety nurse stormed the room and ordered me out. "Go home," she demanded. "You need rest too."

She was downright scary for someone barely five feet tall. She was actually closer to four feet – the thick rubber soles on her shoes added height and kicking power. Protesting got me nowhere. The woman was a tyrant. Ten minutes and two quick kisses from my little family later, I was out the door.

The long drive back to the cottage was made impossibly longer by the mayhem left in the wake of the storm. Branches were scattered all along the highway from Hobart to the Cove, which meant it was ridiculously slow going.

It made me nervous to see what sort of shape the cottage was going to be in. I pulled into the driveway and breathed a sigh of relief at the realisation that we still had a roof.

It had been the longest day of my life. As soon as I was inside, I flopped on the sofa, checked the time on my watch and realised I'd been functioning for nearly two days without sleep. Besides being exhausted, I was starving – but not starving enough to eat any of the fifteen boxes of cereal in the pantry. My wife had a serious addiction to the stuff. Bridget should've been born looking like a cornflake.

Too hungry to sleep, I grabbed my keys and headed back into the night in search of a decent meal.

* * *

Pipers Cove was hardly the food capital of the world. The only hope I had of getting something to eat was at the pub. But as soon as I walked in the door, I realised I'd picked the wrong night to be hungry.

"Adam!" bellowed a huge voice I hadn't missed one bit. Jasmine Tate rushed toward me, dressed in a blue shiny dress and a veil.

I'd stumbled into the bachelorette party from hell.

I stopped dead in my tracks as she threw her arms around me. "Hello Jasmine," I muttered, wrenching her hands free.

"It's so good to have you back!" she squealed. "So much has happened since you've been gone."

"You don't say."

She threw her head back and cackled like a witch. "I do say. Sit with us and I'll tell you everything."

Before I had a chance to protest, she hooked her arm through mine and dragged me to a table in the corner.

"You remember Lily, of course." She pointed at her sister.

"Is she alright?" I dropped my head trying to catch Lily's eyes, which seemed to have rolled to the back of her head.

"She's breathing," Jasmine confirmed, holding her hand under her nose to check. "And Wade," she continued, moving behind him. "My fiancée."

Wade jumped out of his chair. I should've predicted his next move. He hugged me, the same way he had the first time I met him.

"It's good to see you again." He whispered it in my ear. He actually whispered it in my ear.

Somehow I broke free. "Thank you," I muttered. "You too."

"Sit," ordered Jasmine, pointing at the chair next to her paralytic sister.

"No, it's fine," I replied. "I'm just here for dinner then I'm heading home."

"Where's Charli?"

News in this town normally spread like wildfire, but they seemed oblivious. It was a surreal moment. After being kept in the dark for months, I was actually the first to announce Bridget's birth.

"In the hospital. Charlotte had a little girl this afternoon."

I wish I'd taken a step back before speaking. Jasmine's shrill squeal echoed through my ear. Wade lurched forward and I ordered him not to hug me. I must've looked serious because the hulk stopped and thumped me on the back instead. "Great news," he beamed. "I'll bet she's small."

"Babies usually are, Wade," I replied.

"Don't worry about it," he said thumping my back again. "She'll grow. You can never judge a book by its character."

I swear, the man's head would've whistled in a crosswind. Unable to deal with him any longer, I decided to make a run for it and go hungry.

"Attention. Attention!" yelled Jasmine. I spun around to see her standing on the bar. I couldn't help thinking it wasn't her first time up there. "This bloke is Adam Décarie and today he has a brand new baby girl!"

She charged her glass as the whole bar erupted into cheers. Someone shoved a beer in my hand. And that was one of the last things I remember.

* * *

I don't know who called Alex, but I'm glad they did. I don't think I would've survived another round of Pipers Cove generosity. I'd been shouted so many beers that I'd lost the ability to swallow.

Somehow, he managed to drag me out and get me to his car. "Did you at least get some food?"

I couldn't remember. My mind was elsewhere. "Alex, there was a guy in there called Spanner."

He laughed, somehow managing to keep me upright as he threw open the door of the ute. "Yes, I know. Get in."

"Is he a mechanic?"

"No. They call him spanner because he looks like he's been hit in the face with one. He has a brother called Brick."

"Is that because he looks like –"

"No Adam." I was glad he interrupted. Speaking was a chore. "His name actually is Brick. Apparently his mother had a thing for romance books."

"There are strange people in there," I muttered. "Your people are strange."

"The thing is, Boy Wonder," he patted my shoulder, "if you're planning to stay here, they're your people now too."

He slammed the door closed and my day was done.

* * *

I'd been drunk before. I'd been *very* drunk before, but I'd never been so drunk that I had to put serious thought into where I was when I woke.

I eventually figured out that I was laid up on Gabrielle's couch – and then groaned out loud at the hazy memory of Alex dragging me out of the pub.

I staggered into the kitchen and hung my head in the sink, half drowning myself in an attempt to feel human again. It was not a good look for a brand-new father. It wasn't a good look for anyone. And even the freezing cold dousing wasn't going to cut it. I needed a shower.

Mercifully, Gabrielle recognised that I needed clean clothes too. She inched open the bathroom door and thrust some at me.

"*Merci*," I muttered.

"*Imbécile*," she replied, pulling the door closed.

* * *

Despite the early hour, Alex was in the shed. Avoiding him was impossible. I was relying on him to drive me back to the pub to collect my car – assuming that's where I'd left it. I downed two cups of strong coffee before venturing out there. When I did finally face him, I was wearing his shirt. I felt like a total dick, for more reasons that one.

"A bit rough this morning, Boy Wonder?" He barely cast a glance in my direction.

"No, I'm good," I lied.

He laughed, the same evil laugh he'd come out with on the morning he nearly killed me in the surf.

"If you'd told me you were heading to the pub, I would've warned you," he told me. "Not even you deserved to get caught up in the drama of Jasmine Tate's third hens night."

"*Hens* night?"

"Bachelorette party."

"*Third* hens night?"

"Yeah," he confirmed. "It's going to be a regular Saturday night event leading up to the wedding."

I'd never heard anything more ridiculous in my life.

"It was ugly," I said, shaking my head. "I was lucky to escape alive."

Alex laughed his way to the rear of the shed. "I have something for you."

He lifted a surfboard off the rack on the wall and carried it back to me. "This one's much shorter than the other one you used, but the core is thick so it'll sit high in the water."

I had no clue what he meant, but nodded. Charli would translate later.

He laid it on the workbench and I thanked him. If I could've come up with something more heartfelt, I would've given it a shot. Alex was giving me much more than a board. He was giving me permission to stay.

He walked back and grabbed another board. "This one's for Bridget," he proudly announced. "Gabrielle wouldn't let me give it to her yesterday."

The hard line my cousin had taken was perfectly understandable. The surfboard had to be at least five feet tall. Bridget was barely eighteen inches tall.

"You're giving the baby a board?" I asked incredulously.

"No," Alex beamed. "I'm giving her a religion."

The notion slightly scared me, and I got the impression that was the reaction he was aiming for.

Raising Bridget in the Cove meant that she'd probably share Alex and Charli's kinship to the ocean – something I'd never really understood. I'd grown up with an affinity to getting good grades and learning languages.

I casually looked the board up and down, playing down the terror associated with raising a La La baby. "It might be a while before she can use it."

"Trust me," he replied knowingly. "She'll be ready in the blink of an eye."

I believed him, and I was determined not to miss a second of it. I wondered if he knew that. "Just so you know, I'm here to stay."

"Little girls are hard work, Adam," he warned. "Much harder than getting a law degree."

"I'm up for it."

He leaned across the workbench and picked up a strip of black plastic. "What do you think this is?" he asked.

"A cable tie."

"Today it's a cable tie." He waved it at me. "When you're running late on a school morning, it becomes a hair tie."

I shook my head. "I can't tie hair."

Not that it mattered at that point – Bridget had none.

"You'd be surprised what you can do. You can splice rope, right?"

I nodded. "Yeah." I'd done all the rope work on *La Coccinelle*, but I wasn't about to admit that I'd spent a whole day studying a book to learn how.

"Congratulations," he praised. "You can plait hair."

Alex's words of wisdom were hardly life altering, but I wasn't expecting much. Most of the lessons I'd learned from him were silent ones.

"That's it?" I teased. "That's the best advice you can give me?"

"Trust me, Boy Wonder," he chuckled. "You'll appreciate the skill when she goes through her mermaid phase."

June 30
Charli

Being woken by a kiss is the best feeling in the world – unless you've only been asleep twenty minutes after dealing with a fussy newborn throughout the night.

"Hey," whispered Adam. "Where's Bridget?"

"They took her to the nursery so I could sleep," I mumbled.

He swept my hair from my face, settling his hand on the side of my face. "Had a rough night?"

"Not really. You look like you did, though. Is that Alex's shirt?"

He withdrew his hand, smiling sheepishly at me. "I was led astray by the locals."

He elaborated, but the story was short. I suspect that was because he didn't remember most of it. If I'd known he was going to the pub in search of food, I would've warned him that the bride-to-be had been commandeering it every Saturday night for the past month.

"They got you smashed, didn't they?"

"I didn't even see it coming." He shuddered. "Your father had to come to my rescue."

I grimaced and smiled at the same time. "Ouch."

"It wasn't that bad," he replied. "It gave us chance to talk."

I didn't ask for details. Whatever was said didn't seem to have damaged him.

Conversation soon trailed off but it wasn't uncomfortable. I stared at him, trying to figure out how to put my thoughts into words. There was so much that we needed to discuss. Yesterday I'd been happy to go with vague promises of a great life together. I'd had other things on my mind at the time. Today was different. I wanted to know exactly how we were going to pull it together. I knew that regardless of what happened from here on, we were done bouncing back and forth. Babies don't bounce.

Perhaps predicting the heavy turn in conversation, he spoke first. "I love you so much."

"You have to say that," I said wanly. "I just had your baby."

He sat in the chair by the bed and reached for my hand. "No, you had my baby because I love you. There's a difference."

Despite the pretty spin he put on it, I couldn't shake the feeling that Adam had got caught up in the moment. Deciding to stay would've happened quickly. But I wasn't going to dwell. I was used to having him for five minutes at a time. If that was all we were meant to have, I'd deal with it. I'd done some serious growing up over the past few months. As much as I loved Adam, I no longer felt I needed him. I just wanted him. Our future was going to be decided by how much he wanted us.

Nothing was going to be decided that morning. The same nurse who had kicked him out the night before barrelled into the room and ordered him out again.

"No visitors before one," she barked. "Mothers and babies need their rest."

"But I'm not tired," I protested.

"And I just got here," Adam complained. "It took me an hour to get here."

The nurse could not be moved. "And it will probably take you an hour to get home," she replied, moving to the foot of the bed. She tucked me in so tightly that I expected to start turning blue.

"He hasn't seen the baby today," I told her, still pleading our case.

"You may pop in and see her in the nursery on the way out," she permitted.

"Gee, thanks," muttered Adam.

She pointed toward the door. "Out."

He had no choice but to go quietly, but he took his time, just to be annoying. He leaned down and kissed me. "I'll be back later," he whispered.

I threw my arms around his neck, pulling him in closer. "What time?"

"Depends," he replied, glaring at the nurse. "What time is shift change?"

"One. Now go." She pointed at the door again.

I grabbed his hand. "We're going home tomorrow, no matter what. Okay?"

I'd had enough. I had to get out of there.

He nodded, leaned down and quickly kissed me again. "Fine by me."

June 30
Adam

I wanted everything to be perfect when my girls arrived home, and I had less than twenty-fours hours to make it happen. Standing in the doorway, looking at the purple nursery, I realised that was a tall order.

My brother had done a horrible job of painting. I knew he'd done it because he'd gone to the effort of painting his name on one of the walls he'd left half finished. Even more annoying was the way he'd managed to paint over the light switch and outlets.

Repainting the nursery wasn't my only mission. I called on Gabrielle for all things Bridget-related. She seemed happy to help, but I knew I had to tread carefully where Gabrielle was concerned.

I didn't have a clue how prepared Charli was for her early arrival. Gabi swept through the cottage like a pro, taking notes.

"She needs no clothing," she told me. "I've been stockpiling clothes for months."

She threw open the closet door, showcasing a million tiny outfits all hanging neatly. Even she seemed impressed by Charli's organisation.

"So much pink," I noted.

Gabi nodded. "Charli was adamant she was having a girl. Mercifully, her hunch was right. But I kept all the receipts just in case."

There was no need to hedge bets when it came to the universe. I knew that now.

"What else do you want me to buy?" she asked, closing the closet doors.

I shrugged, clueless. "Just get whatever you think we need."

"I'll take care of it," she assured, scribbling something down on her notepad.

* * *

Once Gabrielle left, I made a start on the painting. I'd only been at it for a short while when I heard a knock at the door. Slightly annoyed by the interruption, I abandoned the painting to answer it.

It was Nicole Lawson. I didn't quite know what to say. Charlotte hadn't mentioned her since I'd been back. She didn't look terrified so I assumed they'd sorted out their differences.

"Hi." I held the door open.

"Hey," she replied, walking in. "Alex mentioned that Charli and the baby are coming home tomorrow." She set her bag on the table and glanced around. "I thought I'd stop by and see if there's anything you need."

"How are you at painting?"

She shrugged. "Competent."

"Awesome," I replied, heading down the hall. "You're hired."

* * *

I'd never spent much time with Nicole before and despite her past misdeeds, I hadn't really formed an opinion of her. The feeling wasn't mutual. Before half of the first wall was painted, I'd worked out that she didn't like me very much.

"Tell me again why you're repainting," she said. "It was only done a couple of days ago."

"Ryan did a half-assed job. I want it to be perfect."

She carelessly slapped the roller onto the wall, leading me to think her efforts weren't going to be any better than his.

"Charli's not expecting you to hang around, you know," she revealed. "Her expectations of you are low this time round."

I continued painting, refusing to appear affected. "Things are different now."

"How?"

Her interrogation irritated me. The only person I had to answer to was Charli, and possibly Alex when he was in the mood for holding my feet to the fire. I put the roller in the tray and picked up a rag to wipe my hands. "We have Bridget. That changes everything."

More specifically, it had changed me.

"No, *Charli* has Bridget," she corrected. "Charli's always going to have Bridget. You're only going to have her as long as you're a good boy. When you screw up again, you're out the door."

"I appreciate your concern, Nicole." There wasn't an ounce of sincerity in my tone. "But we don't need your input."

She abandoned the painting and stood, hands on hips. "Charli didn't want to tell you about the baby, no one did. Your brother didn't even tell you, did he?"

I now had a perfectly formed opinion of Nicole Lawson. She was a bitch.

"What's your point, Nicole?"

"The point is, no one has high hopes for you, Adam – especially Charli." She glanced around the room and sighed. "All this effort is wasted. You'll be out the door before the paint dries."

I stared at her, wringing my hands on the rag while I thought things through. I didn't want to accept her words as being anything other than ignorant and mean-spirited – but doubt was already eating away at me. If things had gone my way in the beginning, there would be no Bridget. At the time, I'd considered her to be a terrible mistake that I wanted erased. I didn't deserve a second chance. Perhaps Charli felt the same way.

"I think I'm going to finish this later," I told Nicole.

She carelessly dropped her roller back in the tray. "Fair enough."

"So you can go."

She looked at the floor and smiled. "I'm not trying to hurt your feelings, Adam. I don't really care about you. I'm just giving you a heads-up."

"Go home, Nicole."

"I've got things to do anyway." She headed for the door. "I'm going to Hobart to see the baby."

I shut her down in an instant. "Not my baby."

Gripping the doorway, she turned back to face me. "Excuse me?"

"You're not welcome there."

Her mouth straightened into a tight line. "So it's started already, huh? Charli's going to work you out, Adam. For once, she's calling the shots, not you."

I walked Nicole to the door because I wanted to make sure she actually left. I didn't want to deal with her for a second longer.

I returned to the task of painting, which wasn't necessarily a good activity for someone wrestling with the kind of thoughts that I had in my head. It gave me plenty of time to jump to every horrible conclusion imaginable.

Everything had happened so quickly that Charli and I hadn't had a chance to really talk. Every plan I'd made over the past two days was my own. I had no idea what direction she wanted to go in, and I wasn't sure that I wanted to find out.

* * *

Nurse Nasty had clocked off when I arrived back at the hospital. Bridget was back in Charli's room, sleeping peacefully in the plastic bucket. I didn't know which one of them to kiss first. Charli made the call for me, grabbing me as soon as I was in reach.

"What took you so long?" she asked, pulling me close.

Her enthusiasm sent a rush of relief through me. It wasn't the gesture of a woman with thoughts of cutting me out of the picture.

"I was told not to come back until one," I reminded her, murmuring the words against her lips.

She released her grip, freeing me to sit beside her. "What have I told you about breaking rules?" she teased.

I pretended to think.

"It's good for the soul, Adam," she reminded me.

"I'll try to remember that," I told her, twisting to check out my sleeping angel. "Can I pick her up?"

"She's your baby. I'm pretty sure you can do whatever you want to – except visit her before one."

I laughed, lifting the tiny girl out of the crib. "I can't wait to get you both out of here."

"We're good to go," said Charli. "The doctor came in this afternoon and checked her over."

"And she's okay?"

"Perfect," she beamed.

"And you're okay?"

"I'm awesome," she crowed.

"Yes, you are," I agreed, laughing.

At least she recognised it. Being delicate because she was small was just an illusion. Seeing her bring our baby into the world was the biggest show of strength I'd ever seen.

"I repainted the nursery today," I told her, looking down at the baby in my arms. "Ryan did a terrible job."

"I knew you wouldn't be happy with it. I did warn him."

"Nicole helped me out," I explained, trying to say her name pleasantly. "You never told me you were friends again."

She shrugged. "We are, but it's not the same. I thought she'd be excited to see the baby but she hasn't visited."

I could tell her feelings were hurt. I decided to come clean before Nicole had a chance to twist the story. "She had plans to come today," I admitted. "I told her not to."

"Why?"

"I don't have a lot of patience for Nicole, Charlotte," I admitted. "I don't like her."

I was half expecting her to jump to her defence, but she didn't. "Understandable, I guess."

We were quiet for a minute. It took me that long to work up to asking my next question. "You and I are good, right?" I asked vaguely.

She smiled but it wasn't right. "We have a lot to talk about, Adam."

It was hardly reassuring, but it was all I was going to get from her. I wasn't going to push the issue. There was no way I could push it without making it sound like a political campaign.

I waited until I was leaving that night before giving her the first bit of solid proof that I was all-in. I lowered Bridget into the crib and kissed her goodnight.

"I have something for you," I said, turning my attention to Charli. "Close your eyes and hold out your hand."

She smiled expectantly and did as I asked. I placed the small gift in her hand.

Charli opened her eyes and examined the glassy pink stone. I prayed she knew what it was, because at that moment I'd forgotten the spiel Floss gave me when I'd picked it out of her display cabinet earlier that day.

"Pink tourmaline," she announced. "You've been foraging for rocks, Adam?"

"Yes," I replied, relieved that she recognised it. "I thought it was about time you made a start on your nest."

She let out a quiet laugh. "Do you know anything about pink tourmaline?"

"Do you?"

Her look told me that my question was a ridiculous one. "Tourmaline directly touches the heart." She held it to her chest. "It heals emotional wounds and brings feelings of comfort and safety."

"Is it working?" My voice shook more than I was comfortable with.

"I'm not feeling wounded, Adam." She moved the rock to her lap. "I'm feeling cautious."

"Cautiously optimistic?" I asked, making her smile.

"Cautiously cautious," she clarified. "I worry that you've made a few hasty decisions lately."

I shook my head, feeling mildly hopeless. "I'm not going anywhere, Charli."

She grabbed my hand. "Neither are we."

July 1
Charli

Plenty of things in life are small. Pipers Cove is small. Kittens are small. To me, Bridget was microscopic. That made me incredibly nervous at the prospect of taking her home. Adam, on the other hand, was over the moon.

"What if I drop her?" I asked.

"You won't drop her."

"What if she cries?"

He grinned. "She's going to cry."

"What if I accidentally forget about her and leave her outside?"

"I'll bring her back in," he replied. "No big deal."

I kept waiting for someone at the hospital to come to their senses and demand to keep the baby longer. Not even the mean nurse tried stopping us.

"She should stay a bit longer," I suggested.

"How long do you think she should stay, Charlotte?" asked Adam, stuffing the last of our belongings into the overnight bag.

"She should be good to go in a year or two."

"That seems a waste of a good car seat," he teased, pointing to the baby carrier on the bed.

"I'm scared, Adam," I bleakly confessed.

He abandoned the packing in an instant, pulling me into a gentle hug. "Don't be. We're in it together." He kissed the top of my head. "You, me and Bridget."

* * *

We left the hospital armed with a heap of instructions and a tiny baby. It might have been the first time I realised that the whole Adam-and-Charli dynamic had changed. We were now Adam-Charli-and-Bridget. Extreme selfishness was a trait we'd both been guilty of in the past but something about having a child made me want to be selfless. I wanted to give her everything, and I was a hundred percent focused on doing it.

Adam kept assuring me he was in same frame of mind. I just wasn't entirely convinced. I knew he loved her, but he loved me too, and in the past that had never been enough.

"What are you thinking about?" he asked, as we drove home under a bright sky.

"Huh?"

"You seem miles away."

"What are you going to do here, Adam?" I asked. "What are your plans?"

His answer came easily, which proved he'd at least put some thought into it. "I thought I could find another boat," he suggested. "Maybe restore it over a couple of months and flip it."

"Then what?"

"Find another boat."

"And you'd be happy doing that?"

He took his eyes off the road again. "I'm already happy, Charli. You have to believe me when I tell you that."

"I do believe you," I replied. "But I want you to know that you can change your mind at any time. I'm not holding you to anything."

I saw his expression crumple, but pretended I didn't. It wasn't a look meant for me.

* * *

I had a knack for leaving things to the last minute. I was caught short by Bridget's early arrival, but Gabrielle had picked up my slack in spectacular fashion. She'd gone on a shopping spree the day before, equipping the nursery with a hundred things we needed and a hundred things I was pretty sure we didn't. Surely no one really needed an electric baby wipe warmer.

"Isn't this a bit over the top?" I asked, pressing the button to lift the lid.

Adam lowered Bridget into the crib. "Will a cup fit in there? Maybe we could use it to keep coffee warm."

I spun around, admiring the room. "She's really gone all out, hasn't she?"

"I asked her to," he admitted. "I wanted everything to be perfect."

It was definitely perfect. The lilac room was filled with top-of-the-line white nursery furniture. Mint green bedding and curtains accented it perfectly. It looked like a scene straight out of one of the baby magazines Gabrielle subscribed to.

Adam looped his arm around my middle. It wasn't a comfortable hold. When I wriggled free, he took it personally. "Are you being cautiously cautious with me, Charli?"

I felt foolish explaining. I'd never been a vain person, but at two days post-baby, I had the physique of a retired wrestler. I wasn't feeling huggable. On the plus side, I'd acquired a really great set of boobs.

Ignoring my pleas to keep a distance, he snaked his arm around me again and hauled me in close. I did my best to ignore the contrast of his hard chest against my overly soft body. Adam didn't seem fazed. "You're beautiful," he murmured. "I've never seen you look more beautiful."

"It's the boobs, isn't it?" I demanded. "I have boobs now."

Grinning errantly, he pulled at my collar and peeked down my shirt. "You do have a spectacular rack," he agreed.

* * *

I was so glad to be home. It felt as if I'd been away for weeks. It also felt as if Adam had never been away at all. While the baby slept, we pottered around the kitchen. I made tea and Adam tried to make coffee.

"How long has this been here?" he asked, waving a bag of coffee beans at me.

"Months, probably. You're the only one who drinks it."

He pulled a face and turfed it into the bin. As soon as it hit the trash, I remembered something that could've made ditching the coffee very costly. "No! Don't throw it out." I grabbed the bag. Beans tumbled everywhere as I upended it on the counter and sifted through it.

"What on earth are you doing?"

"Finding these." I waved my curly fry rings at him. "I hid them in there when they got too tight to wear."

"Nice save, Coccinelle. Do they fit now?" He took the rings from me and slipped them on my finger.

I killed the romantic gesture by flapping my hand around. "Perfect."

"Meant to be then, I'd say," he replied, kissing my ear.

I inched my head back to get a better look at him. "Kiss me like you mean it, Adam," I demanded. "I've waited a really long time."

"Like this?" he asked, pressing his warm lips to my neck.

"No," I murmured. "You can do better."

His low laugh tickled my skin as he trailed burning kisses across my jaw. When his mouth finally found mine, I was transported to a place I'd missed terribly.

Adam-and-Charli moments were spectacular but notoriously short-lived. This one was no different, but the reason why was a good one. The tiny cry of our newborn daughter filtered through the baby monitor on the bench.

July 1
Adam

I held off calling my parents until I knew Ryan was home. I expected the conversation was going to be rough and short. I needed him there to fill in the many blanks.

Bridget was settled and Charli was in the shower. I used the minute to text Ryan.

- Baby's here. A little girl.

His reply was almost instant.

- Everything OK? She's early.

- She's perfect.

- Great news. Congrats! Name?

Charli told me about the lecture he'd given about naming her. A smartass reply was inevitable.

- Serendipity Flutterlash Décarie.

I'd barely hit send before my phone beeped.

- ARE YOU OUT OF YOUR FREAKING MIND???

- Kidding. Bridget.

- Almost normal. Happy for you. Don't screw it up.

I chuckled at his comment and planned my comeback. I could've thrown him a snarky comment about the crappy decorating job he'd done on the nursery, but decided to ruin his day in a different way.

- I'm about to call Mom and Dad. Can you go over there?

He left me hanging a long time.

- On my way.

I breathed a long sigh. Ryan knew exactly the level of drama I was facing but still chose to be there for me, just as he always had.

I was still staring at my phone when Charli walked in. "What are you doing?"

"Texting Ryan." I then confessed to trying to work up the courage to call my parents. Charli looped her arms around me.

"You should sit down then," she suggested. "In my experience, tough phone calls are best handled from the kitchen floor."

She was speaking from experience. Charlotte had endured the same terror when calling Alex the day we got married. I thought back. We were blissfully happy and I'd spent a lot of time reassuring her that there was nothing to be worried about. It occurred to me that this situation was no different. Everything was perfect for us. We had a brand-new daughter and life couldn't possibly be any better. For the first time in a long time, I had no worries.

In a surge of bravery, I tapped my father's number on the screen and put in on speaker.

We stared at it while we waited for him to pick up, which seemed to take forever. "Adam." He punched out my name.

I hesitated before answering him, and then warned him that he was on speaker in the hope that he'd keep the conversation polite. Jean-Luc reverted to French and raged for a solid minute, chastising me for throwing my life away and predicting that I'd amount to nothing if I continued down the path I was on. "You'll come to regret it," he roared.

I'd spent six months living with extreme regret. I knew exactly how it felt. This wasn't it. As soon as he paused for breath, I hit him with the news of Bridget.

"A baby?" he asked, stunned.

It made no difference what I said after that. He just kept repeating the word 'baby' until he raised the attention of my mother.

I pinpointed the instant she walked into the room. I'd driven my mother to tears a few times recently. It was a sound I'd recognise anywhere.

I couldn't tell if she was as angry or just overcome with emotion. My father's mood was easy to gauge. He was livid.

I knew my father had a financial obligation to Bridget. It was up to him to ensure she was provided for, just as we all had been. The ancient pot of endless family money had a new taker. I got the impression I was supposed to be eternally grateful that my daughter would inherit an obscene amount of money when she turned eighteen, purely because she was a Décarie.

Financial provisions were the only ones he made for her. He told me that he wanted nothing to do with Bridget until I came to my senses and brought my family to New York.

"Never going to happen, Dad." I spoke calmly. The last thing I wanted was to give the impression that I was affected by his threats.

"Then we have nothing more to say." He hung up.

I stared at Charli in disbelief. My father had just cut us out of his life.

Probably as a comforting gesture, she tightened her hold on me. I gently broke away. "I'm going to go outside for a minute. I need some air."

July 1

Charli

I might not have understood the conversation, but I got the gist of it. I called out as Adam got to the door, "He'll calm down, Adam. He's just hurt."

I'd unwittingly triggered something huge. Adam went from calm to furious in a nanosecond. He marched back toward me, stopping at the edge of the kitchen bench. "Charli, I don't give a damn whether he calms down or not. He just cut us out of his life, wiped us off as if we're nothing because I won't go home. Who does that?"

I hadn't got the gist of the French tirade after all. I'd assumed Jean-Luc was pissed because he hadn't been told about Bridget.

I didn't quite know what to say. While I lived in New York I'd been on good terms with Jean-Luc, but I'd been a good, supportive wife at the time. It would be fair to assume that he wasn't quite so fond of me since I'd lured Adam away with a secret baby.

"He'll calm down." I could hear how empty my words were.

Adam started pacing around the small room. "My kid will never, ever have her worth judged by the size of her bank balance. Do you understand me?" I nodded because I thought he needed to see it. "She's not ever going to feel pressured by us. She'll go her own way." He threw out his arms in exasperation. "Whatever she wants to do. She can dig ditches for a living if that's her bliss. Got it?"

"Yes, Adam," I replied. "I've got it." I wasn't taking his rant personally. It wasn't meant for me. I was hearing all the words his father would've copped if he'd had the decency to stay on the line another few minutes.

Adam's anger faded the second he realised he was taking it out on the wrong person. He stopped pacing, looking lost and in total need of rescue.

"He cut us out." His voice was calm voice but laced with bewilderment. "Who in their right mind would deny a beautiful, perfect child because she doesn't fit in with their master plan? It's the most ridiculous…"

His voice trailed off as he reached a horrible conclusion. "Oh, my God," he muttered. "I'm just like him. I did the exact same thing."

"No, you didn't. You're here."

Nothing I could say was going to be enough to talk him through the light bulb moment that had just gone off in his head, so I said no more. I watched him walk into the cold night air, hoping that time was all he'd need to get back on track.

July 1
Adam

I drove fifty kilometres in a bid to clear my head, ending up at a gas station in Sorell. I headed inside, purchased a huge amount of the chocolate koalas I knew Charli liked, and drove fifty kilometres back. I walked in the door feeling like a total dick. Charli acted as if I'd never left.

"Hi," I said meekly.

"Hey."

I walked over and flopped beside her on the couch. "I'm sorry," I muttered contritely. "I behaved like a child."

Charli twisted and rested her legs across me. "Adam, did you ever get around to reading *Peter Pan*?"

"I did," I admitted. "Twice." She slapped her hands on her knees and I knew there was a quote coming. "Off we skip like the most heartless things in the world, which is what children are, but so attractive, and we have an entirely selfish time, and then when we have the need of special attention we nobly return for it, confident that we shall be rewarded instead of smacked."

She'd recited it in one breath, in a voice like that of a pantomime actress.

"How the heck do you know that by heart?"

She laughed, a sweet sound that I hadn't expected to hear again that night. "It's Alex's favourite quote. He used to quote it all the time, especially when I'd been tormenting him. Basically it's about being a cocky brat."

I reached for her hand. "I was; and I'm sorry."

"Not really." She was far more forgiving than I deserved. "You've got some things to work through, Boy Wonder. What your dad did was hurtful, but not honest. He lashed out because he's upset. We've all been there."

I traced the lines on her palm so I didn't have to look at her. I knew him better than that. My father never said a single word he didn't mean.

Charli took her hand away and sat up straight, resting her head on my shoulder. "I'm glad you came back. There's nothing on TV."

I let out a quiet laugh. "Are you going to reward me or smack me?"

"I'm too tired to smack you."

"How about I reward you then?" I reached into my pocket and dumped a heap of koalas onto her lap.

"Oh, Adam," she crooned, gathering them up. "My hero."

I kissed her cheek. "I would've bought you stars or diamonds, but I shopped at a gas station."

"Good luck finding diamonds at a servo," she replied, chuckling.

Charli scooped up the koalas with both hands, leaned forward and dropped them on the coffee table.

"You're not going to eat them?"

"No. I'm going to save them."

"For what?"

"For the day I can fit back into my skinny jeans," she replied. "I'll be craving a chocolate hit so badly by then, I'm going to need every one of those suckers."

I leaned closer to her and whispered in her ear. "She was a lovely lady, with a romantic mind and such a sweet mocking mouth."

Charli arched back and stared at me, brown eyes bright with surprise. "You *did* read *Peter Pan*."

"I told you. Twice." I held up two fingers. "Better late than never, right?"

"Always better late than never, Adam." She pressed her lips against mine. "Always."

July 2
Charli

By the next day I was going a bit stir crazy. Bridget was hardly a party animal. She slept and she ate.

"I think we should go for a walk," I announced.

Adam was on the couch, patting Bridget's back as she slept on his chest. "I think you should take it easy."

"I don't want to. I've just spent nine months taking it easy," I told him. "Pack your daughter up and let's get out of here."

He continued patting the baby, making no attempt to move. "Yes Ma'am."

* * *

The main street was where we ended up, which wasn't the brightest of ideas. Stopping every two minutes to show off the baby meant we didn't get very far.

"She's lovely, Charli," said Mrs Daintree, abandoning the customer at the counter to come outside. "Your father was very cagy when I asked him about her yesterday."

"Really?" I tried not to smile. "What did he say?"

Valerie pulled a sucking-lemon face. "He told me that she was present and accounted for."

Adam's laugh was cut short by the snarky glare she shot him.

"We should keep moving," I said, tactfully. "You have people waiting on you." I pointed at the post office window, namely the old lady who waiting at the counter for service.

"Yes," agreed Valerie, making no attempt to go back inside.

I saw her customer walk away from the counter. When she got to the door, I realised it was Edna Wilson. Adam recognised her too. He let out a low disgruntled groan.

Valerie pointed at the letter in Mrs Wilson's hand. "Shall I take that, Edna?"

"Thank you, dear." She handed it over and Mrs Daintree disappeared back into the post office, leaving us alone with Crazy Edna.

"How are you, Mrs Wilson?" I asked.

She ignored me, focusing her attention on the baby strapped to Adam's chest. He moved his hand to cradle her head, perhaps to hide her.

"Ah," cooed Edna, leaning in for closer look. "*Post procella phoebus.*"

She glanced up at Adam and he smiled, obviously understanding her mumbo jumbo perfectly. The last time I'd heard Edna say *procella*, she'd been in the midst of predicting doom and gloom. It bothered me to hear her say it again.

The conversation went a step further when Edna reached up and touched Adam's cheek with a shaky hand. "*Si vis amari ama,*" she mumbled. "You do deserve it. Understand?"

He nodded as if in a trance. The moment lasted an uncomfortably long time, then Crazy Edna dropped her hand, wished us well and wandered away.

I gave Adam a moment to recover before grilling him. "Since when do you speak witch?"

"It wasn't witch. It was Latin."

I hooked my arm through his and we continued our slow walk. "What does *procella* mean?"

"Storm," he replied. "She said that after the storm comes the sun."

I could no longer deny that Crazy Edna had epic skills in magic.

"The day Gabrielle and I went to her, she kept harping on about a *procella* baby," I told him. "She knew then that Bridget was a storm baby. She also said I was going to run out of time. Maybe she wasn't banking on Alouette."

He smiled and kissed the top of our baby's head. "Maybe not."

"What else did she say?"

I didn't buy the apathetic shrug he gave. Whatever Edna said had nearly reduced him to tears. I stepped in front of him, forcing him to stop. "Please tell me."

"She said, 'If you want to be loved, love.'"

Then she'd assured him he deserved it, which made me worry because I knew he thought he didn't. "Do you want to be loved, Adam?"

His smile was slight but pronounced enough to make his cheek dimple. "*Ad infinitum*, Charlotte," he murmured.

"And what does that mean?"

"For infinity."

"You *do* deserve it," I promised.

"How can you be so sure?"

"Because I say you do. Stop beating yourself up."

"I'm not sure I can forgive myself." His voice was barely there. "If you'd gone through with –"

I shifted my hand to cover his mouth. I didn't want him to finish the ugly thought. "But I didn't, Adam. She's here and she's fine. Love and you'll be loved for infinity."

It wrecked me to see him looking so tortured. I knew his regrets were huge, and the drama with his father wasn't helping.

"Everything is exactly as it should be," I asserted.

I felt his smile under my hand. I also felt our little baby wriggle, unhappy that we were crowding her space. I took a step back.

"I love you, Charli Blake," he fervently declared, patting Bridget's back to settle her.

I grabbed his free hand to get him walking again. "It's Charli Décarie to you," I replied. "And I love you too. When I can fit back into my skinny jeans again, I'll seal the deal."

* * *

We only made it a short distance when Adam stopped walking again. I was ready to give up and head back to the car. We were getting nowhere.

"Do you want to turn back?"

"No. Charli," he muttered, "what is this place?"

I looked at the old stone building that had caught his eye. "It used to be a bank back in the day – about fifty years ago," I explained. "I've only ever known it to be vacant."

Adam ran his hands along the rough stone wall. He was weirdly tactile when it came to architecture.

"Who owns it?"

"The Tates, I think." They owned the majority of real estate along the main street, derelict or not.

"Can we get in?"

I looked at the boarded windows and padlocked door. "I can get us in."

He returned the wicked smile I flashed him. "I don't doubt it for a second."

We slipped around to the back. Adam unclipped the baby sling and handed Bridget to me while he jimmied the board off one of the windows with a steel rod he found on the ground. "I'm so proud, Adam," I declared.

He was halfway through the glassless window already. "Why?"

"Our daughter's first break and enter is a bank," I replied. "It doesn't get any grander than that."

I heard his laugh echo as he walked through the building. The back door creaked open a few seconds later.

"Ladies," he announced, waving us inside.

Clearly we were the first people to go in there in years. It was a three-roomed derelict shell, but undoubtedly a bank. The old service counter still stood and there was a vault in the back room.

"I can work with this," announced Adam, turning slowly around. "Look at this old fireplace. Why would a bank need a fireplace?"

"It's an old building," I replied. "Probably a hundred years old. They all had fireplaces back then."

"There are no bars on the windows," he noted.

I shrugged. "There's no glass either. We're a trusting lot here."

He turned back to face me, grinning excitedly. "I want it."

His enthusiasm made me smile. "You can't have it. I don't think it's for sale."

"Everything has a price, Charlotte," he retorted. "Besides, Mr Tate owes me a favour. I did him a good deal on the Audi. He promised to return the favour."

I doubt he'd meant it. John Tate was as ruthless as Meredith. But there was no talking Adam out of it. And truthfully, I didn't want to talk him out of it. Renovating the old bank building was exactly the kind of project Adam needed.

* * *

The weather the next day was cool but bright. Adam made the most of the unseasonably calm ocean, talking Alex into giving him a lesson in the surf. It was remarkably generous of my father. Alex didn't usually get out of bed for a less than stellar swell, let alone venture out there to babysit a Sunday surfer like Boy Wonder.

I was enjoying my morning alone with the baby. I wasn't a natural like her father, but as the days passed my confidence grew. I had no choice but to get the hang of it. My little person was relying on me to keep her alive.

When Bridget woke for her morning feed, we headed outside to enjoy the sunshine. "Consider it a picnic, baby," I told her, sitting at the shabby old picnic table. I was concentrating on nothing other than the warm sun on my back and the tiny noises the baby made as I fed her, which is why I missed seeing Flynn cross from his yard into mine.

"Hello, Charli."

He startled me so much that I jerked Bridget in my arms. I moved to rearrange her blanket, making sure I was completely covered.

"Hi Flynn," I replied coolly.

He craned his neck, leaning forward. "Long time no see."

I couldn't work out if he was trying to get a better look at the baby or my chest. Either way, it creeped me out.

"I've been a little busy."

"So I see," he said quietly. "My Grandma told me the baby came early. Congratulations. I hope everything went well for you."

"Fine, thank you."

"And Adam's back, right?" he asked. "That's a bit of a coup. You get rid of one bloke and another turns up the next day. You must enjoy the company."

I could feel bile rising in my throat. I had no idea what he was insinuating but felt sickened by the smarmy spin he'd put on it.

"You seem to know a lot about the goings on here, Flynn," I muttered. "Perhaps you should stick to your side of the fence."

He frowned at me. "I think you and I went a little off track somewhere."

"There was no you and I," I snapped. "I don't know what you want from me."

Flynn took a step back, having the nerve to look slightly wounded. "I don't want anything. I came over here to congratulate you on the baby."

I was tired of treading lightly where Flynn Davis was concerned. I decided it was as good a time as any to lay it all out there.

"Have you been in my house while I'm not there?" I asked.

"Excuse me?"

I knew I wasn't going to get a straight answer. I studied his body language instead, which was pointless. He was nervous and fidgety on his best day.

"You heard me."

"Why the hell would I do that?"

I looked straight at him. "I have no idea. But someone's been going into my house while I'm not there."

His face darkened. "What do you take me for?"

A creepy obsessed neighbour who frightened the hell out of me. I just couldn't bring myself to say it out loud.

I rearranged my shirt under the blanket, cutting Bridget's lunch short. I stood up to leave, ignoring the fact that she'd begun to cry. "Stay away from me," I ordered.

As I passed him, he grabbed my arm. "Charli –"

It was a stupid move on his part. I went from being marginally creeped out to hysterically terrified in two seconds flat. I burst into tears. "Get away from me!"

He held both hands in the air and backed away as if he was trying to escape a cornered animal.

"Don't ever come near me or my house again," I added, rushing to the veranda.

"You're crazy," he told me. "Absolutely mental."

I carried Bridget inside and bolted the door, convinced that I wasn't the crazy one.

* * *

I'd had enough where Flynn was concerned. When Adam arrived home that afternoon, I told him everything – from the very beginning.

"What makes you think he's been coming into the house?" he asked, remarkably calmly.

I wasn't sure I had a decent answer, but I tried. I told him about windows being left open, the flowers he'd sent me and the numerous attempts he'd made at asking me out.

"I would never leave windows open," I told him. "At first I put it down to forgetfulness, but it's happened a few times."

Adam thought it through before speaking again. "Is anything missing?"

"No," I conceded. "Nothing's missing."

He stood up and carefully handed me the baby. I called out as he got to the door, "Where are you going?"

"To sort this out," he replied. "Stay here."

I worried that it wasn't going to end well. I spent the next few minutes trying to work out how much cash we had in the house in case I needed to post bail. Threatening a police officer would probably be costly. If he went a step further and belted him, I'd probably have to consider selling the baby to cover it.

July 3
Adam

Anger drove me as I marched across to the house, but by the time I stepped on to Flynn's porch, common sense kicked in and I slowed my roll.

Charli had been through a lot over the past few months. It wasn't much of a stretch to think she could have blown things out of proportion. A few windows left open hardly constituted a break and enter. She'd said it herself – nothing had been taken. And Flynn was a police officer. As smitten as he might be with my wife, breaking into her home was a little extreme.

By the time I knocked on the door, I was feeling slightly foolish.

Flynn looked less than pleased to see me. "I take it Charli sent you over here," he said sullenly.

"Look," I began. "I don't really know what's going on, but –"

He cut me off. "Nothing is going on. I went over to congratulate her on the baby and she freaked out and accused me of breaking into her house."

I nodded. "Yeah, she did."

"Has your wife always been crazy?" he asked.

"Have you always been in love with my wife?" I shot back. "Because I'm fairly sure that's why she's so sure freaked out by you."

The tables turned in an instant. The look on his face proved that Constable Creepy had just lost the upper hand.

"Charli made it very clear that she wasn't interested me. I sent her flowers once, that's it."

I stepped off the porch. "That was where you went wrong then," I taunted. "She hates getting flowers. You should've sent chocolates instead."

He called out as I walked away, "If Charli genuinely thinks there's a problem, she should make a police report."

I turned back. "Yeah, I'll keep it in mind."

"How long are you in town for?" he asked.

It was the million-dollar question that I was sick to death of hearing. I answered him anyway. "I'm here to stay, Flynn. My wife and daughter live here."

* * *

I wasn't looking forward to dealing with Charli. She truly believed that something underhanded was going on. The problem was, I didn't.

She collared me the second I walked through the door. "What did he say?"

I took her by the hand, led her to the couch and sat her down. She didn't appreciate the gesture one bit. She pulled her hand free the second she hit the cushion.

"I think you've been under a lot of pressure lately," I said gently.

"I'm not imagining things, Adam," she retorted.

"I didn't say you were." I smoothed my fingers through her hair. "I just think you might be mistaken about this."

"I don't think I am."

I wasn't going to win this one. I'd be lucky to escape the conversation unharmed. I continued trying to reason with her anyway.

"I think you should just take a breath and put things into perspective. Flynn is a police officer, Charli. Why would he risk everything by getting caught breaking into someone's house?"

She was quiet for a moment. I hoped that meant she was thinking it through. "I don't know," she conceded.

"And nothing is missing," I added. "It makes no sense."

She nodded. "Did you tell him to stay away from me?"

I relaxed a little. "Yes. I'm sure he got the message loud and clear."

"Fine." She got up. "It's over then."

* * *

John Tate wasn't an easy man to deal with but I was persistent. He'd initially refused to entertain the idea of selling us the disused bank but money talks, and I had plenty of it.

I knew I'd paid more than I should've but was still confident of making a profit when I resold it. The money didn't matter, but making it a successful project did. That was the Décarie way. I wasn't just passing time; I'd stumbled into a new career.

I managed to finalise the sale and get possession of the keys within a week. Work started straight away, meaning I'd created my own nine-to-five.

I couldn't claim to have half a clue what I was doing. I knew nothing about renovating – but I'd known nothing about boat restoration, either. On days when I was at a loss, I called on Alex for advice.

On days when Charlotte was at a loss, she called on Alex too. Not only was he a dab hand at plastering walls, he could settle a screaming baby at a hundred paces.

Gabrielle ran hot and cold, and we did our best to make allowances for that. Some days she couldn't get enough of Bridget, and other days she kept her distance. Either way, I knew that my little girl went a long way toward filling the hole in her heart until she could have a child of her own.

I could never get enough of Bridget – or her mother. Things were finally falling into place for us, and slowly but surely I was beginning to feel as if I deserved to be a part of it.

* * *

For such a little person, Bridget demanded a lot of attention. Her tiny cry was the loudest sound in the world, especially at four in the morning.

Charli sat up in bed, nursing our little girl. "I'm so tired," she whispered.

I reached across and ran my fingers along Bridget's cheek. "I know you are, but you're doing an amazing job."

316

"Do you miss sleep, Adam?"

"No," I whispered, leaning across to kiss her. "I don't miss anything."

We had trouble settling Bridget. Charli was so tired that frustrated tears soon followed. "I just need sleep. You have to fix her," she pleaded.

I lifted the baby out of her crib. "She's not broken," I said quietly. "She's just a night owl."

I carried Bridget back to the bed, switched off the lamp and leaned down and kissed her exhausted mother. "Go to sleep. I'll take her for a while."

"Where are you going?"

"I'm going to teach our daughter how to make coffee."

"Awesome," Charli mumbled. "Just what she needs."

I pulled the bedroom door closed and wandered down the hall with the mini queen of noise. The minute I started pacing the kitchen, she quietened down. "So baby, how do you take your coffee?" I wondered aloud.

I talked Bridget through the whole process of making the cup of coffee I didn't really want – in French because that was our thing. The baby girl wasn't paying attention. She was fast asleep in my arms.

I sat at the table until the first glimpses of the sun appeared over the horizon. It was so quiet that I could hear Bridget breathing. The sensible thing to do would've been to go back to bed and make the most of the peace, but I couldn't move for looking at her. The picturesque view outside wasn't even enough to draw my attention away.

I'd experienced love at first sight once before. I loved Charli from the first minute I laid eyes on her – then spent the next few years trying to get it right. Bridget was my second *coup de foudre*. It was different this time round. It was pure and uncomplicated from the start, which made me unafraid to feel it.

I loosened Bridget's blanket, freeing her little hand. I uncurled her fingers and stroked her palm with the pad of my thumb.

She wrapped her fingers around my thumb and pulled a pouty face I hadn't seen her make before. The new expression brought to light something else she'd been hiding.

Bridget had a deep dimple on her right cheek.

"Them's the breaks, baby," I whispered. "Just don't let your mama see it."

July 11
Charli

Nicole met Bridget for the first time when she was thirteen days old. When she showed up at the cottage armed with a teddy bear and an excited smile, I did my best to hide the fact that my feelings were hurt.

"Where is she?" she beamed.

"Sleeping," I replied, taking the bear from her and ushering her inside.

Nicole walked to the bassinette and peered in. "Wow. She's little, isn't she?"

"Not as tiny as she was a week ago." I turned back to the mound of washing I'd been folding.

Nicole picked up a shirt and started folding. "I'm sorry I haven't been around earlier," she said. "I've been stuck at the café most days. Alex has been taking a lot of time off lately."

It was a perfectly acceptable excuse. Alex dropped everything to come running every time I called, which was often. It hadn't occurred to me that Nicole was picking up his slack.

"It's okay. I'm glad you're here now."

She dropped the shirt on the coffee table and reached for another. "So tell me everything. What's it like?"

I glanced across at the bassinette. "It's nothing like I thought it would be, and exactly what I want. Life is good."

"Wow. That's a bold declaration, Charli," she teased. "How's Adam coping?"

I felt myself cringe at her choice of words. Bridget wasn't something we needed to cope with. She was our biggest joy; but maybe that was a secret that only parents could know.

"He's great. You know he bought the old bank building, right?"

"Yes, Jasmine told me. What's he going to do with it?"

"He's doing it up to sell it," I said proudly.

"Nice." She grinned. "I'm glad he found a little pet project. It might keep your baby-daddy here a bit longer."

I abandoned the folding to glare at her. "Why would you say something so nasty?"

"I'm sorry," she replied, insincerely. "I didn't mean anything by it. I just wonder how long he's going to be able to stick it out here. You have to admit Charli, going from studying law in New York to sanding floors in Pipers Cove is a bit of an anti-climax."

If I'd had the opportunity to defend him I would've taken it, but Adam walked in. I took a few seconds to study him. He didn't look like a man who was having trouble dealing with a slower pace of life. His jeans were tatty, his shirt was filthy, and I could smell varnish wafting off him. He looked grotty and tired, but more importantly, he looked happy – at least until he spotted Nicole parked on his couch.

"Speak of the devil," declared Nicole, less than politely. "Hi, Adam."

Adam looked far from impressed to see her. "Hey," he replied, *almost* politely.

I stayed silent, which did nothing to ease the tension in the room.

"I just came to see your pretty baby."

Adam headed into the kitchen. "Gorgeous, isn't she?" he called.

Nicole grinned at me as she replied. "She must get it from her mother. Her father's just a lowly contractor."

I whacked her with the pair of jeans I was holding, silently ordering her to pull her head in.

"Yes he is," he agreed, reappearing in the room with a bottle of water in his hand. "Great work if you can get it."

"Not a fall from grace?" she wondered.

Adam glanced at me, infinitesimally frowning. In that moment, I knew he wasn't going to let it ride.

"I'm detecting spite, Nicole," he said. "Coming from you, it's familiar, but not a good look."

Nicole dropped the unfolded shirt back on the pile. "You're detecting wrong then," she told him. "Charli's my best friend. I'm looking out for her."

"How, exactly?" he queried.

I wanted the floor to open up and swallow me. I had no idea where the ugliness had come from, or how to handle it. I just wasn't as deft at bitchiness as I used to be.

Nicole shrugged. "I just think it's a bit of a stretch to think you've managed to change your complete outlook on life in a few weeks. You didn't want a baby. Now you're trying to make out that you do. It's confusing."

Adam took a sip of water before replying. "I agree that it might seem disingenuous," he said coolly. "Almost as disingenuous as you working your way back into the fold."

Perhaps realising she'd met her match Nicole didn't bite back. Instead, she worked hard to lighten the conversation, making small talk and cooing at the baby for a few more minutes before making excuses to leave.

Adam's good mood slipped out the door with her. He disappeared to the bathroom, either to shower or get away from me – I couldn't tell which.

* * *

I was putting away the clothes when he walked into the bedroom, wearing only a pair of jeans and mussing his wet hair with a towel. I waited for him to speak.

"What's Nicole's problem, Charli?"

Nicole had been jealous of the time I spent with Adam from the very beginning. It didn't excuse her catty behaviour but it went a long way toward explaining it. Pipers Cove was a lonely place when you spent too much time alone.

"I think she's feeling a little abandoned," I replied, handing him a shirt.

"She needs to grow up."

"Maybe," I agreed.

"Why does she think I'm going to be on my way out the door at the first opportunity?"

I wondered if he thought I'd somehow incited the attack. My friendship with Nicole would probably never recover to the point where I'd confide in her. Adam needed to know that any misgivings she had about him were her own.

"I have no idea why she's running with that idea. We barely talk these days."

"It didn't seem like genuine concern to me," he grumbled. "She's trying to cause trouble."

"Don't worry about it," I said quietly. "I'll talk to her."

"If you've got a problem, talk to me," he ordered. "Not her."

Until Nicole's visit, I didn't think I had a problem in the world – and I told him so. I also told him that I didn't appreciate the attitude he was giving me.

"I'm not giving you attitude, Charli," he replied. "I'm just getting tired of having to defend my decision to stay here."

"You can't blame people for being sceptical, Adam."

He dropped the towel on the floor and followed up with a growl. "Why, Charlotte? Why can't people just accept it?"

"Because you've never wanted to stay here," I replied, raising my voice to match his. "You've never given up a single thing for me. It's really hard to believe that you've abandoned your career plans and life in New York for us. I think you got caught up in the moment when Bridget was born and decided to stay. I'm always going to be waiting for the other shoe to drop."

"Why?"

"Because it always does," I replied, scooping the towel off the floor and throwing it at him. "You've only ever been good for five minutes at a time."

He stared at me, and I realised that he wasn't angry. He was hurt. I bit my lip to stop myself apologising. I couldn't apologise for the way I felt.

"My decision to stay had nothing to do with Bridget. If I prove it to you, will you promise never to question it again?" he asked.

"Yes."

"What did you do with the paperwork the courier gave you?"

"Huh?"

"When he delivered my stuff," he elaborated. "Did he give you any paperwork?"

All of Adam's possessions had been delivered via courier a few days earlier. I still hadn't gotten around to unpacking my New York boxes. I didn't even attempt to deal with his – all twenty-two of them. I just asked the driver to stack them with the others in the spare room. Every time I opened the door, there seemed to be more boxes. I was sure they were breeding. Unpacking was an impossible task.

"I put it on top of the fridge."

I followed Adam as he stormed down to the kitchen. He grabbed the delivery receipt and handed it to me.

"Look at it."

"What am I looking at?"

"Read the date, Charlotte," he grumbled, tapping the page with his finger.

"June twenty-seventh," I replied, reading the date at the top of the page.

"Right. I asked my mother to pack everything up and ship it here on the day I left," he explained. "Why would I ship everything here if I wasn't planning to stay?"

"You wouldn't," I conceded, staring at the delivery receipt.

"Bridget was born on the twenty-ninth," he reminded me. "I knew nothing about her at the time."

A lovely feeling of contentment filtered through me. I hadn't felt it in a long time. The paper in my hand was absolute proof. Adam was exactly where he wanted to be. I had no idea why, and judging by the look on his face, he didn't either.

"Why were you so confident about coming here?" I asked. "We didn't exactly end things on a high note last time."

He looked as conflicted as I'd ever seen him. "I wasn't. I was terrified that you'd turn me away. But I had this overwhelming feeling that I needed to do it."

I wiggled my eyebrows. "Alouette."

He looped his arms around my waist, dragging me forward. The paper fell to the floor and I linked my arms tightly around his neck.

"Maybe," he conceded, focusing on my mouth as he spoke.

I inched my head back. "It's true. Alouette delivered Bridget's soul to you. You had no choice but to bring it to her." I studied his eyes closely. "Everything happens for a reason, Adam."

"I want to tell you something," he said gravely. "And it's probably going to sound crazy."

"Ooh," I teased. "I like crazy."

"I know you do. This one's all shades of crazy. It's a story of magic."

I'd never been more intrigued by anything he had to say than I was at that moment. I nodded eagerly but said nothing, fearing he'd change his mind about sharing. I listened as he explained how he'd stumbled on one of my pictures at Billet-doux – the same picture that had brought him to me three years earlier.

"I took it and hung it in the apartment. It's always been special to me. It reminded me of better times. I spent an abnormal amount of time just staring at it, Charli. I thought I was losing my mind at one point," he admitted. "I had nothing else going on in my life."

"What about school and your clerkship?"

"I graduated in May. I had an opportunity to start my clerkship early but I knocked it back."

"Why would you do that?" It was almost impossible to fathom. I'd been fighting for pole position my whole married life, always coming in second best to his career plans. Nothing had ever been able to shift his focus.

"I don't know. I feel like I just lost my way. I fell off track."

"It might be fleeting, Adam," I suggested unwillingly. "Maybe after all that studying, you just needed a break for a while."

The words tasted sour in my mouth. I didn't want Bridget and me to be his temporary down time. I didn't want him to suddenly find focus and disappear again. I wanted him to stay lost forever.

"It's permanent, Charli," he assured. "I'm sure of it."

"How? How can you be so sure?"

"Because I didn't go with the first thought. Staying in New York and seeing things through would've been the easy option, don't you think?"

I had to agree. From what I'd heard, toeing the line was always easier than going your own way – I'd just never done it.

"What was the second thought?" I asked.

"Coming back here and begging you to let us start over."

I mulled over his confession. "You graduated in May. Why did it take another month for you to get here?"

"Because second thoughts take time," he explained, winking at me, "and I'm a slow learner."

"Coming to your senses isn't magic, Adam," I said, slightly disappointed.

"I haven't got to the magical part yet." His dark blue eyes brightened as he smiled. "You said that Alouette gives you a sign. I got one. I just didn't know what it meant at the time."

Adam wasn't a believer in anything other than proven fact. La La Land was a place he visited – but he owned no real estate there and always made sure he had a return ticket to the real world. I'd told him a hundred fairytales over the past few years – and it took something as simple as a picture falling off the wall to convince him that the universe was sending him a message. I laughed at the irony.

"Don't act like I'm the crazy one," he grumbled. "If you don't believe, what hope is there in the world?"

"I believe," I insisted. "Do you believe?"

He didn't need to speak. As far as I was concerned, Alouette hadn't just given him a sign of Bridget's impending arrival. She'd drilled it into him like a brick to the head, managing to change his whole outlook in the process. "You do believe, Adam," I crooned in my best fairy-tale voice. "You do, you do."

"I'm pleading the fifth," he replied, leaning in to kiss me again.

July 13
Adam

One thing I'd learned from Charli's time in New York was that I could never take her for granted again. It was hard not to get caught up in my renovation work at the bank – I was excited by the progress I was making – but I was careful to clock off at five each day and stay away on weekends. Arriving home to a beautiful baby and her gorgeous (although sometimes strung out) mother was nothing short of a gift.

We'd somehow fallen into the pattern of a very traditional family. Charlotte was a brilliant mother, she just didn't realise it. Every now and then moments of self-doubt would creep in and turn my beautiful wife into a certifiably crazy woman. On days like that, I made sure we got out of the house and spent time together. My suggestion for this day was a trip to the city – not because she was in a crazy mood, but because I was keen to try out the new stroller Gabrielle had given us. Even Alex had been impressed by it.

"It's Italian," he'd noted, whistling in approval. "That means it's built for speed."

It seemed criminal that we hadn't yet tried it out. Bridget was nearly three weeks old. I cornered Charli while she was brushing her teeth. "We can get some lunch, go for a walk along the waterfront and show Bridget the sights," I pitched.

She saw through me in an instant. "This is about the pram, isn't it?" She narrowed her eyes. "You want to test drive the pram."

"Charlotte," I put my hand to my heart, "you wound me. All I want to do is spend quality time with my girls on this beautiful Saturday and you accuse me of having an ulterior motive."

"I'm on to you, Boy Wonder," she retorted, waving her toothbrush at me through the mirror.

"Okay, yes. I want to try out the pram." I badly mimicked her accent, and ended up sounding like my mother.

"Fine," she relented. "But I'm driving."

* * *

The big fancy stroller should've come with learner plates. We had no clue what we were doing, and the steering issues we had as we negotiated the steep Hobart streets made it obvious. With Charli at the helm, I had to make a grab for it more than once to stop our daughter from tumbling headfirst into the gutter.

"You push," she finally told me, handing over control.

I didn't complain. I was seriously fearful for Bridget's safety at that point.

We walked so far that even I eventually began to relax. "See?" I marvelled. "We're doing it. Awesome parenting."

Charli laughed at my cockiness. "Keep your eyes on the road, Boy Wonder."

We headed down a side street, circling back toward the car. The small street was lined with up-market stores and boutiques. Window shopping wasn't usually Charli's thing but something in a window caught her eye. She stopped in her tracks and I halted the stroller.

"What's wrong?"

She pointed at the window. "That's my dress."

"You want to buy it?" I asked, confused.

"No. I already own it. That's my dress."

I looked at the sign on window. Mila's Vintage Haven was a recycling boutique.

"Maybe it's just the same as your dress," I suggested.

She was shaking her head before I'd got the words out. "It can't be the same as mine. It can only *be* mine," she insisted. "It's vintage Oscar de le Renta. Even if there is more than one, it's not likely to surface in the front window of a Hobart thrift store. It's a two thousand dollar dress, Adam," she said, glancing across at me. "Your mum bought it for me." She started toward the door.

"Where are you going, Charli?"

"I'm going to ask them where they got it from."

July 13
Charli

Adam somehow manoeuvred Bridget's pram up the concrete steps and followed me inside. The woman behind the counter greeted us straight away.

"Can I help you?" she asked cheerily.

"Just looking, thanks."

As soon as the saleswoman peeked into the pram, she forgot me.

"Ooh, what a beautiful baby," she gushed.

"Thank you," replied Adam, smiling at her.

She wasn't the first woman he'd made weak at the knees. The gorgeous Décarie grin had been upgraded lately. He now possessed a killer dimpled smile plus a baby. It was a lethal combination.

Bridget and Adam were the perfect distraction. While the sales assistant was occupied with them, I pored through the racks of clothes.

I found six of my dresses. My mind started spinning in all sorts of ugly directions. I hadn't even noticed they were missing. I'd stopped looking at them the day my waistline disappeared. No one needed that kind of torture.

I'd suspected that someone had been breaking into my house for months, and had convinced myself that it was Flynn. Common sense told me that Flynn Davis had nothing to do with it. He didn't strike me a designer gown kind of guy.

"Excuse me," I called, pulling her attention away from the blue-eyed duo near the counter. "Where did you get this dress?"

I fanned out the skirt of a pink James Galanos gown.

"Oh, that one's lovely." She used the same voice she had when gushing over Bridget. "It was actually brought into the store by a lady from Sandy Bay."

Sandy Bay is one of Hobart's more exclusive suburbs. Needless to say, I knew no one from Sandy Bay.

I glanced around the shop, noticing security cameras. It brought me a little hope. I stopped short of demanding to see the footage, deciding to play my cards close to my chest instead.

"She's actually brought in quite a few dresses over the past few months," she added, walking toward the rack nearest the window.

My heart sunk when she held up a black Balenciaga dress. "This one's particularly exquisite."

It was the dress I'd given Nicole.

Speaking took huge effort. "How much are you selling it for?"

She looked at the tag. "Fifteen hundred dollars."

I shook my head sadly. "Just so you know, it's worth twice that. It's vintage Balenciaga."

Our tiny baby began to stir, giving us an excuse to leave. We walked as far as a café a few doors down. Adam ordered coffee while I fed Bridget. When he returned, I filled him in on everything, ending with the obvious. "I'm fairly sure Nicole's been stealing my dresses."

* * *

We went home straight after our pit stop. It was a quiet journey. I had nothing to say, but I suspected Adam was fighting the urge to throw a big fat told-you-so out there.

He'd made no secret of the fact that he didn't trust Nicole. I was the only fool who'd been prepared to give her the benefit of the doubt and I felt brutally angry that I'd wasted so much time defending her.

The cottage was calm and quiet. My thoughts were not. They were reserved entirely for my so-called best friend who'd spent months weaselling back into my good graces so she could rob me blind for a second time.

Adam settled Bridget into her bassinette and I slipped down to the spare room. I pushed my way through the stack of Adam's boxes to get to mine.

As soon as I sat on the floor and opened the first one, my suspicions were confirmed. It was nearly empty. I couldn't work out if I was angry or hurt. Tears won out.

Adam appeared in the doorway a few seconds later. "Are you okay?"

"I feel like such a fool," I blubbered. "I can't believe I let her screw me all over again."

Adam pushed his way through the boxes, pulling me to my feet when I was in reach. "What do you want to do?" he asked quietly.

I could only think of one thing. It involved a trip next door and a massive slab of humble pie.

* * *

Understandably, Flynn wasn't exactly thrilled to see me. He spoke to me through the screen door, refusing to invite me in – just as I'd done to him a hundred times before.

"How's the baby?" he asked.

"She's doing great."

"That's good news."

"Please let me in, Flynn. I need to talk to you."

He folded his arms tightly. "I don't think that's a wise idea, especially given how you feel about me. Perhaps you should've brought someone with you to witness the conversation."

I felt terrible. The hostility was more than warranted. I'd accused him of breaking into my home and tormenting me. I'd been vain enough to believe it was because the man had a crush on me. Clearly, Flynn Davis was over me, and had been for a while.

"Flynn, please. If you don't want to let me in, perhaps you could come to our house and talk?"

He opened the door, enough to stick his head out and see Adam's car on the driveway. It gave him confidence that there wasn't anything underhanded going on. "Okay," he relented.

The inside of Flynn's house was ridiculously neat, much like the rest of him. Not one thing was out of place. Even the newspaper on the dining room table was perfectly square.

I sat at the table. Flynn sat opposite, looking as if we were about to begin a police interrogation. I guess we were.

He sat in silence while I told him everything I knew. "The store has security cameras. If we can get hold of that footage, I'm sure I'll be able to nail her."

He nodded. "I can certainly check. If it is Nicole, are you sure you want to pursue it?"

I'd never been surer of anything in my whole life.

"Collectively, those gowns are worth thousands of dollars. They're couture. And it's not the first time she's stolen from me."

Flynn stood up, opened a drawer on the sideboard and grabbed a notebook. He sat back down and spent the next half an hour taking notes.

"I'll look into it," he promised.

"Great. Thank you," I breathed, relieved.

He walked me to the door.

As I stepped onto the porch, I took one last shot at apologising to him. "I was wrong. I'm so sorry."

"I'm a police officer, Charli. It's my job to uphold the law, not stalk spoiled little princesses who live next door."

I nodded but said nothing. The last word was his.

July 20
Adam

There was tension in my little household over the next week, and it pissed me off. Charli was on tenterhooks waiting for Flynn to come through with video evidence that Nicole was a traitorous thief. I didn't need proof. As far as I was concerned, she was one of the most despicable people I knew, and I knew some despicable people.

Mercifully, she seemed to be steering clear of us. Perhaps she'd taken everything worth stealing.

Bridget seemed to pick up on the tension. She'd had an unsettled few days and Charlotte was at her wits end. We sat at the table, half-eating breakfast while we dealt with a cranky baby.

"I need you to make her to stop crying, Adam," begged Charli, resting her elbows on the table and covering her ears.

"She's okay," I assured. "Just take a breath."

"I have to cut my hair," she babbled, confusing me.

"Is it a Samson and Delilah thing?" I teased. "Will Bridget lose her strength and stop crying if you cut your hair?"

She twisted her long blonde hair into a pile on top of her head. "I haven't washed it in two days. I haven't had time. I'm turning feral."

I bounced the baby on my shoulder in a bid to settle her. "You're the most beautiful creature I've ever laid eyes on."

"Creature?" she asked, eyes wide. "Like something out of a swamp?"

"No," I amended, trying not to smile. "You're lovely. End of story."

334

She released her grip and her hair tumbled over her shoulders, proving that lovely was an inadequate description of her. "We're married. You're legally obligated to say that."

"I don't remember studying that particular section of family law, Charlotte."

She stood to clear the table. "You must've missed it," she replied. "It's in there somewhere."

Ordinarily getting a haircut would be trivial. But I wasn't getting that vibe. Something told me that going with the first thought on this one might be a recipe for disaster. "Look, just think about it for a day or two," I suggested. "Don't rush into anything."

She dumped the dishes in the sink. "I have thought about it. My hair grew five inches while I was pregnant. If I don't like it short, I'll just get pregnant again." I couldn't be sure she was joking. "Problem solved."

That was as close as I'd ever come to dropping the baby. Bridget was not amused at my near slip. Her grizzling grew louder.

Charli came and draped a blanket over the baby. "You're going to work on the bank today, right?" she asked.

"Yeah," I replied, glancing at my watch. "I'm having all of the new windows put in today."

The look she gave me was very familiar. I guessed her question before she asked it. "Will you stay here with us instead?"

I'd been waiting a week for the glazier. I couldn't progress any further until the windows were in. Putting it off would mean another week of waiting. It was the making of a costly and aggravating delay. "Yes," I replied without hesitation.

I'd learned a few lessons on the way to becoming more like the man I wanted to be. My time was the most valuable thing I had to offer Charli and Bridget.

"What about the windows?" She was grinning as she said it. Charlotte didn't give a damn about the windows.

"I'll reschedule."

"Have I told you how much I love you today?" she asked.

"No." I grinned at her, ignoring my phone, which had started vibrating on the table. "Feel free to elaborate."

She took Bridget from me. "Answer your phone first."

I read the number and cancelled the call.

"You're not going to take it?"

"It's my father." I hadn't heard from him since he'd hung up on me. As far as I was concerned, that was the end of it. I wasn't in the mood for another screaming match.

"You're just going to ignore him?"

"He can't have it both ways, Charli," I pointed out. "He can't cut us out of his life and then call me."

"He'll calm down, Adam," she said quietly. "He's just hurt."

July 20
Charli

Jean-Luc's decision to banish us from his kingdom had seemed like a rash decision to me. It was a prime example of what happens if you go with the first thought while angry and hurt. I wanted Adam to take his call on the off-chance that he'd calmed down and thought it through.

Adam tried to play it down, but it had rattled him. When he left the room, I grabbed his phone and scrolled through his endless contact list, searching for his father's email address. It took forever. Adam knew a *lot* of people. My contact list consisted of ten numbers, and Alex was listed twice. I transferred the address to my phone, attached a few photos of Bridget and emailed them to her grandfather.

All I could do then was wait and hope that my meddling didn't backfire.

* * *

Once Bridget settled, I reconsidered my plan of keeping Adam holed up with us. He didn't exactly try talking me around. He was almost smiling as he pulled on his boots. "If you need me to come home, just call me," he instructed. Adam pulled me into his arms and planted a firm kiss on my lips before making a bolt for freedom. He swung the front door open just as Flynn was about to knock. It was the first time I'd ever been pleased to see him.

"Are you on your way out?" asked Flynn. "I can come back later."

I'd been waiting a week for him to get back to me about the theft of my dresses. He wasn't going anywhere.

"No, stay," Adam wisely replied, inviting him inside.

Flynn came bearing good news. He'd gone to the boutique and managed to get hold of the surveillance footage. As suspected, the well-to-do lady from Sandy Bay was none other than Nicole Lawson.

I was gutted but not surprised. My usual modus operandi would've involved plotting her demise in my head, but this time I wanted to see her receive a more traditional punishment. I was prepared to let Flynn handle it.

"So what happens now?" asked Adam.

"If you press charges, I'll go and pick her up now," replied Flynn.

I didn't want him to arrest her at her mother's house. There was only so much poor Carol could bear. She was going to have plenty of opportunity to be embarrassed and humiliated in the coming days.

"Can you pick her up here instead?" I asked. "I'll call and see if she'll come over tomorrow."

Adam frowned, clearly unhappy with my plan. "I don't know if that's a good idea, Charlotte."

"She's not violent, Adam. She's just a low-down dirty thief. I want to be there when she gets what's coming to her."

It wasn't my usual game plan. My acts of revenge were usually carried out on the sly, and were so perfectly executed that there was no need to hang around to see the fallout. I'd decided to take a step back this time. Nicole was playing in the big leagues now. She deserved to be punished at the same level.

* * *

For once my lack of sleep had nothing to do with the baby. I lay awake for hours that night, unfairly weighed down by thoughts of Nicole's epic betrayal.

Adam was fast asleep and perfectly still, which blew my mind. I'd only ever known him to toss and turn all night, no matter how exhausted he was. I spent a long time just staring at him, first to make sure he wasn't dead, then to admire how freaking perfect he looked.

I'd gone through some huge changes lately but I'd had the benefit of time to get used to them. Boy Wonder's life had spun in a completely new direction in a matter of weeks. Sometimes it was easy to forget that, mainly because he'd handled it so effortlessly. I no longer worried that his presence was temporary or coerced. Adam was calm, content, and sleeping peacefully for the first time in his life.

* * *

I felt no better by morning. Bridget was having another cranky episode. Perhaps she knew Nicole was on her way over.

I called her early, making up a lie about needing her to drop off some milk on her way to work. "I'd really appreciate it," I told her. "It's a mission to get the baby out of the house to go shopping."

"No worries," she replied. "I'll let Alex know I'm going to be a bit late."

A couple of years late with a bit of luck, I didn't reply.

The next half hour dragged. I was in the kitchen making up a bottle while Adam paced the lounge with Bridget in his arms, trying to settle her – or at least to buy time until her bottle was ready. This charming domestic scene was ruined by the arrival of my ex BFF. She let herself in, which I found very ironic.

"Hey," she greeted, making a beeline for Adam and Bridget. "Can I hold her?"

Adam glanced at me and I nodded stiffly. He reluctantly handed her the baby. Bridget kept crying and Nicole paced the room trying to calm her. It took all I had not to march over and rip her from her arms.

"She's so cute," she cooed. She was probably totting up how much she could sell her for. I palmed the baby's bottle to Adam and slipped down to the bedroom to call Flynn.

"She's here now," I whispered.

"Okay. Just keep her there," he replied. "I'll be there in five minutes."

It was a long five minutes. I didn't want the lying rat anywhere near my family. Adam clearly felt the same way. By the time I returned to the room, Bridget was back in his arms sucking on her bottle.

Flynn finally arrived and I rushed to let him in. Nicole looked understandably stunned. As far as she knew, I was terrified of Flynn, and no one had encouraged that more than her.

Flynn walked straight to Nicole. There was no greeting or kind words. "Nicole Lawson, I'm arresting you on suspicion of burglary and handling stolen goods."

"What's this about?" she whimpered. "Charli?"

I couldn't find my voice, but Adam had no problem bringing her up to speed. "You've been stealing from us, Nicole," he said flatly. "Did you really think we wouldn't find out?"

Her expression changed from bewilderment to fury in a flash. "You've got it all wrong," she shouted.

Flynn spun her and snapped cuffs on her. I was amazed at how quickly he did it. So was Nicole. By the time she'd started resisting his hold, it was too late. She was trussed up like a true crook.

She turned back to face me. "Tell him it's a mistake," she begged.

A small part of me wished I could. It was the part of me that remembered us as eight-year-old girls lying in the sand dunes planning our travel adventures. Those girls were long gone.

"I found my dresses at a boutique in Hobart, Nic," I muttered. "How could you do that?"

"I would never do something like that," she protested. She sounded believable but her expression gave her away. So did the video evidence.

"I'm not just going to forget about it this time."

She dropped the innocent act dizzyingly quickly. Perhaps she knew it was hopeless. "It was a handful of dresses," she spat. "You didn't even miss them."

"What did you do with the money?" I asked out of curiosity. She hadn't been flashing cash around.

"I didn't do anything!" she screamed.

"Get out of my house, Nicole," said Adam, perfectly calmly. He sounded more bored than outraged. "You're pathetic."

"I'm pathetic? You think I'm pathetic?" She spoke with pure contempt. "Your whole life is pathetic, Adam. You'll realise it sooner or later. A year or two in this town will destroy you. You should take your kid and make a run for it while you can. That's what you do best, right?"

"Why are you so bitter and twisted?" asked Adam.

I was sure his calm voice was riling Nicole even more. Her next words were spat out with pure hatred. "Go to hell!"

"What did I ever do to you, Nic?" I asked quietly.

Nicole smirked at me. "I've told you before, Charli. Not everything is about you." She shifted her venomous glare to Adam. "You'll realise that when you're left holding the baby he never wanted."

"Give up, Nicole," murmured Adam. "You don't even sound convincing."

Flynn picked that moment to lead her out of the house. Our tiny cottage fell silent. All I could hear was Bridget making tiny little mewls as she drained her bottle.

"Charlotte, I will never leave you or Bridget again," Adam promised.

"I know," I whispered.

He leaned across and kissed the top of my head. "*Ad infinitum.*"

"We're good, Adam," I assured. "For infinity."

Nicole's rant should've reduced me to tears but it didn't. Jealousy and spite had been driving her for a long time – probably years. I had no idea that she'd been so resentful toward me, but I could understand it. I was the lucky one. I'd stumbled into a life I didn't even know I wanted. I had more than I could ever have hoped for – and she hadn't damaged it at all, despite her best efforts.

* * *

Nicole Lawson didn't make bail. She was remanded in custody awaiting her court appearance because, unbeknown to everyone, she was on probation at the time of her stealing spree. It turned out that she'd been busted in

Queensland the year before for passing bad cheques that she'd stolen from some other sucker. I no longer believed any of the sob story she'd fed me. I had no idea if she'd really made it to Fiji or just stayed on the mainland wreaking havoc. It made me wonder if I'd ever truly known her at all.

Alex was horrified when he heard what had happened, especially when I came clean about the fate of the boat money she'd skipped town with three years earlier.

I summoned him to the cottage to break the news.

"Why didn't you tell me?" he asked, sounding more hurt than angry.

My answer came easily. "You wouldn't have let me go with Mitchell if you'd known I was broke."

He blinked at me – too many times. "You're right," he said finally. "I wouldn't have."

I pointed at the tiny baby in his arms. "And if I hadn't gone, I wouldn't have gone to Adam and you wouldn't be holding that little girl. No lying, thieving Nicole, no Bridget."

Alex looked down at granddaughter he wasn't even old enough to have. "Your logic is skewed, Charlotte."

"And you're only just realising this?" I asked, trying to raise a smile out of him.

He glanced up at me, still looking deadly serious. "You're a good girl. I'm very proud of you."

It wasn't like Alex to be so sappy, but I let him have his moment. I understood his mindset. Nicole and I had been joined at the hip since kindergarten. I hadn't always known she was shady, but knew I sometimes was. Staying on the good side hadn't always been easy for me. Mercifully, Alex had reined me in and Adam had held me there.

"You did good, Dad," I praised, albeit jokingly.

His expression didn't waver. "Thank you," he whispered.

* * *

The whole town was buzzing at the news of Nicole's arrest. My father never usually surrendered to gossip but surprisingly, he had no qualms about setting people straight where Nicole was concerned. If anyone asked him, he told them everything he knew.

I tried to put the whole sorry saga behind me. I'd already wasted too much time thinking about it. Laying low meant I didn't have to deal with anyone. Spending time at home with Bridget wasn't a chore, especially now she was back to her sunny self.

Having a baby was an adventure far different from the one I thought I wanted. Nothing dulled the thrill of seeing her do something new or unexpected, which seemed to happen daily. Life was good. The only thing I wished for was more hours in the day. If I'd had them, I would've spent them washing my hair.

I'd taken Adam's advice and held off getting it cut for a few days, and was now more determined than ever to do the deed. Fearing he'd try talking me out of it, I didn't mention my plans. His mind was elsewhere, anyway. His windows were in, meaning he'd moved on to phase two of the restoration. He'd left the cottage that morning babbling something about crown moulding.

I called on Gabrielle for moral support.

"Are you sure you don't want to go to the city and get it done?" she asked as we walked down the main street. "We'll find a nice salon."

"We have two here," I reminded. "One of them should be able to get it right."

The Parisienne halted the pram and put on the brake. I didn't even know the thing had a brake.

"So which will it be, Charli?" she asked, staring in the direction of the salons further down the road. I could hear the smile in her voice.

My choices were limited to say the least but I had no trouble deciding. I wasn't prepared to face Carol Lawson.

According to Alex, she hadn't handled Nicole's shenanigans well. She'd had the nerve to front up to him at the café, screaming about *his* daughter's lack of compassion. Alex gently reminded her that her daughter was a no-good, sneaky thief who deserved no compassion. I suspect he got the last word in.

"I'm going to let Jasmine cut it," I told her.

"Are you mad?" gasped Gabi.

I grabbed the handle of the pram, kicked off the brake as if I knew it was there all along, and steered it toward The Best Salon In The Cove. "It's only hair, Gabs. What's the worst that can happen?"

"I suspect we are about to find out," she replied.

The only person more shocked by my choice of stylists than Gabrielle was Jasmine. "Are you sure you want me to do it?" she asked, furiously fluttering her caterpillar lashes at me.

I wasn't brimming with confidence but I forged ahead. "Of course."

I couldn't look in the mirror as she cut. I just focused on the long blonde hair piling up on the floor beneath me. After what seemed an eternity, Jasmine spun my chair around to face Gabrielle.

"Ta-daa!" she crooned.

Gabrielle's hold on Bridget seemed to falter.

"Please don't drop her," I whispered. "Adam would kill me."

"What do you think?" asked Jasmine. She didn't give Gabrielle time to respond. She pinched at wisps of my new fringe and continued her nervous babble. "I think it's pretty. All she has to do now is drop a few kilos and she'll be gorgeous again."

I ignored her almost-compliment and focused on Gabrielle's expression, which finally shifted into a warm smile that reassured me just enough to keep me from bolting out of the salon.

"A yummy mummy," she praised, making it sound weird purely because of her accent.

I put my hand on my head, feeling the strange sensation of having shoulder-length hair for the first time in my life.

Jasmine spun me back to face the mirror. "Well?" she asked.

I deliberated for a long moment.

"Are you going to cry?" she asked, sounding worried. "I can order in some hair extensions if you don't like it."

I shook my head, trying to hide the fact that I was nearly in tears. I didn't hate the haircut. It was just a bigger deal than I'd expected it to be.

"It's great," I mumbled. "Thank you."

* * *

Gabrielle and I parted company outside. She had an art class to teach and I needed to go home, have a good cry about my haircut and get it out of my system before Adam got home. He hadn't been convinced that it was a good idea in the first place, and witnessing a meltdown would confirm it. I put Bridget down for a nap, had a good sook and managed to pull myself together.

Everything was fine until I got a phone call from Jean-Luc. I stared at his name flashing on my phone for a long time before working up the courage to answer it.

I was feeding Bridget at the time. I was convinced she could feel my heart thumping through my chest.

"Hello."

"Good afternoon, Charli." His formal tone and diction did nothing to calm me. "How are you?"

I answered his generic question with and equally generic response – then got down to business and asked why he was calling.

I hoped to hear that he'd had a change of heart regarding the hard line he'd taken with Adam, believing there was no way he wouldn't have melted at the sight of his pretty granddaughter in the pictures I'd emailed him.

But his call had nothing to do with Bridget. His focus was solely on his errant youngest son – and I couldn't deny that what he had to say was very enlightening.

I knew Adam had blown off his clerkship. What I didn't know was that he'd blown off sitting the bar exam too.

"He never told me," I admitted.

"I suspected as much," he replied gruffly.

It was almost maddening to think that our lives together had been put on the back burner time and time again for something he'd never actually managed to complete.

I looked at the baby in my arms and gently ran my fingertips across her head. "Why are you telling me this?"

"Because I want you to talk some sense into him," he replied. "You seem to be the only one he listens to lately."

"What are you asking me to do, exactly?"

I didn't give him a chance to explain. Bridget began to fuss. I told Jean-Luc to hold on and set the phone down while I repositioned the baby.

"Are you still there?" I asked, bringing the phone back to my ear.

"Yes," he said after a long pause. "Is that the baby I can hear?"

The hard Décarie shell cracked – just a little. It was spectacular.

"Yes," I explained, "I just had to swap boobs. She's impatient."

"Oh, I see," he stammered.

The mention of boobs fell into the too-much-information category. I didn't care. As far as Jean-Luc was concerned, Bridget's existence was in the too-much-information category.

After a long silence, he cleared his throat and went back to laying out his master plan. Just a few minutes later I found myself agreeing to something I never thought I would.

"It's for the best, Charli," he assured me.

"I know."

I ended the call feeling uneasy. Bridget didn't seem to pick up on my stress. She was milk drunk and fast asleep. I was glad. It meant she didn't hear me when I told her that we were going to have to let her father go.

July 24
Adam

As soon as I walked through the door, I knew something was going on. Charli stood in the centre of the room rocking Bridget in her arms. It didn't seem like a soothing gesture, more like a nervous one. Perhaps that's why I didn't venture much further than the doorway.

"You've had your hair cut," I noted, wondering if that was the root of the tension. "It looks great."

I wasn't just trying to be nice. She looked gorgeous, but it had little to do with the shorter hair. I was distracted by her beautiful form. She was wearing a blue dress that I vaguely remembered from her New York days. The way the skirt flowed around her legs as she stood rocking our child practically set me on fire.

"Thank you. I'm not sure if I like or not."

I kicked my boots off at the door and hung my coat on the hook. "Well, if you want me to knock you up again so it grows back faster, just say the word. I'm game if you are."

She laughed, but nothing about it sounded genuine. Something was going on. I just had to figure out what it was.

I walked over to her, leaned down and kissed her forehead. It was the best I could do considering I was covered in dust. I held off touching Bridget but noticed that she was dressed to the nines too.

"Wow. Both of my girls have gone all out tonight," I said, peering down at her. "She has no hair, Charlotte. How did you manage to get the bow to stay on her head?"

She grinned, more genuinely. "Blu Tack," she replied. "I couldn't find any glue."

* * *

Pretty outfits weren't all they had going on that night. Charli had cooked dinner. It was a sure-fire sign that something was in the wind.

I managed to hold off quizzing her until we were at the table. "What are you up to?" I asked suspiciously.

Charli jumped up as if the question had freed her to confess. "I have something for you," she blurted.

She headed to the kitchen and snatched an envelope off the top of the fridge, her makeshift filing cabinet.

"Good something or bad something?" I took it from her.

"Just read it."

It was an airline ticket. *One* airline ticket.

"I want you to go back to New York. You leave tomorrow."

"Why, Charli?"

My expression must have looked dire because her answer came at warp speed. "I want you to sit your bar exam. If you go tomorrow, you'll make it in time. You can only sit it –"

"Twice a year. Yes, I know." I folded the ticket and dropped it on the table.

"I don't want you to miss it," she replied. "If you don't see this through, all the angst and separation we've been through has been for nothing."

"There's no need for it, Charli. I'm happy here."

"How do you know you're not going to want to go back to it some day?" she asked, sounding frustrated. "At least keep your options open."

I stared at the ticket.

Charli wrapped her arms around my neck from behind. "Please do this."

I slid my chair back and pulled her onto my lap. "You've been speaking to my dad, haven't you?" It was a redundant question. She couldn't have known about the exam otherwise.

She nodded, twisting a button on my shirt so she didn't have to look at me. "It would mean a lot to him."

"I'm not going to fly half way around the world and sit a two-day exam to please him, Charlotte. I've spent too much of my life trying to please him."

"Don't do it for him then." She shrugged. "Do it for yourself."

Nothing about leaving Charli and Bridget seemed like a good idea, but I couldn't deny that there was a small part of me that wanted to pass the bar and end my years of study properly.

I stared at the ticket and deliberated. "You'll be okay for a week without me?"

"We'll manage."

I leaned forward and kissed her before resting my forehead against hers. "I don't like who I am without you," I whispered. "That guy from New York is an ass."

She put her hand to my face, predictably poking my cheek with her thumb. "So, don't be him. Go back, wrap him up and come home to us."

July 26
Charli

Besides sitting the bar exam, a chance to make peace with his father could only have been a good thing. Both men were stubborn but this was a disagreement that Jean-Luc wasn't going to win. For once, Adam was following his heart instead of his over-educated private school mind.

Fiona was in Adam's corner, despite the fact he'd ignored her pleas to ship his family back to New York. She called me every day, but I suspect Jean-Luc knew nothing about it. The queen gave up on the idea of Bridget being raised caged instead of free-range remarkably early. I guess Ryan had something to do with talking her round – she'd once referred to moon ducks when wailing about our settlement in the boondocks.

She'd also stopped threatening to visit. No amount of planning on my part could prepare for a visit from the queen. Pipers Cove was definitely not Fiona Décarie's scene. I could picture Jasmine Tate cornering her on the main street to give her fashion advice.

Confident that Adam would sort out his differences with his father, I made the promise of visiting her instead, when Bridget was a little bigger and able to travel. It was a compromise I was happy to make. Occasional jaunts to Manhattan weren't going to kill me. I was a hundred percent confident that Pipers Cove was where Adam wanted to be. If that changed in the future, we'd work it out together.

* * *

A couple of days after Adam left I found my feet. The house was almost in order and Bridget was sleeping. For the first time since she'd been home, I was able to pick up my camera, slip outside and take some pictures.

I wheeled the pram onto the veranda so I could keep an eye on her. It probably wasn't the best day to have the baby outside. There was a dark sky moving in from the east. I hoped the little Cove wasn't about to cop another pounding from the elements. The clean-up from the last one had only just finished.

I loved the squally winds. The bed sheets, towels and baby blankets hanging on the line were the perfect muse. I stood in the yard snapping away at the linens flapping wildly. As the wind picked up, so did the clothes.

I was about to move to a different vantage point when something came into sight through the viewfinder.

My blood froze in my veins.

Ethan Williams stood on the porch, holding my daughter.

I glanced toward Flynn's house. His patrol car wasn't on the driveway, which obviously wasn't good. I was on my own.

I had no idea what Ethan wanted. I wondered if he was looking for Nicole. Perhaps he didn't know that she was punching out numberplates in jail.

I walked to the veranda, doing my level best to play it cool.

"Ethan. How are you?"

"I'm alright. Your baby was crying."

That was a lie. She was still sleeping, despite the fact that he'd taken her blanket off her.

Bridget was within reach but I decided against making a grab for her. I didn't know what he was capable of. Nicole had told me some horrific stories, but I had no clue whether any of them were true. She was hardly a reliable source.

"We have to get her inside," I said. "It's too cold for her out here."

He gave an upward nod toward the door as if he was giving me permission, but didn't hand me the baby. I breathed a silent sigh of relief when he followed me in.

All I wanted to do was get Bridget away from him. I didn't care what happened after that. I grabbed a blanket off the couch and held it out. Bridget wriggled in his arms, letting out a tiny little mewl that seemed to scare him. Ethan handed her over and I wrapped her up in record time. If ever there was a moment that I was truly in danger of dropping her, that was it. I gently laid her back in the bassinette and turned back to Ethan.

"Why are you here? We haven't seen you in a long time." I made it sound like a casual, friendly question but my heart was in danger of exploding right out of my chest.

A grin crossed his face. "I've been here for a while. I keep visiting you but you're never in."

Although vague, his comment answered a hundred questions I'd had burning at me for days. I'd never understood why Nicole got into the cottage by jemmying windows. She didn't need to have me out of the house to steal my dresses. She probably could've bagged them up while I watched and I wouldn't have noticed.

"*You've* been the one breaking into my house?"

"So many freaking times, Charli." He sounded put out, as if I'd made him burglarise my home over and over.

"You have great taste in clothing. You took all the best dresses."

"I didn't take the bloody dresses." He grimaced. "That was all Nicole."

I wasn't surprised that she'd rated a mention. It didn't take a genius to work out that she was probably at the root of things.

"So what did you take?" I asked, trying to sound relaxed.

He took a step closer to the bassinette and I moved to block him.

"I never found what I was looking for. That's why I'm here now."

"So, what do you want?"

Ethan pointed to my left hand. "Nicole reckons that ring is worth twenty grand."

I glanced at my curly fry rings. "At least," I muttered foolishly.

He shrugged. "So, hand it over and I'll leave. You won't ever see me again."

As if! I'd mellowed lately, but not that much.

"What's the plan, Ethan?" I hissed out the question.

I wasn't expecting him to tell me anything. Nicole had given us no explanation whatsoever. I realised that was because she was the smarter of the two. Ethan laid out the entire plan, which turned out to be as moronic as he was.

Nicole had come up with the bright idea of stealing my rings the second she'd laid eyes on them.

Her whole sob story about being used and abused by Ethan was a big fat lie. They'd never even been apart. Nicole had no choice but to come back to the Cove. Part of her probation conditions from Queensland was that she lived with her mother, which only proved that Carol had known what a wretch she was all along. Ethan had been lying low at a doss house in Sorrell, killing time until her probation was over. I suppose her getting arrested put a dampener on things.

All the day trips to Sorrell to take care of her bogus restraining order issues were a crock. When she wasn't checking in with her probation officer, she was meeting Ethan, whose only job for the last six months was to steal my wedding rings.

How frustrating it must've been to spend months searching my house and coming up empty each time. I wanted to tell him what a dick he was, but thought better of it. I don't think he would've appreciated hearing it.

"We needed money," he explained. "That's why she sold your clothes." Nicole Lawson wasn't a refined fashionista. She wouldn't have had a clue about their worth until I gave her the Balenciaga dress. "I couldn't believe they were worth so much," he continued. "You should be ashamed of yourself."

Pot. Kettle. Black.

"How do you figure that?" I asked sourly.

"You're the original earth child, Charli. You used to be all about living simply and freely. I was really surprised to hear that you turned out just like every other girl in this town, knocked up and married before your time. You just have a bigger bank balance than the rest, that's all."

"And I'm supposed to just give some of it to you?"

"Consider it sharing the love," he suggested. "I still like to live simply and freely."

It didn't sound like a very simple life. The pressure of being as crooked and underhanded as Nicole and Ethan must've been enormous.

"Nicole's going to do time, Ethan," I warned. "She won't get out of it this time."

He shrugged. "I'll go on without her."

There truly was no honour among thieves. I was actually a little appalled.

Ethan reached toward me and I instinctively flinched. Then I realised he wasn't reaching for me. He leaned down and stroked Bridget's head. "Just hand the ring over and I'll go," he said quietly.

I realised that there was something odd about his tone. He didn't sound menacing. He sounded tired.

"You're stuck without her, aren't you? She's gone and you're still stuck here."

"I just want the ring, Charli," he replied, dodging the question. "Then I'll leave."

I didn't have a clue what to do, but I wasn't going to just give in. Ethan Williams wasn't getting another thing from me.

"Come outside and I'll give it to you," I told him.

He didn't question why. He just followed me outside. I wasn't scared of Ethan, I just didn't want his grubby paws anywhere near my daughter.

As soon as we were both outside, I took a quick step back and pulled the door shut, locking Bridget inside. Ethan had been in my house plenty of times, never once going through the front door. The ancient old windows slid open with ease. If he wanted to get back in to her, it wouldn't be hard – but at least I'd slowed him down.

Ethan didn't seem to notice my strategy. He gestured with his fingers. "Now, Charli."

"Are you going to fight me for them?" I asked. "Rough me up and make me hand them over?"

Ethan actually seemed a little revolted. "I don't hit girls."

"Not what I heard," I taunted. "Nicole said you were pretty vicious to her."

He glared at me, aghast. "Is that what she told you?"

I nodded. "She told me plenty of things."

And I was beginning to realise that very few of them were true. Ethan wasn't the brute she'd made him out to be. He was just desperate, and had made the mistake of putting too much faith in her. Somewhere along the line, the simple plan of travelling the world had been tainted by greed, making the easy life not so easy. I almost felt pity for him.

I reluctantly twisted the rings off my fingers, pretending they were a tight fit. He held out a hand in anticipation.

Stupidity often dictates my actions. It's been that way my whole life. It's the only excuse I can come up with to explain my next move. I drew my hand back and threw the rings as far as I could into the garden. They landed somewhere in the mass of flowery bushes at the edge of the lawn.

"You want them, you find them." I said, dusting my hands as if it was a job well done.

Ethan looked across at the garden before turning back to me. "Well, that was a dick move." He spoke as if he couldn't believe I'd done it. He also looked completely beaten.

"Not from where I'm standing," I retorted.

He sat on the edge of the step, dropped his head and ran his hands over his head. Game over.

"I just want to get out of here, Charli," he muttered.

I sat beside him. "Then what?"

"I just want to be free and travel. I haven't felt free in a long time. Don't you miss it?"

It was the first time I'd really thought about it. I realised that I didn't miss anything. My dreams weren't unfulfilled. They'd just changed – so gradually that I hadn't even noticed it happening. Wanderlust was always going to be embedded in my soul, but for now I just wanted to settle and build a cosy nest of rocks.

"I'm happy here," I told him.

He looked out at the yard, shaking his head. "Nothing turned out like we planned."

"That's because your plans suck," I told him.

"Nicole made it sound pretty simple," he replied, glancing across at me for only a second.

"You love her don't you?" I asked.

He gave a twisted smile. "Look where it got me."

Love makes us do all sorts of unreasonable things. I didn't think for a second that Ethan was an innocent victim, but I knew things had gone terribly awry for him.

"Nic told me horrible stories about you. She sold you out at every opportunity," I muttered. "She's no good, Ethan." I stopped short of telling him he could do better. I didn't think he could.

"She's paying for it now, I guess."

"Do you have a criminal record too?" I was curious.

He shook his head. "Not so far. I'm sure Nicole will eventually sell me out over the boat money. I'll have to cop to that one probably."

As if on cue, Flynn Davis's car pulled onto the driveway next door. Ethan's body went rigid. I could almost feel his panic. Flynn seemed to sense something wasn't quite right too. He called out to me as he got out. "Okay, Charli?"

I kept my eyes on Flynn but could feel Ethan's nervous glare boring into the side of my head.

"Fine, thanks," I replied cheerily. "How are you?"

He nodded and kept walking toward his porch. "Good, thank you."

Ethan didn't say anything until Flynn was out of sight. "Why didn't you call him over?"

"Why would I?" I asked. "Do I need police assistance?"

After a long pause, he shook his head. "No."

"You're a dick, Ethan. I've always thought that about you," I told him, taking my phone out of my pocket. "Which is why doing this makes absolutely no sense."

"Doing what?" he asked, confused.

I tapped away at my phone, leaving him hanging for a long time before replying. "I'm booking you a one-way ticket to a new life," I said finally.

"Where?" he asked incredulously.

"Kaimte. Mitchell is there," I explained. "Go to him, stay with him and learn how to be a decent person."

"Why would you do that for me?"

I wasn't sure I knew. We'd all grown up together, and most of us had taken wrong turns at some point. Some of us lost our way, some found our way back. I saw it as giving Ethan a chance to find his way back. My actual explanation was much simpler and far less maudlin.

"Because I'm not a dick," I said. "Your flight to Melbourne is at seven with a connection to Cape Town at ten. Don't miss the plane and don't come back here. Deal?"

"Yes." he choked. "Thank you."

"Don't thank me," I warned him. "Mitchell is going to kick your arse."

* * *

Ethan left the cottage leaving me feeling almost glad that he'd come. He'd filled me in on many blanks regarding Nicole, which somehow brought me closure. It meant I no longer had to waste another minute of my life thinking about her. I doubted she was feeling the same level of peace. I liked to believe she'd spent a lot of time thinking about me over the past few weeks.

The downside to foiling his robbery attempt was the fact that I now had thousands of dollars' worth of diamonds lost in my garden. I wasn't worried at first, but when I hadn't found them by the next day, I began to panic.

I roped Alex into helping me search when he turned up that morning to mow the lawn.

"Tell me again how you managed to lose them?" he asked, staring at the mass of flowery bushes.

I managed to tell my lie with a straight face. "They fell off."

"Both of them?"

"Yes." I pointed to where I thought they were. "They landed there somewhere."

His frown grew more concentrated as he thought it through. "And you didn't think to pick them up at the time – you know, when they fell off?"

I abandoned the stupid play at innocence. "Look, please just help me find them. Adam gets home in a few days and I don't want him to know."

Alex let out a hard laugh. "I think Norm has a metal detector. I'll see if I can borrow it."

"Best. Dad. Ever," I breathed. "Thank you."

* * *

Alex returned a short while later armed with Norm's metal detector and the Parisienne. Gabrielle fussed with Bridget while I oversaw the mining expedition in the garden. I gave up after half an hour and joined Gabi and the baby on the veranda. Alex persevered, not even a little bit discouraged by the fact that all he'd managed to find was some rusty nails and a ten cent piece.

"Adam is home soon isn't he?" asked Gabrielle, pulling my attention from the beeping detector being waved through the garden.

"Yeah. I can't wait."

"Bridget will be excited to have her daddy back," she said, speaking down to the baby stretched across her lap.

"She will be," I agreed.

Dealing with Gabrielle was tricky. She loved hanging out with Bridget but there was always an underlying sadness. I hadn't discussed her baby issues with her for a long time. For some reason, I chose that moment to be brave and ask her about it.

"Alex has given up on the idea," she said quietly, "but I haven't."

I looked at Alex, deliberating. I knew something that might make her rethink his stance. My father wasn't one for deep and meaningful conversations and he was notoriously private. It wasn't up to me to tell her anything he hadn't chosen to share with her, but I had a big mouth and I couldn't help myself.

"Alex hasn't given up."

She hunched forward and lifted Bridget up, cradling her against her shoulder. "What do you mean?"

"He reburied my box." She looked at me, puzzled. "My box of wishes. I didn't spend them. I would've been happy to thank my lucky stars and chuck the shells back in the ocean but Alex took the box and reburied it in your garden."

She shook her head. "It was a box of shells, Charli. He was humouring you."

"No, Gabrielle. It's a box of hope, and Alex kept it," I insisted. "He hasn't given up. He's just saving wishes for another day."

Something about her whole demeanour changed. She stared across at Alex, who was oblivious to the attention he was receiving.

"There's always hope, Gabi," I continued. "Even when it doesn't feel that way."

July 27
Adam

Returning to New York didn't feel like going home. It felt like backtracking, but I was there for a reason. I hadn't been away long enough to miss anything other than the coffee.

I avoided my parents, electing to stay holed up in Ryan's apartment to cram some serious study in before my exams. I hadn't picked up a book in weeks, and the ill preparation was beginning to stress me out.

"You've got this, Adam," encouraged Ryan. "Stop worrying."

I thumped the book on the coffee table and leaned back, watching my brother swiping through pictures of Bridget on my iPad.

"Pass or fail, it doesn't really matter in the grand scheme of things," I reasoned.

He glanced at me. "What is the grand scheme? What are you going to do in the Cove? Pick flowers and count stars?"

Ignoring the dig, I told him about the bank renovation. "I can't wait to finish it," I said. "It's a lot more rewarding than studying. I like watching it take shape."

I'd given Ryan the perfect opportunity to throw a sarcastic comment, but he didn't. He's seen the magic of Pipers Cove first hand. My brother knew exactly the kind of life I'd found there. He focused back on the screen in his hands. "She looks more like Charli than you."

I grinned at him. "Well that's good news considering she's a girl."

"Is it weird?" he asked, lowering the iPad to his lap. "Having a kid, I mean."

His serious expression demanded a serious answer so I thought carefully before replying. "I used to think I had it all figured out but I don't know anything any more. When Bridget looked at me for the first time, I realised that's how it's supposed to be."

"What do you mean?"

I shrugged. "I don't even know how to explain it. It was as if she knew I was her dad."

"And she didn't burst into tears, totally devastated?"

I laughed at his stupid comment. "No, she saw the deeper picture."

"Of course she did," he replied dryly.

"It's true, Ryan. She knew I'd finally come through for her and she knew how much I love her mom. Nothing else matters."

His smirk morphed into a thoughtful stare. "You're such a dick, Adam. She used to cry over you," he revealed. "Charli thought I didn't know, but I used to hear her."

Pure agony coursed through me, throwing me straight into defence mode. "I'm not the only dick. If you'd bothered to call and tell me about Bridget, I would've gone sooner."

"Charli would never have trusted it," grumbled Ryan, pulling a face. "She spent six months waiting for you to come to your senses and go to her. If she thought you'd only gone because of the baby, she would never have believed it was real."

"I know," I conceded. And if I hadn't been able to prove it with the delivery receipt, she probably still wouldn't believe it.

"You're lucky she even let you back in the door."

I grinned at him. "I know that too."

"I'm glad it worked out for you," he muttered, turning his attention back to the screen in his hands.

I swiped both hands down my face. "I'm not sure it has yet. I still have to face Mom and Dad."

"We should probably talk about that," he said ominously. "I changed the story a bit, which means you have a bit more studying to do if you want to stick to the tale I told them."

I groaned, fearing the worst. "What?"

"I told them that you knew about the baby all along," he confessed. "They think you made a last-minute decision to man-up take responsibility."

"What?" I practically shouted. "Why would you do that?"

He shrugged as if it was no big deal. "I didn't think it was fair that Charli should take on the role of bad guy. You were the asshole here, not her."

He was right. He was absolutely right; but it wasn't going to make placating them any easier. Not only did they think I'd bailed on my career; they thought I'd spent six months bailing on my child.

I let out a long sigh. "I can't deal with them right now."

He continued scrolling through the pictures. "You don't have to. Concentrate on passing the bar, stop by to see them on the way to the airport and go back to your family."

He'd broken it down in such a simple way that I realised he was right. If my father never forgave me, it wouldn't be my problem. My life would continue in the same perfect direction I'd been heading in since Bridget was born. It was up to him whether he wanted to be part of it.

* * *

I ended up caving in and going to my parents' place on the night before my first exam. Ryan gallantly suggested coming with me but I declined, worried that he'd twist the story even more. I had enough ground to make up as it was.

Mrs Brown met me at the door with a tight hug and a gift for Bridget. I thanked her and made my way through the glass doors into the lounge. Obviously they were expecting me. The scene had been perfectly staged. My dad was standing at the windows with his back to me. He didn't even turn to greet me. My mother was sitting on the very edge of the sofa, already blubbering.

I felt like a little kid in trouble.

"Hey, Ma," I greeted her.

She walked over and threw her arms around my neck. "I am so upset with you, you horrid boy." She broke her grip to whack me, swatting her hand hard against my chest.

I was in an impossible position. There were two different reasons for the anger in the room. My mother was furious for no other reason than Bridget, thinking I'd spent months denying her. My father didn't give a damn about Bridget. His fury stemmed solely from the fact that I'd shut down my career before it even got started. Both were disappointed beyond belief, and I felt hopeless knowing I wasn't going to be able to make either of them happy.

"Are you prepared for tomorrow?" asked my father, finally turning to face me.

"As best I can be, I think," I replied.

He shook his head. "Not good enough."

I pulled in a long breath to make sure the next words out of my mouth were calm. "I'm probably never going to be good enough for you, Dad. But I'm not trying to be good for you. Bridget thinks I'm good. Charli thinks I'm good. That's all that matters to me."

My mother gripped my arm pulling me closer to her side. "Charli sent us pictures," she told me. "She's such a lovely little girl, Adam."

"She's perfect, Mom," I beamed. "She looks just like her mama but she has my eyes, *your* eyes."

Mom gripped me tighter and I realised I was probably holding her up at that point.

"The child will be taken care of," my father announced mechanically.

"Yes, she will be," I agreed. "By me. She's going to have the best life imaginable and it's going to be nothing like mine was." I pointed at him. "If you want to know her, you're going to have to make allowance for that."

A flash of anger crossed his face. I was impressed by how well he was holding it together, considering he wanted nothing more than to rip me apart.

"How can I make allowance for the fact that my son has thrown away his entire career? Surely your child would benefit from her father's success."

I wondered how. My father's professional success had only ever set the bar impossibly high for Ryan and me. Growing up under that kind of pressure had been unimaginably hard to stand. It had very nearly ruined me and I vowed to never subject Bridget to it.

"I've thrown nothing away," I responded. "I'm still here. I'm still your son."

"You should want to give your daughter the very best," he said sourly. "A good strong foundation to –"

"I will give her everything. I will teach her French, and I will bring her back here to see my city in every season," I said strongly. "And if you'll just soften a little bit, I'll make sure she has a decent, loving relationship with her grandparents."

"We want that," insisted my mother, tugging hard on my sleeve.

"Of course we want that," agreed my father, no louder than a mumble.

"Good," I choked. "I want that too."

"The child will always be welcome here."

I groaned, wondering if I was making any headway at all. "Say her name, Dad. She has a name."

Jean-Luc took a step back, seemingly taken aback by my rough tone.

"Bridget," he announced. Not that I'd ever admit it to him, his thick French accent made it the best rendition of her name I'd ever heard. "Bridget will always be welcome here."

I felt as if I'd gone ten rounds in a boxing ring. I also felt immense relief. We were never going to be a perfect family unit. It was a complex mash up of two completely different worlds, and it had been that way from the very second I'd nearly run Charlotte down with my car. My life forever changed that day. My only regret was that it took me so long to realise it.

* * *

I aced my exam, just as I'd spent years hoping I would, which pleased my father no end. It meant that whenever Jean-Luc was asked what his sons did, he could quite honestly answer that both were attorneys.

Like my brother, I was now a licensed but non-practising lawyer in the state of New York. I didn't know if I'd ever return to that life, but passing the bar meant the door had been left open.

I was excited to be going back to the Cove. Mom sent me home with a small fortune worth of excess luggage – gifts for Bridget, clothes for Charli and junk food for me. My father took the extraordinary step of seeing me off at the airport. Not once did he try talking me out of going. Instead, he wished me well and made me promise to bring my girls back to visit sooner rather than later.

I left my city finally feeling as if all loose ends had been tied, and I was no longer in danger of being strangled by them.

August 3
Charli

I'd never been more excited to see Adam's car pull onto the driveway. He didn't even make it to the veranda before I pounced. Mercifully, he caught me as I launched myself at him.

"This is exactly the kind of homecoming I was hoping for, Charlotte," he murmured, walking us up the path toward the house.

"I aim to please," I replied, making him laugh.

I finally let him go once we were inside because I no longer had dibs on him. I now shared him with a little person who was wide awake as if she'd been waiting for him too.

Adam scooped Bridget out of her bassinette and showered her with a week's worth of missed kisses. "She looks bigger," he said glancing at me.

"That's because I've been feeding her," I explained, putting my hand to my heart. "Didn't forget once."

He chuckled his way back to me, babe in arms. "I am so glad to be home," he said, leaning to kiss me.

"Tell me about your trip."

He shrugged. "Passed the bar, handled my parents, hung out with Ryan. All boxes checked."

I smiled. "Great. So now we have your undivided attention."

"Forever, Charlotte," he replied, sounding absolutely sure.

* * *

Alex hadn't had any luck finding my rings, which meant I had no choice but to fess up to Adam. Like a true coward, I picked my moment to tell him, waiting until late that night when he was nearly asleep.

I held off explaining why I'd thrown them in the garden. Ethan didn't need to rate a mention.

"You lost them?" he mumbled.

Adam didn't notice me cringe. His eyes were closed.

"Not exactly. I *almost* know where they are."

He thought for a moment. "So, after all your searching, you *almost* found them?"

"Exactly."

"I'm sorry you lost them, Coccinelle," he slowly murmured, on the very edge of sleep. "I'll buy you new ones."

I reached across and turned off his bedside lamp.

"No, they're not lost," I whispered, resting my head on his shoulder. "They're in the garden."

He wrapped his arm around me. "We'll keep looking then. Go to sleep."

"Are you mad?"

"No."

"I love you, Adam," I said quietly.

"I love you too, Charlotte. Go to sleep."

"Okay."

"Charli."

"Yeah?"

"Shut up and go to sleep. We'll talk tomorrow."

I smiled into the darkness, realising that I had thousands of tomorrows to share with this man. And we were going to spend every one of them foraging for rocks, searching for diamonds and raising our baby.

August 20
Adam

Most days were perfect – except this one. We had a wedding to go to. The mere thought of it made me shudder.

Everyone in town was expected to be there, except Alex and Gabrielle. According to Alex, his wedding allergy was as severe as his dog allergy. I wish I'd thought of it first.

Charlotte couldn't have gotten out of it if she'd tried. And she did try exceptionally hard when Jasmine had turned up at our door a few days earlier begging her to take on the role of bridesmaid number six.

"I'm desperate, Charli," she wailed. "My cousin Vicky was supposed to do it but she backed out at the last minute."

"Why on earth would you want me to take her place?" asked Charli, doing little to hide her horror. "We're not exactly close."

Jasmine straightened up on the couch, still snivelling. "Well, you have great shoes and you've lost all the baby weight. You're skinny and pretty again."

To imply that Charli had ever been less than beautiful was ridiculous, but I wasn't about to argue the point with Bridezilla. I retreated to the kitchen instead. It was all I could do to stop myself laughing.

Agreeing to play bridesmaid was conditional. Charli wanted no part of the pre-wedding festivities and agreed to do it only on the proviso that she'd meet the rest of the wedding party at the church.

"Oh, come to the house first," begged Jasmine. "We're having lingerie pictures done before we get dressed."

"No chance," blurted Charli, appalled.

Jasmine didn't try too hard to change her mind. She knew she was treading on thin ice already. "Are you sure you'll be there?"

"I'll be there, Jasmine," grumbled Charli. "But I'm not wearing the hat."

* * *

She did wear the hat. And as expected, it looked ridiculous. I just wasn't brave enough to tell her. I caught my first glimpse of it when I returned to the cottage after dropping Bridget at Alex and Gabrielle's for the day.

"If you laugh, I'm going to kill you," she warned, running her hand across the top of the feathers sprouting from the tiny top hat.

"I wouldn't dare," I replied, holding up my hands.

There was something remarkably odd about seeing her all gussied up, Beautiful style. I hadn't known a dress could be glittery, pink and shiny all at the same time. She looked radioactive.

"I can hardly breathe in this thing," she said, putting her hands to her stomach.

"Maybe I should help you take it off, then," I suggested, swooping my arms around her and dipping her backwards. It was a good move on my part. The stupid hat fell off and hit the floor.

She put her hand to her head. "You broke it," she moaned. "Do you know many hot pink chickens had to die to make that hat?"

I righted her, threw her over my shoulder, and carried her to the bedroom. Jasmine's decision to put the zipper on the front of her trashy bridesmaid dresses helped me immensely.

"Adam," breathed Charli, "I just got dressed."

Her protest was weak considering she did nothing to stop me. "So did I."

She dragged off my tie. "Who taught you to tie a tie?" she asked irrelevantly.

"I don't know. I can't remember," I mumbled against her skin. I was a Décarie. I was probably born wearing a tie. "Who taught you to be so lovely?"

Both of her hands moved to my face and her warm brown eyes locked mine. "You did."

I couldn't speak. I could still move, though. I dragged the horrid pink dress off her and tossed it on the floor.

"If you had any idea how long it took me to get that contraption on, you wouldn't have done that," she told me.

"I'm pretty sure I would've, Charlotte," I replied dropping my head to kiss her.

* * *

I'd been to a lot of high society events in my time but nothing compared to the wedding of Jasmine and Wade.

It was taking place at the local church. The limestone building had the same old-world charm as the bank, which meant the wedding should've been equally as elegant and classy. I realised early on that this wasn't going to happen. The pink carpet path leading to the door was the first giveaway.

Meeting the rest of the bridal party at the church wasn't conventional, but it was the only way Jasmine was going to get her sixth bridesmaid. I offered to wait outside with Charli but she insisted I go inside. "They'll be here in a minute," she assured, fussing with her stupid chicken hat. She looked like she was gearing up to run.

"No flee-itis?" I teased.

Charli handed me her bouquet to free up her hands while she straightened my tie. "None. I'm cured."

I wasn't convinced but I left her there anyway, armed with nothing more than a good luck kiss.

I regretted my decision to go inside the second I walked through the door. Pink flowers, silver streamers and glitter decorated every surface. It was sensory overload. And never before had I seen an arbour of balloons decorating an altar.

I had no idea which side of the church to sit at. The choice was made for me when a lady wearing a big straw hat shuffled along the back pew and patted her hand on the space she'd made.

It seemed a long time before the show began. Someone hit play on the sound system and a mediocre version of Ave Maria filled the air. Everyone turned their heads toward the back of the church in time to see the first of the wedding party come in. Bridesmaids one through five floated through the door, arm in arm with their partners. They looked like amped-up showgirls, and every groomsman looked as if he'd rather be anywhere but here. Groomsman number three seemed to be handling it best, mainly because he looked drunk.

My eyes were glued on bridesmaid number six. It didn't even bother me that she'd been partnered with Flynn. My beautiful girl looked poised, confident and totally unfazed, despite the two-dollar hooker look she was working. She winked as she drifted past, sending my thoughts in a totally inappropriate direction considering we were in church.

I quickly recovered when the bride walked in. Cracked-out Scarlett O'Hara looked like she'd been hit at close range with a shotgun load of chintz and diamantes. Her dress was so wide that her father had to walk behind her so she'd make it up the narrow aisle. Everyone oohed and ahhed, probably in disbelief, and I had no problem hearing Meredith's attention-seeking sobs from the back pew.

The ceremony began and my interest waned. Things dragged on forever, making me wish I'd brought a book or Bridget to keep me company. By the time it ended, I was happy to get out.

My plan to reclaim my wife and make a run for it didn't happen. Part of Charli's bridesmaid duties involved sticking around to have her photo taken. She didn't look pleased, and who could blame her for not wanting photographic evidence of the day? I kept a safe distance as the photo shoot got under way in the church gardens. Four photographers clicked away at the bridal party. Perhaps realising it was as close as she'd ever come to being sought by the paparazzi, Jasmine relished every second of it.

Charlotte did not. As soon as she could escape, she picked up the hem of her dress and bolted toward me, waving her bouquet.

"Quick! Let's go!"

I couldn't help laughing at the urgency. "Are you sure you can leave?"

She hooked her arm through mine and tugged me toward the parking lot. "Yes. We don't have to be at the reception until six."

The second we pulled out of the parking lot, Charli lost the hat and dumped her bouquet on the back seat.

"Where are we going, Coccinelle?"

"Well, let's think about this for a second," she began. "We're baby-free, have two hours to kill and I'm dressed like a whore. Where do you think we should go?"

I glanced at her and was met by a wicked smile. "Somewhere quiet?"

"Yes." She giggled. "Take me to the café and I'll make you coffee."

"Not exactly what I had in mind, Charlotte."

"I know," she replied still laughing. "But if you think I'm putting this dress back on for a third time, you're mistaken."

* * *

I'd never seen the town so quiet. Stores were shut and the main street was deserted. The Tate wedding was a big deal to everyone in town except us.

The café was closed too, but it had nothing to do with the wedding. The owner had chosen spending time with his grandbaby over making a living that day. Going there must've been pre-planned. I'd never known Charlotte to hide keys in her bra before, but that's where she pulled them from. I didn't question it. I'd never known her to wear chicken hats before that day either.

Time alone with Charli was a rare treat. It was the first time she'd been away from Bridget for any length of time and I could tell that she was itching to have her back.

"Do you think she's okay?" she asked quietly.

"I'm sure she's fine," I assured her. "Alex hasn't called us and she's too young to start fires or steal cars."

Charlotte slid a cup of coffee across the counter. "Bridget wouldn't do that." She looked so pretty when she smiled but I was still fighting the urge to lurch forward and wipe the thick makeup off her face. "She's going to be a good girl."

"You think so?"

She walked around the counter and levered herself onto the stool beside me. "I think she's going to *try* to be good," she clarified. "It might take her a while to get it right."

I reached for her hand and held it in place on my knee. "She'll work it out."

"In the meantime, she'll probably put her father through years of hell," she warned. "Are you prepared for that, Boy Wonder?"

I took a sip of coffee. "Nope. That would require planning. I don't make plans. Whatever will be, will be, right?"

August 20
Charli

The reception was at the restaurant at the vineyard. When I heard that it had been closed all week in preparation, I knew it was going to be extreme.

I made sure Adam got us there on time. My first ever bridesmaid job was nearly over, and I'd come close to pulling it off like a pro. We walked into the small foyer to find Lily standing near a table of gifts, marking off names on a clipboard. The look of concentration on her face led me to believe she was taking the task very seriously.

"Do you need to see our invitation, Lily?" queried Adam as we approached.

She looked up and smiled. "No. Just your gift."

Her businesslike approach was almost scary. I wondered if she would've turned us away if we'd shown up empty handed.

"Of course," said Adam dryly. He reached into his welt pocket and produced an envelope.

"Just a card?" she asked, taking it from him.

"Don't worry," he said, continuing with the run of sarcasm. "There's a cheque in there."

"Not a very personal gift," she harrumphed.

When it had come to choosing a gift, I couldn't think of a single thing to give them beside his-and-her hair straighteners. Adam argued that they'd already have them, so we were back to square one. It highlighted the fact that we weren't friends. I tolerated Jasmine and Wade bewildered me, which made serving as an attendant at their wedding positively bizarre.

Adam leaned close to her and spoke quietly. "It's a big cheque, Lily."

Instantly appeased, she stepped aside and let us proceed.

Adam started laughing the second we got through the door. I knew why. At the head of the room stood two giant gold thrones. I shushed him, trying desperately hard to hold back a giggle of my own. It was cheesy, self indulgent and very Jasmine.

I was pleased to see that there was no bridal table. The other bridesmaids were scattered around the room and there didn't seem to be a seating plan. Adam and I found a small table near the window and hurried to claim it. No one paid us any attention, which was wonderful. All eyes were on the happy couple perched on their thrones like the king and queen of sparkles and trash.

Even Nancy, the Pomeranian, had made the guest list. The little dog was scurrying around the room in a tutu that covered the worst of her bald patches.

Meredith kept approaching the bride to tug on the hem of her dress or position her better while the hired paparazzi continued clicking away.

Jasmine was in her element, and I felt happy for her. As vulgar as they were, she'd worked tirelessly for months to pull her wedding plans together. Wade seemed to relish the attention too. I watched him for a while. The stupid grin on his face was permanent, and every minute or so he'd charge his glass and wink at random people.

People milled around, shuffling from table to table for a switch in conversation. We stayed put, dealing only with those who approached us. Floss joined us for a while and we both made an effort to appear interested as she gushed about her new granddaughter-in-law. A few others stopped to chat, mostly to Adam. He'd come a long way in the past few weeks. He was no longer considered a blow-in from out of town with a funny accent. He'd met a lot of people, mainly because of the bank renovation, but I was surprised when Spanner Padgett approached our table and greeted him like an old friend. Spanner had gone all out that day. He was wearing a tie with his flannelette shirt.

As soon as he'd gone, I quizzed Adam. "How do you know Spanner?"

Adam leaned back in his chair, his dimple deepening. "Spanner and I go way back," he replied, making me laugh. "And his brother, Brick."

* * *

I barely ate any of my dinner. The food was fine but I couldn't concentrate on anything other than the sight of the bride and groom on their thrones, eating their first meal as a married couple off TV trays on their laps.

"Charlotte," murmured Adam, drawing my attention back to him. "You're staring."

"I know." I gave a nod toward the happy couple. "Have you ever seen anything like that?"

He dropped his head and laughed. "Never in my life."

Jasmine and Wade eventually climbed down from their thrones to cut the cake. It was the highlight of my day. The three-tier monstrosity with the white icing and edible glitter had been teasing me all evening.

"Can we leave now?" asked Adam.

"No chance," I told him. "They're about to cut the cake. I've been waiting hours for a piece of that bad boy."

"If it's a bad boy you're craving, I could –"

"Stop right there." I cut him off, inciting a blinding half-dimpled Décarie grin. It confirmed that his intended sentence wasn't wedding-friendly.

Adam didn't have a chance to speak again. A waiter sidled up and placed two massive hunks of cake in front of us.

We stared at our plates. The cake didn't look so appealing any more. It looked like road kill.

"How do you think they made the cake pink?" I whispered, turning the plate full circle.

"Beet juice," Adam stated.

"Beetroot juice?" I was aghast.

He shrugged. "That's how Ryan makes pink cake."

As confused as I was, I didn't ask for an explanation. I just pushed the cake to the centre of the table, suddenly unenthused by the prospect of eating it. When Nancy the dog approached a short while later, I figured I'd give her a treat. I broke off a morsel of cake and fed it to her under the table. Apparently, Nancy had a thing for cake. Within minutes, she'd polished off the whole piece. "Are you going to eat that?" I asked, pointing at Adam's plate.

He slid it across. "Knock yourself out." I continued feeding the little dog until Adam's plate was nearly cleared. "I'm not sure you should give her any more, Charli," he warned.

"Why not? It's a celebration. She deserves a treat." I hadn't always been kind to the ugly little pooch. In fact, I'd often laughed at her misfortune. Nancy was Jasmine's baby. I wouldn't like it if Jasmine was mean to my baby.

Adam pointed out that it was an unlikely scenario. "Your baby doesn't have an overbite."

"No," I agreed, grinning. "But she is bald."

With two slabs of sickly sweet pink cake under her furry belt, Nancy scurried away and headed for Jasmine. She jumped up on the self-proclaimed queen's lap and that's where she stayed while Wade made his ridiculous speech.

Adam had trouble keeping a straight face from the first line.

"Our love is like a murial painted on the wall of life…" Wade began.

Jasmine was so focused on her new husband's declaration of love that she didn't notice Nancy retching on her lap. By the time she did it was too late. The little beast had thrown up a massive slab of pink cake on her stark white dress. Jasmine's bloodcurdling screams suited her new look perfectly. She looked like she'd just been stabbed.

Nancy took off. Meredith and Wade ran to Jasmine's aid and the room erupted into sympathetic gasps and groans.

Not so long ago, I would've been thrilled by such a turn of events. Not anymore. I felt terrible. I'd inadvertently ruined tramp-Barbie's dream wedding.

August 20
Adam

I had to laugh, which meant it was time to leave. Charli didn't protest when I pulled her to her feet. In fact, she didn't say a word until we were out of the room.

"I can't believe that just happened," she choked, wide-eyed and worried.

She looked absolutely horrified and I felt the need to reassure her. "It wasn't your fault," I lied.

"It was ninety percent my fault."

It shouldn't have mattered but I was interested to know how she'd worked out the ratio of blame. "Who's responsible for the other ten percent?"

She widened her brown eyes. "Did you see her bouquet? Putting foxgloves in your wedding bouquet is begging for trouble."

"Of course," I agreed.

"I need to make this right, Adam."

I was used to crafty, criminal Charlotte who would've taken great delight in using Nancy as a Pomeranian weapon of mass destruction. The girl with me didn't look too delighted. I could see her mind ticking over as she tried coming up with a way of atoning.

"We'll pay for the dry-cleaning," I offered.

Her head whipped up. "No! Then she'll know it was us."

I overlooked the fact that she'd implicated me her crime. She wasn't completely reformed. Charli might have been remorseful, but not remorseful enough to own up.

"So, what's your plan, Charlotte?"

She put her hand on my shoulder to steady herself while she took off her heels. At first I thought it was so she could run faster, but she walked to the table of gifts, shamelessly swiped a bow off one of presents and tied it around her shoes.

"Shoes?" I asked incredulously. "That's your atonement?"

She positioned her impromptu gift on top of the pile. "They're not just shoes. They're twelve hundred dollars worth of awesome and Jasmine will love them."

The level of fascination I felt for this girl was practically a disability. I stepped forward, gearing up to kiss her half to death. The embrace was cut short when the not-so-happy couple appeared in the doorway. Jasmine was gripping the skirt of her dress and puffing like a fire-breathing dragon. Wade looked suitably terrified.

"Charli," she huffed between blubbers.

I glanced at Charlotte, immediately noticing the trapped expression on her face.

"Oh, Jasmine," she said pitifully. "I am so sorry."

Both of us stared at the huge stain on her dress. Jasmine stalked toward us, looking so menacing that I pulled Charli closer to my side to protect her if it turned physical. But Jasmine wasn't heading for Charli. She made a beeline for the gift table.

"Louboutins?" she squealed. "You're giving me your Louboutins?"

Charli stiffly nodded. "I know you like them."

Jasmine glanced down at Charli's bare feet before unceremoniously launching herself at her. Charlotte tried wriggling free, and for a moment, it looked like she was having a punch-up with a marshmallow. Finally Jasmine let her go. "You've just made this day the happiest day of my life!"

She tore the bow off the shoes-of-awesome and swapped them with her own. The puke on her dress was forgotten. Her tears were now tears of joy. It was unfathomable.

"I really love you, Charli," she declared. "And you, Adam. I really love you. And your little baby," she added as an afterthought.

"We love you too, Jasmine," replied Charli in a strange monotone voice.

The bride squealed, gathered up her filthy dress and took off back into the reception to show off her shoes. Wade made no attempt to follow her. "Thanks, Charli," he said. "That was a really nice thing to do. She was really upset when Nancy chundered. I wasn't looking forward to spending the rest of the night being her escape goat."

Charli half smiled. "No worries, Wade. Congratulations, by the way."

Wade thanked her and headed off to find his bride, leaving me alone with mine. "Did he just say *escape* goat?" I whispered in her ear.

"Yes." She chuckled. "Yes he did."

December 2
Charli

After five long months, the bank renovation was finally finished. I hadn't visited the bank often during its revamp. It wasn't the best place to hang out with a baby who'd developed a fondness for putting things in her mouth. But now Bridget and I had the honour of being the first to see it. Adam started bombarding us with builder's jargon at the door. I wasn't interested in hearing that the antique mortise lock on the door had had to be sent to the mainland for restoration. I didn't even know what a mortise lock was.

"So it opens and closes now?" It was the best I could come up with.

He smiled. "Yes, it does."

"Awesome. Can we go inside, please?" I asked impatiently, bouncing Bridget on my hip.

Adam stretched out his arms and Bridget mimicked him, giving him permission to take her. Baby transfer complete, Adam opened the door and ushered me in.

It took me a long time to find the right words to describe the place. It was completely transformed. The hardwood floors were so dark they looked almost black. The dull lacquer was in keeping with the age of the building, and was offset perfectly by the stark white walls.

Everything looked perfect and, more importantly, authentic.

I stood in the centre of the main room, trying to notice every detail.

"What do you think?" asked Adam.

"I think you're amazing," I declared, turning to face him. "I love it."

"I love it too." Well deserved pride saturated his tone. He dropped his head, speaking only to Bridget. "What do you think, Bridge?"

Supremely comfortable in her father's arms, her little legs were wildly kicking.

"I think she's impressed," I told him.

"I want to show you something," said Adam, holding out a hand. "A surprise."

He led me through to the back room. Near the old vault was a paint-spattered tarp. In my experience, any surprise hidden under a tarp was a good one. "What is it?" I asked eagerly.

"Curious little thing, aren't you?" He spoke slowly but there was underlying excitement in his voice.

As expected, the big reveal wasn't dragged out very long. He pulled the tarp away revealing a painting set up on an easel. I leaned down. Instantly I knew it was one of Gabrielle's masterpieces. It took me a bit longer to work it out – too long for Adam. He explained, rushing to get the words out. "I know the plan was to sell this place once it was finished, but I have a better idea. I think it would make a great gallery to display your work."

I kept my focus on the painting. It was a picture of the outside of the bank, complete with a sign at the door.

"Galerie Décarie," I announced, leaning to get a closer look.

"If you don't like the name, you can call it whatever you want."

I hoped my poker face had improved since the last time I'd attempted it.

"Well?" he asked nervously. "What do you think?"

"What do *you* think?"

"I think there's a fine line between encouraging and pushing where you're concerned," he replied. "In my experience, you tend to resent pushing and ignore encouragement. I'm trying to work out which line I've crossed."

"Really?" I asked dryly.

"Absolutely, and I'll have you know that I'm prepared to use my daughter as a human shield if necessary." He held Bridget in front of him to validate his claim. Our little girl madly kicked, cooing like a little pigeon trying to take control of the room.

I tried not to smile, but once he cracked I couldn't hold back. "You want to know what I think, Adam?"

"Tell me," he replied, repositioning the baby on his hip.

I stepped closer to him. "I think you're the best person I know."

He leaned forward, pressing his lips against mine. Bridget grumbled, making the embrace short but perfectly sweet. "Don't get out much do you, Charlotte?" he teased.

I giggled my way over to the small room. "Do you really think I could open a gallery here?"

"I think you could open a gallery anywhere, but here is as good a place as any."

I took some time to think things through. Opening a gallery would be a great next step for me, and something I would never have considered if not for Adam's support. It was a telling sign. As much as I'd grown in the past few years, I still needed the occasional push to move forward.

"I like the name," I said finally.

His eyes brightened. "So you'll do it?"

I nodded, inciting a lovely Décarie grin. "You know what this means, Adam?"

"Tell me," he urged.

I threw my arms wide. "You're done. You're going to have to find a new project to keep you occupied."

"I'm way ahead of you, Coccinelle," he replied wryly. "I've found another boat. It's being delivered to the shed as we speak. It's old and rundown and needs a lot of work. It might take me years to restore."

I needed the occasional push, but Adam needed the opposite approach. He was still a perfectionist, driven to put everything into whatever he was working on. It was up to me to rein him in and slow him down. Dragging him away from his renovation work at a reasonable hour of the day was something I'd had to do more than once. Knowing I'd only have to walk as far as the other side of the yard to do it from now on brought relief.

"Years? Really?"

"Years and years and years."

I smiled at him, realising that for the first time ever, I felt like I fitted my life. Charli Blake grew up, took a wrong turn by becoming Charlotte Décarie, and finally found her feet as Charli Décarie.

After spending far too long trying to pull each other in opposite directions, Adam and I had found balance.

Our child was our middle ground. She was Bridget by name and nature. The impossible deadlocks that forced us apart over and over were bridged by a mutual desire to be deserving of her. She made us both want to be better people, and as long as we continued to walk the same road, our happy ending would always be in reach.

Three Years Later
Adam

We spent a long time looking for Charli's wedding rings – three years, to be exact. I offered to replace them a hundred times but she refused, settling for the simple gold band she'd started out with instead.

"You wear the rings you're married with. That's it," she told me.

She didn't have much time to devote to searching the garden these days. Her gallery had taken off in the past few years, as I knew it would. She'd sold pictures to buyers all over the world and had been published hundreds of times over. She was continually surprised by the interest in her work. I wasn't. It confirmed something I'd always known. She was talented, creative and a genius.

My workload was a little more subdued, and I loved every minute of it. After the bank renovation I moved on to a fifteen-metre sloop in dire need of some TLC. Six months later I flipped it for a tidy profit and moved on to another. Working from home had its advantages. It meant I could spend days hanging out with the chatty whip-smart toddler we had on our hands.

A cottage at the top of a cliff wasn't necessarily the best place for a curious little girl with a penchant for adventure. As soon as Bridget started to crawl we erected fencing around the yard to contain her, but I was still nervous. I knew that if she could find a way over it, she'd be rappelling to the beach in a second.

A strong sense of adventure wasn't the only thing Bridget had inherited from her mother. She was a little too young to grasp the concept of wishes and never-done lists, but glimmers of La La Land were already shining through. She'd learned to swim before she was two, insisted on wearing galoshes to bed, and vehemently maintained that her favourite number was yellow.

I connected to her on a different level. Bridget loved books, which was a coup because I loved reading to her – mainly in French. She floated between two languages with her toddler chatter and I never got tired of hearing it.

Fearing she'd spend a lifetime being tortured by secret conversations, Charli finally made an effort to learn the language too – at Bridget's pace. Her pronunciation was terrible but I didn't care. She had a way of making the most botched word sound gorgeous.

Everything about Charli was gorgeous, especially that morning. I was sitting on the deck of the dry-docked yacht when she appeared in the doorway of the shed.

"Adam, I have to go," she called. "I can't be late."

I backed down the ladder and walked toward her, making no secret of the fact I was looking her up and down. Her anxious, fidgety mood didn't quite match the stylish grey suit she was wearing.

"Look at you," I crooned, drawing out the words.

She nervously smoothed the front of her straight skirt. "It's my hard-arse Wall Street look," she joked. "Do you think Art Bloke will be impressed?"

A very keen buyer on the mainland had contacted her the week before to set up a meeting. Charli was so taken aback by his call that she hadn't caught his name. We'd been referring to him as Art Bloke.

I leaned forward and kissed her, making sure that was the only contact we made so she'd stay tidy. "Knock 'em dead, princess. You look beautiful."

Her meeting was in Melbourne, which meant Bridget and I were being left to our own devices for a whole night. I was sure it was adding to Charli's nervousness.

"I'll be back in the morning, okay?"

I nodded.

"Bridget is still in bed," she continued. "Don't let her con you into giving her cake for breakfast. I already told her no last night."

"Okay, I've got it."

"And don't forget her dance class at three. Don't be late or Mrs O'Reilly will lock you out."

I wished Mrs O'Reilly *would* lock us out. Bridget's dance class was the longest hour of the week and I always left with a headache. "We'll be there," I promised. "Now go. You're going to miss your flight."

She smiled and held up her hand, crossing her fingers. "Wish me luck."

I blew her a kiss. "You won't need it."

* * *

I was the one who needed luck. Sleeping in had done Bridget no favours. She woke up cranky and wanted her mother. I calmed her down, carried her down the short hallway and sat her at the table. "Mom had to go on the plane, baby," I explained. "It's just you and me today."

"I can go too?"

I kissed the top of her head. "Not today. She has to work."

Bridget took a long moment to think things through. "I like planes," she said finally. "You like planes, Daddy?"

I nodded. "*Oui.*"

"You like cake?" she asked.

I knew exactly where she was headed. The only hope I had of winning was to shut her down early. I filled a bowl with cereal and placed it in front of her. "*Aimes-tu les céréales*, Bridget?"

She pushed it away. "Non," she grumbled. "I just like cake."

"You're not having cake." I slid the bowl back to her. "You're having cereal."

Bridget melted down. Tears began to flow – the awful kind – the snotty, world-is-ending kind that made me think we were in for a very long day. Fearing the worst, I caved and broke her mother's one and only rule.

She had chocolate cake for breakfast.

We ended up spending a great day together after that, right up until dance class.

We sat in the car until exactly three o'clock. I didn't want to spend a minute longer than necessary in that hall. Bridget didn't complain. It was a routine she was familiar with.

Charlotte rarely attended dance lessons. She still held the title of being the only child ever to be expelled from Joyce's class. It bothered her more at twenty-three than it had when she was five. That meant dance had become a daddy and daughter activity.

Once the other tiny dancers started filing into the hall, I unbuckled mine and held her hand as we walked across the parking lot, stopping twice so she could pick up rocks off the ground.

Bridget liked Mrs O'Reilly's dance lessons, but she was no Anna Pavlova. Her choice of footwear and pocket full of stones might've had something to do with her lack of grace. My mini ballerina was the only kid in class wearing a tutu, a hoodie and galoshes. I thought she looked cute but Mrs O'Reilly didn't. She greeted us at the door with the blistering look of disapproval that we were used to.

I sent Bridget off to join her posse and joined the other parents on the row of plastic chairs lining the side wall. No one seemed to notice me, which suited me fine. The mothers were too busy catching up on gossip and bitching about those who didn't show up that week. I did my best to block them out, focusing on my little girl thumping around on the wooden floor, doing her best to dance like a butterfly.

"That's lovely, girls," praised Mrs O'Reilly, throwing her voice across the echoey hall. "Nice, poised butterflies."

I doubt she was praising Bridget. I chuckled as I watched her flapping around and stamping her feet. She looked like she was trying to put out an invisible fire.

Her technique didn't improve when they moved onto fairy dancing. Each girl was handed a glittery wand. Most waved it through the air and kept dancing. Bridget used hers to practise her golf swing. I silently took the blame for that one. Bogan-golf sessions with her grandfather were a common occurrence for us.

Poor Mrs O'Reilly was at the end of her tether, and she wasn't backward in coming forward and letting me know. She yelled at me to stay back after class.

Everyone else eventually cleared out, leaving just the three of us in the hall. Bridget continued her solo golf tournament, now sporting a wand in each hand.

I dealt with Mrs O'Reilly at the doorway.

"Little girls are like flowers," she declared, throwing her arms wide. "With a little encouragement, they usually bloom."

"But?"

"But, your daughter is nothing like a flower." She didn't even try to let me down gently. "If you want Bridget to be graceful and ladylike, maybe you should consider dressing her appropriately for dance."

"With all due respect Ma'am, she's three," I replied. "I don't really care how ladylike she is at this stage."

"Her mother was just the same, you know," she informed me, looking at me through narrowed eyes. "Boisterous and unpredictable."

The comparison made me smile. "I'm thrilled to hear that."

"Perhaps – like her mother – Bridget isn't cut out to be a ballerina," she suggested.

My little girl picked that moment to take an impressive swing with her wand, sending a small rock ricocheting off the wall above our heads. Bridget started giggling, a gorgeous cheeky sound that I never got tired of hearing, no matter the circumstances.

Mrs O'Reilly was unamused. "I don't think she's ready for dance classes," she said through gritted teeth.

I nodded, hoping I looked disappointed. "I understand."

"I hope Charli will understand too," she replied.

"Well, if she doesn't, I'll be sure to get her to give you a call."

I might as well have threatened her with bodily harm. Mrs O'Reilly looked terrified.

I walked to Bridget and scooped her into my arms. As we got to the door, I asked her to give the wands to her teacher, which she did without fuss.

Mrs O'Reilly thanked her and said goodbye. "We'll see you in a year or two, Bridget, when you've outgrown the boots."

I was strapping her into her car seat when Bridget finally spoke. "You like my boots, Daddy?"

"I love your boots, baby."

She reached up and pressed her little fingers into my cheek. "You like cake, Daddy?"

I countered by poking her dimpled cheek. "Yes, Bridge." I laughed. "I like cake."

* * *

Separating Bridget from her prized boots usually didn't happen until she was asleep. Tonight was a little different. As I was tucking her into bed she lifted one foot and asked me to take them off.

"Are you sure?" I asked.

"Hurts," she complained.

I wasn't going to argue. I grabbed the boot and wrenched it off her little foot. The reason why her feet hurt became clear in an instant. As I pulled it off, something flew out and tinkled across the wooden floor.

I stooped down and picked up Charlotte's wedding rings. Even when they were in my hand I couldn't quite believe it.

They were filthy and looked a little worse for wear, but they were found. I couldn't begin to fathom the level of magic involved. To find one would've been a coup. To find both was nothing less than miraculous.

"Where did you get these, baby?"

"In the dirt," replied Bridget casually.

"When?"

Her longwinded explanation was neither French nor English. I shook my head, not even trying to follow. Instead I tucked her up and kissed her perfect little head. "I love you, little treasure hunter."

* * *

Charli's business meeting continued the next day. I took it as a sign that things were going well. On the downside, she missed her scheduled flight and arrived home hours later than expected.

I met her at the door and pulled her into my arms the second she was within reach.

"I'm so tired," she complained.

She *felt* tired. I steered her across the to the couch by her shoulders. Charli kicked off her heels and grabbed my hand, yanking me down beside her. "How's Bridge?"

"She's good. She's been asleep a while," I replied, moving her so her head rested in my lap. "She missed you."

"I missed her too," she replied, mid-yawn. "What did you do while I was gone?"

I tried to play it down, speaking very quickly as if that somehow dulled the drama. "Nothing much. Yesterday we played for a while and got kicked out of dance class. Today we went to the beach, then visited Floss at her store."

She didn't seem tired any more. "Got kicked out? Oh no. What happened?"

I smoothed her worried frown with my fingers. "It's no big deal, Charli. She's just not ready for dance classes." I wasn't sure that the dance world would ever be ready for Bridget Décarie – but I left that part out.

"Was she sad?"

"She's over it," I assured her.

"It was the gumboots, wasn't it?"

"It might have been the boots. It could also have something to do with her awesome golf swing." Charli sighed but still looked concerned. "She's fine," I repeated. "No tears, I promise."

"Okay."

"What about you? How was your trip?"

She stared up with tired eyes, seemingly thinking my question through. "Can we talk about this tomorrow, please? I want to go to bed."

I didn't push. I had more pressing things on my mind. I expertly untucked her shirt and trailed my hand across her stomach.

When my fingers slipped under the waistband of her skirt, she grabbed my hand. "Cool your jets, Boy Wonder." She flashed me a lazy smile. "I want to go and kiss our girl first."

"Fine." I slipped out from under her, scooped her up and threw her over my shoulder. "Let's go."

She must've really been tired. She maintained her ragdoll position the whole way down the hall. When we got to Bridget's room I lowered her to her feet.

I stood watching from the doorway as Charli crept across the room and gave our little girl a quick kiss and a fresh tuck up. Once she started picking toys up off the floor, I moved quickly to reclaim her.

The hold I had on Charli as I carried her down to the bedroom was much better suited to the mood I was trying to put her in, but she felt so limp in my arms that I was sure the play at chivalry was wasted on her – right up until she turned her head and kissed my neck.

One day apart was too long. I'd barely handled it, and the way I kissed her as I lowered her to the bed made it obvious. Her body was pinned beneath me but I was the one who was captured.

Charlotte was my other half – the better half who constantly reminded me of all that was good and beautiful and special in the world. She'd loved and believed in me, even when I didn't deserve it. And she'd recognised how much I loved her when I wasn't able to prove it. I was the richest man on earth, and it had nothing to do with money.

"I love you, Charli," I whispered in her ear. "So much."

She pulled me in impossibly closer, raking her nails up my back as she pulled my shirt over my head.

"I know you do," she replied, sounding a little breathless. "That's why you're mine."

Being hers was a position I intended to hold for the rest of my life, and I spent the rest of the night convincing her of it.

* * *

I spent the next morning working on the boat, trying to pull the perished rubber moulding off the gunwales. It was a task that required plenty of curse words and more patience than I had.

"Filthy mouth you have there, sailor," teased Charli, appearing in the doorway.

I smiled down at her. "Have you come here to taunt me, Charlotte?"

"No. I came to pacify you with café coffee." She waved the cup at me. "Permission to come aboard?"

I made my way along the messy deck and grabbed the coffee from her as she climbed the ladder. When she neared the top, I reached for her hand and helped her on board.

"Where's your kid?"

"At the café. I took her down there to get you coffee." She brushed sawdust off a seat. "She decided to stay and hang out with Rex."

Alex encouraged Bridget to call him by name, mortified by the thought of being called Grandpa. Rex was the best she could do. Gabrielle had ended up with the unfortunate title of Prizzy. She was mystified as to how Bridget had come up with it. Charli and I theorised that it was a shortened version of Parisienne, but we didn't dare tell her.

"So we're home alone?" I asked, wiggling my eyebrows at her.

"All morning. I told Alex we'd pick her up this afternoon."

"Excellent." I set my coffee on the deck and leaned over the side of the boat. "You can help me pull this stripping off."

Charlotte let out a quiet giggle. "I was hoping we could talk, actually. It's important."

I straightened up. "Of course. What's going on?" Her mouth opened as if she was going to speak, but gave me nothing. I tried to help her out. "Is it about your meeting yesterday?"

She nodded.

Charli had barely mentioned her trip to Melbourne. I found it odd considering she'd been so looking forward to it.

"Tell me," I pushed.

"Art Bloke has a gallery," she began. "Every piece in it is some form of motion photography. Gorgeous, beautiful pictures of things like sports and concerts and the ocean."

I pulled a crate across the deck and sat opposite her. "Okay."

"He really liked my oceanic photography, especially the ones of the surfers at Cobb beach."

"So he wants to buy them?"

"Not exactly," she hinted. "He wants me to consider taking on the position of curator at his gallery. He offered me a job."

I stared at her lovely face for a long time, pondering what that meant for our little family. Unless Art Bloke had opened a gallery next door to Charli's, the position wasn't local.

"Are you thinking of taking it?"

She shrugged. "Maybe. I think it's an amazing opportunity, but it's a big deal because it's so far away."

I reached, tangling my hand through her long hair before resting it on the back of her neck. "Melbourne is an hour by plane. It's not that far."

She shook her head and I lost her eyes as she looked to the deck. "Adam, have you heard of Bronson Merriman?"

The name sounded vaguely familiar but I told her no.

"He's an art dealer in Manhattan," she explained.

"Oh, yeah," I amended. "I have heard of him. He has a gallery on Madison Avenue, I think."

"Yeah, he has."

As soon as she looked up at me, the penny dropped. I released my hold on her and straightened up. "Art Bloke is Bronson Merriman?"

"Yes. He first saw my work at Billet-doux," she explained. "He came all this way just to meet me. I guess I impressed him."

Of course she'd impressed him. Charli Décarie was the most beautiful, talented girl on earth.

I took a few seconds, trying to come to grips with what she'd told me. "You want to take a job in Manhattan?" I asked, making doubly sure I had the story straight. "You want us to go back to New York?"

She shrugged again. "Only if you do."

I could hardly make sense of it. We'd only been back a handful of times to visit my family. Bridget had experienced white Christmases, my parents had spoiled her rotten and my brother did his best to corrupt her. As much as we enjoyed it, we were always glad to get home. Unless I could be absolutely certain that Charli was going to be happy there, I wasn't even going to entertain the idea of moving back there permanently.

"I'm not sure, Charli," I admitted. "Why would it be different this time?"

"Because I think I'd really like the job," she reasoned. "I couldn't hack New York before because I had no place there. A job in a gallery could be my place."

I smiled at her and she grinned back at me. "Can I think about it?" I asked.

"Yes, it requires going with the second thought."

"Is going to New York your second thought, Charli?"

She slapped her hands on her knees, dusting them off. "It was my first and second thought. I can't see a reason not to do it."

As she stood, I reached for her hand and pulled her onto my lap. "I love you very much," I declared, making her smile.

She linked her arm around my neck. "I know. Tell me something else that's true. Tell me anything, as long as it's true."

"Bridget had chocolate cake for breakfast while you were away."

"I know that too. She told me. Tell me something else."

I pretended to think, leaving her hanging for a long moment. "We're going back to New York," I said finally.

"Really?" she asked, her bright eyes shining.

"Sure, why not?" I shrugged. "I'd go anywhere with you."

I meant it. Having a good life had nothing to do with geography. It was about being whole. As long as the three of us were together, we were whole.

Her lips pressed against mine. "Inside will be fine, for now," she breathed, breaking free for only a second.

Three Years Later
Charli

Because getting out of Dodge is best done quickly, we needed to tell Alex we were leaving. We drove to the house that afternoon to collect Bridget and to hit him with our news.

"How do you think he'll take it?" asked Adam.

"He'll be devastated," I replied quietly.

We pulled onto the long driveway, immediately noticing that the ute wasn't there.

"Do you want to wait?" asked Adam. "It doesn't look like they're home yet."

I pointed to the little red Mazda parked near the garage. "Gabi's here. We'll tell her first."

We hadn't even made it to the house when the Parisienne came rushing out.

"No! No! No!" she ranted, wagging her finger at us. "You can't be here today. Go home."

"We're just here to pick up Bridget," Adam told her. "Then we'll leave."

"Fine," she relented. "They will be here in two minutes. Take your baby and leave. Come back tomorrow."

I'd seen Gabrielle in some strange moods before but nothing like this. Adam grabbed her hand.

"Stop," he ordered. "Calm down. What's wrong?"

Her smile was blinding, even for a Décarie. "Nothing. Absolutely nothing. I just don't want visitors today."

Alex pulled onto the driveway and Gabrielle clapped her hands. "Oh, he's home." She took off, leaving us standing at the base of the steps to the veranda.

"What the hell is going on?" Adam whispered.

"No clue," I muttered.

Our little girl caught sight of us and started running up the path toward us. I couldn't help laughing. She was all gumboots and crooked blonde pigtails.

The amped-up Parisienne collared her as she passed and gave her a quick kiss before letting her continue on her way. Bridget took a flying leap at Adam and he caught her in mid-flight.

"Prizzy crying," she told him in French.

Both of us stared at Gabrielle as she made her way to Alex. We were too far away to hear their conversation, but she seemed to have calmed down.

Bridget wriggled free of Adam. We were so engrossed in the muted conversation taking place on the driveway that neither of us noticed her go into the house. We did, however, notice her when she came back out, mainly because of what she was holding. I took it from her and waved it at Adam.

It was a positive pregnancy test. Finally, after nearly five long years of waiting, my father and the Parisienne had got their wish, and the timing couldn't have been better. Nothing would ease the pain of us leaving town more than a new baby.

Our news could wait a day or two. We slipped away without a word to the happy couple. I turned to them as we got to the car. Their position hadn't changed. They held each other tightly while Gabrielle sobbed. I'd seen this before, usually accompanied by a woeful expression on Alex's face. He wasn't stricken this time round. My dad looked happier than I'd ever seen him.

* * *

I didn't feel like going home. Bridget fell asleep before we hit the main road.

I rested my head on the window, watching the trees whizzing past. "Do you want to go somewhere special, Adam? To a secret place?"

He reached for my hand. "Somewhere new?" he asked.

"No, somewhere old," I replied, glancing at him.

He smiled, the gorgeous half-dimpled smile that I'd been besotted with since I was seventeen-years-old. "Lead the way, Coccinelle."

We hadn't been to the top of the cliffs in years, and if Bridget hadn't been strapped into her car seat fast asleep, we wouldn't have been there that day either. Adam wound her window down a little so we could hear her and we got out of the car.

"We can't leave her here, Charli," said Adam, frowning.

"I know. We don't need to go down the trail. We just need to listen."

"To what?" he asked.

"Shush. Close your eyes." Mine were already closed. I took a peek to make sure his were too. "What do you hear?"

"The ocean," he replied, breaking a smile. "We haven't been up here for a long time."

"I know. It's still amazing, right?"

"It's not my favourite place," he admitted.

"No? Why not?"

"Well…" He snaked his arm around me and dipped me backward. I ignored the fact that my ponytail was sweeping the ground. I was too focused on his eyes to care. "Last time we were here you broke my heart. I'm hoping you didn't bring me back here to do it again."

I gripped his forearms. "No. You have a daughter now. It's Bridget's job to break your heart from here on in."

Adam chuckled and righted me, but his hold didn't waver. He brought my hand to his shoulder and before I knew it, we shuffling in the dirt, slow dancing to the sound of the waves crashing against the base of the cliffs.

"Are you sure you're okay with going back to New York?" I asked.

"As long as you're happy, I'm happy," he replied making me smile.

"What will you do there, Adam?"

He barely hesitated. Perhaps he'd already put some thought into it. "Well, I have a law degree," he replied, grinning. "I could probably put that to use." He held my hand above my head and twirled me around before drawing me back in close. "I have something for you."

"Really? Where?"

"In my pocket." He glanced at the top pocket of his shirt.

"Can I have it now?" He let go of my hand, freeing me to reach into his pocket. I was absolutely dumbstruck to find my wedding rings.

"Bridget found them," he told me. "I don't know how long she had them before I found them. She'd hidden them in her boots."

I looked at the rings in my hand, suddenly blinking away tears.

"They were a little worse for wear after years in the dirt so Floss cleaned them up for me."

When I studied them closer, I discovered something even more special. "Did she engrave the billet-doux too, Adam?"

"There's a billet-doux?" He failed miserably at sounding surprised. "I hadn't noticed. What does it say?"

The words hitched in my throat. "I will love you always, wherever *we* are."

Adam put his hands to my face and brushed my tears away with his thumbs before moving in to murmur his next words against my lips. "Even if it is New York City."

I inched my head back. "You did this yesterday?" He nodded. "You didn't know about New York yesterday."

He smiled wryly. "Don't know what to tell you, Coccinelle. It must be magic."

THE END

Made in the USA
Lexington, KY
05 June 2015